When the Trees Started Falling

Falling
A Climate Chaos Thriller

A.D. Popovich

A.D. Popovich

Cover Art

Dedication

Dedicated to our magnificent Earth.
May we heal our Goldilocks climate before it's too late
. . . for Humanity . . .

Chapter 1

Luna Lewis bolted up from her childhood bed and kicked away the sweaty sheets clinging to her legs like an alien form of plastic wrap. "So much for getting any sleep." It didn't help that she was still furious with her irresponsible parents for bullying her into babysitting Rogue the next three days. They had even left her ten-year-old brother alone in the house, as if expecting her to bow to their beck and call. Even worse, her boss hadn't been too happy about her so-called family emergency.

Luna's parents were dictating her life once again. And she was letting them. *Well, this is the last time*! Simple. She would ghost them for a while after they returned from whatever protest event they had disappeared to. Even more puzzling was why they hadn't taken Rogue to their protest.

At twenty-seven, Luna was more responsible than her parents. She cringed at their lack of integrity for shamelessly using their own children for shock and awe. Simply because viral posts, videos, and podcasts gained more paying sponsors for their ever-expanding social media platforms, they exploited under the pretense of "documenting" their radical save-the-planet escapades.

She fanned herself with the pizza flyer on the nightstand, which she intended to cash in for lunch. "Why's it so freakin' hot?" That was when Luna realized the ceiling fan had stopped working. She flipped the switch. *Damn, power's out.* Mom and Dad relied on crappy solar power grid-tied into the utility grid, so when the power company went dark, so did they. Off-grid solar was the way to go, but it had been far too expensive to install at the time.

To this day, Luna loathed solar power. It wasn't reliable; something always went wrong, and it had seldom produced enough power during her carbon-footprint-guilted childhood. After living on her own, she had rejoiced in the indulgences of carbon consumerism by living like a *normal* person, consuming all the energy and high-carbon footprint products she could afford. Guilt-free.

"Phew." She waved the flyer faster, inches from her face. Her internal ranting wasn't resolving anything as she impatiently wiped away the beads of sweat dribbling down her forehead. It was ninety-three degrees at three minutes to midnight, according to the funky water-powered clock on the nightstand.

The National Weather Service had issued a Heat Advisory for most of California, thanks to the unprecedented heat dome lingering over the Western U.S. the past three days. It had her wondering how Southern California was coping.

Overwhelmed with angst, Luna stormed out of her old bedroom with the sudden urge to check on Rogue in the next room. An instant smile replaced her angst at the sight of her little brother lying spread eagle in his rocket ship bed, wearing his favorite spaceship pajama shorts.

She hoped their fanatical parents hadn't brainwashed Rogue into a mini-version of their eco-freak selves. But they probably had. Especially since her super-smart and attention-craved brother was eager to please Mommy and Daddy.

Unable to shake her angst, Luna decided to take advantage of the solitude to rehearse her upcoming job interview notes on the patio, hoping for a breeze. It would be her only opportunity. Once Rogue woke up, he would demand constant attention. She tugged on a pair of designer skinny jeans under the faded Alanis Morissette T-shirt she had downgraded to a sleepshirt. She slipped on her glitzy pink Betsey Johnson sneakers, thinking she should check the solar inverter for error code messages first.

During her teenage years, Luna had learned various troubleshooting hacks for the temperamental solar unit. Dad had constantly preached, "This is a new world, and you better learn to figure things out and adapt accordingly. Or die."

Yeah, right.

She was downing a glass of warm water from the obtrusive Berkey water filter contraption on the kitchen counter when—*boom*! The entire house quaked, sending water splashing down her chin and neck.

"What the hell was that?" Her frustration morphed into confusion. *Wait.* She sniffed the air. "Is that smoke?" She checked the stove and the oven. They weren't on.

Another explosion had her running to the front of the house. She thrashed open the living room's ultra-ugly, hemp blackout curtains. Outside, the red-glowing hillside roiled in an ocean of flames lashing at the midnight sky. The neighbor's house on the plot across from theirs was totally engulfed in the flames' fury.

The propane tank must have exploded. Had they escaped the inferno? She didn't know who lived there now. "Rogue!" Luna shrieked, running back to the kitchen.

She swung away the vertical bamboo blinds to the kitchen patio. "Damn!" *The backyard's on fire, too*! They had to get out of there. She turned around to find Rogue yawning with furrowed brows as the amber light's eerie glow bounced in between the swinging blinds.

Recognition settled in before she had to explain. "The go-bags are in the hall closet," a solemn Rogue mumbled while he put on the sneakers left under the kitchen table.

Of course, Mom and Dad had go-bags prepped for practically every Shit Hits the Fan scenario, which they had never used in an actual emergency. "Go for it. I'm getting my purse and suitcase." She wasn't leaving the house without her car keys, cell phone, and the super expensive Bebe suitcase that she had scored at Nordstrom Rack last month. Luckily, her coveted designer shoe collection was safe in her Sacramento apartment.

"Getting the car now. Meet me outside in ten seconds," she yelled over her shoulder, toting her rose-gold suitcase and Versace purse. She scrambled out of the house, unable to get through to 9-1-1.

"No!" The fire flickered at the outer wall of the garage. So quickly?

"Rogue," she shouted into the house, "hurry!" At the fire's ferocious speed, the house would be torched in minutes.

For some reason, Rogue dropped the armful of go-bags on the front porch and ran back into the house.

"What are you doing?" Luna yelled and parked her luggage on the edge of the driveway. Momentarily torn, she decided to move the car to safety first—then get Rogue, since the house wasn't on fire. Yet.

She rolled up the garage door with one hand and fumbled frantically for the Nissan Leaf's key fob with the other. She hopped into the car, despite the flames scorching the wall. *Unplug the EV charger cable, you idiot.* It had been close to dead by the time she had arrived. With the crappy Level 1 wall outlet charger, it wouldn't be fully charged. But enough to get them out of there.

What? The cable wasn't plugged in. "Rogue!" Last night he had begged incessantly to play table tennis despite the hot garage. After winning the best two out of three matches and exhausted from the heat, she had taken a cool shower. As usual, her ever-helpful brother had promised to charge the car.

"Dammit, start!" Flames roiled over the garage's ceiling.

She blamed herself for relying on someone else. *Can I push the car out?* The wall next to her burst into flames. Far too close. The blasting heat seemed to sear her skin, foretelling a grisly fate.

She scooted to the passenger side, jumped out of the car with her purse, and just stood on the cemented driveway completely spellbound as the car morphed into a fiery ball. She backed away, worried the lithium battery might explode.

Rogue was suddenly by her side. "Stay back," she yelled.

"The bus!" Rogue yelled back.

Stuck in a loop of this-can't-be-happening, Luna stared in disgust at the keychain Rogue shoved into her hand. She hated the funky old school bus.

He reshouldered the go-bags before snatching back the keychain. "Forget it. I'll drive." And he raced for the bus parked on the far eastern side of their property, as if he were in total control of the situation.

"But my car . . ."

It's okay. Breathe. I have insurance.

Hot erratic winds spurred the fire on. The blue gable shutters she had helped paint that last summer at home glowed crimson red. *It's go-time!* She ran for the bus with sanity seeping into her veins. By the time she tromped onto the bus with her bulky suitcase, Rogue had started the bus.

"Move," she ordered.

"Do you even remember how to drive it?" Rogue snarked back.

She flashed him a cold-steel glare before scanning the gauges. God, she better. She had wiped her mind's hard drive free from those annual off-grid survival camping trips. Determined, she sat behind the wheel and firmly shifted it into gear.

"Hey, you gotta wait for the airbrakes to prime and the—"

He shut up when she head-jerked toward the fast-moving flames. The bus spluttered in protest when she feathered the gas pedal and forced it to roll. But, where to? They were trapped on both sides by walls of flames ravaging the parched grasses of February still brown from a rainless winter.

"Rogue, run to the back of the bus. Tell me if I can back out to the road."

He took off, hurdling over a pile of stuff left in the aisle. Dad and Mom were notorious for starting projects they never finished. The bus had undergone constant renovation for as long as she could remember. What could they possibly be working on now?

The flames grew wilder, faster, higher in the rearview and side mirrors. But it was Rogue's scream that sent a rash of goosebumps stinging her arms. Her worst fear realized. The fire had reached the rear of the bus, totally blocking the road. The only way out was straight ahead—blocked by a fence.

She revved the engine. "Hold on!" Luna slammed the bus through the old wooden fence Dad had threatened to replace since she had been in grade school. She swung the bus around and headed for the fallow field that had once been a walnut orchard. The Shearers had moved years ago; they wouldn't mind. Besides, after the fire's devastation, no one would know she had been the culprit.

Rogue plopped onto the bench seat behind the driver's cockpit. "Where the heck are you going?"

Like she knew. Luna reined in her panic. If they were lucky, the fire hadn't reached the old mill, and from there, she could cut across the apple orchard to the paved road that led into town.

"Stop!" Rogue went soprano. "We have to warn Mr. Fox. And, and, Mrs. Romero. And Stevie, Branden . . ."

She didn't have the heart to tell him that if the rural residents of Valley Pines hadn't already escaped, it was probably too late. *Hope their smoke alarms worked.* Knowing the tight-knit community, one of the neighbors would have warned them of the approaching fire. The fact they hadn't received a warning call or text meant the Northern California neighborhood was just now finding out about the fire—trying to escape. Just as they were.

"Surely the explosions woke them up," she said to ease his worries. "Send a group text."

"Aw, shit!" He stomped his feet. "I can't believe I forgot my f'n phone."

She caught the reflection of Rogue's watery eyes of anguish in the rearview mirror with the help of the interior lights. "Here, try calling on mine." She didn't bother telling him that he wouldn't get a signal. She couldn't bear his despair. He was close with the neighbors, raking in the bucks doing odd jobs for his college fund.

Focusing in, Luna maneuvered the full-size bus over the plowed clumpy fields and raced the flames edging closer on the right. *If I can just pass that line of fire . . .* She could cut across to the road.

"I can do this!" She drummed her fingers on the wheel. But the bus hadn't warmed up yet. All she could do was stare out the ash-speckled windshield at the fiery hillsides and keep her foot on the pedal. And hope they made it to the paved road before the fire swallowed them. Bus and all . . .

Rogue cried out, "I can't get a signal!"

"Keep trying. We're going to Bobcat Creek," Luna decided after assessing their viable options. She remembered reading an article about a family surviving a wildfire by wading in a creek until firefighters had rescued them.

"The creek's dry." His voice went monotone.

"Impossible—"

"Look, by that car," Rogue shouted. "Someone's waving us down."

The vehicle's emergency flashers finally registered amongst the fiery horizon. Someone definitely needed help. Otherwise, they wouldn't be standing out there in all that smoke with the fire so close. *Can I cut across the field before the fire totally surrounds us?* She had a bit of a head start now that the bus was warming up.

"Don't think. Just do it!" Rogue hollered, as if reading her mind. "I'm pretty sure that's Mrs. Romero. You gotta save her."

True, they had to save someone. She gauged the quick-spreading flames and blasted the horn like a road-rage addict on crank. With gritted teeth, she cut across the field to the paved road, chancing the flames. Because she *knew* Mrs. Romero. The woman, who must be in her sixties now, used to babysit her. And to this day, sent Luna homemade fudge and snickerdoodles every Christmas.

Luna leaned forward in the seat, as if it made the bus go faster. One of the sprawling oaks lining the roadside next to the car, Mrs. Romero's Subaru, if she remembered correctly, burst into flames.

"Faster!" Rogue bellowed.

"Almost there," she said more calmly as sobriety took control. Sparks from the oak tree sizzled and zizzled in the air, dazzling the sky, and ignited the ground before her. But she was not stopping. She drove right over the flames.

"You rock!" Rogue yelped like a crazed little man.

Luna parked the bus in the middle of the narrow two-lane road several yards in front of the car. "Rogue, do you really know how to drive this?"

"Duh." He sat with his butt on the edge of the seat. Surprisingly, his little legs reached the gas pedal.

"Okay, move the bus up if you need to. And stay ahead of the fire." Luna leaped down the bus steps to the pavement, feeling like a horrible parent for letting him drive.

"Mrs. Romero?"

"Is that you, Luna?" Mrs. Romero grappled a lumpy bag to her chest with both hands. "Old Betsy died on me. Never did get that bloomin' alternator fixed."

A crackling pop, followed by a snap, had them jumping back as a fiery limb crashed down between the two of them.

"C'mon," Rogue yelled out the door.

"You don't have to tell me twice." Mrs. Romero disappeared to the other side of her car.

Luna ran the long way around the flaming branch and rushed to the older woman's aid. Rogue pulled the bus up a few yards just as a thick cloud of smoke descended upon her. She pulled her sleepshirt over her nose and avoided the orangish flames glowing through the smoke. At least Mrs. Romero had thought to wear a face mask.

Unexpectedly, Luna lost her sense of direction, overwhelmed by the swirling smoke. Seconds later, Rogue tapped out a series of honks. She followed the honks with outstretched arms, walking by braille on the sticky pavement until colliding with Mrs. Romero.

"Heavens," Mrs. Romero husked. "Thought I lost you."

Relief flooded through Luna when a clearing in the smoke allowed her to see the bus's flashing taillights. *Thank you, Rogue.* "This way," Luna said, choking down gulps of smoke. She fumbled around for the older woman's hand and realized they were full. She must have salvaged her suitcase from the car before it had gone up in flames.

Luna herded Mrs. Romero toward the bus, senselessly attempting to wave away the smoke. Don't panic, she kept telling herself. The bus was only a few yards away, although she no longer saw the faint glow of the taillights. She just kept following her mental compass.

She knew they'd be okay when her hand hit the bus. "Just a few more feet," she encouraged, gingerly sliding her hand along the side of the hot bus. The smoke thinned out with each step. They must be on the edge of the fire. For now.

The accordion door squeaked open. "Get in!" Rogue urged.

She was never so happy to see her little brother. She bustled a disoriented Mrs. Romero up the steps, all the while Luna hacked, gasping for a breath of untainted air. Her former babysitter barely made it to the bench seat behind the cockpit when Rogue hit the gas. Luna landed on all fours next to Mrs. Romero's suitcase. She was too relieved to get pissed after a terrorizing realization flittered into her mind: she could have died of smoke inhalation. Or burned to death out there.

She continued coughing out her smokey lungs. The more she tried making sense of their hellish escape, the more she realized this must be some shroom-tripping nightmare. Raging forest fires didn't occur in February. Bobcat Creek had never been dry for as long as she had lived there. And Rogue, couldn't possibly know how to drive yet.

"Luna, bless your heart. You and Rogue saved my life," Mrs. Romero babbled in the background.

Luna went with the terrifying dream and continued hacking.

Mrs. Romero pulled her mask down under her chin. "For heaven's sake, hon, drink some water before you go into convulsions."

"There's water in the fridge," Rogue said from the wheel, driving much faster than a kid, or anyone should drive a school bus on a winding rural road in the middle of the night in a freaky firestorm.

Luna stumbled to the fridge to find a chilled glass bottle of water. She guzzled down the ice-cold taste of pure splendor, not questioning why the fridge was on. This didn't need to make sense. It was merely a dream. She politely offered the bottle to Mrs. Romero, who was still in her nightgown.

"Thought you'd never ask." Mrs. Romero took a long swallow. "I take it your parents are still gone?"

"Yes. Did they tell you where they went?" Luna asked.

"No. And I didn't ask. Lord knows they were up to something."

"Just another protest," Luna mumbled with repulsion. Her parents were notoriously known as effective Protest Consultants when they weren't sidetracked with championing their own causes.

"Uh-uh," Rogue whispered. "It's something huge. They even prepped the bus. They grounded me and told me to get ready to bug-out."

Mrs. Romero flashed her a look of concern.

Luna shrugged. "You know my parents. They're probably protesting that water company that's been siphoning more than their contracted share from the California side of the Sierras. It's even made the Sacramento news." Since she had written off the fire as a dream, she quickly indulged in the "everything's-going-to-be-okay" state.

Until the bus skidded to a stop.

"You drive like Rusty Wallace," Mrs. Romero jabbed.

Playing along, Luna asked, "When did Dad teach you to drive?"

"We're trapped!" Rogue shrilled.

Luna sprang from the bench seat behind Rogue with a ricocheting heart threatening to leap out of her chest as the hellacious firestorm shrieked at them from the left side of the road. But it was the downed, sparking power line blocking their path that sent her back into panic. The heat blasting in from the windows shouted this was all too real.

"I don't like the looks of that," Mrs. Romero bemoaned.

"How far are we from the creek?" Luna asked, needing validation she knew where they were. With all the smoke it was disconcerting.

"I told you, the creek is toast!" Rogue roared. "Just like we're gonna be."

"It's just that way a bit." Mrs. Romero pointed. "A five-minute walk."

"And the creek bed's sorta flat. Right?" Luna questioned, trying to remember.

"Why, it certainly is," Mrs. Romero said, rubbing Luna's shoulders. "You're a genius. If we can just get this big thing there."

"If we can't, we'll make a run for it," Luna chirped optimistically in an attempt to soothe the fear oozing from her brother's startled eyes. "Move." She motioned Rogue out of the seat. "I'm driving." Courage raged through her. "Does Dad still keep the bus stocked with shit-hits-the-fan crap?"

"Duh." Rogue rolled his eyes.

"Find the masks. Get some wet towels. Do we still have those fire blankets? We might have to outrun the fire on foot." Luna sat behind the wheel, confident. Dream or no dream, she wasn't letting this hell-storm win. She seldom lost a battle of wills; inheriting her parents' tenacity had its benefits. So, if this was her freaking nightmare, she vowed to be the damn hero.

"On it," Rogue boomed.

"Mrs. Romero, hold on!" Luna revved the engine while her former babysitter clutched a bulky bag to her chest, which she realized was a pink pillowcase. Mrs. Romero must have stuffed it with valuables before escaping her house. "Damn!" *Why didn't I grab Mom's scrapbooks*? All those photos . . . And Dad's antique book collection. All gone.

The fast-moving flames seemingly tried to lash through the windows while fiery embers streaked across the road, pelting the bus. For a millisecond, Luna thought the fire would engulf the entire bus. The wild intoxicating inferno reminded her of a lucid out-of-body experience, sucking away her willpower.

"The power to prevail lies within you," Luna chanted as if words actually held power, silly as it was. Odd, how quickly she had reverted to her metaphysical upbringing, if only to get through their dire situation. This moment required all the skills she had learned from her far-left metaphysical mother and her far-right apocalypse-now father.

The swirling smoke dissipated to reveal a backlog of fire evacuees stuck on the road in their vehicles as clusters of spot fires spawned in the hazy distance.

Mrs. Romero sighed deeply. "Careful, hon, I think there's an accident up ahead. Heavens, the Post Office is on fire."

"So is Dollar General," Rogue exclaimed.

"What a travesty," Mrs. Romero said. "It took us five years of pandering to get the bloomin' board to approve that Dollar General."

"Luna, don't stop!" Rogue ordered. "The fire's on our ass! Remember that hella-fire in Paradise? People burned alive! In their cars . . ." His words faded into foreboding silence.

Luna had no intention of stopping in the middle of the road. No longer disoriented, she knew exactly where they were. She veered to the right, off the road, and plowed the unwieldy bus through the hot spots like a badass Charlize Theron in a *Mad Max* flick.

"Rogue, bring me a mask," she yelled, dodging downed fiery branches and burning bushes. All they had to do was get to that creek, drive about a mile, well, maybe two to three miles, and cut back to the road leading to the center of the small town. They could get help there. Maybe then this wicked nightmare would finally end.

An unusually subdued Rogue handed her an N95 mask, which she strapped around her wrist for later. According to Dad, N95s were the best paper-like masks for smoke. And he only bought the best. Luckily, Dad had bought cases of them before the tripledemic had hit a few years ago. Despite her eco-crazy parents, they were always ready for The End of The World As We Know It, otherwise referred to as TEOTWAWKI during their frequent and often volatile dinner debates.

Yeah, her parents were fanatics, but that didn't mean she didn't love them.

"There's the creek," Rogue shouted as if she couldn't see it.

Luna slowed down for the creek's embankment. It didn't look all that steep, but she didn't want to risk rolling the bus.

"I still can't get a signal. I can't even get nine-one-one. I thought the SOS thing was supposed to work in emergencies. F'n liars!" Rogue wailed. "Mrs. Romero, did you"—he paused—"call Mr. Fox?"

"Lord knows I tried." Mrs. Romero shook her head. "But the landline was down as well. When that new telecom company took over the phone lines, they did away with the battery backup system we used to have. That's why I didn't get the bloomin' Code Red Alert on my landline. I told them last summer at one of the town hall meetings that we needed to start a petition. But, did they listen to me? No," she rambled on.

Absolutely no one Luna knew used landlines; hard-wired phones were practically extinct. Like cable TV, those old boxy computers, and 3G. *Mrs. Romero should keep her cell phone on during fire season* was Luna's first thought. Wait, fire season hadn't started yet. Luna had only signed up for Code Red Alerts in Sacramento. Surely, Rogue had signed up for the alert system, and yet his phone hadn't warned them. Then again, Mom and Dad had probably told him to turn off his cell at night. A lot of people did.

Luna harnessed her will to maneuver the bus down the creek's embankment, praying the damn bus didn't roll over. Or get stuck. To her surprise, there was no mud. The headlights revealed the dusty creek bed was as dry as the Sahara. How was that possible? They used to raft down the creek every summer. Another clue this was a wonky dream.

"Luna, you did it!" Rogue cheered. "We're in the creek!"

"Hon," Mrs. Romero cooed, "look at you, so calm and collected. You take after your parents."

Yeah, right. That wasn't how Luna saw Mom and Dad. She continued at a mere five miles per hour, avoiding the debris of shredded tires, scrap metal, and tons of plastic crap littering the creek. *Why do so many people litter*? Disgusting. She pondered why no one had cleaned it up—instead of their narrow escape.

Mrs. Romero tapped Luna's shoulder. "You want to turn out before the bend in the creek, otherwise you'll run into a muddy section. Which is all that's left of Bobcat Creek. I took a stroll down here just the other day, thinking I should bring my metal detector out here. Planned to organize a clean-up party at next month's town hall. Lord have mercy on Mr. Fox," Mrs. Romero chattered on. "Who knows how many were sleeping snug in their beds. Ooh, that damn telecom company!"

Wow, she had never heard Mrs. Romero swear. Another clue this was *not* happening.

"Here we go." Mrs. Romero pointed to the right. "You want to pull out right about—here."

The incline was steeper than the bus liked as the wheels churned in the sandy embankment.

"Put it in the lowest gear," Rogue nagged.

"I know how to drive," Luna snapped. Dad had spent endless hours teaching her to drive this whale every summer during their mock SHTF camping trips. That was how jaded her parents were. Fake evacuation drills, camping with crappy tent toilets and solar-powered shower water bladders before the bus had been fully converted into a house on wheels. After eating all that high-sodium, freeze-dried prepper food, she was lucky she didn't have high blood pressure.

Fishing hadn't been so bad. It had been a good excuse to work on her tan. Gosh, those endurance runs, push-ups, no wonder she had rebelled by seeking asylum as an overindulgent consumer. If the world's economy and climate were on the verge of going "cray-cray" despite the global activists' forewarnings, she might as well live it up. And she had been. Her maxed-out credit cards were proof.

The tires slipped. The bus slid backward down the slope.

"You're gonna get us stuck!" Rogue scolded.

"I have this under control," she said more to herself than to him. The glow of headlights in the rearview mirror revealed other vehicles were using the creek as an escape route as well. Which made her all the more determined to get the bus out of the creek. She tried going up the embankment again, faster.

When the bus made it out of the creek, Mrs. Romero clapped loudly behind her. "Bravo!"

"So, that's Pioneer Avenue just ahead?" Luna asked, wanting confirmation. A long line of four-wheel drive vehicles clogged the road.

"Uh-huh." Rogue hovered over the window next to Mrs. Romero. "Hey, look, that's Mr. Fox's truck."

"Would you look at that?" Mrs. Romero gushed. "That lucky geezer made it out."

"Awesome, Pietro's Pizza didn't burn down. Did you bring the coupon?" Rogue quizzed as if they were stopping to eat.

Luna ignored him and tapped the horn before cutting into a break of the traffic-stalled road. They inched along as if stuck in Interstate 80 rush-hour traffic. Luckily, the wind was blowing the fire away from them, or they'd be in deep shit. "Rogue, try calling Mom." Time to end this tiresome dream.

"Still no signal," Rogue said with desperation. "Mrs. Romero, can I use yours?"

"Sheesh, wouldn't you know. I left my phone in the car. Thanks to the both of you, we'll be just fine," Mrs. Romero assured.

"I guess," Rogue said. "But where do we go now? Our house—all of them on Orchard Lane are—" There was no mistaking the grief in his voice. "Gone . . . gone . . . gone," he chanted like a spooky ghost.

Damn, where should we go? Luna hadn't thought that far ahead. The dream usually decided what to do next.

"Not to worry, hon," Mrs. Romero said. "We're fine now."

Mrs. Romero seemed stuck on being "fine." Based on Luna's churning solar plexus, it wasn't over just yet.

"But what are we gonna do without our house?" Rogue whined louder.

"Dear heart, that's a problem for the adults," Mrs. Romero said. "I'm sure your parents have ample insurance—"

"Wrong!" Rogue blurted. "The shitty insurance company canceled us."

"Oh my," Mrs. Romero muttered.

"Really?" Luna questioned. Mom hadn't mentioned anything.

"Get this," Rogue raged on. "They said we had to cut down all the trees within fifty feet of the house. Yeah, Dad was *hella* pissed."

"Sheesh, we live in a forest," Mrs. Romero lamented. "I suppose they're planning on sending me a non-renewal notice as well. I'll tell you, this world's a rotten mess."

So, that was it. "Maybe Mom and Dad are protesting the insurance company," Luna wondered out loud, trying to make sense of it. Which didn't help because she had no idea what insurance company they used. The traffic finally increased to thirty miles an hour. She couldn't wait to get out of there. Out of the dream.

"So, *where* are we going?" Rogue asked.

"My apartment," Luna decided.

"Hon," Mrs. Romero said, "isn't that all the way in Sacramento? Why don't we stay the night in Gold Town? Ooh, at that swanky hotel. Always wanted to stay there. It'll be my treat. Then, in the morning, with a clear head, we can make our plans."

"Sure," Luna said dreamily. She hated the idea of driving the clunky bus to Sacramento. Besides, there was no place to park it at the apartment complex. Maybe she could rent a car. Might as well break in that new credit card with zero interest for twelve months. She cringed; at the rate she was going, she'd never get out of debt. Unless she got that awesome buyer promotion. She was one of the top three candidates, according to her friend in human resources.

"We gotta call Mom and Dad from the hotel," Rogue said. "They'll freak if they see the fire on the news. Oh, shit, I can't remember their new phone number."

"That's the thing with these darn cell phones," Mrs. Romero said. "You don't have to remember phone numbers anymore. To this day, I keep a list of contact numbers in my wallet, ever since my last phone died on me."

"But, I wanna talk to Mom. Right now!" Rogue wailed.

Mrs. Romero snuggled up to Rogue. "Let's wait until morning. You don't want to wake them up," Mrs. Romero said sweetly.

"I guess," Rogue said.

Luna was relieved they had figured out a plan. She drove in a sort of numb, zombie state and stopped trying to make sense of their fiery escape. The traffic jam of fire evacuees thinned as most took the junction to Lodi and Stockton.

After an excruciatingly surreal two-hour drive, Luna squeezed the bulky bus into the Gold Rush Hotel's narrow parking lot entrance, so exhausted the parking space markings seemed to bounce off the pavement.

"Luna, do you mind staying here while I see if I can book us a room?" Mrs. Romero asked. "No sense in lugging everything 'til we know there's a vacancy."

"Sure," Luna squeaked out. She just wanted to sleep. The survival adrenaline rush had totally worn off.

"I wanna go with you," Rogue announced.

"Then you best not doddle or wander off," Mrs. Romero said firmly to Rogue.

Luna nodded it was okay when Rogue turned to her with questioning eyes. She could use the solitude.

"Hold this." Mrs. Romero shoved the lumpy pillowcase she had been clutching into Luna's arms before stepping down the bus steps in lavender sweats she must have changed into at some point.

Luna didn't bother changing out of her sleepshirt and jeans and stretched out on the bench seat, when the pillowcase she had scooted to the corner came to life. Startled, she tried to catch it before it hit the floor. A fluffy ball of fur peeked out. The multicolored cat took one look at her and jumped like a crazed Halloween cat: arched back, puffy tail, and all.

"What the—" *Really, Mrs. Romero saved a cat*? Didn't she hate cats? Nothing made sense. Too exhausted to think, Luna couldn't wait for the morning light to bring back normalcy. All she wanted was air conditioning that actually worked and a comfy bed . . .

Chapter 2

Jackson Jones, locally known as Handyman Jack of Amador County, tried massaging away the hackles quivering down the nape of his neck. Something didn't seem quite right. Furthermore, it wasn't like him to get anxious in the middle of the night. Reluctantly, he forced himself out of bed for a quick walk-through of his rustic hand-built cabin on the off chance an intruder was on the prowl.

Perplexed, he snuck around the cabin in alert-mode. After he double-checked the doors and windows, nothing appeared amiss. The outdoor solar-powered motion detector lights revealed no signs of an intruder lurking outside as they intermittently blinked on-and-off due to the unusually gusty morning.

Much to his dismay, Jackson's adrenaline rush warned he wasn't getting another wink of sleep, despite the L.E.D. clock glaring 2:02 a.m. Might as well get an early start on the day. It was going to be another hot one. A buddy up in Oregon had called out of the blue yesterday and needed a hand clearing his property after a freak windstorm had taken down several old oaks on his property.

Splitting wood wasn't Jackson's favorite pastime. Fortunately, Chip had a decent log splitter, which was far easier on his old back and saved him from buying a case of Arniflora to squelch the aggravating pains of old age, or longevity, as he liked to say. After the split and stacked wood seasoned for a year or so, they'd sell however many cords they got out of it for some quick cash under the table, which Jackson planned to squirrel away for his annual summer trip to Canada.

Jackson coddled a cup of morning joe on his way to the back deck, switched on the solar-charged lantern he kept on the barbecue grill, and sat in a tattered rattan chair, relishing the unseasonably warm February morning. Good thing his buddy had called. The isolation had been getting to Jackson.

Lost to an onslaught of regretful memories, Jackson pondered why all his good memories seemed to have occurred in his first thirty years, when he noticed the absence of twinkling stars. A stormfront must be moving in. Interesting, there hadn't been any mention of it on *The Weather Channel*. With spring just around the corner, Northern California was long overdue for its so-called rainy season. Even more disturbing, this month was the hottest February on record. Which had him already dreading summer.

The faraway howling of dogs echoed through the Sierra canyons, disrupting his quietude. They seemed ill at ease as well. Time to get moving. He hated doing nothing for long. Might as well head up to Oregon. He'd text Chip in a few hours to let him know he was arriving sooner than expected.

After packing a duffel, he grabbed the .45 Colt revolver stashed in the sock drawer for a just-in-case scenario before filling the thermos with the last of the coffee. At this rate, he could stop for breakfast at one of his favorite haunts along Interstate 5 for a mouth-watering dose of high cholesterol. Things were shaping up, despite the peculiar notion something was off-kilter.

Jackson strolled into the cluttered but organized toolshed for any last-minute tools that might come in handy. He had already loaded the brand-spanking-new gas-powered chain saw that had set him back a pretty penny. His old one seemed to cry out, "Take me too." Might as well.

Scanning the workbench, he grabbed the safety goggles, his go-to pair of leather gloves, and chainsaw chaps from their prospective hooks along with a canvas bag loaded with spare doodads and gizmos he hadn't found a place for as of yet. One never knew what might come in handy in a pinch. He kept the truck's side mount toolboxes well stocked. Hence, he prided himself on being perpetually prepared for just about any odd handyman job he might encounter.

It took another trip to add two jerrycans of gasoline for the chainsaws. *That reminds me. When I get back home, ought to hit the flea market for another gas-powered chainsaw.* They were getting harder to find. Chip had been sold on the idea of doing his part to save the planet and had reverted to electric chainsaws last year. That was until his buddy had found out the hard way. It took nearly a dozen battery chargers for a good day's work instead of a few gallons of petrol.

It had Jackson wondering how those independent landscapers were squeaking out a living if they had to invest in dozens of chargers for their crew and then waste time keeping them charged. Why pick on the little guy? The fossil fuel giants created this mess; let those greedy bastards foot the bill for going green.

A blustering wind whistled through the towering pines and cedars adorning his property as he finished loading the trusty Ford F-150 with the *HANDYMAN JACK* logo emblazoned on the doors. He reflected on that pivotal day he had gone up and quit his foreman construction job to go solo as a handyman soon after that devilish tripledemic had taken the world by storm.

Fed up with the pandemic's politics such as "to mask or not to mask" and "to vax or not to vax," which had trickled down to his bosses, fellow contractors, and suppliers, Jackson had simply retired early, sinking half his 401(k) into his handyman venture.

He had been born with the knack to fix darn near anything not requiring a computer chip. Turned out, his timing couldn't have been better. With the great resignation and all, more people than ever had stayed home, hence, more repairs and home improvement jobs and such had been in high demand. Things had slowed down since, giving him time to work on more gratifying projects.

He tossed the duffel into the passenger's seat before patting down his pockets to make sure he had his wallet and phone. *Good to go.* He caught a slight whiff of aromatic smokiness and realized Old Man Granger was likely pulling an all-nighter, smoking one of his to-die-for briskets. Jackson ordered one on occasion. *Maybe when I get back*, he decided, suddenly famished.

He started the truck, took a swig of coffee from the thermos, and was off. Jackson found the handyman stint challenging and reliable, working on the cheap since most folks in his area of Northern California lived near the poverty level. Especially since a glut of investment property owners rented their homes as short-term vacation rentals, triggering a housing shortage. Which raised the rates on the few long-term rentals available. A perpetually vicious cycle.

Based on his thrifty budget and pension, he only needed two to three jobs a week, leaving him ample time for hiking the western slope of the Sierra Nevada Mountains for unusual pieces of wood for his latest venture: medieval-hobbit dog houses. He had sold out at the local Christmas Fair and was working on two- and three-story catio versions after receiving several requests. All in good time.

He turned out of his long dirt driveway onto California State Route 88 when a strong wind gust took him by surprise. It could have been the Santa Anas the way the wind carried on out there. He shrugged it off. After all, it was February. This side of the Sierras had its share of blizzards. Of course, with this god-awful heat dome, it wouldn't be snowing any time soon. But any precipitation would be a godsend.

He grabbed the first CD his fingers found in the bin and was pleasantly surprised when a soothing Fleetwood Mac melody filled the truck, calming the uneasiness settling over the peculiar morning. Unfortunately, the CD reminded him of his ex-wife. After busting his butt building her dreamhouse, their eleven-year marriage had ended abruptly.

His ex had found a more amorous relationship with someone else while he had labored the weekends away building their home. But he was over that. Nowadays, the carefree bachelor life suited him just fine. Albeit, the loneliness could be difficult to shake at times.

Making excellent time and enjoying the empty roads as he passed through Gold Town, Jackson shuffled through the bin of CDs until he found Nicolette Larson. He took another swig of coffee and let himself enjoy a sweet ballad. That was, until an approaching vehicle flashed its high beams at him, briefly blinding him.

"My bad," he said aloud as if they could hear and quickly switched to low beams.

He was about to switch back to high beams when another oncoming vehicle blasted him with high beams and emergency flashers to boot. *Must be deer up ahead* was Jackson's first thought. Folks around there warned one another of such things. He slowed down, ready to break as he approached what the locals called Seven Curves, a series of sharp turns cutting a swath through the steep canyon.

He took it nice and easy, scouring both sides of the road for deer. To his surprise, a bear and three cubs scampered along the road, heading right for him. The unseasonably warm winter played havoc with the wildlife as he had noted on several occasions. The bears scurried down the opposite lane, not giving him a second glance.

The glinting sky caught Jackson's eye. The day seemed as impatient to get started as he did. The dashboard clock reminded it was too early for sunrise. "Hold on, that glow's coming from the west." He realized the anomaly a few seconds too late while taking the final curve.

"Good God!" That's what those drivers had been warning. A power pole transformer had exploded. *With sparks raining down!* But it was the down limb hanging precariously from the power line that had him concerned as a vicious wind whipped across the road, sending flurries of sparks over the two-lane country road.

He slammed on the brakes, speculating if a fire extinguisher could put it out. But it would be too risky standing that close to the transformer. He reached for the cell phone instead. *Figures, no signal.* He loved the boonies, but the cell service was spotty at best.

To his disbelief, the sparks ignited the dried-out underbrush lining the shoulders on both sides of the road. Clearly, it wasn't safe to continue. Next on his agenda, the volunteer fire department he had driven by minutes ago. Without missing a beat, Jackson made a quick U-turn and raced back toward the sleepy town, muttering a slew of obscenities to no one in particular.

He made it back through Seven Curves as fast as he dared, swerving to avoid the bear family. And wouldn't you know, the blaring of fire engines advised help was on the way. He pulled over as the firetrucks approached. Two firetrucks ought to contain it, he mused.

Jackson headed to Gold Town, thinking it would be a while before he could continue his trip. Up ahead, two vehicles were stopped side-by-side in the middle of the road. It could very well be the same folks who had flashed their high beams. *Better see what they know.* He pulled over to the side of the road, did a quick smoothing down of his unruly mustache, which he kept meaning to shave off, and walked up to the vehicles.

"Figured you'd be back," the man in the Bronco said.

"Thanks for the warning earlier. Any word on that fire?" Jackson asked.

"I just got back from the volunteer fire department in Gold Town. I reported the fire—in person," the man in the Kia said with an obnoxious fake-laugh, as if he were the hero of the day.

"Saw the two firetrucks—" Jackson noted needlessly.

"We drove right by that sparking transformer. But when we couldn't get through to nine-one-one, I turned around," the large man in the Bronco said.

"I told him not to get so close," the woman sitting next to him scolded. "We could've been electrocuted!"

"Exactly," the woman passenger in the Kia said.

"Did the fire department give an ETA as to when they might open the road?" Jackson asked.

"Said they'd knock out the fire real quick," the man in the Kia said. "Apparently, they've been having pop-up fires all week due to these crazy-ass winds. The ground's too damn dry."

"We might have to move to North Dakota at this rate," the man in the Bronco said.

"I hear ya," Jackson commented casually. "Don't think I can handle another fire season like last summer." It had been a killer, the smoke so bad it had reached Canada. Nowadays, no place was safe from wildfire smoke.

The men in the vehicles were busy talking to their apparent significant others. "Well, take it easy," Jackson said before turning toward his truck.

"Excuse me?" the man in the Bronco called out behind him.

Jackson turned around expectedly.

"Is there any place we can grab a coffee? This early? See, we can't go back home. We need to get to Auburn."

Based on Jackson's frequent trips through the area, the mom-and-pop restaurants didn't open until lunch. And the one twenty-four-hour gas station was on the other side of the fire. "Only place I know around here's that expensive buffet at the hotel. But as I recall, they don't open 'til seven."

"Oh, Cupcake," the woman sitting next to the man in the Bronco said. "I've always wanted to try their buffet. I heard they make the best crepe suzettes."

"Sure, if we're still stuck here by the time they open," the hefty man said, all too amicably.

The woman sitting next to the man in the Kia butted in. "Butch, I want to try the buffet too."

Her significant other shook his head adamantly. "You want to spend sixty-something bucks for breakfast?"

"Please . . ." the woman squeaked out in an intolerably high pitch.

Jackson stifled a smirk. He remembered those days when the missus usually won.

"Okay, but don't give me any shit the next time I want to go to Hooters," the thin man in the Kia said somewhat begrudgingly.

"Feel free to join us, uh—I didn't catch your name." the hefty man said.

"Jackson."

"I'm Levi, and this is my wife, Linda," the man in the Bronco introduced.

"I just might do that," Jackson said noncommittally.

"Race you to the hotel," the man in the Kia said to Levi before squealing off.

Looked like Jackson wasn't getting to Chip's early, after all. Rather than parking on the side of the road, he headed for the hotel a few miles down, debating on postponing the trip to tomorrow. An alternate route to Oregon would tack on a considerable number of miles, not to mention hours, up and down the mountains.

It wouldn't hurt to wait it out for an hour or so. The plywood for the Beasley job wasn't due to be delivered until next week, but it reminded him to stock up on basic building materials. Supplies were getting harder and harder to come by, sometimes taking weeks. Not to mention the constant inflation spikes. The supply chain had yet to recover from the tripledemic, and now with the cargo ships getting hijacked or blown up in the Red Sea, future shipments might get dicey until that situation settled down.

Still undecided, Jackson coasted into the entrance of the hotel's large parking lot. The magnificent hotel from days gone by sat farther back, nestled under a canopy of trees. The two couples he had spoken to had parked next to each other at the far west end of the lot, apparently socializing. Jackson wasn't in the mood for small talk with strangers who called their significant others *Cupcake*.

He dug through his duffel. Might as well get in a few chapters of his favorite Tony Hillerman series, needing to soothe his jangled nerves. If they hadn't extinguished the fire by the time the hotel opened for breakfast, he decided to splurge on their pricey breakfast buffet as well.

Page after page, Jackson found himself checking his watch. Occasionally, an early westbound traveler, who had driven by minutes before, joined the other travelers in the parking lot, apparently with the same idea of waiting out the fire.

Too antsy to read when two more firetrucks whizzed down the main road, Jackson closed the novel and grabbed the bundle of tattered maps rubber-banded together in the door's side cubby. Common sense told him he shouldn't worry; the fire was a good hundred miles from his cabin in Shake Ridge. Still, his nagging gut had him thinking he should map-out an alternative route in the off-chance things went south.

Nowadays, one had to be prepared for—anything.

Chapter 3

ROXIE ROMERO AWOKE TO the horrendous shrieking of sirens. Pixie, who had snuggled under the covers with her the moment she had hit the sack, frantically clawed at the sheet until scrambling to the floor, fishtailing around the hotel room's bathroom door only to slam into the wall. Poor thing. No telling where she had done her business without a cat box. However, that was the least of Roxie's concerns.

"Turn that thing down," Roxie groaned, unable to keep the irritation from her voice. Rogue had insisted on sleeping with the television on after their madcap escape from the fire in the wee hours of the night. The background chatter had served as a distracting comfort, buffering the patter of footsteps and constant commotion of closing doors, for the hotel had bustled with late arrivals. Apparently, others had taken refuge at the Gold Rush Hotel. Too bad she was too exhausted to admire the room's exquisite antique décor.

Between bouts of sporadic sleep, Roxie had mentally planned out her list of phone calls. Once she bought a new phone. She needed to let her sister and brother know she was fine before they heard about the fire on the news. She also wanted to check in with her Valley Pines friends to make sure they had made it out. And then there was the dreaded call to the insurance company. Had they issued a non-renewal notice, and she had somehow missed it?

There was no way her home of more than thirty years and her Subaru had made it through the fire unscathed. Still, she refused to fret over the loss of her entire household of cherished items. *Not today.* There would be plenty of time to dwell on that. If she let herself.

The shrieking did not stop. Roxie was too pooped to drag her aching bones from the luxurious pillow-soft bedding; instead, she propped her elbows on the pillows to see the blank television screen was not to blame. She turned to the adjacent queen bed to find Luna and Rogue gawking in a state of apparent bewilderment.

"Must be a false alarm. It can't possibly be *another* fire," Roxie said with a vocal yawn after a glance at the nightstand's clock indicated it was barely five in the morning.

Roxie hobbled out of bed and ignored the fear emanating from Rogue's face. Luna appeared annoyed at the world as usual. It must be a generation thing: rankled at every blooming thing that didn't suit her. With so much wrong with this world—indignation must serve as a coping mechanism.

Curious, Roxie drew the curtains. "Heavens! The sky's on fire!"

"What?" Luna grumbled behind her.

A pounding at the door nearly gave Roxie a heart attack. She swung open the door to find a harried yet pleasant-looking sheriff deputy. "Evacuate. Now!"

She stood at the door in her not-quite-see-through nighty, speechless.

"Is your vehicle in the parking lot?" the deputy continued.

All she could do was nod.

"Ma'am, are you here with someone who can drive you?" he asked rather slowly, as if she were an invalid.

For a moment Roxie was taken aback by his insinuation. Until she happened to catch her reflection in a shabby chic mirror next to the door. To be fair, with her silvery hair floating around her face, she looked like a banshee.

Luna rushed to the door. "What's going on?"

"Mandatory evac! Got a hell of a firestorm on our hands. Go! Before it takes the entire town." The deputy turned his back on them and banged on the door across the hall.

Roxie shook her head. "The same fire?" The hotel was a good seventy miles from Valley Pines. Furthermore, out-of-control wildfires didn't occur until summer. Not February. Then again, there was nothing "usual" about the weather, except that it seemed to become exceedingly more unusual with each passing year.

Luna threw up her hands in obvious disbelief. "Impossible."

"Hey!" Rogue shouted from the balcony. "The rooms on the end are on fire!"

Upon hearing that, Roxie was done questioning the plausibility of it all. It was happening whether it sounded plausible or not. "Pixie?" she called out to no avail. Her spooked tortoiseshell hid in the nook between the sink cabinet and toilet just out of her reach. She wasn't leaving without Pixie. Her quirky cat's caterwauling had awakened her in time to escape her house with her suitcase long before the smoke alarms had gone off.

"Rogue, be a dear." Roxie tossed him the embroidered pillowcase she had managed to stuff Pixie into before leaving her home. "Put Pixie in this." Sadly, the precious pillowcase was the only heirloom she had left of her mother's.

"Zip up your suitcases," Roxie urged, back in adrenaline mode. "We'll change on the skoolie." Good thing she had been too exhausted to unpack, and even more fortuitous, she had packed her suitcase just yesterday for the Reno trip with her Bunco girlfriends. *That reminds me, the Reno trip's today.* She needed to add Flora and Izzy to the list of phone calls. *I do hope they weren't affected by the fire.* They lived in a fifty-five-plus community in the next town.

Rogue returned with Pixie in the pillowcase as she and Luna finished zipping their suitcases. Seconds later, they scurried down the stairwell with their luggage in tow along with dozens of others. Several from her fire-ravaged community based on the familiar frenzied faces. But there was no time for chit-chat in the smoke-shrouded corridor.

Sheesh, for the second time that morning, she was forced into making a spectacle of herself by fleeing in a flimsy smocked nighty. Not that anyone would pay any mind to a disheveled woman of her age, one of the few benefits of being a senior citizen.

Roxie let her suitcase bounce wildly down the stairs while Luna gingerly coddled hers down. Rogue had slung the pillowcase over one shoulder and lugged his backpack on the other. Roxie kept one hand on the railing and followed the crowd down the stairs when the stairwell plunged into darkness. A series of groans and gasps echoed off the walls.

"There goes the power," someone announced needlessly, seconds before the backup lights' glow guided the way.

Momentarily dazed, Roxie stopped for a second, only to get shoved from behind. She caught herself on the railing and continued flying down the stairs as fast as she could to avoid becoming a stampede casualty—one of those odd events that seemed to pop up in the news these days. Now she understood how such a thing happened.

"Mrs. Romero?" a concerned Luna called out.

"I'm fine." Roxie's shout disappeared into the clattering of feet and luggage.

Once out of the stairwell's mob, they found the smoke-filled parking lot wasn't much better. The deputy hadn't exaggerated the situation. The sky blazed in whirling flames that had to be a hundred feet high. The wild inferno whipped at the pre-dawn's black sky like an evil demon devouring the planet. She shivered and shook away the eerie thought. *Roxie, you done good so far. Don't lose it now.* As the eldest, she needed to present a calm demeanor for Rogue and Luna.

Once they made it to the skoolie, Luna feverishly dug through her purse. The young woman looked up at Roxie with fear-laden eyes. Eyes that screamed, "*Where the hell are the keys!*"

Roxie wanted to say, *"Please, don't tell me you left the keys in the room."* Instead, she calmly said, "Keep looking, hon." Roxie nodded encouragingly while eyeing the parking lot of shambling guests clad in sleepwear, as they loitered about with cell phones and luggage.

"Dweeb," Rogue yawped. "They're clipped to the side pocket."

"Yes!" Luna's eyes lit up with her usual smug confidence once again.

Roxie was now wide awake and raring to go. "Splendid. No time to dilly-dally. Go! Start the darn thing. I'll take your suitcase," she said, grabbing the handle. As she recalled, the skoolie took time to warm up. Meanwhile, a rush of vehicles fled the scene.

Luna finally released her reluctant grip. It had Roxie wondering what was in that fancy-schmancy rose-gold suitcase. Must be a status symbol, an expensive one at that. It definitely wasn't the homely earth-friendly sort, which was bound to raise a heated discussion once the young woman caught up with her parents. She could already hear Crystal and Forest admonishing the lavish purchase.

Luna had started the skoolie by the time Rogue helped Roxie onboard with the luggage, all the while the parking lot swarmed with the frantic escapees shouting if they should go east or west. It was impossible to tell. The sky flurried with embers in every direction, igniting the huge billowing trees bowing to the wind's fury.

Roxie surveilled the roaring inferno from the bus windows. A smoky haze of headlights clogged the road as the town's residents fled, a stark reminder that only one main road went through the small Sierra town.

A jarring boom rattled the skoolie. Unfortunately, Roxie knew that sound—the petrifying reverberation of one of those humongous pines thundering to the ground. These winds were bound to take down the dead wood overrunning the thirsty forests as of late.

In year five of a five-thousand-year drought—there was no denying it. The forests were dying. Despite the government's never-ending politicking that they were on target to stave off the severe effects of climate change while others vehemently denied climate change even existed. A useless debate that served no one except for those gaming the system for their own pocketbook.

"Holy balls!" Rogue shrieked. "The tree's blocking the exit."

"There has to be a back way out," Luna admonished. "There always is."

"Duh, didn't you see the evacuation diagram posted on our hotel door?" Rogue clapped back.

"This place was built before all the modern building codes," Roxie said, staring at the iridescent-red trees surrounding three sides of the hotel. What had once been the hotel's most spectacular feature—taunted them with a fiery death.

The blaring of horns responded, as if everyone became spontaneously aware—there was no way out of the parking lot.

That didn't stop an onslaught of vehicles racing for the hilly, landscaped boulevard separating the parking lot from the main road. The grinding of engines revealed they couldn't make it over the steep boulevard. The remaining hotel guests and employees weren't going anywhere.

Luna and Rogue stared speechlessly out the windshield when the boulevard's shrubs spontaneously ignited into a blazing blockade. Roxie studied their options, or lack thereof as the parking lot turned into a quagmire of panic. Still, a surge of determination kept her sane, for it was her responsibility to keep the neighbor's children safe. So what if Crystal and Forest were nuts, fighting lost causes. They were good people. With good family values.

"Luna . . ." Roxie started.

"Yes," the young woman said in a faraway voice.

"Pull the skoolie next to that water fountain in the middle of the lot," Roxie said firmly. "Out of the path of those power lines." The power lines were bound to be the next casualties.

Rogue furiously shook his head. "Let's just ram over the hill and through the bushes to the road. The bus can take the fire."

What was he thinking? The boulevard was too steep. The bus would get stuck like the other vehicles. "Not with all those decorative boulders. The safest thing to do is wait for help—"

"But—" Rogue groaned.

"We're staying here. And that's final," Roxie said curtly.

"That's sooo stupid!" Rogue's nostrils flared with blatant disgust.

"If we had an off-road vehicle, I'd chance it," Luna said evenly. "But we barely escaped last night. These roads are even narrower, and with this big bus—in this wind—with all the other cars clogging the road. It's too dangerous."

Thank you, Luna. Roxie sighed internally. Rogue could be rather demanding at times. And his parents' view of discipline, or lack of, was an issue as far as she was concerned. But who was she to judge? Luna had turned out well.

"You know"—Luna turned to her—"if everyone helps, we can probably shove the tree out of the way."

"Yeah, we have fire extinguishers," Rogue said, still gung ho.

The harsh reality hit her; not everyone was making it out of Gold Town that early February morning. "It will take a lot of fire extinguishers to put out the tree," Roxie countered. But what really worried her were images of getting trapped in a colossal traffic jam with vehicles bursting into flames, stranded there to melt until fire crews pushed their way through. Stuck in the smoke and the heat—she didn't foresee a happy ending for those who chose that course of action.

Rogue skittered about the bus and returned brandishing two fire extinguishers. Luna nodded to Roxie knowingly, as if recognizing Roxie's despondency in the matter.

"Rogue." Luna's tone deepened. "Mrs. Romero's right. Too many cars. Only one road. Do the math!" Luna snatched the fire extinguishers from her insistent brother and then gave him a loving hug.

"Now that that's settled," Roxie said with finality, "we simply wait for the fire department to do their job." It was a ridiculous thing to say when horrific images depicting death by fire invaded her mind. Perhaps facing the possibility of death twice in the past few hours had messed with her sobriety.

Horrific screaming from outside had them glued to the windows. "Heavens!" Some unlucky person pinwheeled around, engulfed in flames. That gruesome image that had flittered into her mind moments ago unfolded right before her. "What can I do?"

Rogue patted her shoulder when she stood up on wobbly knees to go outside. "Don't worry, Mrs. Romero. I'm not gonna let him die," he proclaimed in a tone twenty years his senior. He snatched one of the fire extinguishers Luna had put on the dinette table.

"Wait!" Luna grabbed his arm. "Wear a mask."

It was pointless trying to stop him. "Hon, do be careful," was all Roxie managed to say as Rogue ran outside with an N95 in one hand and the extinguisher in the other.

Rogue, along with two other men, rushed to help the person flailing around in flames. An older man with a mustache rolled the injured person into a blanket before Rogue had a chance to fire the extinguisher. A sheriff SUV pulled up from behind the hotel and went to the person's aid. Quickly, several men maneuvered the injured person into the backseat.

The deputy who had evacuated them raced for the hilly boulevard. But he wasn't going anywhere with all those vehicles stuck. To Roxie's surprise, the sheriff SUV pushed several vehicles out of the way. And he sped off with his siren blasting.

"Yes!" Luna grunted.

"I do hope they get to the hospital in time," Roxie mumbled.

Luna shrugged. "Probably. I'll move the bus before somebody else parks there."

In a somber moment, Roxie didn't think she would ever forget, she found herself questioning the decision to wait for the fire department. Would it be better to hike out on foot? Had she issued their death warrants by remaining in the parking lot as wild flames took over the sky, the trees, the hills, the hotel, and just about every combustible object in its path?

Chapter 4

Luna Lewis cringed at the suffocating sensation, as if the heat vaporized the air out of the bus, right out of her lungs. Just an illusion, she reassured, then readjusted the N95 mask, unable to take a deep breath. Damn, she hated wearing those stupid masks.

Masks reminded her of the lost pandemic years that had robbed her of the carefree college life she had hungered for during high school after enduring a guilted childhood where comfort and consumerism had been considered evil planet killers.

She had been anxious to explore the frivolous luxuries life had to offer. And then, wham! The tripledemic had come out of freaking nowhere. Even worse, she had been fresh off the heels of a painful breakup with what's his name, whom to this day, she had adamantly redacted from her life. Because the eco-punk hadn't deserved a place in her memories.

Freedom had finally found her that last year of college when the tripledemic had turned endemic and in-person classes had resumed. From that point on, she had bloomed into a social butterfly by joining every club and social event her schedule could fit in. Simple things, like playing on the volleyball team, the debate team, sneaking beers at weekend parties, even dating. And most amazing, shopping for fabulous clothes without Mom's disapproving intervention.

Despite her hectic senior year, Luna had graduated college with honors with a BA in Fashion Merchandising and Management, focusing on Eco Apparel Engineering and Fashion Journalism.

From then on, she had been an unstoppable force in the relatively overlooked niche of non-toxic, eco-chic activewear. Even creating her own organic cotton and bamboo line.

It had been the perfect time to market toxic-free sports bras and leggings. Turbo cancers were on the rise, affecting people in their twenties and thirties. Her clothing line had also served to educate: the toxic chemicals in petroleum-based fabrics leached into the body when sweating, meaning that high-intensity workout did more than burn fat.

Mrs. Romero's shaky hands snapped Luna out of her funk. This must be terribly stressful for the older woman. "Are you okay?" Luna asked. "Did you bring your meds?"

"No worries there." Mrs. Romero pulled down her mask. "I'm pretty healthy for my age. I stick to natural remedies when possible. Like herbs, homeopathy, and vitamins. Believe it or not, I even dabble in CBD oils. That stuff works wonders for those odd pains I get every now and again."

"Cool." Although, holistic herbalists irked Luna. All she needed was an occasional Aspirin or Motrin. If that didn't work, she sucked it up.

Mrs. Romero inhaled deeply. "Hon, this bus must be airtight. I'm not smelling any smoke now."

That was just what Luna needed to hear. They had donned masks earlier when the bus had turned smoky. She tore off her mask and took in all the clean air her lungs could hold. The smoke must have come in when Rogue had opened the door to help the guy on fire.

"Don't you remember?" her maskless brother chided. "Dad installed double-paned windows and caulked the seals. You know, in case of a gas attack. So, as long as the vents are closed, we're super safe."

"Why didn't you tell me?" Luna protested.

"Duh." Rogue threw up his arms. "You never listen to me."

Luna nodded feebly. "Oh, you did say that." But she hadn't believed it at the time. Rogue must really be freaking without Mom's pampering.

"Your dad's always working on something clever," Mrs. Romero cut in. "We'll try calling your parents again when we get to the next town. I can't believe the hotel's phones were out. The hotel clerk said even the nine-one-one system went down."

Yikes, this was going to be a long, boring wait on the bus—when she had so much to do. Since leaving home, Luna had been non-stop, working hard all week, shopping the weekends away, and partying hard Friday and Saturday nights. No wonder she was in so much debt. Well, if she did get that promotion, she'd be out of debt in two years. *Unless I book that Hawaiian cruise with my friends in accounting . . .*

Trying hard not to notice the smoke-laden sky, Luna questioned if they had made the right decision to stay in the hotel's parking lot instead of outrunning the fire. But the answer stared her in the face when she counted the vehicles in flames on the main road. Who knew how many people were stranded out there? Walking around. With no place to take shelter.

"Mrs. Romero," Luna asked, "how far do you think the fire will go?" Once Luna had moved to the city, she stopped paying attention to the wildfires the past few summers. Ignorance was bliss. With all the craziness in the news, she found it best not to dwell on it. The only way to do that was by not caring.

Mrs. Romero shivered, despite the heat. "Heaven knows. Last summer the fire situation was record-breaking. Fires in Oregon, Idaho, Texas, Montana, Hawaii, Alaska—and just last week, Florida had a wildfire. It's burned several thousand acres last I saw. They can't seem to stop them."

"Even Siberia was on fire," Rogue butted in.

"Sacramento doesn't get these insane fires. Just all the residual smoke from the surrounding fires." Her city seemed to be a safe zone, despite its crazy-hot summers.

"By the way," Roxie said. "You two might as well call me Roxie. It looks like we'll be cooped up together for a while. The whole missus thing makes me feel like an old lady."

"But you are an old—" Rogue clasped his hand over his mouth when he caught Luna's disapproving frown.

Roxie chuckled. "That I am. I just don't need to be reminded of it every bloomin' minute of the day."

Luna nodded. "No problem." It seemed odd calling her Roxie after knowing her as "Mrs. Romero, the babysitter who lived down the street" her entire life.

They sat in silence as the smoke thickened. *Thanks, Dad.* He definitely had been right about the windows. She vaguely recalled the heated argument the day Mom had grilled him over the credit card charge for the replacement windows. Dad had prepped for just about every SHTF possibility, perpetually adding more safety features. The bus was to be their bug-out vehicle in the event of an actual end-of-the-world scenario.

"No way . . ." Luna gasped at the meteoric flash igniting the sky—turning the smoky dawn into daylight. She marveled at the flaming sky until realizing the hotel raged with flames. She hoped nobody had stayed behind to grab the computer hard drives and paperwork. It sounded like something her demanding boss would expect.

"Would you look at that?" Roxie exclaimed. "Who'd a thought it would go up lickety-split? The rooms have sprinklers. Just goes to show, we can't control nature."

"Like, where are the f'n firefighters?" Rogue drawled.

"They probably sent them to Valley Pines," Luna speculated, hypnotized by the roiling flames.

"It's a shame, my sister's wedding reception was here . . ." Roxie's words faded off, as if she were lost in remembering. "Rosa moved to Palm Springs a few years ago. I need to let her know I'm fine. She doesn't do well in stressful situations like this. She'll need a Xanax when she hears about the fire."

Luna worried for Roxie, angry by the lack of firefighters. Especially since the hotel was practically famous. A popular venue for weddings, birthday bashes, graduation parties . . . It had been there since the California Gold Rush era. The bathroom was especially fancy with gorgeous gold fixtures. Even the old-fashioned claw-footed bathtub had been painted antique gold. The bed had been ultra comfortable. Better than the Hyatt's. Surely, they would rebuild it.

An SUV, a car, and two trucks squealed around from the far side of the hotel. Right for the bus. "That can't be good," Luna muttered.

"They must think it's safer in the center of the parking lot as well," Roxie commented.

From out of nowhere, a microburst of flames mushroomed over the hotel and blossomed into a fantastical fireworks display as a barrage of debris rained down on the bus. Seconds later, the bed of the Ram truck spontaneously ignited.

Sick of this crazy shit, Luna begrudgingly slipped on the N95 she had tossed onto the dashboard earlier and snatched the extinguisher from Rogue's hands. "My turn." She knew the drill after taking fire safety classes, CPR training, even basic Hazmat protocol. Every summer her parents had thought up another SHTF survival scenario. On the plus side, the drills had made interesting essay topics for "What did you do during summer vacation?"

Once outside, startling heat singed Luna's fair skin while acrid smoke penetrated her eyes like vicious minuscule barbs. She should have looked for the face respirators. *Did Dad still keep those on hand?* she wondered while pulling the extinguisher's pin.

A man with his T-shirt pulled up over his nose waved her over from the tailgate of his truck. She planted her feet firmly on the ground and stood a good six feet from the blaze and aimed the spray at the base of the fire, sweeping the nozzle from side to side. An older man with a mustache hurried out of a handyman truck and grabbed an extinguisher from the side mount. Together, they extinguished the fire.

"Thanks," the guy using his T-shirt as a mask rasped.

Another guy donning a blue medical mask joined them. Medical masks were basically useless for wildfire smoke because they didn't keep out the harmful smoke particles, but she didn't bother telling him that. When the men started talking about how bad the fire was, it was time to leave. "I'm on that bus over there if you need help with more fires," she said, jogging off.

The wild winds whipped at Luna's unbound hair, telling her it was time to bun it up before it caught on fire along with everything else. Even the shimmery red pine needles soaring through the air had ignited, pelting her skin with tiny burns. She sprinted faster for the bus, worried her hair might catch on fire. If her hair was damaged, it would be the perfect excuse to get that bob she had debated on getting last summer. Low maintenance and cheap for those hot Sacramento summers.

"Bravo." Roxie clapped when Luna hopped onto the bus.

"You forgot to put the pin back in the fire extinguisher," Rogue scolded.

She responded by handing him the extinguisher, knowing the OCPD in him would get a thrill from completing the unfinished task. Rogue had been diagnosed with several disorders, from Obsessive Compulsive Personality Disorder to Borderline Personality Disorder to Attention Deficit Hyperactivity Disorder, and more, according to Mom. Although Mom had refused all medications, due to their long list of side effects.

After their mad fire escape, Rogue would probably have PTSD. So, despite being super-smart, her oversensitive brother had a long battle ahead. To this day, she guilted over moving to Sacramento, and not being there for him, if only for moral support. At least Mom had the patience to indulge him and keep him constantly engaged in activities.

"You and Rogue are so brave." Roxie beamed. "I'm nominating you both for the Good Samaritan award. Once things return to normal."

Not wanting to appear disrespectful, she offered Mrs. Romero a polite smile. Her parents had received the honor one year after their aggressive campaign had stopped a logging company from buying a defunct resort, which would have been logged of its trees. Luna didn't have time for silly awards; she'd rather be shopping. *Damn, wasn't Nordstrom Rack having that sample sale today?*

Ugh, I can't stand another freakin' minute on this bus. Impatiently, she watched for that first glimpse of a firetruck or Caltrans, or whoever cleared the roads and deemed it safe to leave.

She caught Roxie leaning against a window with closed eyes with Rogue curled up beside her at the kitchen table. Asleep. Luna's adrenaline rush had completely worn off. With barely two hours of sleep, she needed a quick power nap as well. She stumbled through the cluttered aisle to her old bunk bed just beyond the kitchen area. After all, this was merely a fire, not TEOTWAWKI.

Luna sluggishly opened her eyes, completely disoriented. She patted around the bed in the dark, relieved to find her cell. *What the hell?* Luna tossed her phone onto the bed. Still no cell service. Even 9-1-1 was down. What good was having an emergency call center, if it didn't work—in an actual emergency?

She was more pissed at not being able to contact Sheree in human resources, dying to know if they had scheduled the buyer position interviews. No matter what, she wasn't letting this damn fire screw her out of her dream job.

Unable to stretch out completely, she kicked at the covers at the foot of the bed without any luck. When she flicked on the lithium bunk light, she recognized her old, olive-drab rucksack at the foot of her bunk. No wonder she didn't have room. It must have been there since their last family camping trip, still crammed with survival gear.

Luna shoved it to the side just enough so she could stretch her legs. And sulk. Lying on her back with her hands tucked under her head, she stared blankly at the collage of ripped-out magazine pages glued to her bunk's ceiling. Brad Pitt's smoldering eyes smiled back.

You need to snap out of this funk. The fire was only a temporary setback. Her life would return to normal. Any minute. On that, she smiled back at Brad Pitt and let herself reminisce over those family road trips. She had loved those adventures at Rogue's age. *When did I start hating them?* Really, her childhood hadn't been horrible.

After all, her parents were practically famous, more like infamous, loving people dedicated to saving the planet. At the expense of everything. Including their own children. *Urg*! It was time to let go of such adolescent resentments. If she hadn't had activist parents, she probably wouldn't have been granted that life-changing Sustainable Fashion scholarship, which in turn had lured her from the boring eco-friendly and sustainable clothing industry to designer fashion.

She decided to rehearse the interview questions Sheree had slipped her in exchange for setting her up with the hot, new guy in the mailroom. "Damn." She couldn't access the cloud. She could hear Dad's admonishment loud and clear in her mind. "Always print a hard copy. One day the Internet will go down." So true. Lately, someone was always hacking the system.

Sick to her stomach, Luna wondered what her parents were going to do without homeowner's insurance. Without a house? And why had they planned a family road trip in February? They couldn't expect her to hit the pause button on her career. Especially without advance notice. She had her own awesome life now, one that absolutely did *not* include any SHTF or activists' activities. *Period*!

Luna went back to berating herself for succumbing to Mom's beckoning call when an abrupt creepy feeling warned something was terribly wrong. Thinking about it, Mom had seemed desperate, even panicky when Luna had told her it was bad timing to take time off work. Mom had persisted, saying Rogue was having a crisis. Which had been the only reason Luna rushed home.

One last family vacay? Don't tell me Rogue's ill? Please don't let it be cancer . . .

Her mind raced with the possibilities, all bad. "Stop," she muttered to herself. The new, improved Luna strove for a positive outlook on life—of the world. The world was her oyster, her therapist used to say during those two years of therapy to eliminate the doomsayer scenarios her parents had ingrained into her. From rogue asteroids to global climate collapse and crop failures to worldwide economic collapse . . .

I'm so done with all that end-of-the-world catastrophizing.

Granted, a tripledemic had occurred. The viruses had never completely gone away, thanks to those first leaky vaccines, which had perpetuated countless virus mutations. But the tripledemic had been over for several years. She merely accepted the new norm: people still seemed to get sick. A lot. And were often out for several weeks. Luckily for her, she had a strong immune system.

Tired of wallowing in self-pity, Luna slid open the curtain to her bunk, wanting company. Odd, the bus was dark, as if the windows had been painted black. Had she slept the day away? Knowing Rogue, he had turned off the interior lights to save the battery. She grabbed a solar lantern from the shelf and tip-toed to the kitchen to find Roxie asleep at the dinette table using her purse as a pillow.

Still curious, she crept to the driver's seat. The waning glow of the solar lantern illuminated the black snow raining on the windshield. "So bizarre," she croaked out. She flipped on the headlights, relieved to find the black snow was actually ash.

A vehicle across from the bus flashed its lights, which started a chain reaction of flashing headlights from two other vehicles that had remained in the parking lot. Where had everyone else gone? There had been at least a dozen cars and trucks. "Did we sleep through the rescue?" How idiotic would that be?

"Uh, Rogue?" Luna called out.

"Hon, what's wrong?" Roxie rushed to her feet.

"Rogue?" Luna called out again, hopping over the bags in the aisle. When she found him in the upper bunk bed with the curtain closed, she automatically checked his pulse.

"Hey!" Rogue slapped her hand away. "Don't be weird. It's not like I'm dead."

"Luna . . ." Roxie faltered. "What time *is* it?"

Luna's thoughts exactly. The digital clock hanging on the wall showed twelve fifteen.

Rogue rubbed his eyes. "Time warp?"

She and Roxie held each other's stare for a long uncertain moment when banging on the bus door sent her heart thudding.

Rogue started laughing. "You guys are scaring me. It's just someone at the door."

Roxie shook her head. "He's right, you know. We're spooking ourselves. Maybe help is here."

Luna nodded and shook away the tendrils of insanity attempting to take over and rushed to the door with Roxie and Rogue on her heels. With all that ash outside, she donned a mask before opening the accordion-style bus door.

A large man hurried up the steps, not waiting for an invitation. "Excuse me," he spluttered, coughing. "We want to hold a group meeting. In here, where we can all talk." The middle-aged man slid the blue medical mask below his chin.

Roxie eagerly asked, "Have they cleared the roads?"

He shook his head slowly. "Hate to be rude. We thought this might be one of those renovated buses. My wife and the others wanted me to ask if they can—" He paused.

"Use the restroom?" Roxie finished.

"If it's not too much trouble. The guys don't have a problem taking care of their business outside. The women, not so much." The man shifted from foot to foot, as if his request made him uncomfortable.

Roxie held Luna's questioning look. Right, it wasn't Roxie's decision. "Of course," Luna said. He didn't look like a carjacker.

"So—there's a total of five of us. The others four-wheeled it over the boulevard. Some made it across. Some didn't. And they left on foot. Looks like we're the only sane ones that stayed behind. Um, we could use some water. Maybe something to eat? If you can spare it." He pulled out his wallet. "I can pay."

Rogue held up two bulging grocery bags from the floor. "Sure. We have tons of stuff."

Luna instantly regretted the invite. One of the first rules of any SHTF situation was not to disclose one's stockpile. But, hey, this was merely a temporary crisis. "No problem, although I don't know what we have to eat."

Roxie tried smoothing over her silky, silvery, flyaway hair and said, "Can't believe it's midnight."

The man's jaw dropped. He looked outside and then back at them. "It does seem like that. Actually, it's around twelve o'clock. Noon, that is."

"Holy balls!" Rogue exclaimed.

"Sheesh, I think we're still frazzled after our rather harrowing escape last night. Have you heard when we're getting out of here?" Roxie asked.

"It looks like we're gonna be here a while."

"But what have you heard?" Luna pressed, trying not to feel like an idiot for thinking it was midnight.

"Absolutely nothing—"

"What about the fire?" Rogue interrupted. "Like, is it huge?"

"For heaven's sake, why isn't the fire department here?" Roxie's panicky tone rose above them all.

For the first time, fear seemed to register on the man's face. "No one can get through to the outside." His voice cracked. "If we hadn't stopped here when we did—" His deadening pause said it all.

"Okay, well we have *some* food," Luna clarified. "And of course, you guys can use our bathroom. But we can't keep opening the door with all the toxic smoke and ash." She thought about it for a millisecond before saying, "You guys are welcome to hang out on the bus." From the man's relieved expression, it was the perfect thing to say.

"Your granddaughter's an angel," the man said before hurrying off the bus.

Roxie beamed at her. But, deep down Luna pondered what was really happening out there . . .

Chapter 5

Roxie Romero spooned out three cans of corned beef hash into the cast iron skillet after popping a quick batch of biscuits into the skoolie's mid-size oven. Meanwhile, Luna scuttled about tidying up and explaining the workings of the compost toilet. Hopefully, the rather odd toilet contraption could handle the traffic surge.

There hadn't been much time for formal introductions when the five spur-of-the-moment guests had made a beeline for the tiny bathroom. They fidgeted awkwardly in the narrow walkway by the bunk beds and awaited their turns. Apparently, the men hadn't been too keen on relieving themselves outside after all. She couldn't blame them. It was too smoky out there. It must have been unnerving for them to sit in their vehicles—in the thick ominous air—waiting for help.

"Luna dear," Roxie asked, "do you happen to have butter?" Might as well live it up. Her cholesterol had been within the limits after last month's annual blood test.

"I doubt it," Luna called out from the cozy bedroom in the rear of the bus.

"Yeah, we bought some organic butter," Rogue said. "'Cause, get this, Luna," he shouted back to his sister, "we don't have to eat vegan junk anymore. Mom let me pick out tons of stuff. Hey"—Rogue stared at the skillet—"I wanted to see what SPAM tastes like. That's why I put the cans on the counter."

"Next time, kiddo," Roxie fibbed, hoping they wouldn't resort to that. She planned on eating dinner at the first Marie Callender's she came to after renting a car in Stockton or Sacramento. Wherever they ended up.

"If we're still *alive*?" Rogue spouted with mocked exaggeration.

One of the guests, a middle-aged woman with short curly black hair frowned quizzically at the boy as she limped to the dinette table. "Do you want some help?"

"Oh no, have a seat," Roxie assured. "Don't pay any mind to Rogue. One never knows what he's going to say next."

Luna nodded adamantly as she shoved a stack of storage containers next to the small woodstove, making more room in the walkway.

Feeling like a 1960s homemaker in the charming, retro, turquoise-themed skoolie, Roxie would have fancied vacationing in something like this in her younger days. Despite growing up in the country and used to roughing it, she preferred the modern conveniences, especially air conditioning. A must since the last few summers had turned out to be horrendously hot. This February heat dome had her concerned what summer might bring. Every year the temperatures broke more records.

One by one, the group of strangers took a seat at the dinette booth across from the micro kitchen. Unfortunately, the booth would only comfortably fit two people on each side. Where would they seat eight?

As if reading her mind, Luna announced from the closet, "Getting chairs. Some of us can sit in the aisle."

"Thank you," Roxie said, banging through the cupboards, looking for paper plates. "Rogue, plates?"

"Right in front of you," the young boy replied as if she had gone senile.

Roxie put her hands on her hips. "Pa-per plates," she enunciated like a first-grade schoolteacher.

"You'd murder trees 'cause you're too lazy to wash dishes?" Rogue's glowering glare stung sharper than his biting tone. "*Woke* people use plates made from wheat straw. They're BPA-free, so they don't poison the environment with forever chemicals. You have heard of the plastic invasion taking over the planet?"

"Rogue, stop with the snark." Luna came to Roxie's aid, lugging folding lawn chairs in the crook of one arm. "You know my eco-eccentric parents." The young woman sighed.

"Oh that," the woman with the curly hair sitting at the table said. "We've been trying to cut our waste by following the guidelines. You know, buy this, not that. There's a different article every week, contradicting the prior dos and don'ts. It's impossible to decipher. Imagine my surprise when I found out they don't bother recycling most plastics. It's cheaper to ship our shit off to some third-world country."

"Such absurdity," Roxie said absentmindedly, still appalled as to why the burden fell on the consumers instead of the manufacturers who made the toxic mess in the first place. They should be the ones held accountable. They had to know how toxic their actions were. "Our small rural community doesn't even recycle." However, it was on the town hall's agenda. It seemed these days the city council demanded action without offering feasible solutions, just so they could claim they had addressed the issue when in reality they hadn't accomplished a darn thing.

"That's no excuse," Rogue interjected as he jaunted down the aisle. "Everyone must do their part. That means compost, compost, compost. And boycott the greenwashing corporations who don't give a crap about the environment."

"Then there'd be nothing to buy. The shelves would be bare," the woman with brassy blond hair and glasses, finally said.

A tall gangly man stomped his way to the dinette's booth and slid into the seat next to the brassy blonde. "Damn hippy toilet," he muttered as if accidentally on purpose.

Not that Roxie especially liked the compost toilet. But, it was better than no toilet. She made brief eye contact with Luna, hoping Rogue hadn't overheard the ungrateful man. Fortunately for everyone's eardrums, the outspoken boy was now fiddling with a portable radio at the front of the bus.

"You're right," the brassy blonde said. "They make it so dang hard. Recycling, that is. We stopped trying. All these new laws." The woman waved her hand in the air. "As long as California doesn't go New Zealand on us and try to ban cigarettes."

"Aw, hell no. Those fascist pigs can't tell me what to do," the gangly man lashed out.

"I'm Linda by the way, and this is my hubby, Levi," the black-haired woman said as the heavy-set man who had first knocked on the door squeezed into the seat beside her. "I'll chip in with the dishwashing after we eat."

"Are you sure, Cupcake?" Levi asked, rubbing the back of her neck. "I don't want you to strain yourself."

"The doctor says it's important to get in some exercise no matter how bad I'm feeling. Recovering from knee surgery," Linda explained as she looked out the window with a harried expression. "I need to do something to fight off my nerves."

"Why, thank you." Roxie enjoyed entertaining when a dishwasher other than herself was involved. She focused on the skillet of corned beef hash to avoid catching a glance at the daunting darkness hovering outside. As if the darkness could somehow consume her. She tugged down the window shade over the farmhouse sink.

"Rogue," Luna called to the front of the bus, "help me move the rest of the grocery bags out of the walkway."

They had been maneuvering around the rather large grocery haul, and with this many people, someone was bound to stub a toe or trip.

"You do it. I'm busy," Rogue shouted back.

The last of the five guests made his way to the table. It was the man who had helped Luna put out the fire earlier. Which had her wondering if the man with the Ram truck had made it over the boulevard.

"Handyman Jack, at your service. I'll help with that," the rather spry and rugged gentleman with a scraggly mustache said to Luna.

"Let's eat first," Roxie said, eyeing him from the corner of her eye. With a name like Handyman Jack, he must be a bit of a character, which she found intriguing. Even if he chose to wear that silly mustache.

"I'm for that," the gangly man said with the butt of his fork clanging the table. "Ready for some of grandma's cooking."

The brassy blonde by his side nudged him. "Butch, manners," his wife whispered not so softly.

Roxie hadn't bothered telling the visitors she wasn't related to Rogue and Luna. Why bother? It wasn't like they'd be socializing after this.

"Are you all traveling together?" Roxie wondered.

The guests answered with the shaking of heads.

"We met on Route 26, AKA Main Street when the fire first broke out," Handyman Jack said. "Can't believe how quickly it got out of hand."

"Yeah, I reported the fire first," Butch said. "If we hadn't driven back to the local fire department, we wouldn't be stuck here."

"That's what you get for being a Good Samaritan," Levi apparently joked.

"Wait—" Luna stopped with her hands full of cloth grocery bags. "You actually *saw* where the fire started?"

"Yeah, a transformer blew. A few miles down the road," Butch said.

"You should have seen it!" Linda exclaimed. "This huge fireball was racing along the power lines. And exploded when it reached the transformer."

"You'd think the power company woulda shut off the power in these winds," Levi said.

"Feel bad for the power companies," Handyman Jack seemed to say to himself. "Damned if they do, damned if they don't."

"We tried calling—" Butch started. "But we couldn't get a signal."

"That's when I remembered passing the volunteer fire department in Gold Town a few minutes earlier," Butch's wife said.

"Anyhoo, we sped back to the fire department. Wish we had just barreled past the fire," Butch reiterated.

"Think of all the people you saved," Roxie said. The man didn't seem to care. Then again, he was probably still in shock, same as everyone else. Getting trapped in a parking lot for hours on end surrounded by a wildfire had a way of fraying one's nerves.

"That's when we saw your flashing headlights." Levi pointed to Butch across the table from him. "I slowed down, thinking there was an accident up ahead. Then we came face-to-face with the exploding transformer."

"We couldn't get a signal either. By the way." Linda turned to Handyman Jack. "Did you see that momma bear and her babies running down the road like they owned it? I counted three cubs."

"Wasn't that something?" Handyman Jack noted with raised brows.

"Bears?" Roxie gasped. It made her think of all the wildlife that had perished in her community. Especially her favorite doe, Minnie, whom she had thrown apples to the past couple of years. She choked back the urge to tear up.

"That's when I came into the picture," Handyman Jack continued. "Butch and Levi warned me something was up with their high beams. By the time I reached the blown transformer, sparks had ignited the underbrush. Suppose by that point, it was already too late to stop the fire. With these winds and all." Handyman Jack let out a long whistle. "Still can't comprehend how the fire blew up so damn fast."

"Yeah," Levi said, "when that deputy got here to evacuate the hotel, he told us to go east. But we had to turn around. It was just too hairy out there. People—driving like maniacs. I saw a pickup truck slam into a firetruck. In the middle of the road. Thought Cupcake was going to have a heart attack."

"We couldn't go around the accident—the fire was everywhere," Linda blurted.

"We barely made it back to the hotel." Levi's words trailed off when he looked out the window.

"We were right behind you," Butch's wife said to Linda. "We turned around as well. I pray the people around here know where to go. Like a lake or something."

"Damn," Butch muttered. "If you hadn't taken so long getting ready this morning, we'd be in Sacramento now," he said in condemnation to his wife. "Now I'm missing the dang monster truck show at Cal Expo."

A sudden hush befell the bus. Butch wasn't all that nice to his wife, calling her out in front of strangers.

Roxie went back to stirring the corned beef hash.

"I personally think it's best we stayed put," Handyman Jack said boldly. "See, Main Street, which includes this stretch of Route 26, curves around and up and down these canyons. And fires, well, they just go where the wind and fuel take them. They jump across roads, don't adhere to the speed limit, and can turn on a dime. It's not like you can outrun a wildfire on these winding rural roads."

"I get what you're saying," Levi said. "We could be driving along, go around a hillside, and get boxed in by the fire."

Both women at the table groaned at the same time.

"Roxie, I want to thank you for taking us in," Linda said, changing the subject. "My knee couldn't take sitting in the Bronco for much longer."

The tension slowly eased. Thank goodness. Roxie didn't need any more stress.

"Looks like you're on a long road trip with all those grocery bags?" Butch's wife commented rather snidely.

Once again on the verge of tears after hearing about the guests' narrow escapes, Roxie fiddled with dishes in the sink before finally finding a steady voice. "Something like that—"

"We had to evacuate two times. Since midnight," Luna interjected before walking by with an armful of toilet paper.

"Another fire?" Linda asked. "Where?"

"Valley Pines," Roxie said, unable to keep the quiver out of her voice. "I'm afraid it took our entire neighborhood. We made it here in the wee hours of the morning. Thinking we'd be safe."

"Good God," Handyman Jack whispered. "The three of you escaped two different fires in one night?"

All Roxie could do was nod. Afraid if she said another word about it, she might burst into tears.

"Un-fuck-ing believable," Levi drawled.

"What's happening—" Linda choked up, unable to continue.

"You want to hear another bizarre coincidence?" Levi asked eerily. "We were on our way to get our daughter in Auburn. Her apartment complex burnt down to the ground early this morning. Marta even lost her car. She was staying with a friend until they received the Code Red text to evacuate. For a second time. We never heard back from her."

"Oh, Cupcake, what are we going to do?" Linda said with teary eyes. "We don't even know where Marta and the grandbabies are."

"Heavens," Roxie drawled. "The fire spread all the way to Auburn?"

"That has to be a different fire," Handyman Jack said.

"Yes, of course," Roxie said, feeling like a nitwit.

Roxie didn't know what to think. Three fires, one in Valley Pines, Gold Town, and Auburn in the past few hours? No wonder they hadn't seen any firefighters; they couldn't be everywhere at the same time.

A formidable silence seemed to suffocate the conversation, as if they were all thinking this was the end of the world. Silly nonsense, Roxie scolded and turned back to the stove to flip the corned beef hash crunchy side up. She sure missed cooking on cast iron, the way it sizzled. *I should dig out my old ones from the back of the cupboard.* The thought had popped into her head before realizing she no longer had a home.

"Rogue, what the hell?" Luna went off. "Why do you have twenty boxes of Pop-Tarts in your bunk?"

Roxie burst out laughing along with the guests, instantly lightening the mood.

"Hey," Rogue yelped, "who said you could snoop around my bunk? Besides, they aren't Pop-Tarts. They're Trader Joe's *Organic* Frosted Toaster Pastries. Dad said I could buy whatever food I wanted. Yes, even junk food. And Spam," he blurted, as if anticipating his sister's response. "Without bioengineered crap, of course."

"A must for any road trip," Handyman Jack remarked playfully.

"I can't believe Mom and Dad are so easy on you," Luna berated.

Luna seemed more upset over the junk food than the fires. Perhaps her generation had been desensitized by the constant catastrophes in the news these days.

"That's how it goes," Butch's wife said. "The first child takes the brunt. By the second one . . ." She tossed her hands in the air. "We're done dealing with grumpy kids."

"I know what you mean. We gave our second child more leeway," Linda said. "See, you start off trying to be this perfect parent. After a while, you get tired of the flak. As if we're the bad guys for trying to do what's best for them."

The wind-up rooster timer on the counter went off. Their tentative conversation abruptly halted when Roxie pulled out a cookie sheet crammed with two-inch-high biscuits. The spectators aahed with anticipation. Nothing like a room of hungry bellies to get one's undivided attention.

"The aroma's killing me," Handyman Jack exclaimed, patting his well-trimmed torso.

"Just a mix I grabbed from the cupboard. *Organic*, by the way," Roxie added with a giggle, which was followed by chuckles from the group. "Go ahead and get started on these." She dumped the biscuits into a bowl before setting it in the center of the table. "The corned beef hash will be ready in a bit." Cooking had been a much-needed distraction. But sooner or later, they needed to come to a consensus on what they should do next.

"Oh, I forgot." Rogue dashed to the adorable turquoise Galanz refrigerator. "Here's the organic butter." He plopped into a lawn chair and finally joined the group.

"I feel like I haven't eaten in days," Levi said.

"Amazing what skipping one meal does. How'd they do it back in the pioneer days?" Linda asked.

Once again, the conversation stopped. Everyone was too busy eating once Roxie divvied out the corned beef hash onto the pastel-colored plates. She seemed to sense the tension melting as appreciative "yums" and grunts took over the conversation.

After their plates were scraped clean, and the biscuit basket sat empty, and they discreetly burped into cloth napkins, Luna asked, "So, does anyone know how long it usually takes for rescue units or Caltrans to clear the roads? After a wildfire."

"Good question. I assume they send in an initial team to check for hazards like downed power lines, trees, and whatnot," Handyman Jack said first. "Still, you'd think we would have spotted a crew by now."

"The air quality might be too hazardous." Butch's wife said with a shaky voice. She turned to the window and dabbed her eyes with her napkin. "Pardon my allergies." She sniffled into the napkin.

Roxie could not remember the woman's name for the life of her but was too embarrassed to ask. Especially since the woman seemed to become increasingly more neurotic by the minute—staring blankly out the window at the horror show.

"The air quality is probably like three hundred," Luna said, rushing through her words. "But why hasn't the fire department been by? I haven't seen any firetrucks."

"Actually," Handyman Jack said, "I saw a few headin' westbound when the sheriff deputy and EMT were here." He stroked his mustache as if lost in thought. "Good God, hope the volunteer fire department didn't get hemmed in by the fire."

Roxie didn't like the sound of that, nor did anyone else based on the squirming in the booth. She wasn't the only one stressing over the lack of emergency personnel. She recalled the nice-looking deputy who had told them to evacuate that had sped off with the burned victim, bless their souls. She kept praying they had made it to the hospital.

"Well now," Roxie intervened, if only for her peace of mind, "I'm sure help will arrive any minute. They must have their hands full with fires from Valley Pines to Gold Town to Auburn—"

"The land 'round here's bone-brittle dry," Levi said. "Ash can travel for miles in these winds. I'm sure it started a shitload of spot fires."

"So." Handyman Jack spoke up, clearing his throat. "Levi mentioned it would be okay for us to ride out the wait on your magnificent bus?" He placed two twenty-dollar bills on the table.

Levi added cash to the ante. "Of course, we'll pay our share."

Luna glanced at Roxie, as if asking if it was all right.

"It's your parents' skoolie," Roxie reminded. Letting them stay on the bus was certainly the decent thing to do.

"Yes. It's not safe out there," Luna finally said. "But you don't need to pay us."

"That's mighty big of you," Handyman Jack said. "Still, we talked it over earlier. We prefer paying for the food, the propane for the stove, and whatnot. No one likes freeloaders."

Their guests nodded adamantly in apparent agreement.

Luna shrugged while Rogue swiped the money from the table. "Hey, you guys, wanna play poker?" Rogue asked innocently enough.

What a shyster. Rogue had won ten bucks off her the last time she had watched him for the day. "Later, hon." Roxie was anxious for any tidbits of good news now that everyone seemed to be in better spirits. "Has anyone tried calling out lately?"

Their guests answered with a round of solemn headshakes. "No Internet or cell service as of yet," Handyman Jack confirmed.

"I heard someone say the fire took out a cell tower on Ray Ray's Ridge," Levi said.

"Sheesh." Roxie's heart sank a little further. "That deputy sheriff knows we're here. Surely, he'll send help."

"You betcha," Handyman Jack said with a ring of optimism. "He had a four-wheel drive vehicle. Expect he'll send help in no time."

"That was hours ago," Butch's wife said in a faraway voice, still avoiding eye contact by staring out the ash-laden windows.

"What if the forest fire rages on for days?" Linda's voice wavered. "We could be trapped here. For a week. Or longer." There was no denying her forlornness. The light over the table dimmed as if confirming their fate.

Levi patted his wife's hands. "Don't worry, Cupcake. We'll get to Marta and the grandbabies soon. Auburn must have a shelter for the people with no place to go."

"What if the fire wipes out all of Auburn?" Linda bemoaned.

"Maybe that's where they sent the emergency personnel," Luna said. "They're trying to save Auburn."

The lights flickered off.

"Now what?" a whisper of a whisper croaked.

"Sorry, we're out of solar power," Luna announced. "The panels on the roof aren't getting sun."

"Wait—" Rogue flicked on the flashlight necklace around his neck and lighted his face while making ghoulish grimaces. "What if . . . we just got nuked! And nobody's coming for us. Ever." That gave the attention-depraved boy a round of harried looks.

"Now, sport, I don't think Russia nor China would waste a multi-million-dollar nuclear device for this part of the Sierras," Handyman Jack dismissed good-naturedly.

"But, but, I even tried sending an SOS message from Luna's iPhone."

"Um, yeah, didn't you hear us say the cellular and Wi-Fi systems are down?" Butch chastised.

"Duh, SOS messaging uses a satellite connection," Rogue blasted with matching disdain. "But I couldn't connect. No matter how many times I tried."

"As I recall," Handyman Jack said, "a satellite connection requires a clear view of the sky. And with all this smoke. And trees . . ."

"Yeah, but don't you know, with everything going on in the world, the Doomsday Clock's at like thirty f'n seconds to midnight?" Rogue proclaimed like a deranged scientist in a fifties science fiction movie.

"The Doomsday Clock is just some left-wing propaganda bull-crap scaring us into thinking global warming is real," Butch seemed all too eager to point out. "And to sucker us into buying ridiculous prepper shit."

Rogue made a scrunchy sour face. "Only dipshits and Flat Earthers think climate change is a hoax."

"Rogue, hush," Roxie reprimanded gently, as if they didn't have enough to worry about.

"Don't tell me you're one of them woke, eco-nazi, commie-socialists?" Butch brazenly denounced.

"You say that like it's a bad thing," Rogue quipped back. "Only commie doesn't go with that sentence. Besides, someone's gotta clean up your toxic shit, since your generation is too stupid to comprehend that climate change is for real."

Roxie hands fall into her lap with a thud. Once Rogue was on a roll, there was no shutting him up. Luna had either not overheard Rogue's outburst or had chosen not to intervene while she cleaned the bathroom.

"Sport, one thing you should consider," Handyman Jack said rather patiently. "It's hard for folks to care about the planet when they can barely afford rent, utilities, and food. They expect the average Joe Schmo to make these monumental sacrifices for the sake of the planet while those making the rules jet around the globe. Now, that sorta changes the little guy's perspective."

"Too bad they didn't know how bad fossil fuels were when they started off," Linda said.

"Oh, no, the f'n Fossil Fuel Industry knew way back in the fifties," Rogue countered, back to championing his cause. "But we can fix it, just like we fixed the ozone layer. Well, almost. I think the ozone hole's supposed to close up in the twenty-sixties," he said, as if it were a long-term road construction project.

"If you say so, Mr. Thunberg," Butch said snidely. That man sure loved to antagonize.

Time to start the kettle. Roxie needed a cup of chamomile tea to ease her rankled nerves. Mama used to say, idle chit-chat and a good cup of tea served strangers best, whereas politics and religion were sure to lead the conversation astray.

"You guys should listen to me. I'm a genius," Rogue insisted.

"You don't say," Handyman Jack said as if indulging him. "What's your IQ?"

"Oh, I can't get tested. 'Cause, you know, then the secret government will abduct me."

Laughter roared through the bus.

"Luna," the boy cried out, "tell them. Tell them it's true."

Luna nodded with wide, round questioning eyes as she walked by with fresh hand towels. "If you say so."

He slugged his sister in the arm. Poor kiddo. His parents shouldn't lead him on so.

"Go on, then, tell me something—I don't know," Butch demanded in a rather haughty tone.

"Duh, there must be tons of stuff *you* don't know," Rogue clapped back.

"Rogue, stop being a PIA," Luna scolded.

"I got one," Rogue said triumphantly. "Did you know CO_2 emissions are sooo bad now the Atlantic Ocean current is close to its tipping point? If it collapses, then we're screwed. Like, we'll have tons of badass storms and, and, major flooding—and then *boom*! We'll be stuck in an ice age."

"Hey, Mr. Thunberg here just solved global warming," Butch announced sarcastically.

"No, you're not listening. If the AMOC, as in the Atlantic Meridional Overturning Circulation collapses, it will screw up the planet so bad, we won't be able to grow food. Everyone will starve."

"Well, you can't have everything," Butch quibbled back like a schoolyard bully.

Luna turned around with narrowed eyes aimed at Butch. "Rogue, help me with the solar lanterns." The ever-levelheaded Luna took control of the conversation. "We should conserve as much as we can. Don't worry, we still have propane for the stove, and the portable power station has a full charge."

"We have tons of cool lithium battery camping stuff. You know, stupid prepper stuff that will save your sorry white ass," Rogue snarked.

A powerful blast of wind rattled the bus and no doubt its passengers based on the leery, open-mouthed faces silently questioning one another. On instinct, Roxie grabbed the counter, not sure what to expect next. That doomsday nonsense had her on edge. It required all her effort not to look out the windows at the red-glowing hills. The entire town must be on fire.

"That one was a doozie." Handyman Jack winked at her. "With this wind—"

"I'll start the dishes now," Linda cut in. "Should I use hot water?"

"Sure. Sparingly," Luna added, setting out several lanterns around the bus. "These solar lights still have a charge. I'll be organizing the food haul. To see what else you bought. Can't believe Dad let you buy junk food. I used to have to sneak Hostess Cup-Cakes."

"Whatev," Rogue groused. "Mom and Dad gave up being vegans in January. You would know if you ever came to see us. They said it didn't matter anymore what we ate."

"Are you serious?" Luna stomped to the back bedroom with an armful of bags, mumbling under her breath.

That was the second time Rogue had mentioned giving up veganism. Which was quite peculiar for the obsessive, health-nut family. On the other hand, Rogue was known for his attention-getting antics. The child had issues, and one couldn't always rely on his viewpoint, however true it might be from his perspective.

Another wind gust assaulted the skoolie. Followed by a crash.

"Shit!" Luna yelled from the window. "There goes one of our solar panels."

"Dad's gonna be super pissed." Rogue darted for the door. "I'll get it!"

Handyman Jack nabbed the kid by the back of his shirt. "Sport, no solar panel is worth dying over."

"You're not my boss!" Rogue pulled free.

"Young man." Roxie finally lost her cool. "Sit your scrawny butt down. This instant."

A blazing projectile streaked across the sky, coming closer. And closer. Directly for the bus.

Someone cried out, "What in the hell—is that?"

"It's gonna hit us!" Butch wailed.

They all ducked as if that would do any good.

The object crashed into the water fountain a few feet from the bus.

"Wow, a flaming trampoline," Rogue gushed. "I wish I had my phone! That video would have gone viral."

Handyman Jack let out a long low whistle. "Never seen anything like that. That's precisely why we're sheltering in place, as they say. And *not* going outside," he said pointedly to Rogue.

Roxie agreed wholeheartedly. It was hellacious out there.

Butch's wife no longer attempted to hide her crying spells and bawled all the way to the bathroom while Butch ignored her despair. Linda and Levi stared intently at each other before collapsing into an embracing hug.

Roxie wanted to say something reassuring, something like they were all going to be just fine. But she couldn't. Instead, she stared out the windows, waiting for the next projectile. Finally, the tap, tap, tap of Luna putting away the groceries brought Roxie back from her moment of gloom and doom.

Roxie quietly cleared the table while Linda washed the dishes. Rogue went back to fiddling with the emergency radio, and the men idly chatted about baseball, or was it football? This was starting to resemble a creepy *Twilight Zone* episode about a band of strangers stranded together at the end of the world with the noonday sun looking more like a red-glowing full moon engulfed in flames in the dead of night.

With not a single sign of life beyond the sanctity of the skoolie's walls . . .

Chapter 6

JACKSON JONES SAT BEHIND the wheel of the meticulously refurbished school bus and stared at the soot-stained windshield, trying to shake away the foreboding apprehension snaking up his torso. It appeared as if the fire department had their hands full or worse yet, had been cut off from the isolated town located along Route 26.

The god-awful truth was, in these blustering winds, there was no way a small-time volunteer fire department could contain a fire of this nature. Not without a hell of a lot of backup, including aerial support. He hadn't heard any planes or helicopters. It was too windy for that.

He couldn't stop replaying the scene in his mind of the sheriff vehicles racing down the main road with sirens and loudspeakers ordering folks to evacuate. Seconds later, flurries of embers had showered the hotel, igniting the restaurant canopies. He'd never forget that look of primal fear on the deputy's face, as if the man had known it would take more than one person to evacuate a hotel that size in the dead of night.

Jackson had made the rash and fateful decision to help clear the hotel's first two floors while the deputy and hotel staff had evacuated the upper floors. *Shoulda headed back home when I first encountered the fire*, Jackson berated, staring through a small patch of clean window at the smoldering pile of bricks of what used to be the historic hotel.

According to the map he had studied earlier, Route 26 was the only way in and out of this section of town. No doubt the locals knew the intricate network of side streets and dirt roads. That was what he told himself instead of thinking the alternative: the locals hadn't made it out. No telling what Route 26 was like at this point. He had half a mind to go see for himself.

Butch sauntered down to him. "Jackson, you look like a man deep in thought."

"Tired of waiting for help to find us." Common sense would be to wait for emergency personnel. "They should have been here by now," Jackson said. "The sheriff, Caltrans, fire department, the power company." *Hell, somebody . . .*

"You'd think," Butch said, using his sleeve to wipe the windshield.

"No use. The windows are mucked up." Jackson resisted hitting the wiper switch, thinking the gunk might damage the wiper blades.

"If you ask me." Butch hesitated before saying, "We're on our own."

Precisely what Jackson was thinking. "What d'ya think of taking a hike to the volunteer fire station up the road? That way we can check out the road conditions."

"I'm in," Butch said. "It's better than sitting 'round with my thumb up my ass."

The hyperactive boy who had been napping on the bench seat behind Jackson barged into the conversation with, "I wanna go, too."

Jackson wasn't so sure. "It's awfully smoky out there."

Butch waved him off. "A little smoke won't hurt."

"Don't you know *anything*?" the smart-aleck kid badgered back. "It's called 'particle pollution.' The toxic particles in the smoke penetrate the lungs, and like, really screw you up. That's why firefighters wear respirators."

"Respirators would do the trick," Jackson said idly to placate the kid.

"Well, we don't got any. So, if you want to go out there, put on your big girl panties," Butch goaded.

"Hunh!" Rogue took off toward the back of the bus.

"That brat has some serious issues," Butch carped.

Jackson spotted several N95 masks hanging from the sun visor. "These will do in a pinch." Although, they wouldn't last long in the thick smoke.

Levi must have sensed something was up for he hurried toward the front of the bus. "Do you see someone?"

"Thinkin' we ought to see what we're up against," Jackson said. "Maybe we can get an update from a firefighter or deputy. Technically, we shouldn't be out there in such conditions. But—"

"With communications down, it might take them a while to find us," Levi finished.

The kid returned, rudely squeezing between the men. "Found 'em!" Rogue held up several respirators by the straps, along with a handful of filters.

Levi offered a disapproving frown. "Really?"

Jackson recognized the brand and took the liberty of grabbing one. "They ought to do the trick."

"See, we even bought the smoke and carbon monoxide filters." The kid went on like an overeager used car salesman. "You screw them on. Like this." The boy proficiently attached the filters to each of the respirators.

"Why didn't you tell us you had respirators?" Butch pestered.

"You didn't ask," the kid said with a goofy smirk.

"Damn," Levi said. "And *why* do you have full-face respirators?" Levi held out a hand expectedly.

Rogue rolled his eyes to the ceiling. "Only losers aren't ready for SHTF."

Jackson stifled his chuckle. The kid wasn't one for diplomacy, which was liable to get him into a lot of trouble at school. Still, the kid's innocently frank attitude was starting to grow on him.

"Heavens," Roxie declared. "Don't tell me you're going out there—in all that smoke?" Her admonishing tone said it all.

Jackson's attention quickly shifted to the attractive grandmother as she strutted toward them with hands on hips with her lustrous silvery hair bouncing in the amber lights of the bus.

"Don't worry—" Rogue started.

"No one's going anywhere without me," Luna boldly announced. The headstrong beauty in her twenties approached in glitzy attire, including flashy nails, hot-pink lipstick, and glittery sneakers that would likely melt on first contact with the hot asphalt.

Butch and Levi's tentative smiles quickly transformed into tight-lipped grimaces; apparently the men were taken aback by the young woman's demand.

"What a bimbo," Butch mumbled.

Luna flashed Butch the evil eye. The granddaughter definitely had some cajónes. That, or she was PMSing. Before trouble ensued, Jackson said, "With these, thanks to your brother." Jackson held up a respirator. "We're good."

"Are you sure?" Linda approached. "I know this sounds trivial, but I haven't seen a single bird. It's just"—she shivered—"spooky out there."

"We can't sit 'round on our asses," Butch clapped back. The fellow always seemed primed for an argument.

"We'll do a quick recon of the situation," Jackson stated casually. Although, he didn't know how long Levi would last. The red-faced fellow was always out of breath, not to mention carrying a good thirty pounds of excess baggage around the middle.

"Well, I'm going out there. And if you want to use *our* respirators, wait while I change," Luna commanded with full authority.

"Honey," Butch cut in, "you need to let the boys handle this."

Luna gave Butch the Medusa death stare after his biting chauvinistic remark. "If you get off *my* bus, without me, you're *not* getting back on. And don't open the door until I'm ready." She practically ran down the aisle, jumping over the lower kitchen drawer that Roxie must have left open.

"Roxie, say something to her," Levi said.

Roxie grimaced. "I wouldn't argue with those young hormones, if you know what I mean."

"Yeah, my sister's hella tough. Even if she dresses like a Barbie. So, stop messing with her!" Rogue seemed to dare.

"Okay, so we wait," Jackson said coolly, maintaining eye contact with Butch.

"I can't watch. It'll make me a nervous wreck. I'll whip up a batch of tuna sandwiches for when you get back. That's what I'll do." Roxie sashayed back to the kitchenette.

Jackson tried his best not to ogle Roxie's shapely derriere. *Stop it, you old fool*, he chastised.

"I'll help you, Roxie," Linda said. "But, Levi, be careful. You know what the doctor said."

"Sure thing, Cupcake." Levi smiled sweetly at his wife.

"Women . . ." Butch scowled in obvious contempt.

Minutes later, an unrecognizable Luna returned, decked out in camos, a camouflage ballcap, and military boots.

Jackson offered her an approving smile. "What d'ya know? You're a regular weekend warrior."

Luna barely nodded. "Rogue, give me the respirators. All of them."

"Hey, I need one." Rogue hid them behind his back.

"Absolutely not. If you get hurt, Mom and Dad will hate me forever," Luna said with finality.

"Roxie," Rogue whined, "Luna's being mean to me again."

"Don't put me in the middle of this. Listen to your sister," Roxie responded sternly.

"This is so not fair," Rogue huffed, begrudgingly handing the respirators to Luna.

"Guys, your attention," Luna said. "First, adjust the head harness straps, then just put your chin in, and slip the harness over your head." She demonstrated with ease. "The speaking diaphragm works decently."

"One more thing. With this smoke, it could get dark real quick out there," Jackson said. They should be back before dark. But with the way the smoke shrouded the sun, he wasn't so sure.

"Rogue, flashlights." Luna beckoned with her hand.

"So, I was thinking," Jackson started carefully, not wanting to appear as if he were in charge since that was apparently Luna's job. "Why don't we see if we can make it to the volunteer fire department? They ought to have some info. Can't be more than three to four miles."

"Levi, can you walk that far?" Luna asked point-blank.

Ouch, that one had to hit below the belt. Before Levi could take umbrage with her remark, Jackson said, "If anyone finds the hike too tough, we'll pair you up with someone to go back with."

A pouting Rogue dramatically moped toward them with the flashlights. "These are fully charged LED solar flashlights. Use the hand crank if the light starts to fade," the kid said devoid of emotion as he handed them out.

Jackson tousled Rogue's curly mop of reddish-brown locks. "Thanks, sport. You must have cool parents to have all this neato gear. How's about you sit in the driver's seat and keep an eye on us? Honk the horn if you see anyone."

Rogue shrugged. "Okay," he said, back to his excitable self.

"Hurry back. And don't make me send the cat after you," Roxie called out as Jackson descended the bus steps.

Ah, so there is a cat. Jackson thought he had heard the faintest of meows. Roxie was a trip. His smile quickly faded once stepping outside into the whirlwinds of ashy air.

He took it upon himself to take point, and not so surprisingly, Luna fell into step beside him. They headed for the parking lot's blocked entrance where a charred pine that had to be a hundred feet tall still burned in spots.

The men kicked at the felled tree the way men do when they don't know what else to do. It did not budge. It was a problem for later. Now, Jackson needed to see the road conditions. He stepped lightly over the scorched boulevard between stranded vehicles reduced to solidified pools of melted metal and rubber. Where had these people fled?

Once on Main Street, the fire's devastation resembled the aftermath of a Ukrainian warzone. Piles of brick rubble left stark reminders of the specialty shops lining the street hours ago. This section of the historic town utterly decimated. What about the residents? Had they made it out of the inferno?

The four of them stood in silence, as if paying homage to the refurbished gold-rush-era buildings that had survived nearly two centuries. Until the fire.

"The fire department's this way," Jackson muffled, pointing west of what remained of the spongy asphalt.

"Yeah, 'cause we sure ain't going the other way," Butch shrilled.

Jackson spun around at the man's cynical remark. That can't be. He puzzled over the blurry disfiguration. He rubbed away the soot already collecting on the respirator's shield. And squinted harder.

"Fuuuck!" Luna blasted through the respirator.

She must have realized at the same time he had that the blurry disfiguration was actually the remains of two blackened firetrucks that had evidently crashed into one another, completely blocking eastbound traffic. How far east had the fire gone? All the way to his cabin in Shake Ridge?

Jackson found himself spellbound at the desolation of it all. He regained his composure and headed west toward the low-hanging burnt-orange sun casting that same ominous orangish glow to everything from the sky to the air to the ground. They crept along the disintegrating two-lane blacktop with spot fires dotting the outskirts still searching for something to ignite.

As they turned a bend in the road, the smoke waned enough to recognize a sheriff's SUV ahead. But as they approached, the telltale signs that something wasn't right churned Jackson's gut. No tires! That was the first clue. The vaporized windows and windshields, another chilling clue.

Butch ran to the vehicle. He kicked at the vehicle and shouted obscenities.

"That doesn't look promising," Jackson husked under his breath.

Still, everyone had to see for themselves, to see if anyone was inside—had been. One by one, they circled the charred vehicle as if in a state of sheer disbelief. Thankfully, no one was inside. He didn't think he could stomach finding human remains. He wiped the respirator shield clean again, concerned at what toxic soup of chemicals had been unleashed into the air.

Luna tapped his shoulder and pointed to a vehicle farther down. Another sheriff's vehicle? Jackson stopped running when he noticed the absence of tires. With Levi lagging behind, Jackson took his time, concerned for him. The out-of-shape man should have stayed on the bus. He was slowing them down.

Jackson caught up with Butch and Luna as they paced around the second sheriff SUV in an odd stupor-like state. Jackson peeked inside, greeted by a charred skeleton crumpled on coiled metal on what remained of the backseat. The burned victim? His gut flipped-flopped.

The men big-eyed one another before continuing down the street, finally letting Luna take the lead. Jackson was no longer in a hurry, afraid of what they might find next as he gawped at the line of burnt vehicles heading westbound on both sides of the two-lane road.

By the time they reached the traffic jam of burnt-out vehicles, Jackson braced for the horrors he might encounter. But, the vehicles were empty. *Is that what I think it is? Good God, don't tell me . . .* That was when reality hit him—like the cold of a steel blade pressed against his larynx. "Everyone, hold on," Jackson warned, stepping over a pile of ash.

Butch ignored him and stomped on.

"Stop," Jackson shouted sternly before kneeling. With his pocketknife, Jackson poked at a glinting object catching the light in a mound of ash.

Luna was at his side first. And knelt beside him. "Is that—" She looked away quickly, refusing eye contact.

Butch glared down at Jackson. "If you can't hack it, go back," Butch berated.

"A-hole," Luna muttered.

"What's wrong?" Levi stumbled toward Jackson, nearly tripping.

"Folks, you might want to avoid any mounds of ash," Jackson said, poking at the melted metal. "This is the remains of someone's bridge. As in dental work."

Levi gaped.

Butch kicked at the ashes. "Don't be a pussy."

Luna went ballistic and locked the SOB in a chokehold in mere seconds. She held him against a car for a long palpable moment. Finally, she let go. Letting him fall to the ground. Butch sprang to his feet like he was about to coldcock her.

"Settle down," Jackson said firmly with the four-inch-blade knife still in his hand. Not that he intended to stick the fellow. But, if it came down to it, he was ready. *Hell, today, he was ready for damn near anything.*

Luna returned Butch's glowering stare. Without flinching. That girl was tough.

"We're walking on—dead people?" Levi gagged.

"Yep, it appears as if some people were so desperate, they escaped on foot," Jackson said somberly. "Best we don't muck it up so the cadaver dogs can do their thing. For the sake of these folks' families."

"Hey, I see someone." Luna took off in a dead run for what looked to be a person crawling on the road up ahead.

Unable to match the girl's pace, Jackson wiped away the ashy residue sticking to the eye shield and tried to make sense of the odd-shaped person in the middle of the road. But something wasn't quite right.

"Luna?" Jackson shouted about five seconds too late.

From out of nowhere, a pack of mangy coyotes snarled and growled with blood dribbling down their quivering jowls. The young woman froze in mid-step. After a quick recon, it came to him loud and clear; Luna had interrupted their dinner. At least she had the common sense to freeze as the apparent leader inched closer, revealing a vicious set of jagged fangs.

Jackson crept up to her. "Easy now, no sudden moves." Slowly, he pushed her behind him. "Now let's back up. Slow and steady." Levi and Butch were behind them somewhere. They must have spotted the pack by now. All Jackson could do was try not to threaten the pack to reduce their chances of getting mauled. Or becoming the second course.

Too late. The leader of the pack lunged at Jackson. Mere feet away. The coyotes must think he and Luna wanted to steal their dinner. Jackson reached for the gun tucked in the back of his jeans.

Bang! He let off a round, hoping to intimidate the pack.

A scuffle behind him had Jackson wondering if a coyote had flanked them.

"A-holes," Luna hissed. "Can you believe those two just left us."

What? Butch and Levi had run off? Leaving them with the angry coyotes. *Guess I underestimated Levi.* Rabid-like coyotes had a way of jumpstarting one's adrenaline. Well, Jackson wasn't abandoning Luna. Although, he didn't have enough ammo on him to take down the pack. Nor the shooting skills for that matter.

"We're good. Just stay by my side," Jackson cautioned.

Luna stepped beside him and held her ground with brandished arms. He kept yelling while bending down to grapple the ground for anything within throwing reach. The road had buckled in the perfect spot. And he began throwing chunks of rocky asphalt at the pack, yelling and acting more like a deranged man than anything else. Luna responded in the like.

Together, step-by-step, they backtracked while the wild animals went back to feasting on some poor creature. When a man's boot fell from one of the coyotes' mouths, he realized it was—had been—a person.

The coyotes glanced warily at them every few seconds, growling to reveal gnarly meat-encrusted teeth. "We're doing good," Jackson kept jabbering if not for Luna's sake, then his.

When they made it back to the first sheriff's SUV, Jackson figured the two of them were safe. Still, without another word, they alternated between walking backward and forward, making sure they were out of the danger zone.

That was when Jackson knew beyond a shadow of a doubt this had to be the worst day of his life.

Chapter 7

Roxie Romero hummed a long-forgotten sixties ballad while straining four cans of wild albacore tuna in the skoolie's farmhouse sink. She didn't know why the love song had popped into her head and could not for the life of her remember the lyrics. Nevertheless, the bit of comforting nostalgia brought a smile to her, the perfect distraction.

Rogue sat in the cockpit and kept her posted on Luna's expedition, thanks to a pair of expensive-looking binoculars. *Let's see. What can I add to the tuna?* She perused the cupboards to find a jar of vegan mayo and organic pickle relish, happy for the black olives as well.

She cheerfully chopped away at the olives, expecting Luna and the men to return with help any second. With everything going on, the fact that the authorities hadn't arrived must have been an oversight. She was anxious to get going with the phone calls: the insurance company, the utility companies, her friends, not to mention let her brother and sister know she was fine. Chances were, Rosa and Roberto had heard about the fire on the news by now and were worried sick.

From what Roxie had heard, it took several years to rebuild an entire community after a wildfire due to the arduous clean-up, repairing the utilities, obtaining the necessary permits, and rebuilding the infrastructure, not to mention building the homes. She wasn't looking forward to juggling the red tape.

I better start looking for an apartment and beat the rush, Roxie mused, dumping the strained tuna into a blue cornflower CorningWare dish, the same print her dear grandmother used to have. It would be cheaper to rent a studio apartment for a while; after all, it wasn't like she had anything to put in it. But where? She certainly didn't want to move to the city.

Pixie brushed against her legs, meowing until Roxie let her sniff the empty tuna can. Tuna fish had a way of bringing out the wildcat in her. She added a forkful of tuna to a saucer. "Here you go, Pixie girl." Her skittish cat had spent most of the day hiding in the back bedroom until the men had ventured out. Poor kitty.

Without further ado, Pixie had a sudden case of the zoomies and raced down the aisle, parkouring off the dinette table, the kitchen cupboards, the hall closet, and then back past her to the front of the bus. *What a goofball*. Roxie should count her blessings she still had her kitty. Not that she could say she had saved Pixie, for Pixie had ended up saving her the night of the fire.

Dread started setting in at the thought of calling Rosa and Roberto. They'd been pestering her to move out of the rural area and to the city for some time—while she still had a house to sell. They had been right. But Valley Pines was where her life was. Along with fleeting memories of her children and the sporadic happy years of her marriage.

She certainly didn't see herself living near Rosa in Palm Springs or Roberto in Delaware. They were entrenched with their own families. Rosa took care of her grandchildren after school, since no one could afford daycare these days. And though Roberto would offer her the guest bedroom, his wife was difficult to tolerate even on a good day.

Sadly, Roxie had lost her children to the three Cs: one to cancer, one to a car crash, and one to COVID-19. Why the universe had taken all her children before giving her a single grandchild still kept her up in the lonely nights. Which was probably why she kept such a hectic schedule volunteering in her community. Why, she had jumped through hoops to get the Dollar General approval. And now it was gone.

Roxie went back to humming, but the unyielding stream of worries continued plaguing her. *Hmm, where can I find an apartment?* There weren't many apartment complexes in the rural areas. With so many displaced people, the competition would get stiff, and rents would be high. A colossal headache.

She could take the insurance money and walk away. Start a new life. Someplace pleasant. Perhaps by the ocean? Like Santa Cruz or Half Moon Bay. Of course, she wasn't so sure she had coverage. The fleeting daydream vanished when she wondered what people like Luna's parents were going to do. What if the insurance companies couldn't handle the surge of claims with all these fires? Who would bail out the homeowners? She wouldn't count on the government. Not after they had bailed out the banks—and not the homeowners during the early 2000's subprime mortgage crisis, leaving families homeless.

Roxie took a pinky taste of the organic mayo and decided it wasn't half-bad before stirring in several spoonfuls into the tuna. She shouldn't abandon her community; they needed her all the more now. Besides, she thrived on any worthy cause that needed championing. While some had labeled her a busybody.

She couldn't help it; her DNA seemed encoded with the urge to help those in need, while others chose to judge the less fortunate as losers. Her mind busied over starting a *GoFundMe* campaign for the Valley Pines residents without homeowner's insurance. Even before the fire had hit her town, poverty had been hitting the middle class with more and more familiar faces timidly popping by the Wednesday food pantry.

She dumped in the chopped olives, irritated for letting her troublesome thoughts interrupt her peaceful humming. Couldn't she have just five minutes of peace? As for losing a life's worth of belongings, she found it almost liberating. Except for her cherished keepsakes and scrapbooks.

Life goes on. Good thing she had gone through the laborious task of scanning a life-long collection of family photos onto those nifty flash drives last year. She always kept a flash drive in her purse, and Rosa and Roberto kept copies for safekeeping as well.

Roxie thanked her lucky stars she was financially stable, thanks to the hefty worker's comp settlement after Hank had died on the job due to faulty equipment. Oh, Hank she missed. But not as much as most people presumed. He had been a wonderful provider and considerate husband, more dedicated to football, baseball, and basketball than her.

With spoon in hand, she reached for the pickle relish.

Bang! A gunshot rang out.

The spoon clattered into the sink.

"Rogue? What's going on?" Roxie scuttled to the front of the bus.

"I can't see anything. They're too far away." Rogue flashed her a wide-eyed look. "I'm going after them."

"Young man"—Roxie's tone deepened—"stay put."

Roxie stood in the bus stairwell with her face glued to the accordion door's smoky glass pane.

"Hey, I see someone," he exclaimed between excited gasps. "Running this way."

"Luna?" Roxie worried.

"Un-uh." Rogue adjusted the binoculars. "I don't see her military cammies. Uh, it's a skinny person."

"That's my Butch. That man can run," Butch's wife announced as she ran out of the bathroom.

"What about my Cupcake?" Linda hurried out from the back bedroom. "Do you see Levi—"

"Where's Luna?" Roxie worried out loud.

Butch stopped on the road by the hotel entrance. And just stood there. Waiting. And waiting.

"Hey, I see the big guy!" Rogue said through binoculars.

"Cupcake?" Linda asked. "Thank you, Lord Jesus."

Levi made it to Butch, and the two of them waited by the downed tree. Then they pointed toward the parking lot and awkwardly hiked over the hilly boulevard toward the bus.

"Hon, any sign of Luna?" Roxie asked, her apprehension growing.

"There she is!" Rogue shouted. "And Handyman Jack, too."

Roxie patted her fluttering heart. She certainly didn't want any harm to befall Luna. Forest and Crystal had enough problems.

Levi and Butch stood outside the bus and brushed off their ash-covered clothes. Butch knocked on the bus door. "Remember what Luna said?" Rogue yelled through the glass door. "I'm not opening the door until all of you are here."

Butch responded with vulgar sign language. Which apparently didn't faze Rogue, because the boy responded passionately by flipping off Butch. With both hands.

"You should do something about that little monster," Butch's wife pestered.

"Not today," Roxie said with a slight smile before swiftly closing the blackout curtain that divided the cockpit from the rest of the bus in order to keep the smoke at bay when Rogue decided to let them inside.

"Was someone actually shooting at you?" Rogue was the first to ask as they boarded.

Roxie listened breathlessly on the other side of the curtain along with the wives.

A grim-faced Luna flung back the curtain, mumbling, "A-holes!"

"Is everyone all right?" Linda asked.

Luna's ice-cold glare refused eye contact as she marched to her bunk. Her scrunched mouth and creased brows indicated their scouting trip had not gone well.

Roxie beckoned the three men to take a seat at the dinette table and fussed about filling the glasses with lukewarm lemon tea, anxious for some news. Anything.

"They could have killed us," Luna spouted, immodestly changing into her jeans in the aisle. Luna had never been one to mince words.

"Look," Levi said, "we thought you and Jackson were right behind us."

Butch snickered. "You're the ones who stayed behind like dumbasses—"

"Time out!" Roxie spoke over the escalating argument, gesturing the referee signal. "What on earth happened?"

"The crux of it"—Handyman Jack took over—"we ran into a hungry pack of damn coyotes. Protecting their supper."

Roxie and the wives groaned.

"You *never* run from coyotes." Luna fumed.

"She's right," Handyman Jack said. "You gotta stand your ground. And yell and wave your arms. Throw things—"

"It's called hazing," Rogue butted in. "Everyone knows that."

"You sure as hell can't outrun a pack of 'em," Handyman Jack continued in an agitated tone. "Unless safety's a few feet away. They can run upwards of sixty miles per hour."

"A pack of coyotes?" Roxie was astounded. She had seldom caught a glimpse of a coyote in the distance the entire time living in the country.

"The fire must have brought them down from the canyons," Handyman Jack said.

"Why the hell didn't you tell us you were packing some heat?" Butch quizzed.

Handyman Jack ignored the question.

"You guys didn't kill any, did you?" Rogue said, choked up.

"Coyotes! What's going on out there?" Linda shrilled on the verge of hysterics again.

"You won't believe what we saw . . ." Luna shared a tense glance with Handyman Jack.

"Well, spit it out," Roxie implored, tired of the suspense.

"Let's just say"—Handyman Jack paused—"those coyotes have gotten a taste of *people* meat."

"Ew!" Rogue gagged dramatically. "But did you kill one?"

Handyman Jack shook his head. "Fired a warning shot to scare them off when they attempted to encircle us. I didn't have enough rounds on me to take out the entire lot. Not that I would want to," he said directly to Rogue. "The problem is, scared and hungry wildlife only add to our situation."

Roxie's heart sank a little further. "I take it you didn't find help." Knowing the answer, she leaned back against the kitchen counter.

Luna and the men shook their heads grimly. Linda softly wept on her husband's shoulder while he caressed her back lovingly.

"I'm sorry," Levi said with blinking, watery eyes. "I panicked and hightailed it out of there."

"What are we going to do?" Butch's wife blubbered.

"Simple," Handyman Jack said. "We take matters into our own hands."

Roxie smiled inwardly. She was starting to like this man. "What do you have in mind?"

Handyman Jack grinned wryly. "I just happen to have my chainsaws with me. Fact was, I was on my way to help a buddy clear his property up in Oregon."

"Interesting," Levi said. "You're suggesting we cut back that tree blocking the exit?"

"Sounds like a lot of work," Butch said coolly.

"It's better than staying here," Roxie snapped back. Just looking at the blood-red sky put her on edge. As if the haunting, smoky air gave her a new kind of paranoia-laced claustrophobia.

"This is absurd. Why didn't that sheriff send us help?" Butch's wife ranted. "I'm filing a complaint. He knows we're here. I even gave him a bottle of water this morning."

The men seemed to share the same ominous knowing expression.

Luna made her way to the crowd and whispered, "I don't think the deputy made it out. We found two sheriff vehicles."

"Ah, please say you didn't find that nice deputy who evacuated us?" Roxie murmured.

"Who's to say?" Handyman Jack said. "Nevertheless, we came across a body in the road. And the coyotes were gnawing on—someone. The deputy wasn't in the front seat. Meaning, he ventured out on foot."

"Pfff." Butch's wife set down her glass a bit too hard. "You'd think a deputy would have the brains to stay in the safety of his vehicle."

Levi shook his head. "There was a . . ." He went silent for a long moment. "A skeleton in the backseat. Probably the burned victim."

Roxie went back to patting her heart, trying to slow the rapid beating.

"Roxie, you were right," Luna said. "You saved our lives. If we had tried to escape in this bus—well, we wouldn't have made it very far based on all the abandoned burnt-out vehicles we saw."

"Surely, the residents and hotel guests made it to safety," Roxie said. No one bothered contradicting her.

"Who's with me on cutting up the felled tree, section by section, until we can get our vehicles through?" Handyman Jack asked.

"What's the point? Main street's blocked with burnt vehicles," Levi said.

"Spotted a Cat at Mannie's Hardware, bulldozer that is. The building's toast, but the heavy equipment in the back gravel lot appeared intact," Handyman Jack said.

Butch grunted like a Marine. "Now we're talking."

"We can push the vehicles out of the way if we figure how to start the Cat," Handyman Jack said.

"I can hotwire anything," Butch said.

Why was Roxie not surprised?

"What about the coyotes?" Rogue asked.

"I'm sure they're long gone," Butch said.

"Wouldn't bet my life on that," Handyman Jack countered.

"I'll take point somewhere and shoot at them if I have to," Luna said. "My dad's rifle is in the closet."

"Yeah, right," Levi mumbled.

"Hey, don't be dissing my sis," Rogue barged in. "That's my job. Besides, she's an awesome shot. She took the Sharpshooter award at Apoc Junior Training four summers in a row."

Luna's lips quivered in the beginnings of a smile, which she quickly stifled.

Roxie never knew what to think of the girl. Such a paradox, dressed like a model but hard as nails. Probably rebelling her parents' strict upbringing by glamming it up. Who could blame her?

"But I'm not killing anything. If I don't have to," Luna quickly added.

"No worries there," Handyman Jack said. "As you saw, shooting at them dissuaded their curiosity. They tend to be nocturnal. But the fire's aftermath is sure to shake up their behavior and put them in defense mode."

"Okay, so how long you think it'll take to move the tree and clear the road?" Linda asked. "We have to get to our daughter and grandbabies."

"Depends. Can any of you work a chainsaw?" Handyman Jack asked.

Levi waved his hand in the air. "Been there, done that."

"With two of us, we can cut the tree out of the way in a few hours," Jackson said. "Wide enough for our vehicles, including this big ole bus."

"Meanwhile, I'll clear a path down the road with the dozer," Butch said.

"Please say you can start—right now," Linda groaned.

"Best wait 'til morning," Handyman Jack said. "It'll be dark soon. Other predators might be lurking about. Say, bear, mountain lion, and the like. And they're scared. Hungry. And downright dangerous as we've witnessed."

"Don't forget Bigfoot," Rogue interjected enthusiastically. His remark was followed with a nervous round of laughter much to the boy's chagrin.

"I'm sure Luna and I can find places for everyone to sleep tonight," Roxie said reassuringly.

"Also," Handyman Jack continued, "thinkin' it wouldn't be a bad idea to rotate, say two-hour watch shifts. On the off chance of spotting an emergency vehicle. Maybe a Caltrans crew. Or others who hunkered down during the fire. The cockpit's driver seat is the best place for that. We can flash our lights and honk if we spot any activity on Route 26 AKA Main Street."

"Awesome, I call first dibs," Rogue quipped.

But the real question lingering in the back of Roxie's mind, one that no one had asked: was the fire still raging out of control? She kept her mouth shut, not wanting to be a Debbie Downer, especially since the wives had finally stopped sniveling.

"How about those marvelous sandwiches you promised?" Handyman Jack winked. "The aroma's killing me." He rubbed his belly.

It had been ages since anyone had offered Roxie a flirty wink, even if it was over silly sandwiches.

Chapter 8

Luna Lewis sat cross-legged on top of the cab of Handyman Jack's truck, with her father's Remington rifle cradled in her lap, and methodically scanned the perimeter for predators. As if expecting something to happen. Almost knowing it. She was astonished at how quickly she had reverted to survival mode. Relying on years of mock SHTF training instilled her with a sort of calming numbness once she had been thrown into their precarious grid-down situation.

Meaning, she knew better than to let down her guard.

Handyman Jack and Levi worked at cutting the fallen tree into chunks small enough to roll out of the way. Unlucky tree. As much as she snubbed her radicalized environmentalist upbringing, she still revered nature. Trapped in the parking lot of the forgotten ill-fated town surrounded by blackened trees destined to suffer a slow agonizing death, she struggled not to become victim of the forest's pain. "Trees have a consciousness," Auntie SunFlower used to say.

Beyond the brattling of chainsaws, the distant clattering of metal hitting metal announced Butch's progress as he cleared the road with the bulldozer. She panned to the main road but couldn't catch him in the binocular's viewfinder, even though the smoke had dissipated. Still, the dark smoky horizon cautioned they would be back to wearing respirators when the wind shifted again. To be on the safe side, she had an N95 strapped to her upper arm, ready when needed since the respirator restricted her aim.

A movement between the trees on the opposite side of the road snapped her into full alert-mode. She adjusted the binoculars and focused in on a regal eight-point buck followed by a timid doe. She let out a long deep breath of relief. So many lives disrupted. Not just people. It brought back the gruesome image of the mangled body they had encountered yesterday. In a way, she hoped the deputy, or whoever it was, had died of smoke inhalation *before* the coyotes found him. She shivered despite the balmy morning.

Luna almost regretted inviting the guests to stay on the bus due to the undertones of environmental and political differences spurred by Rogue's outspokenness. Then again, they were all under duress. As a civilized person, she was obligated to help strangers, even if they didn't share one another's beliefs. They were definitely conservatives, which was fine; she had a lot of conservative work friends, and they didn't get into heated arguments. To this day, she didn't understand how people let their political views dictate their personal beliefs—defining who they were.

Linda complained nonstop about her recent knee surgery and limped around, dusting every surface of the bus, and swept the floor every hour on the hour. Mrs. Butch, as they called her, since no one remembered her name—and it seemed stupid to ask now—spent most of the time weeping in the bathroom, blaming her puffy eyes and red nose on allergies. *I'd cry too if I was married to Butch.*

Roxie remained cheery despite losing her home to the fire and catered to the guests' needs, including the cooking, not one of Luna's attributes. Handyman Jack was their best asset. He seemed to maintain order in a casual way and always regarded their safety first. Whereas Luna had to be mindful not to tell them to just shut the hell up when they didn't immediately agree to her decisions.

Then there was Rogue, emotionally fragile. Sometimes she thought Mom and Dad had only exacerbated his mental issues with all their save-the-planet-before-it's-too-late crap. And now, after losing the only home he had ever known, Rogue was bound to be more fragile than ever. And, well, Luna wasn't so good at pampering. Not after being raised in a tough-love environment. However, she should be thanking her parents for inadvertently preparing her for the ruthless fashion world.

Escaping the fires, trapped on the bus, man-eating coyotes—was this too much for Rogue? He hadn't endured the rugged training she had. To her, this might as well be one of those hateful apocalyptic summer camps, only this time their weapons were loaded. "This is not a drill," she could almost hear the camp's over-the-top drill sergeant ranting while she fired tracer rounds at stuffed dummies from a hand-dug foxhole.

Her parents must be freaking out by now. Had they seen the fire on the news? *What if they think we're—dead*? How horrible was that? Damn cell phone towers. No Internet. No SOS messaging. No nothing. "Modern technology is only reliable to a point," Dad used to say.

Everything had gone so wrong so fast since yesterday afternoon when Mom had practically bullied her into babysitting Rogue. Knowing them, her parents had been jailed for chaining themselves to—something. Like the time they had chained themselves to a two-thousand-year-old redwood tree in Guerneville while live-streaming to gain Patreon supporters and donations.

Luna would always remember that wondrous feeling of saving the tree. That day. The next week the amazing old-growth forest had been logged. And her wondrous feeling had soured to "What was the fucking point?" Corporations won most of the time.

"Not again?" The faltering grinding of a chainsaw warned it was having problems. Handyman Jack gave Levi the cease signal. If they lost a chainsaw, it would take twice as long. She didn't want to stay there a second longer than she had to. It was just creepy sitting there amongst the dying trees with the reddish-black sky closing in on them.

Besides, she absolutely could not miss that job interview. Her friend in HR could only cover for her so long. Luna really was the best candidate for the San Francisco branch buyer position. Her knack for predicting trendy shoes for the Sacramento region had proven successful, even though she only served as a backup to the shoe department when the boss worked the L.A. region.

She was bored with managing eco-chic activewear. With her shoe fetish, breaking into the designer industry would be her absolute dream job. However, transitioning from activewear to designer shoes wouldn't be easy. Which was perfect. She loved a challenge.

A flickering shadow blotted out the ominous doomsday sun for a second. She followed the shadow with the binoculars and zoomed in on the eagle as it perched on a scorched tree limb. After blinking away the red-glowing sun from her watery eyes, she gasped at the bald eagle's magnificence.

The eagle stared back with piercing, knowing eyes, eyes that screamed, "Look what you stupid humans did to our home!"

"So sorry," Luna whispered, unable to shake away its pain, as if its sorrow leached into her own heart. She needed to snap out of her funk and not let her metaphysical side take over. As she had learned, there was a time for battle and survival and a time for compassion and healing. Survival always topped her list.

"Hey!" Rogue banged the side of the truck. "Roxie said I could hang with you as long as I wear a mask. *If*, you say it's okay," he quickly added.

Because you're driving Roxie crazy, Luna wanted to say. "Sure," she said as upbeat as she could, unable to bear the fire's desolation. "You monitor the east end of the street, and I'll watch the west." She should get in some much-needed bonding time with him. She hadn't visited much the past two years.

Rogue plopped next to her on the truck roof with his own set of binoculars. "Sweeet, they're halfway done. We can leave by lunch."

She pointed to Handyman Jack, who was in the middle of disassembling the chainsaw. "If he can fix it."

"Ooh, Handyman Jack can do anything," Rogue gushed. "Like a superhero. For old guys, you know."

"He is pretty awesome." Roxie must think so too. She had caught Roxie sneaking intriguing glances at him. They were about the same age . . .

She and Rogue sat in silence, scouring the scorched landscape while she tried to think of something nice to say. She had never been good at playing sister. Probably due to their ten-year age difference. He used to love hearing Mom and Dad's comical retelling of Rogue's namesake after he had spontaneously burst into this world eight and a half months after her parents' weekend retreat to rekindle their twin-flame soul-connection. But Mom and Dad were much better at storytelling.

She wanted to grill Rogue on why Mom and Dad had allowed him to buy junk food. Why had they stopped eating vegan? Had Rogue just made that up? It reminded Luna of the time she had sent out birthday party invites to her third-grade class. Before asking her parents. Bamboozling her way into getting the McDonald's birthday party she had wanted. Sort of. If meatless burgers with only lettuce, tomato, and pickles on a bun were considered a win. But it had been the crappy vegan birthday cake and fake ice cream that had totally ruined the party.

Unfortunately, the party had only accentuated her crazy parents, and she had cried the entire night. Of embarrassment. At that crucial age, Luna had just wanted to fit in with her classmates. Even if pretending for just one day, that she'd had normal parents. So, on that level, she could empathize with Rogue.

"So, you doing okay?" Luna finally asked. "Freaking out or anything?"

"Meh, this is like some screwy Netflix series," he said in a faraway voice. He put down the binoculars. "Don't get mad, uh, there's something I should tell you—"

Luna rushed to her feet. "Guys! Guys! The coyotes are back," she shouted to no avail.

"Holy balls!" Rogue pointed to the coyotes creeping over the boulevard. Straight into the parking lot. He waved his arms, yelling for the men to take cover. But Levi was busy cutting with the chainsaw. Handyman Jack, about six feet from Levi, appeared immersed in taking apart the other chainsaw.

There was only one thing she could do. Take a shot. That would get everyone's attention. She aimed, held her breath, and gently squeezed the trigger, aiming for the tarnished *WELCOME TO THE GOLD RUSH HOTEL* sign on the boulevard.

"You can't just shoot them," Rogue screeched.

The ping of the bullet hitting metal announced she hadn't lost her touch. Handyman Jack dropped the screwdriver and reached for his gun. Levi looked at her and then followed her gesture toward the approaching pack. She stopped counting at eight. "Rogue, get inside the truck!"

"No way! Not if you're going to kill them."

"I don't *want* to kill—" Four more skulked over the boulevard. She squeezed off another warning shot, this time intentionally hitting a burnt-out vehicle.

Handyman Jack held his ground and patted the asphalt, probably for something to throw. He tossed a pinecone at the lead coyote slinking down the entrance. It let out a high-pitched *yippity-yip-yip* when the pinecone hit its mark.

Levi bolted for the bus in a hobbling-cartoonish run. Leaving Handyman Jack as bait. Handyman Jack had no choice but to run. Although he would have no problem outrunning Levi. Leaving Levi as bait, she thought sardonically.

"Wussy!" Rogue heckled to Levi's back.

The no-longer-hesitant pack took off after its prey. Too many to shoot at once. She pivoted toward the bus, about a hundred yards away from the truck, in time to spot a lone coyote prowling at the rear of the bus, ready to pounce on Levi or Handyman Jack. Whoever made it to the bus first.

She had to do it. Good thing she had zeroed the rifle scope earlier. Moving targets were trickier than street signs. But with no windage and her expertise, it was an easy shot. In that heart-stinging moment she pulled the trigger, the wild creature yelped as scarlet red instantly stained its splotchy-brown hide.

Rogue girly-punched her arm. "I hate you!"

So much for bonding. "Chill! Handyman Jack's in trouble." Luna tried blocking Rogue's fist with her back as she pivoted toward Handyman Jack.

Handyman Jack must have realized he wasn't making it to the bus in time. He turned as if in mid-step, straight for the truck, which was slightly farther away from both the bus and the pack.

With her eye glued to the scope, Luna followed the coyote on Handyman Jack's heels. "Please, don't make me do it." But the coyote quickly gained yardage on Handyman Jack. In that millisecond as it lunged—she gently squeezed the trigger, this time bracing for the regret pinching her heart.

Rogue screamed when the coyote fell flat onto the asphalt with a heartbreaking yap. Surprisingly, her brother didn't cuss her out. He seemed caught in a loop, staring in utter disbelief from her to Handyman Jack to the crying coyote.

The other coyotes hesitated as if unsure of continuing their pursuit. "Any more by the bus?" she shouted, keeping Handyman Jack in the rifle sight while he sprinted for the truck.

Seconds later, Handyman Jack climbed over the truck's tailgate instead of taking refuge inside the truck. Rogue jumped from the truck's roof to the bed of the truck and nearly knocked down the man with a clingy hug.

"Uh, guys—" Luna stood on the truck's cab, eyeing six of them circling the truck. Staring at their prey with yellowish bone-chilling eyes. It was too late to get inside the truck or the bus.

"Easy now," Handyman Jack said. "Unless you can hit them all in seconds, think we ought to wait it out for as long as we can."

"I, I think they want to eat us," Rogue blubbered.

The coyotes stopped circling. And blatantly stared up at them, drooling with quivering curling lips. Oh, they were ready for another human kill. As if Luna had tuned into their desperate hunger.

"I don't think"—Luna's gravelly throat revealed her uncertainty—"we can wait them out."

"Getting that feeling myself," Handyman Jack said calmly, checking the chamber of his gun. "On my mark . . ."

Luna swallowed hard, ready to take them out. But not wanting to. Ultimately knowing that a single miss could be deadly for the three of them.

Four more appeared from nowhere. "Luna," Rogue cried out, "what are we going to do?"

Without warning, the bus horn blasted! And did not stop. Confusion replaced the coyotes' hungry glares as they craned their heads, searching for the source.

"Son of a—I do believe that's Roxie behind the wheel," Handyman Jack marveled.

"Way to go, Roxie!" Luna exclaimed.

When Roxie started the bus, the pack scampered off with cowering heads to the other side of the bus. Not far away enough. "It'll take a few minutes to get the bus moving," Luna advised him.

"Then, we'd best take advantage before we lose this window of opportunity!" Handyman Jack jumped out of the truck bed first.

"Take Rogue. I'll cover you." Luna followed the pack through the scope as the coyotes crouched behind the hotel's rubble. Except the apparent leader of the pack, that stood tall, standing its ground. Its snarling sneer so unnerving, she had to force herself to not look away.

"Rogue, let's go." Handyman Jack motioned to her obstinate brother.

"Not if you're going to kill them!" Rogue's nostrils flared in contempt.

"Stop being a PIA. A second ago, you were scared shitless," Luna reminded. He obviously wasn't going to listen to her. Their senseless arguments used to last hours. Something she was hoping to mend.

The bus door burst open. "Rogue, get your scrawny butt on this bus, this instant. You hear me?" It was Roxie, standing on the lower bus step, ranting like a super-pissed grandmother.

Luna hadn't seen her that angry since that time she had eaten the blackberries Roxie had wild-harvested for the summer bazaar pie auction.

"Whatev," Rogue grumbled, jumping to the pavement.

With gun in hand, Handyman Jack escorted Rogue to Roxie while Luna swiveled side to side, expecting strays to appear from every possible direction.

"Your turn," Handyman Jack shouted. "I'll keep my eye on the front of the bus."

She cringed at the thought of hitting the payment—knowing the rest of the pack might be waiting on the other side of the bus. Ready to attack.

"Say, Roxie," Handyman Jack called out. "See any of 'em on the other side of the bus?"

"Nothing over here," Roxie answered.

While Handyman Jack stood guard at the front of the bus, Luna fought for the courage to jump to the pavement. She didn't understand the profound fear consuming her. In ten to fifteen seconds, she would be safe. As if seeing herself stuck in pause, she couldn't move.

Levi banged open one of the bus windows and yelled, "Haul ass! They're at the back of the bus. Comin' right for you."

"Fuuuck!" Luna's heart seized. But not her legs. And she ran.

She jumped onto the bus just as the pack rounded the corner. Seconds later, Handyman Jack joined her on the bus steps. And Roxie slammed shut the door a nanosecond before a swarm of noses smashed into the glass door.

Mrs. Butch screamed, "We're all going to die!"

"We're good now," Handyman Jack was quick to say. But Luna's brief eye contact with him told her he wasn't so sure.

Meanwhile, Linda and Mrs. Butch would not stop screaming.

"For Christ's sake. Settle down before we all go batshit!" Handyman Jack berated.

Luna caught Roxie's smirk, as she set the rifle down before resting trembling hands on her wobbly knees. She'd always had an unreasonable fear of wild dogs. Something she had never admitted to anyone. But then again, she had never expected to be hunted by a pack of man-eating coyotes. They should contact animal control. Right, if they actually had cell service.

"Are you all right, hon?" Roxie hovered about her.

"Sure," Luna lied, not wanting to look like a wimp.

Rogue stomped down the aisle to Levi cuddling his wife at the dinette table. "You just left us. You f'n jerk!"

"You better watch your mouth," Linda scolded.

"I don't have a gun, now do I, smart-ass," Levi bickered in his defense.

Luna hurried to Rogue, aware of her brother's emotional triggers. He was about to go off into one of his horrific rants. When that happened, he could go on for the rest of the day.

"Leave me alone." Rogue pushed her away and disappeared into his bunk. "You guys suck!"

"That boy needs one helluva whoopin'," Levi nearly spat. "Can't believe you let him talk to me like—"

That's it. She was done tolerating a-holes. She walked up coolly to Levi, grabbed a handful of his cheap, blue-checkered cotton shirt, and held him inches from her face. "Shut the fuck up!" When all she really wanted to do was sucker-punch the bastard. "Or, hey, get off my bus."

"I, uh, apologize for hubby's crass behavior," Linda stammered as if afraid they were getting kicked off. "We know what it's like to have bratty children." She rubbed Levi's back. "Don't we, Cup-cake," she enunciated slowly to her husband.

"All that matters is," Roxie cut in, "everyone is fine."

"Sweet Jesus!" Mrs. Butch's hands flung to her gaping mouth.

Handyman Jack's eyes widened. "Butch!"

In the madness of it all, they had forgotten Butch! He was out there in the bulldozer. He hadn't wanted a spotter. Handyman Jack rummaged through his duffel and pulled out a box of ammo, dumping the bullets onto the table.

Roxie shook her head. "You're not going back out there—"

"Someone needs to." Handyman Jack loaded his revolver. He crammed another handful of bullets into his jean jacket pocket.

"I sure as hell wouldn't go out there," Levi snarked.

"Clearly, you wouldn't," Luna quipped cynically.

"We can't just leave him." Mrs. Butch swooned and grabbed the kitchen counter. "Please, do something."

Linda just stood there, shaking. "He's on his own. There's noth-ing we can do." Linda's heartless words fell flat onto the cork flooring.

"I beg to differ," Handyman Jack said firmly. "First of all, chances are he's all right. The Cat's enclosed."

"He must have heard the gunshots," Roxie said.

"Precisely," Handyman Jack said. "So, he knows there's trouble. He ought to be savvy enough to drive the Cat to the hotel entrance. If he doesn't return in the next fifteen minutes or so—"

"For now," Luna broke into the conversation, "we need to mon-itor the windows and watch where the pack goes."

"I second that," Handyman Jack said. "If need be, I'll sneak my way down to Butch."

"I'm coming with you," Luna said with feigned confidence. She couldn't let him go out there. Alone.

"Doubt anyone could stop you," Handyman Jack muttered.

Only, Luna didn't want to go back out there in the heavy unforgiving air. With mad coyotes hunting them. That would be—idiotic.

Chapter 9

JACKSON JONES, KNOWN TO be light on his feet despite the decades creeping in on him, darted for his truck a good hundred yards away, with Luna matching his pace. Roxie and the others monitored the bus windows to warn them if they spotted coyotes on the prowl. Luckily for them, they hadn't seen hide nor hair of any the last twenty minutes.

Still, he couldn't shake the hinky feeling those hungry creatures lurked about—watching.

Luna was fearless for going back out there. Facing God knows what. Truth be told, it was as if they faced one hell of a grim deadline. Which was the only reason he no longer presumed waiting for the authorities was indeed the wisest decision. Not to mention, the bus was getting overcrowded with—volatile attitudes.

He threw a quick look over his shoulder. No signs of any coyotes.

"This is so weird." Luna's perfectly plucked brows creased closer. "It's like I feel probing eyes, on me. Like they're waiting to attack."

Her chilling words resonated deep within his core. "All the more reason to get this over with." When they reached the passenger side of his truck, he opened the door and kept an eye on his six. "Hop in."

"We're taking the truck?" Luna seemed surprised as she propped the rifle's butt on the floorboard and leaned the muzzle toward the window.

"Might as well see how far Butch cleared the road before chancing it on foot." Jackson closed her door and rushed to the driver's side.

The downed tree in the parking lot had been cut back enough for the truck to make the turn onto the main road. This was the optimum time to see for himself how feasible it would be for the bus to zig-zag from lane to lane. He and Butch had agreed there was no point in clearing an entire lane, only swaths wide enough for the bus to make it through the burn-zone.

Once he was strapped inside his trusty truck, it started right up. He cranked the wheel hard, coaxing it over the boulevard's tarnished stone border to skirt around what remained of the downed tree. *What a fool*, he admonished, for not returning home when first encountering the fire. He could be tinkering around his workshop with a pot of French Roast at his beck and call.

Then again, who was to say his home was still standing. With these erratic winds, the fire could have hopped all over this side of the Sierras. He couldn't imagine losing everything. Like Roxie. Escaping two fires in one night . . . must have been a bitch. He had overheard the women talking about what the poor gal was going to do next. Although one would never have suspected Roxie's loss based on her light-hearted attitude. Nonetheless, he sensed the forlorn pain hidden behind the woman's smiles. Perhaps because he, too, had been lost to hopelessness once upon a time.

"Tell me if you see any coyotes," he muttered, bolstering his ragged nerves. For the most part, Butch had shoved what remained of the melted vehicles into the oncoming lane. Apparently, quite a few people must have heard the sirens and had fled. Attempted to.

"Definitely," she said through binoculars.

"Butch made good progress. Any sign of him?" Jackson rambled, knowing good and well she would inform him of such details.

"Not yet." She let out a heavy breath. "But all these vehicles . . ."

It made Jackson wonder if the evacuees had made it out on foot and were gathered at the community swimming pool, waiting for help to find them. Not wanting to dwell on the morbid possibility of a mass casualty event, he focused on the task at hand and kept the pace slow and steady. Eyes peeled for trouble.

"Fuuuck," Luna whispered. "The pack!"

Jackson caught movement in the right lane several hundred yards ahead and stepped on the gas. He tapped the horn repeatedly, hoping to disperse the coyotes and let Butch know help was moments away.

"Wait, there's the bulldozer—but I don't see Butch," Luna said with icy calmness.

Jackson skidded to a stop. "What the hell?" Butch waved frantically from the top of a melted heap of what looked to be a utility truck. "What's Butch doing up there?"

"Holy fuck," Luna hissed.

The pack had found Butch first. Those demon-like creatures sprang like panthers from a smaller burnt-out vehicle to the rickety roof where Butch stood. Within seconds, Luna positioned herself behind the truck's opened door, resting the rifle's barrel on the downed window frame. And took aim.

"Do you have a *clear* shot?" Jackson cautioned. Had to be a dozen of them. Too many.

Boom! She nailed one of the SOBs. With an agonizing squeal, the coyote slid to the melted asphalt.

Slam! The pack pounced Butch. The man's terrifyingly pathetic scream announced his demise to the world as he landed on the asphalt with the maniacal pack on top of him. He didn't have a chance in hell. Nonetheless, Luna kept shooting. One by one, coyotes collapsed to the ground.

One thing was clear, gunshots or not, nothing was keeping those voracious creatures from claiming their supper. Jackson tentatively stepped out of the truck. He crept toward the pack as close as he dared and fired his .45 Colt revolver at the coyotes on the outer perimeter, not chancing hitting Butch. Late-night target practice with beer cans was one thing, moving targets amongst an actual person was quite another. Though, he didn't see how Butch could have survived such a brutal attack.

The alpha coyote made an ominous appearance, scowling in Jackson's direction long and hard while the rest of the pack yipped and yapped and snapped at one another as if claiming their right to the prize. Jackson took a step forward to mark his ground while yelling obscenities. And tried to steady his nerves to make the shot.

Bam! Luna took out the alpha coyote with a clean shot to the head.

The pack stopped bickering and seemed to contemplate whether or not to wolf-down their fresh kill. Meanwhile, one of the coyotes nudged the smaller one Luna had shot. The dead coyote must have been a yearling based on its smaller size. The coyote glowered at Jackson with the eyes of a devastated mother. He shook away the unlikely notion.

The coyotes swarmed Butch again.

Luna cocked the Remington and fired multiple rounds. Finally, what was left of the pack crept away on lowered haunches. A sickening feeling overtook Jackson upon spotting Butch's mangled body protruding under the heap of coyote corpses.

He and Luna rushed to him.

"Good God . . ." Jackson murmured as they shoved away dead carcasses. He avoided Butch's gruesomely disfigured face and focused on the man's shoulders. He tugged for the arm to check the pulse, only to find the hand gnawed off. Based on the crumpled body, twisted and mauled beyond recognition: Butch had to be deader than dead.

Luna stood there, gaping. Without uttering a word, she bent down and checked the pulse on what remained of the man's bloodied neck. "No pulse." She shoved his body over to its side, probably to check the pulse on his other arm. But it had been bitten clean off.

Jackson grabbed her shaking hands and pulled her to her feet. "We've done all we can." His worthless words made him feel like a failure. The cold-hearted fact was this was his fault for letting Butch go out there on his own. Nonetheless, who would have ever thought a pack of coyotes would kill in broad daylight? Their modified behavior indicated they were desperately hungry. Or had gone mad.

From now on, they needed to pair up. "Let's get back to the bus," Jackson said.

"Shouldn't we take him back—" Luna started.

"In a perfect world, yes." He didn't want to bring back the aroma of a fresh kill to tempt the other hungry wildlife out there. "You don't want his wife to see him like that."

"Hell no." Luna exhaled deeply.

It didn't take much to send that woman over the edge. "Suppose for the sake of common decency and preservation, we ought to put him inside the Cat." Jackson ripped the gold cross necklace from Butch's neck. No doubt his wife would want the heirloom. "You mind grabbing the tarp from the back of the truck while I look for his wallet?"

Stifling his gag reflex, Jackson patted down the mangled man's blood-soaked pockets until finding the wallet. He checked the driver's license. "Sorry, Butch."

Luna laid out the tarp next to the body. Together, in a sort of morbid silence, they rolled the body onto the tarp and, with squinty eyes, they rolled the man in the tarp like a burrito.

"Can you help me lift him?" Jackson asked as he opened the door to the Cat.

What was that? Just the squeak of the door, he told himself. Definitely not a coyote. There it was again, the faraway scream—of a woman? *Good God.* They had to get out of there. Before his imagination drove him insane. Seeing Butch like that had a way of reminding him of his own mortality.

Luna grabbed the end with the feet, and after a couple of thrusts, Jackson lifted his end high enough to get the corpse through the Cat's door.

The agonizing scream of a woman in difficult labor seemed to reverberate through the smoky air, as if he had the ability to perceive the sound waves floating by.

Luna cocked her head and stopped shoving, leaving Jackson with the butt end of the deadweight "What is *that*?"

"I do believe that's the cry of mountain lions courting," Jackson said. And they were too close for comfort from the sounds of it. "We don't want to be here if they come this way."

"Now we have mountain lions?"

They went back to pushing and shoving. "That'll do," Jackson said, fighting off the heebie-jeebies. He left the man's driver's license on the tarp before shutting the door to the Cat.

"Why did Butch let himself get stranded like that—out in the open?" Luna questioned.

"Beats me." Maybe the man had needed to take a piss. "Best we hurry back." Roxie was no doubt worried after hearing the gunshots.

Luna sighed heavily as they jogged to the truck. "Mrs. Butch is gonna"—she twirled her finger around her ear as in crazy—"fuckin' freak."

Funny, no one seemed to recall Butch's wife's name, not even Mr. Know-it-all, Rogue. Now certainly wasn't the time to ask, "*Excuse me, I never did get your name. By the way, your husband's dead.*"

"You got that right. I certainly didn't sign up for this," Jackson said, checking the side mirrors as he quickly backed the truck into a niche between two burnt vehicles. He slammed his fists on the steering wheel. "Five minutes, hell, one minute sooner, and we could have saved him."

"Then, maybe . . ." She paused. "They might have gotten us instead."

Luna's haunting reply seemed to resonate deep within him. A tear slipped down her cheek. She quickly donned the N95 on the dashboard, as if disguising her moment of vulnerability.

"It's a possibility," he said thinly. They needed an excuse to clear them of blame. All this was too intense, even for him: a fire taking the town, trapped in a parking lot with no sign of anyone whatsoever. With killer coyotes on the loose. *Things had gone from bad to downright treacherous.*

Jackson and Luna boarded the bus with eyes glued to them. Roxie, who had been sitting in the driver's seat, didn't say a word. Perhaps she sensed their somberness.

"Did you find him?" Rogue shouted from the kitchen.

Jackson whispered into Roxie's ear, "You didn't happen to see any, uh, libations lying about?" He could use a shot of something strong to calm his tweaking nerves.

"I know just the thing," Roxie whispered back as the three of them walked to the kitchen table.

"I'll be out in a minute, Butch," his wife called from the bathroom.

Jackson braced himself for what was to come. Even Luna seemed somewhat reticent.

"Raspberry tea, anyone?" Roxie asked cheerfully. "Sorry, it's lukewarm." She didn't wait for an answer and went around filling tumblers with a pitcher of her tasty tea. Oh, you need a glass," she said to Jackson before going to the cupboard.

Roxie returned and discreetly set a turquoise glass in front of him. Jackson gulped down half the glass, a top-shelf scotch, based on his tingling taste buds.

"Where's Butch?" Levi asked for the third time.

"Is he still clearing the road?" Rogue asked as the gang looked on eagerly.

Luna's stone-faced attitude wasn't helping.

Jackson downed another mouthful, biding his time, urging the alcohol to kick in.

Mrs. Butch scurried toward them. "Where the hell's my husband?"

On that note, Jackson guzzled the glass. He spent a little too long clearing his throat, stalling. All the ways he had thought to inform Butch's wife seemed to have left him tongue-tied. For he had never been the first to inform someone of a death.

"I'm so terribly sorry," Luna said with the slightest touch of emotion. "He's not coming back."

Mrs. Butch threw up her arms and screeched, "Didn't you tell him how dangerous it is?"

Jackson took off his straw hat and clutched it to his chest. "Sorry to say, Butch is . . . dead." There, he'd said it. Plain and simple. *Best not go into the grim, gory details.* This wasn't the time. Besides, would she really want to know wild animals had mauled her husband to death? She would learn the official cause of death soon enough, once the authorities came through, searching for the dead.

"No-no-no-no-no! You're just being mean." She looked out the bus window, probably looking for Butch outside.

"Stop jerking us around," Levi said. But Jackson heard the consternation in the man's voice, as if Levi wasn't sure.

It took all of Jackson's strength to offer her the cross necklace. *Damn.* He should have wiped off the blood earlier. Silently, he laid the wallet on the table in front of Mrs. Butch.

A rush of red swept over the newly made widow's face. She jumped up from the dinette's bench seat, reached over the table, and slapped him hard across the face. "It's all your fault. Making us stay on this hellish bus."

Everyone seemed taken aback by her outburst, most of all Jackson. Her reaction hadn't been one of the many scenarios flooding his mind. Nonetheless, he had taken the hit like a man both physically and emotionally, empathizing with the woman's grief.

"But the bulldozer's enclosed?" Levi said with the narrowing beady eyes of a hawk.

"Did you bring back—his body?" Linda gawked out the window, as if expecting to find the body in the back of his truck.

This was getting more complicated than Jackson had anticipated, reminding him how quickly one little white lie could get out of hand. "We, Luna and I, wrapped him in a tarp and left him inside the Cat."

"Eww." Rogue gagged.

"You can't just leave him out there . . . Go, bring back my husband," Mrs. Butch screamed all the way to the kitchen sink and splashed her face with water.

"I don't think you're telling us the whole story," Levi said in an accusing tone. "We heard the gunshots. What if one of you shot Butch. Maybe by accident? Think I should investigate this for myself."

"Yeah, right," Luna snapped. "You won't last two fucking minutes out there. Without a gun."

"What are you insinuating?" Linda asked incredulously.

Roxie went up to Mrs. Butch. "You should lie down for a bit."

Mrs. Butch didn't argue and let Roxie walk her to the back bedroom.

No one said anything, as if waiting for Roxie to return. The swishing of the bedroom curtain closing came all too soon. Roxie hurried back to the table, scooped up Jackson's glass, and returned it with a generous refill.

It was time to hash out their plans. Help obviously wasn't coming anytime soon. Not from the looks of the devastation. Realistically, how long could they live on the bus? They'd run out of food and water at some point. Not to mention fresh air, what with all the hazardous toxins lingering out there.

"So, how exactly did Butch die?" Levi pressed.

"Coyotes," Luna mouthed.

They certainly couldn't hike their way to the next town. Not with that pack of killer coyotes stalking them. Not after they'd had the taste of people meat in their jowls. And had learned how easy it was to take down a man.

"Seriously? Coyotes—killed him?" a wide-eyed Rogue questioned, as if just now realizing the god-awful horror of their situation.

"That's it. We're leaving." Levi fumed.

"That's been the plan all along. Just need to cut back the felled tree a few more feet," Jackson said, thinking out loud. "Enough so this bus can make the sharp turn onto the road. Then, I suppose we continue clearing the road to the highway as needed."

"That's a big hell no," Levi blustered. "If your truck made it out, so can my Bronco."

"I wouldn't do that," Jackson suggested, afraid it fell on deaf ears.

"What if Auburn isn't there?" Rogue hauntingly questioned.

"It's Judgment Day! Lord have mercy on us all," Mrs. Butch wailed from the back room.

"Now, hold on," Jackson intervened, wanting to steer the conversation toward a more positive direction while Roxie hovered over them with the pitcher of tea. "I could use some help with the tree. For safety reasons, we should caravan. In the event, one of us has vehicle trouble. Like a flat tire. Lots of sharp objects out there."

Levi and Linda whispered to each other for a long minute, something he couldn't quite catch.

"How far did Butch clear the road?" Levi asked.

"All the way to Bob's Bait Shop. Maybe five miles," Jackson said.

"It's still standing?" Linda asked.

"Naw, just that huge ridiculous fish sign, which collapsed on the road. For the most part, the fire torched everything on both sides of the main road. Figure another couple of hours on the tree—"

"You're an idiot!" Levi abruptly stood up, bumping the dinette table, and knocking over glasses of tea. "Cupcake, we're going to find Marta and the grandbabies—if it takes all damn night. I'll drive us to the bulldozer, and you can follow me as I clear the road."

"Can you," Linda asked, "operate a bulldozer?"

Levi waved her off. "Sure, I used to drive my uncle's tractor. Remember, at the farm? Grab your things," he ordered, grabbing his go-bag.

Mrs. Butch came waddling out of the bedroom with purse in hand. "Don't leave me here with these crazies." And she stomped down the aisle and out the door right behind Levi and Linda.

"Hallelujah," Luna blatantly clapped back with feigned Christian-like enthusiasm.

Jackson was at a loss. It wasn't like he was in charge. They could do whatever they damn well pleased. Which apparently was what they were doing. One would think in a crisis such as this, people would band together. Despite their differences.

"Sheesh, ungrateful jerks. Not so much as a thank you." Roxie leaned over the sink like she was about to faint.

Jackson rushed to her. "You all right?"

"What are we going to do now?" Roxie said meekly.

Rogue tore off down the aisle and yelled out the door, "You, you, you . . . are a bunch of, of fuckeroos!"

"Oh, Rogue!" Roxie quickly covered her mouth, as if holding back a chuckle.

"Well." Jackson took another swig of scotch. "We're not going anywhere until I chop up that tree another few feet. Unless," he threw out there, "you want me to drive to the next *unaffected* town. And bring back help?"

Roxie shook her head defiantly.

"No!" Rogue cried out. "Don't you leave, too."

Jackson looked pointedly at Luna, wanting her feedback.

"The smartest thing is to stay together," Luna said. "There are too many unknowns."

"Then, best I get off my boney butt and get to work," Jackson said.

Roxie grabbed his forearm. "You do know," she said full of compassion, "Butch's wife was wrong. It's not your fault he died."

Jackson wasn't so sure about that.

Roxie continued, "Butch's exact words were, 'I don't need no babysitter.'"

"A part of me knows that," Jackson said. "But another voice says I should have gotten there sooner."

"We had to wait until we thought it was safe," Luna reminded.

Jackson stumbled to his feet. "Best I get back to that tree."

Roxie motioned him to sit. "You should rest a bit."

Just his luck to get stuck with two of the most headstrong women he had ever known. He plopped down in the seat, unable to get Butch's gruesome image out of his mind. How horrific it must have been—knowing he was going to get eaten. Alive!

He looked out the window. "Son of a bitch." He slammed his hand down on the table. "Those bastards stole my damn chainsaw. The one that works."

"Can't you fix the other one?" Rogue asked.

"Suppose so," Jackson grumbled. "Got a bag of spare parts. Ought to be able to piecemeal it." *He damn well better*. They were counting on him. There wasn't enough room for four people in his truck with the two bucket seats. Riding in the back of the truck, even if he dumped half the cargo, was too dangerous with the smoke. Not to mention the flesh-hungry wildlife.

"I wanna help," Rogue quickly offered. "Dad taught me how to use tools and stuff."

"Not with those coyotes out there," Roxie said firmly.

"You won't let me do anything," the kid whined.

"Rogue, if you promise to go inside the truck when I tell you to, you can take guard with me on top of Handyman Jack's truck," Luna offered. "You can even bring your crossbow."

"For real?" Rogue seemed surprised.

"Only if you promise to do what I say," Luna reiterated.

"I promise." Rogue crossed his heart with his hand before taking off for his bunk.

"Don't be aiming that thing in my direction, just saying," Jackson said playfully. Wow, the kid even had a crossbow. Who were these people?

Roxie sat down heavily opposite him. "You're a good man. For not leaving us . . ."

Before realizing it, Jackson reached across the table to pat Roxie's lovely slender hands, all too aware of her gold wedding band staring back at him. "Ah, I'd never do a thing like that. A man's gotta have his principles." However, his past was riddled with more than his fair share of remorseful decisions.

Decisions he wished he could undo . . .

Chapter 10

Roxie Romero's nerves were completely fried as she attempted to distract herself with sanitizing the overworked bathroom. She could not stop stewing over how their guests had deserted them. *Not even offering us a ride*! She threw the pastel-striped Turkish hand towel onto the counter. Not that she would have gone with them even if they had.

Perhaps it had worked out for the best, when a rather wicked thought popped into her mind: what if Levi, Linda, or Mrs. Butch were to get angry with Rogue's volatile outspokenness and kicked them out along the way? In the middle of the devastation. Mrs. Butch had seemed psychotic, even before her husband had died. Roxie certainly wouldn't want to be trapped with her in a basement of sharp, rusted tools. She shook away the unreasonable thought.

Jackson seemed the decent sort, although she didn't much care for his silly hat and mustache. She did, however, appreciate the way his tushy filled out a pair of faded Levi's. She walked to the front of the bus to check his progress. Based on the chainsaw's erratic whirring, he hadn't fixed it.

She had certainly lived long enough to know when to trust her intuition. And that ominous red-glowing sun seemed to warn, "Leave while you still can." Meanwhile, the not-so-faraway chilling serenades of coyotes were starting to sound more like ghost dogs from the underworld planning an all-out massacre. She couldn't get out of that hellish parking lot soon enough.

Roxie plopped into the driver's seat in an effort to calm her mounting anxiety. At least they didn't have to suffer through another awkward slumber party. Last night had been rather crowded with Levi and Linda sleeping on the dinette table that converted into a bed while Butch and his wife slept on an air mattress in the aisle. Jackson had napped on the bench seat behind the driver's seat. He couldn't have slept much with Luna and the men taking shifts watching for passersby.

Luna had been a dear, insisting Roxie sleep in her parents' bedroom in the rear of the bus with her scaredy-cat, Pixie. After their numerous heated conversations, Pixie must be traumatized. "Pixie, Pixie, you can come out now," Roxie called out.

Roxie had filled a cardboard box with shredded paper lined with a grocery bag as the cat box and constantly lit a bundle of dried sage she had found in the bathroom cupboard to disguise the odor. It wasn't like they could open the windows. With so much going on, no one had complained.

"Whoa." A gust of wind accosted the bus. Roxie grabbed the steering wheel, as if she might blow away. She giggled when Jackson's straw hat went frolicking across the parking lot. He chased it like a goofy cartoon character until a garbage dumpster rolled by and kept it from flying into the hotel's smoldering coals.

He tossed the hat inside the truck with apparent disgust and motioned Rogue and Luna to the bus just when another windy wave walloped the bus. They took off running for the bus, as if trying to outrun the wind.

"For heaven's sake," Roxie bellowed, opening the accordion door. "What's going on out there?"

"This weather is whack," Luna said.

Roxie wanted to ask Jackson if he could fix the chainsaw, but the defeated scowl on his face said it all. They scurried to the dinette table, and she followed quickly with the bottle of scotch, which she didn't bother to hide now that the rest of the gang had deserted them.

Jackson didn't refuse it.

"So, now what?" Rogue blurted with despair.

A long eerie crackling had them transfixed in their seats.

Bam!

The entire bus shook.

"There goes another tree," Luna uttered in a faraway voice.

Jackson rushed to his feet. "Not a good sign."

With craned necks, they stared out the windows as gust after gust bombarded the bus.

"Must be one of those Red Flag days," Jackson said. "It's not uncommon for this side of the Sierras to get fifty-mile-plus wind gusts."

Did that mean the fire was still spreading? Roxie winced at the thunderous crackling splintering her ears. Everyone's frantic eyes searched the windows once again. Waiting to see where the unlucky tree crash-landed. And it did, right into the parking lot. Missing the bus by a few feet.

"Sure wish we had a basement to hole-up in," Jackson said with a pulsing jaw. He strode to the front of the bus. "Look how those snags are swaying. Ready to snap."

"Snags?" Rogue frowned.

"Deadwood. All those scorched trees . . ." Jackson's voice faltered. "How tall you reckon they are?"

"At least a hundred feet," Luna said.

Jackson swallowed hard. "Good guestimation. Which means—"

Rogue's eyes lit up. "Holy balls!"

"Fuuuck!" They followed Luna's eyes to the blackened forest enclosing three sides of the hotel's parking lot.

"We're not even safe in the bus," Rogue whispered loud enough for everyone to hear.

Jackson snatched his work-gloves before disappearing behind the black-out curtain separating the living section of the bus from the cockpit.

"Where do you think you're going?" Roxie called out.

"Doing what I should have done in the first place. You all hang back." Jackson stomped off the skoolie, slurring a string of curse words.

"I don't know what he thinks he's doing," Roxie wondered out loud.

Luna grabbed her rifle and mask. "I'll watch for predators."

Roxie pulled Rogue back by the scruff of his shirt when he attempted to follow his sister. "You're not going anywhere, mister." Even if he was only a child, she needed the moral support. This was too nerve-racking.

They watched from the cockpit as Jackson pounded large nails into the sawed-off end of the downed pine. All the while, winds blasted the bus. He scurried back to his handyman truck and shuffled through the utility units mounted to the sides of the truck bed. He finally pulled out what looked to be a rather thick heavy-duty chain.

"Ah, I get it," Rogue exclaimed. "He's gonna pull the tree out of the way with his truck."

"Can he do that?" Roxie said. "Without burning-out the engine."

Boom!

She grabbed onto Rogue. The crash jangled her nerves just a little bit more. They followed the sound to find the tree had landed onto the hotel's rubble. Maybe fifty feet from the bus.

Rogue blinked his eyes repeatedly as if in disbelief. "We gotta get outta here."

Jackson appeared unfazed and continued hammering the nail heads over the top of several links of the chain. After several quick tugs on the chain, he strung the chain to the trailer hitch on the truck's rear bumper before wrapping it around the hitch.

Rogue pointed to the truck. "Told you."

But that was a mighty big chunk of tree. Could the truck bear the burden? They were about to find out. Luna jumped to the pavement with her weapon when Jackson started the truck. He started off slowly with the tires spinning and smoking.

"C'mon!" Rogue yelled.

"You can do it," Roxie cheered on.

Inch-by-inch, the truck nudged the tree. Finally, Jackson stopped. He surveyed his progress and then flashed a smile and two thumbs-up at Roxie and Rogue staring out the skoolie's windshield.

"I don't know . . ." Roxie scrutinized. It would be a tight left turn for the bus from the partially blocked entrance to the road.

"Don't worry, Mrs. Romero," Rogue said. "Uh, I mean, Roxie. It's gonna work. It has to."

Jackson and Luna hurried onboard. "Luna, tell me," Jackson said, "how good are you at driving this monstrosity?"

"She's a pro," Roxie said before Luna could answer.

"Yeah, she's super great," Rogue chimed in.

"Well then, I'll take point. In the truck," Jackson said. "If you can make that turn onto the main road, we're home free."

Roxie didn't see how the bus would make it. But her nerves were ready to take the chance. She could not handle staying there another night with those explosive winds, knowing a tree could crash down on them any second.

Another boom shook the bus. "They're dropping like flies," Roxie muttered. "Rogue, sit with me at the table while the bus warms up. We need to let them concentrate." She was half-tempted to down a shot of scotch. Instead, she and an unusually subdued Rogue sat at the table.

Roxie grabbed the deck of cards Rogue had been nagging them to play and shuffled them over and over. She even dealt out a round of Seven Card No Peek, Rogue's favorite. But he couldn't care less about playing cards.

Finally, the skoolie started rolling. Roxie gripped the edge of the table when Luna forced the bus into the sharp turn. The grinding and screeching of the bulky bus protested it didn't like it.

And then, mission accomplished! They made it onto Main Street.

"You rock!" Rogue jumped up and clapped.

Jackson pounded the bus door and shouted, "Good job, Luna. Best we get a move on. Wind's picking up again. Follow me. Not too closely, mind you. And we just might make it to Olive Garden for a late supper."

"Ew." Rogue gagged dramatically. "Nobody eats there anymore. I wanna try an In-N-Out Burger, since I don't have to be vegan anymore."

Jackson swept open the curtain and yelled, "Roxie, you all right in there?"

"Pleased as punch." Roxie berated herself for saying something so dated.

"Wait, I wanna go with Handyman Jack." Rogue looked from her to Luna, as if not sure who was in charge of him.

"I could use the company," Jackson said.

"Yes! I'll get the Walkie Talkies."

"That kid's always thinking," Jackson said, tapping his temple with his forefinger.

"Oh, before you go." Roxie rushed to the kitchen. Earlier she had filled the metal flask she had found in the bedroom nightstand. "A little something for your nerves."

"Ah, you shouldn't have." Jackson flashed a flirty smile. "Not that I plan to drink-and-drive."

"It's just to keep the edge off," Roxie said.

Rogue ran back down the aisle, sporting a backpack and two radio gizmos. "They're totally charged."

Luna snatched a radio from Rogue.

"Do you even remember how to use it?" Rogue nagged.

Luna flashed him a look of disdain.

"Okay, let's go over our route one last time," Jackson said. "We continue going west on Route 26. Eventually, we'll hook up to

49. Then we take 16 to 50 to Interstate 80. That will get us to Sacramento."

"All of that?" Rogue declared to the ceiling.

"I better write that down," Roxie said, grabbing a notepad and pen from the kitchen drawer. They had decided earlier that Rogue should stay with Luna at her Sacramento apartment until they heard from their parents. The past couple of days must have wreaked havoc on the boy. After all, he was only ten.

Roxie planned on staying the night with them. Tomorrow she'd rent a car, buy a phone, and start the dreaded phone calls. Maybe even stay at a hotel until she found a studio apartment to rent. Jackson had remained tight-lipped. It must be unnerving not knowing if the fire had spread all the way to his cabin in Shake Ridge.

"Honestly," Luna said, "do you think the roads will be clear?"

"That remains to be seen," Jackson said, smoothing down his mustache. "If need be, we can always take a detour. At some point, we'll catch up with Levi, since they'll be stopping to clear the roads with the Cat. And my chainsaw!"

"Rogue, don't be a PIA," Luna urged in a bossy mom voice.

"That goes for you, too, Handyman Jack," Roxie quipped. "Don't take any chances out there."

"Aye aye, Captain." Jackson offered a flimsy salute before the two boys jogged to the truck.

"Hon, need the bathroom or anything before we go?" Roxie asked.

"I'm good," Luna said, adjusting the driver's seat.

"Let me know if you need anything." Roxie parked herself in the bench seat behind the driver's cockpit. Ready to get somewhere—safe.

Roxie stared at the fire's wrath in utter disbelief. All those magnificent pines, cedars, and oaks destroyed. Even sadder, all the pristine cabins that once dotted the countryside had been reduced to mounds of smoking rubble. Lifetimes upon lifetimes of memories—disintegrated. Her heart skipped upon the sudden realization this was how her foothill community must look.

She found it difficult to think the fire had been a result of the highly volatile topic: climate change. If so, the planet was changing more rapidly than the news led everyone to believe. Even so, the so-called devastating weather of climate change wasn't supposed to occur in her lifetime, unless maybe she was in a nursing home. Oblivious to it all.

These recent extreme weather patterns could be a fluke. Nature had its cycles. Even so, hundred-year events, even thousand-year events were now occurring every year in some part of the country. Hadn't it snowed in Las Vegas last week? And the Mississippi River was quickly going the way of Lake Mead and the Amazon River.

What they needed was rain. Lots of it. *If the northwest's drought continues, think how bad this year's official fire season will be.* As of February, the lakes and rivers were running low. Farmers' wells were going dry, leading to historic winter crop losses. Which meant little luck with the summer crops. What if the major rivers went dry? Were food shortages just around the corner? Good thing she kept an ample supply of canned goods in her basement.

Sheesh, Roxie kept forgetting she had lost everything! The reality of it all hadn't sunk in. Must be a protective mechanism, she mused. Pixie butted her leg. "There you are."

Pixie jumped into her lap. Roxie cradled her, when an abrupt bout of joy surged through her. She had never been a cat person, and now she couldn't imagine her life without Pixie. The shivering, starving, half-feral kitten had found its way into her garage two winters ago, and Roxie hadn't had the heart to kick out the adorable thing. At least Pixie was oblivious to the desolation blurring past the windows.

Luna wasn't one for idle chit-chat. She kept the skoolie at a steady thirty-five miles per hour and followed Jackson's truck. Now and again, Rogue quipped something ridiculous over the radio, which only had Luna sulking all the more. This must be hard on the young woman as well. After all, her parents didn't have fire insurance.

Supposedly, FEMA helped the uninsured. But she had heard through word of mouth, based on last summer's wildfires that FEMA and the Red Cross didn't provide all that much assistance. Furthermore, it took years to rebuild. If one could even find a contractor. And with inflation the way it was. What if many homeowners simply couldn't rebuild?

As it was, Roxie's insurance premium had tripled in the past few years. Soon homeowner's insurance would be impossible to afford. And since home loans required coverage, people would start losing their homes. With all the homeless encampments and flash mob robberies, America's downward spiral appeared to be unfolding before her very eyes. If she chose to look in that direction. The government might need to reallocate its preposterous budget to its citizens for once. *What a novel idea, helping our own people.*

As the miles went by, Roxie stared out the windows at the sporadic piles of grayish and blackened hollowed-out vehicles, apparently shoved aside by a bulldozer based on the ashen tire tracks. It was comforting to know Levi, Linda, and Butch's wife had made it that far. Still, it left her wondering where all those people in the abandoned cars had fled. Had help somehow found them? There was no ocean to jump into like Maui.

"We're so f'd," Rogue declared over the radio. "A huge tree crashed in the middle of the road."

"Give me that," Jackson admonished in the background. "Luna," Jackson said. "Hold on. While I check out the damage."

"Fuuuck," Luna murmured as she stopped the bus.

Roxie stood up for a better view. A huge cedar that had to be three to four feet in diameter blocked the entire road. It must have fallen down after Levi, Linda, and Mrs. Butch had made it through.

Luna had just opened the bus door, when Roxie spotted a creature slinking in the charred forest just beyond the road. "Wait!" Roxie pulled Luna back by her arm.

"You guys," Luna shouted into the radio. "Get in the truck! Mountain lion on your three o'clock."

Roxie had never seen Jackson run so fast.

"Phew," Jackson said. "Thanks for the heads up."

"Don't shoot it," Rogue whined in the background.

"Actually, Roxie saw it first," Luna said. "So, what are we doing about the tree?"

"Yep, that *is* a problem. My truck can't budge it. As it is, the tranny's having problems."

Roxie kept her eye on the curious mountain lion and asked, "Can we go around the tree?"

"The terrain's too rough for the bus," Jackson said.

"We're so screwed!" Rogue wailed.

"Take it easy, sport. The only option I see, take that side road we passed about a mile back. Or, hey, we can hang tight here 'til Caltrans finds us."

Luna turned to Roxie with questioning eyes.

"If the winds can take down a tree that size, we're not any safer here than the parking lot." Roxie had said what nobody else seemed prepared to say.

"Question is"—Jackson seemed to stall—"I don't recall seeing a turnout for the bus. And backing up for a mile, maybe two, *and* maneuvering around the wreckage . . . could get dicey."

Roxie downed the last bit of chamomile tea she had been savoring.

"Luna can do that, easy-peasy," Rogue insisted. "Uh, can't you?"

Luna gave Roxie a determined look. "I'll just have to."

"Luna, do you want me to guide you?" Rogue asked a bit too excitedly.

Luna mouthed an adamant "No" to Roxie.

"Rogue, don't you get out of that truck," Roxie ordered. "There's a mountain lion out there. Somewhere." She had lost track of it. "I'll help Luna."

"Okay then, we make one helluva team. Give me a minute to turn around," Jackson said.

Luna let out a long sigh. "Roxie, don't stress. Basically, I have no problem backing up in daylight with two lanes to maneuver in. It's the car pileups and debris I'll need help navigating around. That part I'm not so good at," she surprisingly admitted.

Roxie wasn't looking forward to guiding the bus. "Just be patient with me."

"Sure," Luna said.

Jackson honked playfully as he passed them. This was going to be a long, tedious ride to get to the other road. What if it was merely a dead end? At one mile per hour, it could take one to two hours just to get there. Then what? They had already made several detours. Roxie sure hoped Jackson knew where they were going. Because she didn't have a clue.

Her worries quickly fixated on the power lines swaying precariously low on leaning poles propped up by the skeletons of trees lining both sides of the road. If a tree or power pole snapped at precisely the wrong moment . . .

After hours of detours, they had made it to Route 88, which was still just a two-lane country road. But Jackson knew where they were. Even better, he knew how to get to Sacramento. That was all that mattered. But they probably wouldn't get there until the wee hours of the morning. And Luna was getting tired.

"Hey, Luna," Rogue's voice sang out over the radio, "Handyman Jack wants you to hang back while he checks out this place. The sign says it's open. Like now."

"What?" Roxie said. "Out in the middle of nowhere?" Although they had passed several billboards for Kirkwood, a popular ski resort. It must be up ahead. The fire seemed to have fizzled out in this area, maybe due to the glowing firebreak that cut through the forested countryside.

"Roger that." Luna put on the brakes.

Jackson turned right up a steep hill next to a scorched billboard sign that had fallen to the ground. That was when Roxie spotted the small hand-painted A-frame sign: *WELCOME FIREFIGHTERS! FOOD AND SHELTER HERE.*

The spinning of wheels hinted Jackson was having trouble making it up the grade. "What's going on?" Luna was quick to ask over the radio.

All they heard was Jackson cussing up a storm over the radio.

"Crapola!" Rogue shrieked into the radio. "The truck died. We have to walk. Oh, and Roger that."

Luna tossed her hands into her lap, as if disgusted.

"Maybe the truck's out of gas," Roxie muttered to herself.

Luna grabbed the rifle.

"Hon, stay put," Roxie urged. "Jackson has his gun."

Luna simply nodded.

A long ten minutes passed. Finally, Rogue yelled, "Guys! C'mon, drive the bus up. There's a diner, and it says they're open."

"Is there room to park the bus?" Luna asked.

"No problem there," Jackson announced over the radio.

"Can we make it up that incline?" Roxie wasn't so sure.

"Oh, yeah, it has a low gear," Luna said firmly, as if determination was her middle name. "I've pushed it higher than this."

Guess they weren't making it to Olive Garden . . .

Chapter 11

Luna Lewis waited next to Rogue, Roxie, and Handyman Jack at the counter of the small ski lodge's diner located on the top of a spectacular rock cropping known as Granite Hill Lookout, which jutted above a vast forest. It was absolutely breathtaking. Except for the fire-ravaged acreage glimmering below in the distance.

She leaned against the red sparkly counter and ogled the menu on the wall, not quite believing they had stumbled upon an actual building untouched by the fire's wrath. The two people at the kitchen's order window rushed about, although there were no customers in sight.

Handyman Jack cleared his throat loudly. "S'cuse me. Do you happen to be open?"

A tall Black woman wearing a striking red and black scarf wrapped around her head spun in their direction. "Of course. Sorry, I didn't hear the bell. Y'all take a seat. Be with you all after we put together this bulk order for our amazing firefighters."

"Yes! Chocolate milkshakes, bacon burgers, and onion rings." Rogue practically drooled out loud.

"Wish I could still eat like that," Handyman Jack commented. "Let's grab a booth by the window. I want to keep an eye on the fire situation."

"What are you getting?" Rogue said to Roxie as they snagged a booth.

"Whatever they have, as long as I don't have to cook it," Roxie said with apparent relief.

"Sorry 'bout that, Roxie. You've been catering to us for the past two days," Handyman Jack said. "Thank you again."

Roxie rearranged the salt and pepper shakers. "You and I should be thanking Luna and Rogue. It's their skoolie."

"Our parents' bus," Rogue corrected.

"I thank you all. Dinner's on me." Handyman Jack slapped his American Express card onto the table. "Whatever you want."

"Then I want onion rings *and* fries. And, and, pie. Hmm, or a milkshake?" Rogue squinted at Luna with eager eyes.

"I don't care what you have," Luna said. She was proud of him for owning up to not being a vegan after faking it all these years just to appease their parents. Luna hadn't had a choice until moving out. Mom and Dad had been relentless in those days.

Since living on her own, Luna ate whatever the hell she wanted. Guilt-free. So what if most processed foods contained bioengineered ingredients. Genetically modified organisms were now a part of nearly everyone's diet. Even well-known natural food stores sold produce coated with toxic petrochemicals like Apeel and Edipeel. Eventually, every single plant on the planet would be exposed to the forever chemicals invading the topsoil and water supply. Her body needed to acclimate to the poison. Not avoid it.

Handyman Jack's brows furrowed. "Roxie, I'm confused. Aren't you the grandmother?"

Roxie let out a wide grin. "Ah, no. A long-time neighbor. I babysat Luna when she was little. And Rogue on occasion. See, Luna and Rogue rescued me from the fire after my car died on me. If they hadn't found me when they did—"

Handyman Jack shook his head. "Oof, how terrifying."

Roxie waved him off, probably not wanting to think about it, Luna mused. What if they hadn't gone that way, or what if the smoke had been too thick to see Roxie's emergency flashers? Luna decided she didn't want to revisit their narrow escape either.

"I'm not one for silly superstition," Handyman Jack said, "but the fact the four of us made it this far must be some sort of kismet thing."

"I know, right?" Rogue quipped. "Like we're these super-cool immortal characters in an apocalyptic HBO series: *Humanity's Last Hope*," her brother fantasized aloud.

"I wouldn't go quite that far," Roxie scoffed lightheartedly.

Rogue was always falling for the whimsical, champion novelty conspiracy theories. As long as it was for the greater good of the planet. It must keep his hyperactive persona engaged. Luna had long lost interest in the plethora of whack-job theories she used to buy into, thanks to her parents' influence. As if every single new invention from cell phones and 5G to the entrapment of social media to those bioengineered mRNA vaccines, were evil government plots to control and depopulate Humanity. She was so done with that doomsday crap.

Luna noted how Roxie, Rogue, and Handyman Jack gradually seemed to relax while they chatted nervously when all Luna relished was simple quietude to decompress from the tense drive through miles and miles of charred forest. She needed de-stressing before hitting the road again. Backing up the bus for over an hour had left her ungrounded, as if her eyes wanted to pop out of her head.

But there they were. Sitting in a secluded diner on the top of a random rocky plateau, surrounded by forestland. Which they had luckily stumbled upon before dark. Talk about serendipity . . . if she allowed herself to believe in that stuff.

It reminded her of the "spiritual awakening" road trip to Sedona that Auntie SunFlower had taken her on for her thirteenth birthday. Auntie SunFlower had insisted it had been time to awaken her kundalini in order to discover her spiritual path and spiritual gifts. As if it were a coming-of-age event all children experienced.

Imagine Luna's embarrassment when she had found out spiritual awakenings were not the norm when reading aloud her summer "vacay" essay to the entire eighth-grade class. Her classmates had laughed and laughed. But she had quickly played it as a satire piece. From then on, she had vowed to live a normal life once graduating from high school.

"Luna, are you all right, hon?" Roxie disrupted her thoughts. "You've barely spoken a word."

"Just tired." Luna offered a quick smile. She did miss Auntie SunFlower, the most authentic, happy, fun-loving person she had ever known. And that Sedona trip had been remarkable. Almost mystical. Too bad Luna no longer believed in such whimsy.

Rogue drummed the table with straws. "This is taking for-ev-er."

Roxie squashed his annoying drumming with her hand.

"Be right with y'all," the woman called out as she bagged an extremely large order at the counter.

A lanky Black man burst into the diner and shouted, "Say, Bud, some dumbass left a truck on our driveway."

Rogue went into an obnoxious fit of laughter. "Handyman Jack, he just called you a *dumbass*."

"Been called worse." Handyman Jack waved to the man. "That would be me. I apologize. My truck conked out on me."

"Aw, didn't see you there." The man quickly changed his tone. "That bus belong to any of you?"

Luna raised her hand halfway. "That's ours."

"Wait a minute?" The man turned to them with a puzzled frown. "You all don't look like firefighters. Where the heck did you come from?"

"We finally made it out," Handyman Jack said. "Been stranded at the Gold Rush Hotel in Gold Town since the fire started."

"You shittin' me? You drove through that hell storm?" The man seemed amazed.

"Sanchez, burritos are ready," the waitress in the red and black scarf informed.

"Coming." Sanchez hurried to the counter. "Bro, let's talk when I get back. Need to deliver this to our courageous firefighters on the frontline."

"How admirable of you," Roxie said.

The Black woman approached, wearing a red fifties waitress outfit. "I'm Nina. Did I hear you say you came from Gold Town?" Nina asked with terror-filled eyes.

"Honestly, don't know how we made it," Handyman Jack admitted.

Nina hung her head low. "Sheriff Hooper was here yesterday. Said, hundreds of residents didn't make it out in time."

"I know. Like, we saw tons of burnt-out cars on the road," Rogue said.

"All I can say," Handyman Jack said, "we must have skirted through. With precise timing . . ."

"You all are blessed." Nina flipped open her notepad. "God must have a plan for you."

"They gettin' a handle on the fire?" Handyman Jack asked.

"It's not looking good. I've lived here my entire life. My grandparents built this place. We *never* have fires in February. There should be three to four feet of snow out there."

"This is the perfect location to ride out a fire," Roxie said.

"Granny chose this spot," Nina said. "Five acres of granite, above the trees. We have a generator, propane tank, and two water tanks. We're busy cooking up the perishables before the propane runs out. Still, this fire scares the living Jesus out of us. It burned a swath through the canyon below us last night. I tell you, that fire raged through like the Devil himself."

"Nina, any more eggs?" the man in the back shouted.

"In the back icebox," Nina shouted back. "Now, what can I get you all?"

"What d'ya got?" Handyman Jack asked.

"Burgers, hot dogs, fries," Nina rattled off. "Enough bacon to feed half the firefighters in the county—"

"Milkshakes?" Rogue couldn't wait to ask.

"For you, of course." Nina tousled Rogue's irresistible curly reddish-brown hair. "Got sweet tea, barbecue ribs, albacore sandwiches, burritos, tacos—"

Luna stopped listening at tacos, instantly famished.

After placing their crazy-large order, they sat in the booth, almost giddy, waiting for their food. Until now, Luna hadn't realized how lucky they had been to make it out unscathed.

"I'll turn on the tube for y'all. But the signal's been going in and out." Nina clicked on the huge widescreen TV at the end of the room before handing off the remote to Handyman Jack as she whisked by.

Anxious for news, they watched the fiery scenes they were all too familiar with. A woman news reporter with a nauseating, high-pitched voice braved the elements in a bulky yellow firefighter jacket and N95 and attempted to explain the difficult firefight over the mountainous terrain while drone feed streamed live footage of hundreds of blazing buildings. Probably people's homes. It made Luna sick.

"This just in. Spot fires—"

A blast of wind nearly knocked down the reporter. The woman quickly regained composure. "The Grass Valley Complex fire that destroyed Auburn has expanded to Rocklin, and Roseville. People, this is quickly outpacing the Valley Pines Complex fire that remains at zero percent containment and has devastated most of Amador County. Firefighters— Wait." The reporter grabbed her earpiece. "We have reports of fires in *Sacramento*—" She frowned at the camera. "Is that possible?" she seemed to ask the cameraman. "Yes, that's correct, the City of Trees is currently on fire." She paused again, as if listening to another update. "The entire Sacramento metropolitan area is now under mandatory evacuation. I repeat *mandatory* evacuation. This includes—one moment," the reporter said as if waiting for the details. "Interstate 80 is open only to evacuees and emergency personnel. The governor announced a State of Emergency moments ago—"

A strong gust knocked the woman to the ground, sending her hard hat rolling down the road. A flurry of embers landed on her hair. The camera apparently fell and captured out-of-focus fragments of her crew smothering the fire. The screen went blank.

"Heaven's," Roxie murmured, "I do hope Linda and Levi found their daughter and grandchildren."

"Holy balls!" Rogue exclaimed. "Luna, now we can't even stay at your apartment."

They stared at one another, as if what they had just heard couldn't possibly be true. Sure, forested mountain regions were known for out-of-control wildfires. Not entire cities.

Nina came running out. "Did they just say, Sacramento?"

"Yep." Handyman Jack slammed his hand on the booth's cushioned seat. "Now where do we go?"

Luna's heart sank. "We can stay with my friend in Natomas," she decided.

"I don't know how you'll get to Natomas with tens of thousands evacuating," Nina said. "You all better stay the night here. Or you might get trapped on these winding roads with no place to go. We have one room left that's been out of commission due to some dry rot. But it's functional. I won't even charge you for it. The firefighters have the rest of the rooms. They even took over the pool hall. For sleeping, when they get a break."

Handyman Jack rubbed his stubbled chin. "Not a bad idea."

"Frankly, my nerves aren't ready for another drive like that. Not at night," Roxie rambled. "What if we get trapped again and have to back the bus out?"

They were right. "We definitely should stay here. But I'm sleeping on the bus," Luna stated firmly. She wasn't leaving their only asset unguarded. Not after her parents had lost everything. What if the fire reached her apartment? Or office. *Don't even think that.* The firefighters could stop the fire from taking Sacramento. Right?

"Nina, I don't suppose you have any water to spare for showers?" Handyman Jack inquired.

So glad he asked, Luna thought. The bus didn't have much water left.

"The water tank's half-full," Nina said. "Just go easy on your water usage. We may have another wild night of putting out embers." She looked out the windows warily. "Last night was a nightmare."

"Thank you for the offer," Handyman Jack said. "We'll stay here for a while. Until the firefighters advise it's safe to go on."

"After a quick shower," Roxie said, "I'll stay on the bus."

"I wanna hang out with Handyman Jack," Rogue announced to the empty diner.

Handyman Jack patted Rogue's back. "Works for me. Maybe you can finally talk me into playing some poker."

"Don't let Rogue's boyish charm fool you," Roxie warned with a hint of a smile.

Luna had never realized how savvy and cool Roxie was until now and was really starting to admire Handyman Jack's laid-back persona. They had such a different outlook on life. Unlike Luna's insanely uptight world, where her friends, frenemies, and coworkers tried so hard to be politically correct twenty-four seven, afraid of getting fired if they said something inappropriate. Honestly, with all the societal rules dictating what one could and could not say in the workplace, she never really knew who her true allies were.

A symphony of beeps went off at once, followed by a round of puzzled looks, followed by that "aha" moment when Luna realized what it was. She and Handyman Jack reached for their phones simultaneously.

"Well, how 'bout that. Cell service at last," Handyman Jack said with relief.

Funny, after nearly forty-eight hours, Luna had totally forgotten about her phone. She scrolled hungrily through the texts as they popped up on the screen.

"Like how many texts did you get?" Rogue ragged.

"Miss Popular over here," Roxie said. "Wouldn't you know, I left my lifeline in my car. I need to call Roberto and Rosa."

"By all means, use mine." Handyman Jack offered his dorky-looking android. "Think Luna will be at it for a while," he teased.

Roxie glanced at Nina approaching with an armful of plates. "Thank you. After we eat," Roxie said.

Luna ignored the food and continued scanning through the texts and missed calls. No interview appointment. *Damn*! On the plus side, with the evacuation, the interviews would be postponed. So maybe, she hadn't blown it after all, she thought before re-alizing how selfish that sounded. People everywhere were losing everything. And all she cared about was the interview. Auntie SunFlower would probably insist she needed a two-day cleansing to clear her negative energies.

"According to a text from my friend in Citrus Heights," Luna said, "they're evacuating now." What a nightmare. Rush hour in Sacramento was bad enough. But everyone. Leaving at once. It would never happen. Especially since people blatantly refused to follow the rules. She could see it now, flash mobs of looters robbing for the thrill of it. YouTubers ignoring evac mandates to film live footage just so they could record the chaos to boost subscribership.

Nina cluttered their table with bottles of ketchup, mustard, mayo, and taco sauce. "Holla, if y'all need anything else."

"Thank you," Roxie said.

"What did Mom and Dad say?" Rogue asked.

Luna's heart lurched. She hadn't seen any messages from them. She scrolled through again, guilty for not noticing their messages first. "Nothing. No calls or texts." Her throat went hoarse. Mom was notorious for texting her all times of the day. Sometimes in the middle of the night, for senseless questions like, *Do you still have those hiking boots*, or *Have you read this book*?

"Luna, hon, don't you think that's a bit odd?" Roxie said before sipping iced tea topped with a lemon wedge.

Luna nodded, feeling, more like knowing, something was wrong. But she couldn't think with Rogue squirming around. "Rogue, the restroom's over there," she scolded.

Rogue scowled at her through narrowed eyes. "It's not that—look." He pointed to the television.

She had intentionally ignored the news station announcing another "Breaking News Report" when Rogue turned up the volume. She didn't need more news about the fires. Not after living through it. Really, she just wanted to get it out of her head.

There on the screen, staring back at Luna—were Mom and Dad. ". . . are considered prime suspects along with the members of the fanatical eco-peace New Pangea organization. I repeat, we have confirmation that ten northwestern data centers have simultaneously exploded. Investigators are not ruling out these incidents as vile acts of domestic terrorism."

"Whoa, they finally did something radical," Rogue blathered in awe. "Those super boring, stupid, wussy protests are just a time-suck. But this—"

He shut up when Luna's California Driver's license photo and one of Rogue's school photos unexpectedly filled the widescreen.

"Fuuuck," Luna whispered.

"Persons of interest include the activists' children, who went missing after a suspicious fire destroyed their rural hometown of Valley Pines, which may have ignited the current fires hitting Northern California, spurred by hurricane-force winds during this unprecedented heat dome."

"Hey, that's so not fair. They can't blame us!" Rogue lamented.

"Shhh." Luna tugged the camouflage ballcap lower over her forehead. Although, she was basically unrecognizable without her heavy eye makeup. However, Rogue's unruly curly hair could give them away.

Handyman Jack quickly plopped his scruffy straw hat onto Rogue's head.

Luna was amazed, still not believing it. Mom and Dad had never resorted to violence. It was against their principles. As in totally implausible.

Poor Roxie looked utterly aghast when she turned to Handyman Jack. "That can't be true. Besides, why in heavens would Crystal and Forest attack a data center of all things?"

Rogue's glare shifted from the television to Roxie. "Duh, this is like the worst drought ever. And data centers waste billions of gallons of water," Rogue berated, "every f'n day!"

Handyman Jack's brows furrowed deeper. "How's that?"

Rogue dropped a ketchup-drenched fry onto his plate in mid-bite, splattering ketchup everywhere. "'The Cloud,'" Rogue spouted with air quotations.

Handyman Jack eyed Rogue questionably. "I thought it was a good thing. Saves trees."

"Not so much," Luna said, already bracing for Rogue's tirade.

"Well, by all means," Handyman Jack said sarcastically. "Now I've got to know what's so bad about the cloud."

"See," Rogue started in. "What most people don't get, data centers, you know, the mega-complexes that run the Internet and store people's digital crap, leaves a humongous carbon footprint. To keep all those processors cool."

"Is that so?" Handyman Jack turned to Luna, as if to confirm his statement.

Luna nodded. "It's true. Even worse, they build a lot of data centers in the desert where water is a commodity."

Handyman Jack let out a long whistle. "Guess I never thought of it that way. Idiocracy and bureaucracy always seem to go hand in hand."

"Think about it," Rogue continued. "Gazillions of emails sitting on servers. Some people have so much crap, they actually *pay* for a service to store stupid emails and photos. 'Cause they're too f'n lazy to trash junk emails n' stuff. It's way easy to transfer photos and important documents to memory sticks. That way you always have them. But you gotta store them in a Faraday pouch. You know, for when we get EMP'd."

"Aw, yes the proverbial electromagnetic pulse," Handyman Jack seemed to say in jest.

"Sheesh," Roxie whispered. "So now, even emails hurt the environment? Next, it will be my thoughts."

"Exactly." Rogue seemed oblivious to Roxie's mockery.

"Seems to me the government would do something to prevent this massive water waste," Handyman Jack rebutted.

"Meh, they don't give a shit. The Tech Giants are more powerful than our lame government. Most people think it's cool to have universal access to their data. But if *we* have universal access, so do the tech companies. Access to every photo and document we create. One of the guys I follow on Rumble talks about how the Tech Giants transfer all our personal data into these ginormous think tanks. Then with the help of AI, they put people into basic categories. You know, like an all-knowing cyber-psychologist. With a few keystrokes they can do predictive modeling on us. So, in the not-so-distant future—they can enslave us," Rogue finished out of breath.

"You're a wealth of information," Handyman Jack said. "But I see what you're getting at. What's your view on the subject?" Handyman Jack said to Luna.

It was true. People liked to collect shit. Luna was no exception. And, well, the all-powerful tech companies did whatever they wanted—because the government let them. The average person couldn't grasp the consequences of such power. Which was one reason she had long given up the impossible fight: convincing people to care.

Everyone turned to Luna, expecting her to respond. *Great.* She didn't want to get into a heated discussion. "Ignorance is bliss," she said before taking another bite of the overstuffed taco. She had spent most of her life debating lost causes.

Really, from what Luna had seen, all society wanted was to continue business as usual and spend, spend, spend until there was nothing left to consume. Including her. She had tired of the sky-was-falling conspiracy theories, understanding that society couldn't or wouldn't comprehend Humanity was destroying the earth. It was simply beyond their comprehension. Just like the narrative in that chilling fateful movie *Don't Look Up*.

"Sorry, forgot these." Nina cheerfully cleared a spot for the plate piled with at least three orders of onion rings.

Roxie pretended not to be flustered, looking even more suspicious. "My doctor's going to have a conniption fit after my next blood test. Thank you, this is wonderful."

"You all are welcome," Nina said before walking off.

Rogue shoved the onion rings to Handyman Jack. "I'm not so hungry."

"So, I'm hanging out with a bunch of hooligans." Handyman Jack's slow endearing smile hinted he wasn't ratting them out.

"Wait a minute." Luna stared long and hard at Rogue. "You knew about this?" Things were starting to add up. The urgent call to watch Rogue. The prepped bus.

Rogue was suddenly tongue-tied.

Handyman Jack snatched an onion ring. "Speak up, sport. Dying to know the rest of the story."

"Hey, don't blame me. All they told me was"—Rogue stopped and continued in a whisper—"Mom and Dad were going on the most important protest tour. Ever. I sorta thought they expected it to get ugly. See"—he turned to Luna—"you were supposed to take me to Auntie SunFlower's that next day. Then the fire started . . . and everything went wrong." Rogue covered his face with his hands and stamped his feet.

"Why protest now? This has been going on for years," Luna contemplated in frustration.

"When we lost the fire insurance, they tried to sell the house. But, they couldn't sell it for what they owed. 'Cause they had already re-did the loan for cash to build an underground bunker."

"Refinanced with these extortionist rates?" Roxie asked.

"Wait, a bunker?" Luna went soprano.

Rogue squirmed in his seat before saying, "And, and there's something else—"

"What?" Luna was livid.

"Well, I guess they knew there was gonna be hecka trouble. 'Cause they stopped surfing for bunker plans on the Internet. And, okay, so this is the really weird part," Rogue said. "They switched the bus license plates and registration with Auntie Sun-Flower's bus. You know, the buses sort of look alike. So, if the police ran an APB or BOLO, they wouldn't know it was *our* bus. That way we can live off-grid for a while. Mom said they're on a waiting list to live in a survival shelter. So, I think they spent the loan money on supplies. Then Dad got super pissy at Mom for telling me about the survival shelter. And, and then they wouldn't tell me anything at all."

Luna threw up her hands in despair. Her parents had gone insane. Her face was all over the news and probably the Internet as well. How would she explain that in her upcoming interview?

"One thing's clear," Handyman Jack said. "Your parents, crazy as they sound, are pretty clever."

Roxie just sat there with her hand patting her chest, as if she couldn't process everything Rogue had said.

"So, now what?" Rogue blubbered. "What if we don't ever see Mom and Dad again?"

"Hmm." Handyman Jack hinted at something as he tossed his napkin on the table. "Sounds like you should stick to the original plan."

Rogue's eyes lit up. "So, you're not gonna turn us in?"

"Sport, why'd I do a thing like that? If it weren't for you two, I might have turned into one of these." Handyman Jack held up an extra crispy onion ring. "Besides, if what you're sayin' is true. Your parents are heroes in my book."

"He's right," Roxie said. "Although, I don't condone acts of violence."

"But, what do we do?" Rogue let out a gush of air.

"We're going to Auntie SunFlower's in Mt. Shasta," Luna decided. "And wait for Mom and Dad." And then she'd berate her parents or disown them or whatever.

"She lives sorta off-grid on a little farm," Rogue added.

Handyman Jack waggled an onion ring in the air. "Hold on. No doubt, your relatives will be under surveillance."

Luna let out a wide wicked grin. "We're not related at all. Sun-Flower is an old friend from my mom's hippy commune days. Get this, they're so paranoid about New World Order shit, they only communicate through actual snail mail. Like pen pals."

"How in heavens do we get you two to Mt. Shasta amidst all these fires?" Roxie grumbled.

"No doubt, I can study the map and find a round-about way there," Handyman Jack said, as if deep in thought.

"Roxie, I'm so sorry to get you involved in this. What do you want to do?" Luna asked.

"I'm not sure. I need to start the ball rolling on my insurance claim."

"Roxie, pretty, pretty please, you gotta help us too," Rogue bemoaned. "It will be fun. We can pretend we're on the run from the evildoers."

That had Handyman Jack chuckling.

"Roxie," Luna said, "don't let Rogue pressure you into anything you don't want to do."

Roxie nodded. "I need to talk this out with my sister first. I honestly don't think you need me when you have Jackson," she said, looking out the window wistfully. "I'm too old for this. And I've never been involved in anything illegal."

Relief surged through Luna, knowing Handyman Jack wanted to help. As far as Roxie was concerned, it was her decision. Still, what tore Luna apart was why Mom and Dad had risked it all for a few data centers that, in the grand scheme of things, would barely make a dent in the carbon footprint.

Dragging her and Rogue down with them? It was an inexcusable selfish act. *What were they thinking . . .*

Chapter 12

JACKSON JONES STOOD AT the edge of Granite Hill Lookout's stone wall, mesmerized by the surreal sea of wild flames crowning from treetop to treetop as far as the eye could see, like a Hollywood scene depicting the infernos of Hell. Erratic voracious winds whipped at ferocious speeds, spurring the flames on. Giving the true meaning to the expression "spreading like wildfire."

For the time being, he hoped more than knew the vista point was a fairly safe location, as if the Almighty Spirit had plunked a chunk of granite smackdab into the middle of the densely forested canyons for this very occasion. For it was the only thing saving them.

Despite situated above the timberline, all it would take was one stray ember . . .

Since the morning Jackson had sought refuge in the Gold Rush Hotel's parking lot, he had yet to assimilate the gut-wrenching emotions from being trapped by the fire, to the killer coyotes, to *not* saving Butch. But last night had been the kicker after catching a late-night news update: Shake Ridge hadn't survived the multi-county megafire. His cabin was gone.

To top it all, he was traveling with fugitives wanted for domestic terrorism. Allegedly, he reminded. Nowadays, the news media could spin or rather manipulate the narrative in any direction it saw fit. Rogue was right about that. There would come a point when one wouldn't know truth from fabricated lies. That scared the bejesus out of him. More so than the fires.

Ever since the tripledemic years, it appeared as if old-school investigative journalism had fallen to the wayside. A travesty for the "Free World" so many Americans had sacrificed their lives for. It had him questioning if the world leaders, or those running the show, had instigated the malicious disinformation and misinformation campaigns on practically every subject from politics to childrearing to the possibility of alien life—to keep the population at odds with one another, and moreover, in perpetual confusion so those in control could continue their agendas.

History knew the answer to that one: Divided we fall.

A deafening crack of thunder splintered his eardrums, bringing him back to the situation at hand. He automatically searched the sky for clouds, but the scintillating red sky exploding like a firework's show gone amuck showed no signs of a thunderboomer. Too bad. Mother Nature was probably the only thing that could extinguish a fire of such magnitude. "Must be another tree biting the dust," he said aloud, but his words were sucked out of his mouth by the dry hot winds.

"Whoa!" Rogue backed around in a semicircle, recording the disaster on a cell phone. "That's a, a, a f'n firenado!"

A turbulent column of smoke spun in the distance, resembling the beginnings of a funnel cloud. "Well, I'll be damned!" Jackson had never seen anything like it. The dissipating smoke revealed a long twisting rope of fire extending from the ground to the sky!

With the volatile winds along with the updrafts and downdrafts created by the mountainous terrain, a fire whirl was possible. But this one was a beast. Jackson stood, awestruck by its wicked beauty. Funny how Rogue preferred watching the spectacular fire show from the minuscule phone screen rather than basking in the formidable magnificence of it all. It must be the kid's way of distancing himself from the actual event.

"I think it's coming for us!" Rogue bellowed into the wind.

"Whut?" Jackson tried gauging the firenado's speed and direction as it zigzagged about like a mile-high flamethrower torching everything in its path. It definitely appeared closer.

From out of nowhere, a gust of blistering wind seemed to sear his skin. More than embers, he realized, when a slew of tree limbs—turned projectiles flew in their direction.

"Good God! Those aren't limbs…" An onslaught of trees, roots and all, hurled about helter-skelter.

"Get down!" Jackson snatched the kid to his side. Together, they took cover behind the granite wall.

An uprooted tree with fiery branches landed mere feet from them. "Holy balls!" Rogue roared with the wild eyes of an ape-man.

Rogue tried to run, but Jackson held on to the kid for dear life. Afraid a fiery object might crush him. While the boy quivered in his arms, Jackson gathered the courage for a quick peek over the wall. To his relief, the firenado spun down a canyon in the opposite direction and left a trail of uprooted trees in its wake.

Jackson finally found his voice. "We're good now." Maybe not. The granite outcropping had been overtaken by embers. He hustled to the falling embers and began stomping them with his feet. But there were too many.

"Sport, you okay?"

"I guess."

"I need you to make sure the bus is all right. Use the fire extinguisher on the bus to keep it safe," Jackson hollered over his shoulder as he bustled to help Sanchez when the west corner of the chicken coop's aluminum-like fire blanket flew up in the wind.

"Don't worry, I'll save the bus!" Rogue hurrahed as Jackson grabbed the flapping end of the fire blanket.

"Thanks," Sanchez said, his voice muffled under his mask. He fiercely pounded in nails to secure the blanket to the small wooden chicken coop. "Nina love them chickens more than me." Sanchez laughed madly, adding to the ludicrousness of the moment.

"Who cares about chickens when the world's on fire?" Jackson wanted to say.

"I need to patrol this back area with the propane and water tanks," Sanchez said. "You mind walking around the lodge and extinguishing the embers? They get caught under the eaves." Sanchez handed him a fire extinguisher.

"Do my best." Jackson took the extinguisher, not liking this one iota. *A fine time for those firefighters to leave.* They had left a couple of hours ago, ordered to hold a crucial firebreak near a populated foothill community.

Jackson strode around the lodge and scanned the eaves. The diner and pool hall were on the bottom floor, hotel rooms on the second floor, and the owner's living quarters on the third. Thankfully, Sanchez had placed twenty-foot ladders on each side of the building. Ready for trouble.

He chased a whirling ember as it collided into the side of the building. And wouldn't you know, the wind caught it just so, trapping it under the eave. He shot out a stream of foam. "Gotcha!" Good thing the building had a metal roof.

A flash of light streaked by his periphery. Jackson broke into a run and doused the restaurant's wooden entrance with foam. Seconds later, Nina came running out in pajamas. She grabbed the garden hose and started spraying down the building for a second time since the early morning firestorm had threatened them. But in this extreme heat, it was already bone-dry, which gave him an inkling of how dry the forest was.

Roxie and Luna ran out of the diner, and they all stared in awe at the deadly fireworks dazzling the densely forested canyons below. There was no time to tell them about the hellish firenado. No doubt Rogue would be telling them an animated embellished version later.

"Luna, I sent your brother to protect the bus. You might want to check on him?" It was a lot to ask of a kid. Jackson hustled to stomp out an outbreak of cinders skittering along the sidewalk before they found something to ignite while Luna sprinted off to the bus.

Jackson jogged around the lodge again searching for embers, while Bud tinkered with the snowmaking machine that sporadically sprayed a mist of water on the side of the building facing the canyons. It was a help but not foolproof.

Nina had lined up several buckets and filled them with water while the skyline continued exploding around them. A decorative shrub by the hotel entrance lit up without any warning whatsoever. Roxie was Johnny on the spot, grabbed a bucket, and doused it.

"This is what the firefighters said might happen," Nina said. "When the fire first ripped through here thirty-six hours ago, it hopscotched through so fast it left many parts untouched. But with the wind shift—it's coming back for what it missed."

Nina's haunting tone gave Jackson the heebie-jeebies, as if the fire had a personal vendetta of its own. Against Humanity. Or any living creature. He shook away the absurd notion. Until another burst of embers rained down on them.

It is going to be one helluva grueling night.

Jackson sat in the diner, nursing a second cup of Joe and idly chatted with Sanchez and Bud about the San Francisco 49ers' prospects, as if avoiding last night's firefight. Jackson, more antsy than usual, wanted to get an early start on the day—whatever the gals decided to do. However, they were still getting ready on the bus. He was at everyone's mercy. Something he loathed.

Bud had managed to tow his truck to the top of Granite Hill Lookout before the fire had reemerged. Unfortunately, the tranny was shot all to hell. Towing it to a mechanic shop any time in the near future was out of the question. Once officials came through there, the place would most likely be either locked down until deemed safe or gridlocked from people checking the damages of their ski chalets near the popular Kirkwood Mountain Resort.

Jackson couldn't stop squirming in the booth. It was time to get—to wherever they were going. He could feel it in his aching bones. A glance at the retro Elvis clock on the wall, the kind with the swinging legs and hips, seemed to natter it was half past eight. And he was late. For something important.

Get a hold of yourself, he scolded, unable to wind down after snuffing out little starter fires until damn near four in the morning. Then poof, just like that, the firestorm had abated or had found another canyon to annihilate.

"Say"—Jackson was curious—"do you plan on evacuating the lodge any time soon?"

"Oh, we're *not* leaving," Sanchez insisted.

"Last time we left during a mandatory evac," Bud said, "the place was looted. Man, they cleaned us out. Even ripped out our ovens."

"I'll probably make a trip to Redding to secure a water tank delivery. And get more propane," Sanchez said. The man's haggard voice revealed he was about to keel over from sheer exhaustion after staying up the entire night patrolling his property.

"Redding?" Jackson questioned.

"After last summer's fires, I spent hours on the phone, trying to secure a water truck delivery. Competing with everyone else this side of the Sierras. I ended up going all the way to Redding and renting the damn truck myself. What about you and your family?" Sanchez asked.

Funny how everyone assumed he, Roxie, Luna, and Rogue were related. He didn't bother nixing it on the off chance they had recognized Luna and Rogue from the news reports. "Not sure as of yet."

"I feel bad for those stuck in the Central Valley," Bud said with an ominous note. "I pray it didn't turn into another Maui catastrophe."

"I don't understand what's happening," Sanchez said. "Yeah, I know, the whole climate change thing. But that's not supposed to happen for a few more decades."

Jackson better squash that topic before Rogue showed up. "Do you mind if I leave my truck here? It might take a few days to bribe a tow truck driver here."

"Of course," Sanchez said. "You're certainly welcome to leave it here until you can arrange a tow. You put your life on the line to save our property. We couldn't have done it without your help."

"Ah, here comes the rest of your peeps," Bud said. He patted Jackson's shoulder. "You all are welcome to stay. Free of charge. We have plenty of nonperishable food."

"Thanks for the offer," Jackson said as the two men jaunted off.

Roxie flashed him a lovely smile, a sight to behold with her startling light-blue eyes. Her silvery hair was done up in a style his mom used to wear, a French twist, with wispy strands adorning her face. Meanwhile, Luna's scowl didn't bother hiding she was none too happy. He quickly turned his attention to Rogue, not wanting to appear like a lech when his eyes kept drifting back to Roxie. "How's it going, sport?"

"I put out over a hundred embers last night. Ooh, and I recorded that firenado. I'm gonna send it to CNN—"

"You used *my* phone?" Luna tore into him.

"Can they track you? I mean . . ." Roxie looked over her shoulder at Nina, Sanchez, and Bud deep in conversation behind the diner's counter. "In the movies, they're always tracking cell phones."

"Exactly." Luna held out her hand.

Rogue shrugged and handed her the phone.

"Don't *ever* use my phone. Without permission." Luna adeptly removed the SIM card. Then she dug through her fancy rhinestone purse and retrieved a tool.

"A Leatherman?" Jackson was surprised. Luna was a paradox: her high-maintenance, beautified appearance didn't match her tenacious diehard skillset. Normally, he was good at pegging personality types.

"Oh, yeah, Dad gave you that last Christmas." Rogue stared intently at Luna as she cut up the SIM card with the scissor tool. "Bummer, I was hoping really hard that Mom and Dad would call us today." Rogue's voice cracked.

"We can buy those phones drug dealers use," Roxie whispered with intrigue.

"Like mine?" Jackson held up his burner phone. He was always dropping or losing his. So, he stuck to disposable devices. People in Amador County usually called his landline anyway.

"Hey, we can call Mom and Dad on yours. Can you get a signal now?" Rogue's glumness converted back into enthusiasm.

"Don't be a moron," Luna berated. "They're probably monitoring Mom and Dad's phones. Using his phone to call them will connect Handyman Jack to us."

"She does have a point," Jackson said gently as he turned on his phone to see if Chip had returned his call.

"Which brings us to our next move." Roxie made eye contact with Luna. "We talked about it this morning."

"What? Without me?" Rogue pouted.

Roxie rubbed the kid's scrunched shoulders. This was a lot for a kid his age to cope with. Hell, it was a lot for him, and Jackson had lived through his share of tough situations.

"I really should start my insurance claim," Roxie said. "What a mess of red tape that'll be. Part of me worries I don't have coverage."

"Were you able to get a hold of your husband?" Jackson asked before realizing it. "He must be worried." He had assumed her husband had been out of town.

"Oh, dear." Roxie seemed taken aback. "Hank, God rest his soul, passed on years ago. Thanks, I did try calling my sister and brother last night. I couldn't get through, but I left messages to let them know I'm fine. Not to worry, I didn't say a word about Luna and Rogue."

"Hopefully, they got the message" was all Jackson could think to say, trying to keep the smile out of his voice. He had assumed Roberto was her husband. *So, she's not married. Interesting . . .*

"Now what—" a grumpy Rogue snapped.

"The plan," Luna said, talking over Rogue, "we drive to the first town with car rentals. And we go our separate ways. It's the smartest thing to do."

A puffy-eyed Nina walked up with his breakfast order, a double order of bacon, hash browns, scrambled eggs, and burnt toast. Just the way he liked it. Instantly, all eyes fixated on his plate.

"Are you eating *all* of that?" Rogue zinged.

"What can I get you?' Nina said to Roxie.

"What he's having," Rogue said without skipping a beat.

"Shush." Roxie gave Rogue a disapproving look. "Nina, you must be exhausted," Roxie said.

"I'm too keyed up to sleep. Anyway, I need to cook up the rest of the perishables this morning. Those firefighters are always hungry. I'm making the last of the burritos. Bud promised them he'd make another delivery. So, order up while we got it."

"Maybe just a small plate of whatever you have to spare," Roxie said almost apologetically.

"I want the works." Luna nodded adamantly, still eyeing Jackson's plate.

"Nina, you're such a dear," Roxie said.

"Back in a jiffy." Nina bustled off.

"I'm slipping a hundred-dollar bill in the tip jar," Roxie said in a hushed voice.

"Put that away. Remember, I'm paying," Jackson insisted. "And a hundred-dollar tip seems fair enough."

Rogue gasped. "That's way too much."

"She works hard," Roxie said. "I was going to blow it anyway. I was supposed to be on the six a.m. Reno bus with my Bunco girlfriends. I was packed and ready to go when the fire . . ." Roxie didn't need to finish the statement.

Sanchez walked by their booth before going outside. "I'm going to check the wind. Although, we should be in the clear, since the blaze took out the eastern canyons last night. I don't think there's anything left to burn in our piece of paradise."

"Watch yourself out there," Jackson warned. "We ran into a pack of killer coyotes up in Gold Town."

"Madness," Sanchez muttered as he walked off.

It took all of Jackson's restraint to refrain from eating until Nina had served everyone at the table. Then, just like that, they went carnivorous and chowed down. Still, he kept a leery eye out the diner's soot-stained windows for wayward embers. For some reason, he wasn't able to shake the inexplicable ominous feeling: they weren't out of the woods just yet. That fire was still raging on . . . Somewhere.

A rattling on the table startled him when the paper menu started vibrating across the table.

"It's your phone, silly," Rogue quipped.

"Aw, yes. Must be Chip." He snatched the phone from under the menu. "Handyman Jack at your service. No job's too small," he automatically recited. Not that he was in the position to go on any service calls just yet.

Huh? "Roxanne *who*?" Jackson repeated, perturbed by the interruption. "Sorry to say, you have the wrong number." He was about to hang up when he caught Roxie and Luna's harried expressions.

"Sir, sir, don't hang up," the voice bellowed loud enough for everyone at the table to hear. "Sir, I'm Agent Lasardo with the FBI. We have confirmation this phone was used by a person of interest in a crucial investigation."

It hit him. Like a ton of bricks. Roxie was short for Roxanne, and she had used his phone. Apparently, the FBI had already connected the dots. So much for the burner phone theory.

"Are you BSing me?" Jackson put the call on speaker. *Time to wing it.* "Whut?" Jackson acted flustered. "Come to think of it, I did lend my phone to a distraught woman. We're trapped by the fires—"

"Is she with you, now?" the tenacious agent hammered back.

"Haven't seen hide nor hair of her since. Like I was saying, we're trapped—"

"Was the woman with a younger woman in her twenties and a ten-year-old boy?" the agent badgered on.

"Not that I'm aware of. Sorry I can't be of more help," Jackson jabbered like an old codger.

"Right then. Call me at this number—*immediately.* If you see her again. And whatever you do, do not engage. I repeat, do not engage. She's considered armed and dangerous."

Roxie—dangerous? Maybe if she happened to be wielding a cast iron skillet while someone snitched a slice of her bacon. "Anything to help out." On that note, Jackson hung up, unable to hold back his laughter, despite the agent's chilling warning.

"Holy balls, was that *really* the FBI?" Rogue drawled.

Roxie's face turned chalky white. "Well, that didn't take long." She glanced around the room. "And it's all my fault. Looks like I'm going with you kids after all."

"Yay! Roxie's coming with us." Rogue applauded like it was a spontaneous field trip. "Handyman Jack, you *have* to come with us now. Or they might, you know, waterboard you for intel."

Roxie flashed the kid an annoyed look.

"I guess so. Here I was thinkin' how paranoid we were," Jackson said, biting into a tantalizing slice of bacon.

Luna grabbed her purse. "Rogue, we have to get as far away from here—"

"Now, hold on," Jackson started in. "First, let's think it out for a couple of minutes." He didn't know how far they'd get on these roads.

Sanchez strode back into the diner. "Say, Sanchez, did you touch bases with the firefighters before they left? Wondering how close we can get to Sacramento. They're anxious to get back to civilization."

Sanchez approached their booth. "Passable to Nowhere Junction, which is about twenty miles west of here. Then, it gets hairy," Sanchez said. "Just yesterday, Caltrans started clearing Route 88 from Kirkwood to the Nevada state line due to an exodus of marooned RVers and Airbnbers enjoying the warm winter up here. Hmm." He paused. "If you ask me, Stockton or Lodi's your best bet. Though it'll add some time to the trip. Once there, you should check on the road closures. I mean, one minute it's safe, the next it's not. Day-old news is worthless."

"Thanks. Stockton sounds like good advice. Thinkin' we ought to leave after we eat," Jackson said casually.

"I understand," Sanchez said before going back to the kitchen.

"Hey, like why'd you just say that?" Rogue gawked.

"Because"—Jackson smiled broadly to his newfound friends—"Carson City, Nevada, here we come," he husked under his breath.

"Brilliant." Luna actually smiled. "Rogue, obviously we can't go near Sacramento, even if my apartment did survive."

The phone vibrated on the table, stalling the conversation. They stared at it like it was possessed. Jackson flipped open the phone and recognized the area code. "It's the agent."

Luna finally said in a voice well beyond her twenty-plus years, "You have to answer it. Or it will look suspicious."

Everyone nodded in agreement.

Reluctantly, Jackson answered with the same ole spiel, "Handyman Jack at your service. No job's too small."

"Agent Lasardo again. We need you to ID the woman."

"Be glad to—" Jackson started.

"We're sending a helo to—Manny, where is this place?"—a long silence—"Granite Hill Lookout. Based on the latest weather report, the wind's too dangerous for a helo at this time. Shelter in place. I'll contact you once the helo leaves."

"A helo? Must really be important," Jackson bullshitted.

Click. The call disconnected. "Son of a bitch," Jackson mumbled. "Folks, eat up. We need to go. They're sending in the cavalry for you hooligans." He better ask Sanchez if he could borrow the chainsaw he had spotted in the storage room. Jackson had a hunch they'd be needing it.

"Wow," Rogue exclaimed. "They must be digging into your personal stuff. Like everything you and Roxie ever did your entire life."

Jackson simply nodded. "They won't find much there. I'm pretty much a model citizen. On paper." He winked. Except for that messy divorce years ago.

What the hell did I get myself into? But the relief flooding over Roxie's face assured he had made the right decision.

Chapter 13

Luna Lewis frowned at her chipped rose-gold nails tapping the steering wheel and mentally tried forcing the airbrakes to warm up like a hapless bystander ensnared in a *Jason Bourne* adventure. They absolutely had to leave Granite Hill Lookout before the helicopter found them. She searched the windows, expecting a helicopter to descend upon them—any second.

Her rational mind assured there was no way a helicopter could land in this crazy wind and smoke. Handyman Jack's random decision to go east to Carson City, Nevada, and blend in with the chaos of other wildfire evacuees provided the perfect cover to elude the FBI. That was what she told herself. However, according to the map, Route 88 curved through the Sierras.

With these insane erratic winds, it was possible to run into the fire again. The heat alone could kill if the smoke didn't. It had her wondering what those people on Main Street in Gold Town had been thinking . . . just before. She couldn't bear dying like that. Still, it was reassuring to know eventually they would reach a point where Caltrans had cleared the road. *It shouldn't get that bad. Right?*

Rogue interrupted her from the possible dangerous scenarios they faced with his melodramatic struggle of lugging Handyman Jack's stuffed duffel onto the bus. Luna drummed her fingers faster on the steering wheel. "Where's Handyman Jack?"

"He's loading tools and stuff from his truck to the storage compartment under the bus," Rogue said.

"Great idea." Luna had to force-stop her fingers from tapping. Handyman Jack seemed genuinely intent on helping them. *Yeah, because he's crushing on Roxie.* Based on SunFlower's promiscuous escapades, senior citizens still made out. Even had sex. A thought Luna quickly shoved out of her mind.

Roxie held up a cloth grocery bag as she boarded. "Nina's such a sweetheart. She gave us a mess of breakfast burritos to give the firefighters. I feel horrible for not telling her we're going the opposite direction." Roxie flashed a frown. "Perhaps it's just my guilty conscience, but I think she has an inkling something's amiss."

"Yeah, how many people drive a big-ass bus through ravaged fire-zones?" Luna's sarcasm said it all.

"I know, this is so awesome. The best road trip ever," Rogue gushed.

As usual, her emotionally challenged brother failed to understand the seriousness of their situation. Yes, they were safe at the moment. What about an hour from now?

Handyman Jack finally headed for the bus steps with a toolbox when Sanchez ran up to him. "Now what?" Luna muttered, scanning the red hazy sky.

Roxie sat behind her in the navigator's seat. "How are you doing, hon?"

"Good," Luna said, not admitting to anxiety. She was a pro at managing angst, thanks to all the anti-stress seminars she had attended at work. She was used to hiding her stress and anger. Stone-face, that was what her prior boss had once called her. Internalizing life's pressures came at a price. Depression. Which was diffused by taking advantage of the constant events and activities in Sacramento, with shopping her therapy of choice.

Sucking it up, Luna accepted her fate: doomed to this hateful bus another day. Maybe two. Until she caught up with her wanted parents—before the FBI. Somehow, someway, she had to clear her name from starting the fire in her hometown. Or her career was screwed.

"What did Sanchez want?" Luna asked as Handyman Jack boarded the bus.

"Wished us a safe trip. Okay then, take a right on the main road, Route 88."

"Duh, Nevada's the other way," Rogue blurted.

"Precisely," Handyman Jack said. "However, we don't want anyone figuring out our chicanery from the get-go. We simply make like we're heading west toward Stockton since Sanchez is right there. Watching. We'll just have to turn around when we find a turnout. And pray damn hard he doesn't happen to spot us from the hill when we pass by."

"Let's go." Luna wasn't wasting one more second. Unexpected goosebumps prickled down her spine, as if knowing they were jumping out of the frying pan. Into the fire.

"Are you okay with driving the bus down the steep incline?" Handyman Jack's hesitant tone belied his calm demeanor.

"It's not a problem." Luna put it into gear. "I've been driving this bus since I was fourteen. I drove through Utah, Idaho, Colorado . . ." Driving the bus had been fun back then.

"Guys, guys, get this. Luna got a ticket in Idaho for going like twenty miles over the speed limit," Rogue raved.

Roxie giggled nervously. "Is that supposed to make me feel better?"

"Well," Handyman Jack said, "if you're not worried about driving it, neither am I. Got plenty of other worries on my plate."

"Everyone, hold on." Luna pointed the bus toward the steep exit and tapped a friendly honk to Nina waving by the window.

Rogue plopped down onto the bench seat next to Roxie. Handyman Jack sat on the edge of the stairwell adjacent to the cab's cockpit and grasped the metal pole with one hand while digging through his duffel.

Handyman Jack pulled out a bundle of maps. "I'll start getting familiar with the byroads. In the off chance we need to backtrack. Sanchez said the firefighters are worried about a forecasted wind shift sometime tonight that could send the fire back in our direction again. So, as long as we can stay ahead of the fire—"

"This wind," Roxie blustered, "is ungodly. Sometimes I think it's going to blow me right off this bus."

"Not to worry, I gotcha," Handyman Jack said with a flirty smile.

Luna forced her attention on the narrow two-lane road, trying not to take in the fire's desolation, for every scorched tree seemed to deaden her heart just a little more. For self-preservation purposes, she forced herself to go numb and simply concentrated on driving. Like a seasoned soldier on the battlefield.

She eyed the gauges, aware of every fluctuation. They had a half a tank of gas. Plus, several jerrycans in the storage compartment under the bus. Would that get them to Carson City? Handyman Jack seemed obsessed with the map, when she spotted a side road. "Do you think it's safe to turn around yet?"

Handyman Jack jerked his head up from the map. "Go for it. Sanchez was going to work on the chicken coop, Nina was going to make the rest of the burritos, and Bud's sleeping."

"Uh, Handyman Jack"—Luna freaked—"I meant to destroy your SIM card before we left." Had they just screwed themselves again?

"No worries there." Handyman Jack smiled. "I discreetly tucked my phone in a cranny in the vista point's granite wall. Want them to think we stayed put for as long as possible. Having the phone go dark might rouse suspicion."

"My, aren't you clever?" Roxie said. "I do hate dragging Nina and her family into this mess."

"Same here," Handyman Jack said. "They're good people."

"Rogue, I need a spotter," Luna said. She didn't want to risk backing into the small culvert.

"On it!" Rogue took off to the back bedroom.

Carefully, she started backing up the full-size bus.

"Stop!" Rogue yelled. You're gonna hit a tree."

"I see the tree," Luna groaned. "It's the ditch I'm worried about." She shifted and cranked the wheel, from side to side.

"Okay, keep backing up. Stop!" Rogue was too hyperactive to be any help. "Wait, back up two and a half inches, then turn the tires left. And then right. And then—"

"Hold on," Handyman Jack interrupted. "I'll guide you. We don't want a flat tire."

Handyman Jack scurried outside to the back of the bus and stayed within view of the side mirror. She followed his hand motions until backing the bus enough to make the tight turn.

"Nice job," Roxie said when Handyman Jack hurried back onto the bus.

"Do you honestly think we can make it to Nevada?" Luna finally asked the question she had been avoiding.

"If we can make it out of the burn-zone and past the eastern containment line . . ." Handyman Jack said vaguely. "After that, we make like we're on a road trip, should anyone ask. Might want to think of a cover story while we're at it."

"Ooh, I know," Rogue said. "We were going to pan for gold at that river in Gold Town when the fires started."

Handyman Jack grunted as if not convinced. "Where's the vehicle registration?"

Luna had seen it earlier in a plastic baggie clipped to the sun visor. She handed it to him before concentrating on the winding road.

"So, you're supposed to be SunFlower BlueStone." He didn't bother hiding the chuckle in his voice.

"Yeah, that won't work if we get pulled over," Luna said. "Sun-Flower's in her sixties. Can the police look up SunFlower in their database? Because, if her driver's license photo pops up, our cover is blown. We might get accused of grand bus auto."

"I honestly don't know," Handyman Jack said.

"I know," Rogue exclaimed. "Roxie, you can pretend you're Auntie SunFlower. If you dye your hair blue."

"Now that, I have to see," Handyman Jack remarked flirtatiously-ly.

"My hair color won't matter if we don't get pulled over," Roxie said flatly.

"You and SunFlower are about the same age," Luna said. "Blue hair might help since you can't show them your driver's license."

"On the off chance you get pulled over," Handyman Jack said. "You two should do a quick switcheroo."

"I'll memorize SunFlower's address," Roxie said.

"Good thinking." Handyman Jack handed the registration to Roxie. "One problem solved. Next?"

"The lodge had security cameras. And if they were working, footage will show we left together—on this bus," Luna said with her eyes on the road.

"Right." Handyman Jack seemed to contemplate aloud. "Still with the fire and all, local authorities will have their hands full. Once we make it to Carson City, we'll just have to blend in and hope for the best."

"Oh, no," Rogue moaned. "What about those license plate readers? They could be everywhere."

"Didn't think of that." Handyman Jack fiddled with his duffel. "The upside, the license plates are smeared with gunk. Most likely soot. In fact, I'm thinkin' the forest fire might help our charade. Once we make it to Nevada, I can disguise the bus. Maybe add some stripes . . ."

Rogue giggled. "Like a zebra?"

"Pinstripes, you bonehead," Handyman Jack chastised. "They sell pinstriping tape. Maybe get a few decals and whatnot. We'll just have to see how far a few good choices and some good luck takes us."

It was starting to sound like a viable plan. Still, Luna was furious and embarrassed for involving Roxie and Handyman Jack in her parents' self-righteous escapade. But the real problem nagging her was: Were her parents actually involved in the bombings? Or were they just the outspoken activists catching the blame?

"So, I guess we're really doing this," Luna quizzed. "I mean, going to SunFlower's farm in Mt. Shasta. By way of Nevada?"

"Our best option as far as I can figure," Handyman Jack said.

"It's super ballsy!" Rogue exclaimed.

"Remember, we can't use debit and credit cards," Luna said. She only had like twenty dollars. Plus the cash Handyman Jack, Levi, and Butch had given them in Gold Town.

Handyman Jack pulled out his wallet. "I'm good for one hundred and twenty-two buckaroos."

"I have two hundred cash on me," Roxie said. "Thanks to the Reno trip I didn't make."

"Wait a sec." Rogue ran to his bunk.

He stormed back to the front of the bus, waving an envelope in the air. "I win! I have two-hundred and fifty dollars."

"Where'd you get that?" Luna grilled.

"You know, all the yard work I do for the neighbors," Rogue said.

"You don't put it in the bank?" Handyman Jack asked.

"Duh, Dad says it's not safe to keep all your money in the bank," Rogue lectured. "You gotta have some cash for when the banks start crashing. But, now I only have a hundred left in my college savings 'cause Dad sorta borrowed it. He promised to pay me back. With interest."

"That'll get us to Mt. Shasta and then some," Handyman Jack said as Luna turned the bend to be accosted by a fallen tree. "Guys, hang on!" She screeched on the brakes.

"It's just a small snag. Good thing Sanchez lent me his chainsaw," Handyman Jack said.

The bus skidded to a stop several feet in front of the scorched pine. It all seemed so impossible. Downed trees and power lines. Fires everywhere. Wouldn't someone report a vehicle driving through the closed roads? Running from the FBI was only exacerbating their guilt. Prolonging the inevitable?

Chapter 14

SunFlower BlueStone found herself gasping on the floor beside the bed. The lucid vision had been so intense—as if she had actually died. She clicked on the nightstand's lamp. Nothing. It must need a new bulb, one of the many things that didn't work in the cheap Jacksonville motor lodge where she had been forced to take refuge yesterday afternoon when a series of thunderstorms spawning from a tropical storm in the Atlantic had made driving to Cassadaga, Florida, nearly impossible.

SunFlower gagged. "What's wrong with me?" Even her heart raced. She rummaged through her purse until finding the mini-flashlight and stumbled to the bathroom with an urgent need to puke.

A flash of light streamed through the frosted bathroom window, turning night into day. Seconds later, the deafening crackle of thunder sent her heart racing faster.

After a case of dry heaves, SunFlower splashed her face with water and stared back at the vanity mirror, still dazed . . . when her reflection slowly began to fade. Into nothingness.

What a strange illusion. Perplexed, SunFlower decided to ask Prudence her thoughts on the bizarre vision, even though Prudy hated being summoned in the early morning hours. Or any time for that matter.

She finally thought to turn on the bathroom light. Nothing. "Crappity-crap-crap!" The electricity was out. "Prudy, are you here?" SunFlower whispered.

"*Prudy?*" she shouted in her mind.

Her persnickety spirit guide was likely sailing the higher dimensions, avoiding the low-vibe Earthlings as she so often criticized. Just as well, SunFlower consoled herself while rifling through her suitcase.

After a quick smudging with a sprig of white sage she had wild-harvested on Mount Shasta, SunFlower convinced herself it had merely been a bad dream and not one of her vision messages. And she crawled back into bed.

Despite attempts to center herself, all she could do was toss and turn. The humidity was beyond bearable. And with no air conditioning . . . *Don't be a hypocrite.* After all, she advocated against air conditioning. So much easier to do when living in the northernmost county of California. Not Florida. *How do Floridians cope?*

SunFlower's thoughts drifted to her failing mission. Something was amiss. She had been to eight metaphysical workshops from New York to Florida without making a single contact.

By this point, she should have connected with more than twenty crucial activists who had been instructed to meet her under the guise of the workshops. Her job was to provide them false identities and train tickets to a small town in Northern California, for Devin no longer trusted the Internet and phones. Devin would arrange transportation from the Dunsmuir, California, train station to a secret survivalist bunker. So secret, she didn't even know where it was, although she did have a visual in her mind.

These climate activists with specialized skill sets were on the Activist Hitlist. People Devin's New Pangea organization needed to save before they disappeared from this realm. As in murdered.

Had she made a colossal mistake by accepting such a radical mission? It wasn't like she had any covert skills. She considered herself an ordinary mystic with random but often helpful visions, assisted with esoteric tools like the tarot, crystals, and her cosmically bequeathed yet reluctant spirit guide. Honestly, SunFlower should be editing the final touches of her latest crystal book instead of gallivanting across the country, acting like a secret agent.

It had her doubting if, indeed, Crystal, Forest, and Devin's doomsdayer organization were another one of those conspiracy cults with good intentions but working for the wrong karmic truth.

She inhaled and exhaled deeply with a lapis lazuli resting on her forehead. She tried to block out the raucous thunder as she willed in a visual of Devin's aura. His chakras spun vividly in the depths of her mind. No dark energies. *Oh, except several small fear-based murky spots.* That was to be expected. After all, he was on an impossible timeline. To save the planet!

"Whoa!" She nearly fell out of the bed once again. The crackle of thunder so loud, it scared the prana out of her. The intense energies of lightning storms wreaked havoc with her heightened sensitivity. One of the reasons she avoided the South's thunderstorm season. But the rainy season didn't usually start until May.

"*Wake up*! *Wake up*!" Prudy's raspy scream invaded SunFlower's mind.

"Prudy, how could anyone sleep through this?" SunFlower droned while massaging her third eye. "I would like your translation on a vision—"

"*Leave*! *Now*!" Prudy's words livestreamed into SunFlower's internal hearing. "*Or you shall not escape the deluge. And I, shall be stuck in this doomed realm. For an eternity.*"

Not trusting the ever-pessimistic Prudy, SunFlower lingered, exchanging the lapis lazuli for a nuummite palm stone, when unexpectedly her soul burned, as if it were on fire. The ancient blackish grounding stone seemed to singe her hand. She let it fall to the carpet as its speckled iridescent flashes of gold turned crimson.

A fire? Luna's terrified face filled SunFlower's closed eyes. Followed by Rogue's. But when her dear soul-sister's sobbing face took over the vision, begging, "*Don't let them persecute Luna and*

Rogue for the fires!" SunFlower realized Crystal needed her help. That would mean ditching the mission.

"*Imbecile,*" Prudy roared into SunFlower's head. "*Leave, lest you are prepared to die! As in this very day.*"

"I don't like this raunchy motel either," SunFlower said, changing into a pair of perfectly splattered painter's overalls. Her favorite traveling attire. She tried the lights again to no avail and then grabbed a health juice from the mini fridge. With reluctance, she talked herself into going to Cassadaga, despite the panicky desire to return to California.

"*West, we must go west,*" Prudy demanded. "*That lunatic governor is contemplating when to issue the evacuation order.*"

That had SunFlower laughing. "You mean the Florida governor's sending more illegal immigrants to California?" If so, she'd simply contact one of her activist friends in California to set up a temporary shelter for them like they had last month. On second thought, she wasn't supposed to use a cell phone during the mission.

Prudy's piercing scream had SunFlower holding her head. "*Stop playing with me! You must leave at once!*"

It wasn't the first time her pesky spirit guide had made unreasonable demands in the pretense of her own personal agenda. Like the time Prudy had demanded to watch a particular full moon rise, eclipse, or cosmic alignment in order to bask in the energies.

"*The super-storm in the ocean is spinning back—aiming for Florida in a wrath never to be witnessed in all your written history. Once the evacuation order is proclaimed, ensnared you shall be!*" Prudy continued.

It abruptly came to her; the drowning vision and fading away in the mirror had been warnings. Except for the fire images. Often, SunFlower never made sense of her cryptic messages. She crammed the suitcase with her bag of crystals and decided to skip brushing her teeth and re-braiding her hair. "Bathroom" was all SunFlower said, expecting privacy.

With suitcase in hand, SunFlower was ready to abort the mission when the motel room's door burst open seconds before she reached the doorknob. The constant lightning arrays streaking the sky revealed the turbulent clouds shrouding the earth. The extreme barometric pressure seemingly tried to suck her soul out of her. That was when she connected the dangerous low pressure to the hurricane, the hurricane that had been predicted to fizzle out into the Atlantic. After all, hurricane season started in June, not February. The weather was becoming more and more unpredictable. Volatile. She didn't need a spirit guide or tarot reading to tell her that.

She made it to her Tesla as a meteoric flash singed her retinas. A nanosecond later, the crack of thunder had her rubbing her ears. Conserving her depleted energy, SunFlower asked internally, "*Where to?*" as she strapped on the seatbelt ever so ready to return to her sanctuary, her little farmhouse in Mt. Shasta where cool breezes awaited. She might even have a few guests waiting there, since Devin used it as a temporary safehouse for on-the-run activists. More importantly, she had the urgent need to check on Luna and Rogue.

As for the children's parents, Crystal and Forest were on a different sort of mission arranged by Devin and his New Pangea associates. A far more dangerous one from the images she had gathered. However, SunFlower carefully pushed away those snippets of info attempting to channel through, preferring not to know the details, should the feds ever detain her. Or worse, she was shadowed by dark beings.

Prudy's grating voice pried into SunFlower's mind. "*Take me to Sedona.*"

So, that was what the urgency was all about. Prudy needed some me-time at one of Earth's powerful vortices. "I took you there last month to see the Northern Lights." It had been an amazing once-in-a-lifetime opportunity, thanks to the severe geomagnetic storm that had spawned auroras across the United States.

"*I must go yet again,*" Prudy demanded.

"I grant you permission to go without me," SunFlower blurted aloud.

"*And still, you do not comprehend the karmic laws of spirit guides. I cannot abandon you! Turn here. You need a more, shall I say, effective escape vehicle.*"

"What?" SunFlower scoffed. "Now you're just pushing my ethereal buttons." After all, Prudy had insisted she buy that particular pricey Tesla model years ago. There was no pleasing her.

"*SunFlower, beloved lightworker of All That Is,*" Prudy beseeched with feigned patience as was her way, "*I beg of you, indulge me this—final time. The approaching storm is so vast, it shall inundate the entire landmass known as Florida. Then, it shall spin into the overheated gulf waters, swell even larger, and spin back into land, obliterating a swath through the land you call Texas. Once the evacuation is announced, you shall be stranded in this—this ludicrous contraption. See for yourself—*"

Prudy had conversed more in the past few minutes than she had all week. Usually, her spirit guide just flitted around like a fidgety fairy forever annoying her with sarcastic one-liners that chastised SunFlower's inept metaphysical abilities. For Prudy to express alarm was unlike her.

Miffed, SunFlower snapped, "For the love of the Goddess, why didn't you tell me sooner the hurricane changed course?"

"*Don't blame me for your clairvoyant inadequacies. If you were truly dedicated to your spiritual path, you would see the timeline constantly shifts. Once the dark forces anticipate our path, they alter theirs.*"

Without warning, a pervasive image pushed into SunFlower's mind to reveal an endless stream of vehicles obstructing the highways.

"*Is that clear enough of a vision for you?*" Prudy's sardonic tone invaded her mind. "*The refueling reservoirs shall remain hollow for days.*"

SunFlower's spleen began prickling. Warning of danger. It was time to take her spirit guide seriously. She happened to spot a car rental business and swerved into the parking lot, even though it was only 5:00 a.m.

"*Not here. They shall not have any vehicles for you.*"

"Okey dokey," the ever so patient SunFlower managed to say. Prudy had served her well many times, guiding her to safety when escaping activist's assassins, which was her spirit guide's primary purpose from what she had pried from Prudy. A hurricane was a completely different situation, which may well be just as important as saving activists on the Hit List. For one must save one's self before attempting to save others.

"Lead the way," SunFlower said aloud as she squinted through the sheets of rain slapping the windshield.

"*I find it annoying how you depend on me rather than your own cosmic gifts.*"

Airport signs flickered ahead in the sporadic lightning show. "Are you taking me to the airport?" SunFlower bemoaned, slowing down to a stop at a blinking red-light intersection along with two other vehicles. A group of people stepped out of their car in front of her and waved her down. What a time to have car trouble.

"*Do. Not. Stop.*" Prudy screeched.

Wham! The car juddered. A group of men dressed in hoodies pounced on her car. The next thing she knew, they were rocking the car and yelling obscenities so loud she winced.

"Get out of the fuckin' car!" *Wham*! A baseball bat slammed into the driver's side window.

"*Go!*" Prudy kept screaming in her mind.

To do that, she risked hitting them. Or running over them. Her conscience would never let her commit such a vile act. She mentally scanned the man glaring at her through the side window, thinking he desperately needed healing energies. Instinctively, SunFlower sent him a ray of light, only to feel the shock of hate zapping back at her like a voracious piranha.

One of the men, his aura so shadowy—she had to shove back the darkness, fighting to keep her own light from being siphoned away. Prudy was there, cloaking SunFlower's ethereal body. Protecting her.

"SunFlower, you must not engage these endarkened souls. You cannot heal them. I beg of you—deny their existence!"

Prudy was right. Their lost souls were beyond her healing capabilities. As if on autopilot, SunFlower proceeded through the intersection and down the street until the man with the malevolent energy fell off the car shouting, "Crazy bitch!"

The other one, running beside her like an athletic zombie, finally let go of the door handle while another attacker flung objects at the back of the car. *Thank the Goddess, I made it out of there.* But the cracked windshield made it difficult to see. That was when she realized the billowing crackled driver's side window would shatter any second.

"Now what?" She had never been accosted by a carjacker. Or anyone with such heinous energies.

"You did well," Prudy said without the slightest trace of condemnation. *"Follow this paved path. Soon, we shall be at the place we must be. Once there, you shall obtain a more suitable vehicle. To outrun this cosmic storm of storms."*

SunFlower wasn't exactly sure what Prudy was referring to. But a cosmic rift had apparently opened. She sensed Earth's turmoil scorching her root chakra. The mission she had agreed upon had been hijacked by something far more crucial. She wasn't sure her years of spiritual enlightenment had prepared her for the monumental battle that lay ahead.

All she wanted—needed—was to find Luna and Rogue, for she understood, they were being hunted . . .

Chapter 15

Roxie Ramirez scampered from window to window, as if expecting to see a swarm of black SUVs surrounding the skoolie. Her irrational and almost debilitating paranoia seemed to amplify as the Carson City Walmart's parking lot grew with more people every few minutes. People loitered about outside and mingled with other loiterers, glancing nervously at the store's entrance, as if unsure they were allowed to just hang out.

Roxie inhaled and exhaled deeply several times, unable to banish the onslaught of toxic and anxious thoughts from dominating her. But her usual calming method wasn't working. Not this time.

Jackson and Luna better get their cute little tushies back here. It was the waiting she couldn't take, worried they would get caught. Jackson and Luna had gone inside the store for a few items. Jackson wanted to buy a disguise of sorts, for himself and the bus. Luna had insisted on buying a box of blue hair color much to Roxie's dismay.

After a nauseatingly tense eight-hour drive through a maze of detours of countless miles of smoldering forests resembling an apocalyptic wasteland, they had made it to a major highway and finally to Carson City, Nevada. Where she had expected, more like needed, everything to return to normal. She certainly hadn't expected to find throngs of people milling about as if they had no place to go.

They had parked the ash-covered skoolie on the far edge of a small homeless encampment developing in the Walmart lot alongside scores of RVs, buses, SUVs, and vans. The place resembled a third-world refugee camp. Some even tromped in on foot with overflowing shopping carts while others had pitched tents right on the blacktop, as if it were a KOA campground.

Roxie had seen it often enough on the news—refugees seeking shelter in shopping centers. It always seemed a rather odd solution. Why not seek help from family and friends? Yet, there she was. Another homeless statistic. Apparently, it was some unspoken courtesy that Walmarts across the country tolerated misplaced people seeking shelter in the wake of natural disasters such as hurricanes, tornadoes, and wildfires.

These extreme weather-related events had increased in frequency the past few years. A new normal the media harped, which quite frankly scared the living daylights out of her. Especially now. From what Jackson had overheard, the Walmart evacuees traveling or living near the California/Nevada border had camped there after escaping the California fires, while travelers heading westbound were stuck waiting the all-clear to enter California.

But what about all these people on foot? Had they really escaped with nothing? Perhaps they eagerly waited for family to pick them up? Roxie wished she could help them, but it would be too risky for Luna and Rogue. Surely, FEMA or the Red Cross would set up an information booth advising of nearby shelters.

The mounting tension in the air seemed to be on the brink of imploding. At least that was how her head felt. *I can't believe there's no aspirin or Tylenol on this bloomin' bus."* Roxie ransacked the cupboards once again to no avail.

She stood at the kitchen window, attempting to massage away her headache when a Carson City police car with flashing lights pulled into the lot. "Damn!"

Methodically, the squad car paused at each vehicle it came to, starting at the outer row, probably scanning license plates. Looking for them? Or anyone with a warrant or expired tags? Either way, her nerves were just about shot.

A yelling match erupted at the other end of the parking lot. She grabbed the binoculars and zoomed in on the scene. Two young men embroiled in an animated brawl hit the ground, rolling on the pavement, trying to get in punches. A third man dove into the mix.

The squad car screeched off with its brain-piercing siren. Roxie winced through the binoculars and attempted to massage her temples with one hand as two officers intervened. She sat in the driver's seat. Watching. Waiting. Worrying.

Relief flooded through her when the squad car took off with two of the troublemakers. It was only a matter of time before more police arrived. Still, the switching of the license plates should hold up—unless the FBI had figured out this bus had been at Granite Hill Lookout. The skoolie could have been ID'd by a traffic cam, which had been impossible to avoid once entering the town.

Sheesh, what's taking Jackson so long? Although, the store must be like Black Friday in there. She liked it better when Jackson was near, with his comforting, easy-going attitude. Besides, just sitting in the parking lot—they were asking to get caught. However, Luna had insisted the engine needed a break for a couple of hours, as it had been running hot.

The shower squeaked off. Roxie needed to find those shears she had seen earlier. Still, she couldn't take her eyes off the growing crowd.

Rogue bounced to the kitchen sink. "Okay, I'm ready for my do-over!"

Roxie flinched. *Uh, too loud.*

"Don't tell me you don't wanna do it now?" Rogue bemoaned.

Roxie forced a small smile at his jubilant innocence. To him, this was an exciting adventure. "Are you certain you want me to cut your hair?" She hated to cut off those gorgeous reddish-brown locks.

"I'm so done with dorky hair. Wanna look all badass. Luna's getting me some hair gel. She's gonna give me spikes," he said, pantomiming spikes with his hands.

Her headache stifled the laugh stuck in her throat. "Stand here on these plastic bags."

"It's not plastic, it's—"

"Shush." She waved her hand in his face, tired of the constant corrections. "And for heaven's sake, be still, kiddo." He was such a peppy thing when he talked. She haphazardly snipped away the curls. Crystal wasn't going to recognize her son by the time she and Luna were done with him.

Luna and Jackson clambered onto the bus with arms full of purchases just as she finished sweeping up the hair clippings, all the while Rogue admired his butchered hair in the mirror mounted to the closet door.

"Hey, guys," Rogue said, as if he had an important announcement, "I know what would make an uber-cool disguise. If I totally shaved my head."

"Right, because that's a normal style for a ten-year-old," Luna retorted.

Curious, Roxie reached for Jackson's Walmart bag. "What did you get?"

Jackson jerked the bag just out of her reach with a hint of mischievousness as he strode to the bathroom. "You'll see."

Luna dumped the contents of her bag onto the dinette table. "I can't promise anything. Just bought the cheap stuff." She handed Roxie a box labeled Shocking Blue. "I'm going with Shocking Pink. But I'm only coloring the tips of my hair."

Roxie wasn't keen on having blue hair. *My mother would roll over in her grave,* she mused. Still, blue hair sounded rather daring. "Can you rinse hair dye down these pipes?"

Luna shrugged. "Probably not. But I won't tell my dad if you won't." Luna tore open a box of large trash bags.

"Don't let Rogue see those," Roxie said in jest.

"He's such an eco-warrior." Luna covered the floor with a plastic trash bag she had cut open to make larger. "Ready?"

"Now?" Roxie was taken aback. She assumed Luna would color her own hair first. Her head was pounding so hard she thought it might crack open. "What about Jackson?"

"Oh, I think he'll be busy in the bathroom for a while," Luna said rather elusively.

It had Roxie wondering what the man was up to. However, she preferred a bit of privacy while Luna colored her hair. "Why not?" Roxie found herself crossing her fingers her hair didn't fall out.

"Rogue," Luna called out while unfolding the hair color instructions, "you absolutely cannot wear that Greta Thunberg *Blah, Blah, Blah* shirt. It's too obvious."

Rogue scrunched his mouth at her. "You're not my mom. I can wear whatever I—"

"She's right," Roxie said firmly.

"Whatev." Rogue moped to his bunk.

Roxie attempted to relax as Luna gently applied the hair dye. What day was it? If it was Monday, she would have been returning from Reno. Tuesday, getting her teeth cleaned after Bible Study. Wednesday, preparing for the town hall meeting—not attempting to look like Cyndi Lauper. Thank heavens, SunFlower didn't have orange hair. That would be intolerable.

"Handyman Jack, what's taking you so long?" Rogue pounded on the bathroom door. "Do you have gas or what?"

"Hold your horses!" Jackson clamored back.

Roxie was appalled at the boy's lack of manners. Apparently, encouraging children to be precocious was the parenting trend. What did she care? Rogue was a hoot. Since she didn't have to live with him permanently. She sat at the dinette table with a towel draped around her shoulders and waited for the hair dye to activate, all the while staring out the partially closed blinds. Expecting trouble. As if she sensed it looming in the periphery.

"Rogue, your turn," Luna said, squeezing a handful of clear goop into her hands.

Rogue gave up annoying Jackson and plodded over. Good, he listened for once and had changed into a tie-dye shirt. Luna ran her fingers through his hair and quickly formed tiny spikes. Meanwhile, Roxie closed her eyes and tried relaxing. Just long enough to get rid of that headache.

"Holy balls!" Rogue belted out.

Roxie's head lurched, and her stomach cramped as she frantically scanned the parking lot. No police cars. She swung her throbbing head around to tell Rogue to "shush" when she set eyes on a complete stranger standing feet away.

"Yes!" Rogue went gaga over Jackson decked out in a leather vest, knee-torn jeans, and a bandanna tied around his head. Even more shocking, he had shaved off his scraggly mustache.

"I scored this faux leather vest from the clearance rack. And there's more." Jackson turned to his side and casually flipped a foot-long braid over his shoulder, as if posing for *Vogue*. "Luna picked it out. Granted it's just a corny clip on."

"It's a great look on you," Luna said, cracking one of her rare smiles.

Roxie was rather speechless with his devilishly handsome look. She quickly turned away, embarrassed he had caught a glimpse of her with clumps of pasty blue hair piled on top of her head in a clip.

"Too much?" Jackson fretted, as if his feelings had been hurt by her lack of response.

Roxie clapped at the expense of her pounding head. "Bravo! No one will ever recognize you."

"What about me?" Rogue pouted dramatically.

"Sport, you're looking like a hoodlum, yourself," Jackson prattled.

Rogue strutted down the narrow aisle with jazz hands framing his head.

"The perfect disguise," Roxie said when the timer dinged. Time to see if the dye had fried her hair.

"Guys, I'm craving pizza," Rogue proclaimed, as if everyone had been waiting to hear.

"Now, sport, we should save the rest of our cash," Jackson started. "Don't we still have some of Nina's burritos?"

"There's only one left. I sorta ate two this morning," Rogue admitted. "Hey, I still have gift cards from Christmas." He hurried to his bunk. And just like that, the boy was happy again.

"I'll rinse my hair." Roxie grabbed the flimsy disposable gloves hanging over the faucet.

"You sure?" Luna asked.

Roxie slipped on the gloves. "I can manage that."

Roxie ran her fingers through her matted bluish hair, enjoying the lukewarm water's temporary relief. Unable to ignore her worries, she forced herself to hope for the best. Their situation was impossible. Escaping not one but multiple fires. Along with the incredibly risky decision of helping Luna and Rogue escape the FBI until they made it to Mt. Shasta. *What was I thinking?* She must be losing her mental faculties. Of course, she wasn't hiding forever, just until the kids found their parents.

Roxie was towel-drying her hair when Rogue declared he and Jackson were walking to the Panda Express down the street. So much for pizza. As she recalled, Rogue had painstakingly announced each and every fast-food eatery once exiting the highway to Walmart.

"Uncle Lewie gave me a fifty-dollar Panda Express gift card. So, like, what do you guys want?" Rogue asked.

"Oh, dear," Roxie pondered. "Something mild. Maybe teriyaki chicken." She didn't know what they had. "Does it come with a side of Rolaids?"

Rogue grimaced. "What's Rolaids?"

Jackson winked. "Gotcha covered on that one. Never leave home without 'em."

"No sodas," Luna ordered. "You get crazy-hyper when you have too much sugar."

"Yes, Mom," Rogue nagged.

Off they went.

"While my color is setting," Luna said, "I'll give you a blowout. I do it all the time since it's so freaking expensive."

"Hon, don't bother. Blow dryers use a lot of power," Roxie started in, knowing they needed to conserve the solar battery bank or whatever it was called.

"I just thought of the perfect up-do for you!" Luna whipped out her blow dryer like a zealous gunslinger. "It's cordless. And fully charged," she practically sang.

Roxie wasn't so sure. Still, it was hard to argue with the head-strong woman, especially when she was being so sweet. "Why not? But nothing radical. Tell me, you used to be quite the tomboy. When did you go glam?" Roxie asked.

Luna shook her head. "You know my parents. They were so strict. I wasn't even allowed to wear eyeshadow until high school. Crazy. Right? So, yeah, after I left home, I rebelled. Turns out, I absolutely love fashion and all that Lady Gaga shit I used to scoff at."

"I see," Roxie said, wondering if it was some deep-rooted tactic to irritate her parents. She had seen time and time again, how children often went in opposite directions once leaving the nest. In the girl's case, it was a refreshing change to see she had outgrown her *G.I. Jane* phase.

Roxie closed her eyes, trying to block out the blare of the blow dryer, losing herself to inner solitude while Luna did her thing.

Roxie must have dozed off. She awoke to see a blue-haired woman with a Victorian hairstyle staring back at her, until re-alizing it was her own reflection in the mirror. She was relieved she didn't look like Frenchy, the beauty school dropout in *Grease*. "Mmm, rather sweet and old fashion without looking prim," Rox-ie decided, turning her head from side to side. It didn't look like one of her grandmother's debacles of a beauty parlor treatment gone awry.

"A messy bun. It's absolutely amazing on you," Luna gushed. "You should find something uh, fun to wear in the closet while I rinse my hair."

Amazing? I wouldn't go that far. But Roxie rather thought the style was provocatively feminine without looking like an over-the-hill celebrity trying to look twenty years younger. Like those shameless selfies of Martha Stewart that popped up on Yahoo.

Now for something fun to wear, she mused, rummaging through Crystal's clothes. She finally decided on a darling free-flowing rainbow skirt and a rather sheer gauzy blouse that drifted off her shoulders. Although she wasn't giving up her comfy Skechers. No matter what Luna said.

Shouldn't the boys be back by now, Roxie fretted while Luna primped in the mirror at her new cute pageboy cut with a pink fringe. "That's a wonderful look on you," Roxie said.

"I guess. I wanted a bob for the summer, since Sacramento gets so freakin' hot. I know, let's do your makeup."

"Oh, I don't fuss with that anymore," Roxie protested.

"I have the perfect eyeshadow that will make your blue eyes pop even more with your sexy Helena Bonham Carter updo."

Great, now it's sexy. She preferred amazing. But makeup? Since Hank had passed, the au naturel look suited her. No one ever paid her any mind, anyhow. Which was exactly how she liked it.

"It'll be fun," Luna pestered on.

"What the heck?" Perhaps Jackson wouldn't mind. Roxie resigned herself and sat next to Luna. "Keep it simple," she said, already mortified just glimpsing at Luna's three-tiered cosmetic case that looked like it belonged to a makeup artist.

Fifteen minutes later, Luna said, "Ready for the final result?"

Roxie peered into the mirror. "Oh, my." The catty eyeliner, the enhanced brows that no longer showed any signs of gray, the tinge of rosy blush, and the cotton candy–pink lipstick were a bit much. Perhaps the eyeliner took the focus off her wrinkles and onto her blue eyes and hair.

"So, what do you think?" Luna asked expectedly.

"I think you missed your calling." Roxie didn't want to offend the girl. Even in her younger days, she had never worn so much eye makeup. Still, she rather enjoyed the refreshing change.

Roxie's hands flew to her head. "Sheesh, I can't take this headache another bloomin' minute. I can't find a single aspirin on this bus."

"So sorry. Mom and Dad don't use over-the-counter drugs. I left my Midol at the apartment."

That figures. "My homeopathic headache medicine was due to arrive this week." So much for that. Would Amazon automatically refund her when the package couldn't be delivered, or would she need to request a refund? "Hmm, no sign of the boys. Think I'll dash into Walmart for a bottle of Vanquish or something. It's not like anyone will recognize me in this getup," Roxie said, feeling like a sixties flower child.

"Great idea. We need you at your absolute best. But don't go off with the first guy who comes on to you." Luna walked away, giggling.

Roxie grabbed a twenty from her wallet. "Don't be silly."

Once outside, the oppression lingering in the air seemed to stifle her every breath. *Get over it*, she scolded. It would take five minutes at most, and in twenty minutes, the headache would start subsiding. Scurrying toward the store entrance, she passed loads of panhandlers shaking Starbucks cups at her with blank, blinkless eyes.

Those poor people. Their emotionless faces told her they had lost everything, perhaps even their desire to go on. At least Roxie had Hank's pension. Worst-case scenario, she could afford a small apartment or mooch off her brother or sister. Not that she wanted to impose. She rather relished her simple independent life.

The second she stepped inside the store, an undeniable weight bore down even harder, like her head was locked in a vice. Had she made a grave mistake? Her mind screamed, *Don't be a scaredy-cat*.

During the tripledemic years, Roxie had paraded around in the pretense of being vaccinated after two members of her community had died shortly upon getting the first jab: one with a stroke the day after and the other a heart attack a week later. So, she had faked getting the FDA's barely tested emergency-authorized vaccines, stating she'd had the first two jabs at the mobile health stations at her Dollar General.

When her doctor had asked for her vaccination card, she had gone on and on about all the trouble it had been trying to install the mobile app on her outdated phone. No one had questioned her further. For why would a woman her age fib about a thing like that? Later, she had even gone so far as to buy a phony vaccination card from a friend's son who went to UC Berkeley.

Turned out she must have had an asymptomatic case of COVID-19 due to the antibodies per a blood test a few years back. Still, after losing her eldest son to the Coronavirus, along with several friends, and numerous elderly people in her community, she couldn't quite understand her illogical fear of getting the Dr. Fauci–touted vaccine.

To this day, she avoided crowded places, which had been the primary purpose for the Reno trip—to get over her ridiculous fear. Meanwhile, Mexico's recent outbreaks of H5N2 bird flu kept her on edge. Health experts had said the isolated cases were not a major concern. Hadn't they said the same thing about COVID-19 when it first broke-out in China? In her mind, a thousand cases of human-to-human transmission bird flu was a major concern. Especially with how easy it was to illegally cross the border into the United States.

Her excruciating headache vetoed her fear. However, she found herself holding her breath while navigating through the extremely busy store, as if not breathing would keep her safe. So many people.

She was surprised Walmart let that many inside the store at once. *I'm not liking this*. One thing was evident, there seemed to be a whole lot of crazy out there since the tripledemic.

"There's the aisle I need," Roxie said out loud, hoping the people blocking her path would move. No such luck. She skirted around a flustered mother trying to explain to a group of teenagers that her credit card was maxed out, and they couldn't afford to stay at a hotel another night.

Roxie scanned the sparsely stocked shelves. "There you are." She nabbed a bottle of Vanquish. She seldom used it these days. She had half a mind to open the bottle right then and there and pop two tablets. *Better not*. They might accuse her of shoplifting.

Stuck in a maze of anxious customers, she squeezed through the crowd, trying to find the end of a line to discover the lines snaked around fallen display shelves that no one had bothered to clean up. A man and woman shoving two shopping carts overloaded with camping equipment bumped into her without apologizing. Next thing she knew, they pushed their way past the registers. And out the front door.

Yelling quickly ensued.

"Hey, they can't do that," someone shouted.

"If they can do it, so can we," another shopper yelled.

"Let's go," another voice boomed over the rioting customers.

People just started running for the door. Carts and all.

Roxie spun around at the madness swirling around her. "The nerve of some people—"

Bam! Bam! Bam!

Gunshots?

People hit the floor. And so did she. Others pivoted around in a dazed state.

When the screaming started, it became real, sending her heart racing. Roxie lay on the floor next to an endcap of toilet paper as more gunshots hammered her ears.

A panicky mother with a baby sling around her neck and two kids in tow ran by calling, "Leeza."

"Get down!" Roxie warned.

Roxie crawled toward the front of the store, angling for a view of the exit several meters away. Too many people crammed the exit. If she made a run for it, she would surely be a target.

Sporadic gunshots continued. She clutched her heart when two bodies crumpled to the ground at the exit—where she would have been. A lone toddler ran down the aisle toward her. "Over here, sweetie," Roxie beckoned.

"Mommy?" the red-faced toddler blubbered.

"Over here, sweetie. Is your name Leeza?"

The towheaded girl stopped and stared at her inquisitively as Roxie inched on her stomach toward the child. "You want your mommy?"

The pandemonium of desperate cries and yells blasted her headache. But there was no time to open the bottle; instead, she stuffed the Vanquish into her bra. "Leeza, come here."

Nooo! The adorable girl waddled off down the main aisle. That was when Roxie saw the man wielding a gun at a cashier. Or was it the manager? Whomever it was, wasn't doing so well, with a bloodied Walmart vest.

Roxie's heart pounded harder when the child pointed at the gunman and started giggling and looked back at her, wavering from the gunman to her, as if deciding whom to go to.

The gunman jumped on top of a check-out counter conveyor belt and shouted, "Thank you for shopping Walmart. Nobody's leaving here. Ever!" The man's demented grin stretched from ear-to-ear.

Roxie told herself she didn't have time to be scared. She had to save that child. Somehow. Of all times not to have her purse. Of course, she didn't have a cell phone anyway. Someone must have called 9-1-1 by now. The police would storm the shooter in a matter of minutes. Wouldn't they? But that little girl didn't have minutes. Besides, the negotiating process could take a while.

At a loss, Roxie scanned the floor littered with abandoned would-be purchases. A box of pink Little Debbie cakes caught her eye. She slid on her belly until she could scoot the box toward her. "Leeza, do you want a treat?"

The little girl with padded britches stopped and turned around, still sucking her thumb, which probably served as a pacifier. Keeping her quiet. Roxie's eyes locked onto the girl's. "Fun treats?" Roxie quietly tore open the box and held up a package of pink tulip cakes.

The little girl giggled a bit too loudly and waddled to her. "Pink cake, pink cake."

"Shhh," Roxie whispered with her finger to her lips and kept an eye on the shooter, who was preoccupied shouting at the helpless employee.

When the girl grabbed the tulip cakes, Roxie sprang to her feet, swooped up the child, and ran to the back of the store while a teen held up his cell phone at her, apparently filming her. Instead of helping.

Roxie hid behind the endcap along with dozens of people crouched at the back of the store.

"Leeza," the mom cried out upon seeing her child.

"Pink cake, pink cake." The excited little girl ran to mommy.

"How can I ever thank you?" The mom was soon preoccupied with her children.

Well, that was that. Roxie had done her part for the mother-and-child reunion. But what about herself? The realization she needed to get out of that store *before* the police showed up smacked her in the face. Wouldn't they take everyone into custody as witnesses, getting their account of the crime? Eventually, they would discover her identity.

She cringed at what looked to be a dead body covered with a blanket on the cold floor in front of the employees' entrance next to the restrooms. Why weren't the others going out the back exit? She knelt down and sort of duck-walked toward the back door.

Someone tugged her arm. "There's another shooter in the back. And, uh, more bodies," the young man with an attractive five o'clock shadow and glasses warned in a low tone.

Roxie simply nodded. "Two shooters?"

"Pretty sure," whispered someone from behind.

"Maybe three," another panicky voice added.

"What about the Garden Center's exit?" Roxie asked, thinking aloud.

"That's where we were going, but we lost track of the other shooter," the man with glasses said.

"Help's coming. I called nine-one-one. Just stay here," an elderly woman said.

Roxie couldn't stay there, waiting to be the next victim; her nerves wouldn't stand for it. "Which way to the Garden Center?"

"That way." The elderly woman pointed to her right.

Thinking two men couldn't be in three places at once, assuming there were only two shooters, Roxie crept toward the Garden Center. Determined.

"Get back here," a young punk of unknown gender with earrings in all sorts of places scolded.

Roxie ignored him/her/them until the person jerked her back by her arm. "Excuse me, m—" she started. *Better not say mister or lady.* According to the gender seminar she had attended last year, some people became rather angry when one used the wrong pronoun. Staring speechlessly, she stumbled over the proper etiquette to address the person, rather than the current crisis.

Until the next round of gunshots went off. That snapped her back to reality.

Roxie mouthed, "Mind your manners" before darting to the next endcap, hoping the shooter didn't have time to take a shot at her—if the shooter happened to look her way. She peeked around the corner of the next aisle before going any farther, only to see a dozen or so people hugging the blood-smeared floor, some lifeless, others cocking their heads at her as if she were insane.

She smiled blankly at them, questioning if she should encourage them to follow her. But what if she was wrong? If they wanted to stay there and wait to get shot, that was their decision. She could not just wait for someone to kill her. Despite the fear holding her rubbery legs hostage, her instinct was to get out of there, sight unseen. If at all possible.

Roxie crept to the next endcap, when a figure ran by the far end of the store. The other shooter? She didn't want to know. She faltered, thinking of going back to the previous endcap, surprised to find several people seemed to be following her. Silly, but it gave her the ounce of courage she needed to keep going. And she made it to the next endcap.

The group behind her had bunched up to the next endcap like some life-or-death version of Red Light, Green Light, Mother May I, or was it Simon Says? Why was she thinking such nonsense? Her fear seemed to have transformed into giddiness. She smiled back at the group, taking giddiness over fear any day, and crept to the next endcap. Just a little closer to the Garden Center.

The crazed shooter had discovered the store's intercom and seemed to enjoy rapping a dreadful song about dead Walmart shoppers. The louder and crazier he ranted, the longer the line behind her grew. She supposed if an old lady like herself had the guts to sneak out, they could too.

"There it is" her breathless words wheezed out. *The Garden Center*! Should she make a mad dash and run for her life for twenty seconds or sneak her way out of there? The people at the endcap behind her waved her on. Roxie took a hard gulp and whispered, "Stay low."

The shooter's pathetic attempt at rapping morphed into high-pitched squalling, ordering the employee to dance.

This was her chance to get out of there. Roxie scooted across on her stomach and pulled herself toward the Garden Center with her arms. Not thinking of anything. Merely chanting, "You're almost there. You're almost there . . ."

She made it across the finish line! To her amazement, she counted more than twenty people dragging themselves across the floor behind her. Roxie encouraged them with a twitchy smile while keeping her eye on the back and front of the store for the gunmen.

She lent a hand to the first person to reach her, a middle-aged gentleman. "You must be an angel," he whispered into her ear.

All she could do was nod, thinking she better not stick around a moment longer. Out of breath, she ran to the Garden Center's exit for a quick peek outside. A labyrinth of vehicles jammed the parking lot and with so many people running amuck, the vehicles weren't going anywhere. How would they get the skoolie out of there before the police locked down the place?

More gunshots rang out. The group that had followed her rushed the exit, and it was a free-for-all. She ran.

Confusion set in. "Where's the bloomin' skoolie?" Wasn't it parked by the RVs? At a loss, she ran across the parking lot, straight for the sidewalk, dodging tents and people and vehicles. All she wanted was to get out of that parking lot. Then, well, she would speedwalk along the sidewalk, trying to look like a bystander, not a victim. Which was a rather stupid idea, considering the mayhem surrounding her. *Damn, where is the Panda Express?*

Roxie made it to the boulevard's sidewalk, about to faint as her blood sugar had plummeted, muddling her mind. This was all—too much. She just plopped onto the sidewalk with people running around her like she didn't exist. Not a single soul stopped to ask if she needed help.

"Roxie?" a familiar voice called out. "Is that you?"

She looked up to see a dashing older man in a leather vest lending her a hand. "Jackson?"

"With that blue hair, figured it had to be you." He pulled her to her feet. "You all right?"

What a loaded question. No, she was not all right. The world had gone mad. And she was caught in the middle of it all, no matter where she seemed to go.

"Let's get you on the bus where you can relax," Jackson said, as if reading her mind. "Luna, the clever girl she is, moved the bus to a strip mall down the street when she heard gunshots. Even radioed Rogue. Good thing he takes that damn radio with him everywhere he goes."

"And Rogue?" Her thin voice cracked.

"No doubt he *and* the egg rolls are safe and sound on the bus by now."

Not wanting to appear so fragile, Roxie struggled to find her normal voice. "Can you believe that? A shooting? Here? What's this world coming to?" Roxie rambled as her legs seemed to crumble like Feta cheese. But Jackson was there. Helping her. She was going to be just fine. Once her heart stopped thudding.

"News travels fast nowadays." Jackson winked. "The woman in front of us at the Panda Express was showing everyone a live video call from her husband stuck inside the Walmart. Saw you save that toddler! You are something else, you little spitfire."

"You saw that?"

"You betcha. I hightailed it back to the bus while Rogue waited for the to-go order. Didn't waste my breath arguing you are more important than egg rolls."

Roxie couldn't get a word in edgewise, good thing, because she was completely breathless.

"Must say, got my jogging in for the year," Jackson said, patting his heart. "Heck, you might be on the six o'clock news. And with your *stunning* new look"—Jackson's eyes seemed to take in everything from her quivering smile to her racing heart—"you might go viral on Chitter, or is it Chatter, FaceTock, TimeTic, whatever the hell they call them."

You mean X, formerly Twitter, Facebook, and TikTok, she wanted to say, still unable to find her voice. Knowing Jackson, he was intentionally botching it up to amuse and distract her. That rascal certainly could be quite charming.

Despite it all, the fires, losing her home, the precarious road trip, the FBI, even the traumatic Walmart shooting, Roxie couldn't stifle the wave of electricity that seemed to spark unexpected delight. A delight she hadn't experienced in years. Was it because her new look had revitalized her from the inside out? Her adventurous escapades?

Or, the way Jackson had gazed into her eyes, as if delving into her? Soul-searching . . . for a kindred spirit.

Chapter 16

JACKSON JONES HAD RECALCULATED their route so many times his brain hurt. They certainly couldn't return to California using the same route. It was nothing less than a miracle they had made it to Nevada unscathed. The fire-ravaged areas along Route 88 and Route 89 were far too dangerous. Furthermore, he was damn tired of outrunning the fires and chainsaw-ing downed trees. Interstate 80, for the most part, was also out of the question. Which had him wondering if the Sacramento fires had been contained.

The plan was to take Highway 50 and then head north on Route 28, skirting around the north shore of Lake Tahoe back into California. From there, well, it depended on how far the fires had spread. According to the map, they could take a meandering series of rural highways and byways, which would take most of the day until eventually hooking up to Interstate 5 around Redding. From there, it was a straight shot to the city of Mt. Shasta.

Before leaving Nevada, they had parked on a secluded dirt road off Highway 50, where he and the gang had gone to work disguising the bus as best they could with their limited budget. Notable details the traffic cam operators might have identified earlier, like swapping out the Greenpeace doodad hanging from the rearview mirror for one of those tacky pine tree air fresheners.

Luna had eagerly ripped off the colorful dingle ball fringe dangling from the top of the windshield. He had adhered a set of nifty blue vinyl pinstripes to each side of the bus, and Roxie had attached the large starry forest wall sticker to the back of the bus that he had found in the Walmart camping section. Luna and Rogue had also covered the solar panels on the roof with a brown tarp. That way the panels didn't stick out like a sore thumb.

Luna had even bought one of those family stickers for the back window, only this was a Big Foot family of four. Rogue had gotten a kick out of that. And last but not least, the bus had lost a hubcap somewhere along the way, so Jackson had popped off the other hubcaps and sprayed the rims blue.

Surprisingly, with a little effort, it looked like a completely different bus from the outside. Of course, if a suspicious law enforcement officer pulled them over. And compared the license plate and vehicle registration with the actual Vehicle Identification Number on the bus. They were screwed. He figured the Feds must have ID'd the bus at some point. Probably not at the Walmart, because despite all the cameras, the multitudes of RVs had most likely blocked the view. That was what he was counting on. Anyhow, chances were they wouldn't get pulled over if they obeyed the traffic laws, thereby making it to Mt. Shasta sometime that day.

"Running from the FBI is so crazy fun," Rogue gushed. "I think we totally fooled them!"

"Don't get cocky," Luna said before taking a bite of a leftover eggroll.

"Do you think the FBI helicopter made it to the lodge yet?" Roxie asked, nibbling away at the last of Nina's breakfast burritos.

"Yeah," Luna muttered.

"Poor Nina," Roxie said. "I hope they didn't interrogate her. She was such a dear to us."

"What if they wrote down our license plate?" Rogue said.

"Remember, the plates were smudged over with sooty gunk," Jackson reminded. He had wiped down the plates and the sides of the bus during the revamp. "Think Bud and Sanchez were more concerned with protecting their property. We helped them as much as they helped us."

"But they know we're on a school bus," Rogue said.

"On the upside," Jackson said, "it's common to see old school buses like these thanks to the tripledemic's biggest side effect. Hyper-inflation. I've seen more homeless people the past couple of years than I ever thought possible."

"Duh, it's politically incorrect to call them homeless." Rogue rolled his eyes theatrically. "They're called "Unhoused.""

"Potato, pa-ta-to," Jackson sing-songed. "Changing the name doesn't change the fact that these folks must be at their wits' end. Eventually, whatever label they slap on it will end up having the same negative connotations as the word 'homeless.'"

"All those people camping out in Walmart," Roxie said, "reminds me of the stories my granny used to tell. The Dust Bowl era was harrowing back then. The homeless migrants seeking shelter were branded as Okies. Treated like criminals. Starving to death. I see it happening again. Rather than treating the *unhoused* as pariahs and pretending not to acknowledge there's a problem, the government should help them get back on their feet. Get jobs. And pay taxes."

"People forced to flee their homes due to the f'd up weather are called—climate nomads," Rogue eagerly corrected once again.

Jackson quipped, "You're a regular walking encyclopedia—"

"You mean, *Wikipedia*," the kid sassed back.

He caught Roxie giggling before quickly covering her mouth. There was no winning with that kid.

Jackson sat on the bench seat behind the cockpit and pretended to study the map while Luna kept a steady hand on the steering wheel. Truth was, he preferred being in control of dicey situations like this, including the driving. However, Luna had insisted on driving.

The young woman seemed adept at tackling darn near every situation thrown at her. A surprising and rare trait this day and age. It appeared as if the younger generations couldn't make a decision without referring to their cell phone. He had a nephew who regularly asked his phone where to eat. The grand ole U.S.

of A. seemed to be breeding dumb-downed generations reliant on technology, not basic know-how. *What will these young people do when the blasted Internet goes kerplunk?* Intentionally or not.

It didn't take a genius to realize disabling the Internet would be the most effective weapon in the history of modern society. Hell, with the press of a few buttons, the collapse of the power grid infrastructure and supply chain could take down an entire country. Without Wi-Fi, the younger generations would no doubt need therapy for years. He envisioned the headlines: Wi-Fi dependency leaves fifty percent of the Western population traumatized. Scarred for life.

Who was he kidding? He took advantage of the Internet as well, checking sport stats, the weather, and whatnot. The local newspaper had gone extinct years ago. Even more frustrating, a non-digital subscription to bigger newspapers like *The Sacramento Bee* and *San Francisco Chronicle* were no longer available in his neck of the woods.

Stop complaining, you old fool. There would be plenty of time to agonize over Humanity's downfall *if* it occurred in his lifetime. Jackson needed to focus on the situation at hand. Like it or not, he felt inexplicably compelled to get Luna and Rogue to safety, even though their shenanigans were none of his business and were liable to get him into a big pile of smelly shit. He supposed the real question running around his head was "why" he seemed so compelled to help.

Begrudgingly the truth was, he couldn't get Roxie out of his mind. As if he had dreamt of her—this quintessential woman—his entire life. The way she laughed and smiled. At him. Sure, she was a looker but not a beauty queen. She was pleasant but tough when the occasion warranted.

Perhaps something more profound called to him like God Almighty saying, "Hey, bonehead, Roxie's your soulmate." Thing was, he had never put much stock into such nonsense. Ah, but every time he looked at her, his heart seemed to burst with delight, despite these past few horrid days. If he had left his cabin later that fateful morning as intended, he would have seen the fire-scorched sky and returned home. Their paths never to cross . . .

"*Fate*," his conscious seemed to shout back at his denial.

Fate was about the only thing that explained his undeniable and inexplicable longing reverberating with every heartbeat—like his first adolescent sweetheart crush. As if his heart physically hurt with desire, aching to be in her presence. He promised himself he would not take advantage of Roxie's hapless situation. He had sensed the silent pain screaming from her lovely baby-blues when he had tried to talk to her about losing her home to the wildfires. So, he kept his distance.

A practical man, Jackson realized that once they went their separate ways, odds were, they'd never see each other again. If all he could do was help her get to safety, then so be it. Luna, on the other hand, what a polar opposite; no vulnerabilities exuded from her persona. A real ballbuster when she had the mind to be. She was determined to clear her parents of the bombings. It was a lot for a gal her age to tackle. Still, he wouldn't put it beyond her capability.

Jackson's stomach flip-flopped when the engine faltered, synchronizing with the engine's reluctance. He craned over Luna's shoulder to check the speedometer. The needle hovered in the forties. Realizing they were heading up another incline, he reminded, "The summit is another thousand feet or so. You think this monstrosity can handle that?" *Damn, wish we could take a different route.*

Rogue came skipping toward him. "Sure, Dad says the engine's super strong. We were gonna go on an uber-awesome trip to the East Coast before fossil fuels are totally banned."

"Sport, that won't happen for several decades," Jackson carped. Or hell, he'd be moving to Texas.

"Who knows." Roxie sighed. "They keep banning things. Like gas stoves. I don't know how to cook on anything else."

"You still use gas?" Rogue groaned. "Haven't you heard? Fossil fuels are killing the planet. We're running out of time. The amount of carbon dioxide in the atmosphere is like the most it's been for nearly four million years. And—" Apparently, Rogue hadn't finished his tirade as he stopped to take a big gulp of air. "Last year was the hottest *ever* recorded since humans were invented. And, and, the temperature already increased by two degrees. If it goes up another two degrees, we're f'n toast. Literally."

"And driving this big-ass bus around is eco-friendly?" Luna said it first.

Rogue seemed stuck on that one. "Well, I mean fossil fuels are good *sometimes*. Until we have enough renewable resources," the kid quickly backtracked. "Besides, it's not *my* fault. Dad wants to buy an electric bus or RV. But they cost hella bucks."

"That's another thing, sport," Jackson said. "Why does the government and media advocate EVs are our Hail Mary pass out of this global energy crisis?"

"Renewable energies equal a lower carbon footprint," Rogue spouted in contempt.

Jackson stifled his sudden anger. "Perhaps you're the one in need of a lesson in supply and demand. Lithium batteries are not, I repeat, most definitely *not* renewable. As in there is only a limited supply, which will likely quadruple in price the next few years. Just because those greedy SOBs can get away with it. In all probability, the planet will run dry of lithium long before the average citizen is on their second round of EVs."

"Duh, lithium batteries *are* recyclable," Rogue shot back.

"Huh," Roxie retorted. "I wouldn't be surprised if it ends up in the same place as plastic."

"Yeah, that's so sad," Rogue admitted. "But, but, that's why we need to mine lithium from asteroids."

"Right, because space travel doesn't leave a carbon footprint," Luna quipped cynically.

"Why is everyone picking on me? It's not my fault the planet's dying," Rogue whispered woefully to the ceiling. "I wish *Young Sheldon* was for real. He could invent nuclear fusion."

Jackson shook his head at the thought of driving an electric RV, stopping every few hours to charge it. Like it or not, EVs seemed destined to take over the roads. Maybe Jackson was just too old for this exponentially changing world. He would feel vulnerable without a trusty combustion engine. Who knew how to work on those lithium battery contraptions? Probably had to hire an expensive master electrician mechanic to tinker with them. No doubt they had some snazzy name for it, just like everything else nowadays.

The bus faltered again. The speedometer stuck at the thirty-five mark. Not a good sign. They couldn't exactly call a tow truck.

Roxie stood up from the dinette table. "Can we make it to the top of the pass?"

"Uh, huh," Luna grunted and leaned forward, as if encouraging the bus along.

The green road sign seemed to taunt, *SIXTY-FIVE HUNDRED FEET*. "Almost there," Jackson said more optimistically than he felt. "Once we make it to the top of the summit, best we pull over at the first out-of-the-way spot we find."

"Yeah, the engine's running hot," Luna said. "But if I stop now, we'll never make it to the top."

Jackson's thoughts exactly. He stared down the needle slipping to thirty miles per hour, all the while shivering up a storm.

"What in heavens?" Roxie's hand flew to her mouth. She clutched the afghan blanket draped around her shoulders and sat down beside him.

"Holy balls!" Rogue exclaimed. "It's actually snowing."

Jackson had been so focused on the dashboard console, he hadn't noticed. "What d'ya know?" After a winterless winter, it was finally snowing. They must have reached the outer edge of the storm.

"This is so freakin' bizarre," Luna said with a gasp.

As they climbed in elevation, a good inch of snow was already sticking to the roads. "Granted, we are above six thousand feet," he mumbled to himself, trying to make sense of the abrupt weather change.

"Yes! We made it to the top," Rogue broadcasted loud and clear when the road leveled out.

Jackson spewed out a long sigh of relief. The worst was over. Until the bus skidded around the slight curve in the road.

"Take it easy," Jackson urged through clenched teeth. All at once, the sleety-like snow turned into fat fluffy flakes that seemed to encase them inside a traveling snow globe.

"Fuuuck." Luna's voice cracked. "I can't drive—in snow."

"Sure you can," Jackson quickly countered. This wasn't the time for Luna to lose her confidence. "But we'll find a spot to pull over. Ease up on the gas. We're about to start the decline." Jackson glanced from side to side for a turnout area to park. "You happen to carry chains?"

"Dad keeps the tire chains and snow gear in one of the outer luggage departments," Rogue said.

"Anyone else notice," Roxie said eerily, "there are no other cars on the road?"

"Come to think of it, nobody's passed us in the past twenty minutes or so," Jackson said. Troubling.

Rogue scrambled to a closet and fumbled around with a crash of supplies landing on the floor. Luna didn't seem to notice. That was how focused she was on driving.

"Uh, guys, I can't slow down," Luna uttered in an icy thin tone.

"Downshift," Jackson said as calmly as he could muster as the bus slid past a bottomless cavern to their right. "Take your foot off the gas pedal. The slight incline coming up will slow us down. Avoid the brakes as much as possible."

Rogue came running to the bench seat. "Guys, guys!" The kid fiddled with one of those bright yellow storm radios. "You gotta hear this. It's an f'n bombogenesis! For the western slope of the Sierras. Uh, is that for us?"

"What?" Roxie's eyes couldn't possibly get any rounder.

"You know, as in bomb cyclone—it's sorta like a hurricane. Only with snow," Rogue explained. "'Cause the temperature suddenly drops. A hella lot."

"Now, we get snow?" Roxie seemed to chastise the weather.

Jackson was familiar with bomb cyclones, the powerful fast-forming storms had a way of taking people by surprise. Especially those without Internet access. "No wonder we haven't seen any traffic. We must be the only boneheads on the road."

Luna took the slight curve at twenty-five miles per hour. They were bound to come across a runaway truck ramp or turnout any moment. The speedometer finally dropped to twenty. But the snow drifts piled up as they ventured farther into the storm. He couldn't help but admire the conifers adorned in powdery white elegance standing tall along the rural byway, with no evidence of the wildfires they had driven through earlier.

Then he spotted it. A building surrounded by a flat treeless area up ahead. "Looks like a gas station just ahead." Jackson pointed over her shoulder. They might as well top off the tank. "Try coasting to a stop into the parking lot."

"See it," Luna husked.

"Feather the brakes nice and easy," Jackson said matter-of-factly. "Let's see how the tires grip the road." He cringed inwardly when the rear tires started slipping. "No problem. Steer into the slide."

Rogue shrieked, "We're gonna crash—"

Jackson peered over his shoulder to give the kid the "zip-it" scowl just as Roxie clamped a hand over Rogue's mouth. They nodded at each other knowingly. The kid's excitable behavior was too much at times.

The speedometer inched down to ten mph. They might just pull this off. "You're doin' good," Jackson encouraged. "Get 'er down to five miles per hour and be ready to coast to a stop." The windows started icing over; that was how cold it was out there.

"The gas station looks abandoned," Rogue decried.

On closer inspection, the snow-covered Chevron sign was shattered. "All the better." Jackson exhaled a long heavy breath. "Try the brakes once you're under the awning. The tires should have no problem gripping." Unless the ground had already iced over as well. At least the awning would provide the bus some shelter.

"On it." Luna's tone returned to her usual take-charge self.

Luna turned into the lot at two miles per hour. Once the bus came to a complete stop, it was as if the air pressure instantly dropped considerably—like his ears were about to pop. And he could not stop shivering.

"What a wonderful job, Luna," Roxie cheered lightheartedly, but Jackson recognized the worried creases highlighting her forehead.

"Bummer, you didn't even crash once!" Rogue zinged with a toothy grin. "Get this, it's going down to like minus twenty degrees tonight. And, and, the windchill might get to forty below. Is that even possible for California?"

"Nowadays, anything's possible," Jackson grumbled. "How long is this arctic blast lasting?"

"Like, it might snow for days . . ." Rogue drawled.

"Wait"—Luna spun around in the cockpit—"forty degrees *below* zero?"

"For real," Rogue said as serious as ever.

Luna mouthed an obscenity. "We need to start the Grizzly. Now! Please tell me Dad stocked wood for the cubic mini stove."

Roxie's brows creased further. Jackson quickly turned to the woodstove situated on a hearth built over the wheel well surrounded with bags of supplies. Roxie was there by his side, and together they shuffled the supplies to the dining table.

"I guess. You know Dad and his preps," Rogue said, without any inkling of concern.

"So, that's a Grizzly," Jackson said. "Heard those things really kick out the heat." But would it keep them warm in sub-zero temperatures? Surely the kid had been exaggerating.

"Rogue," Luna called out. "Help bring in the wood blocks. If Dad didn't stock the bus, we'll freeze to d—"

"Coming." Rogue grabbed a pair of boots from the storage compartment under his bunk.

Roxie shook her head. "I feel like a doomed character in an Irwin Allen disaster movie. One minute everything's on fire. The next, it's snowing."

"Ditto. By the way, how you doing?" Jackson asked casually, not wanting to appear overly concerned. She had brushed him off earlier after he had expressed concern over her mass-shooting ordeal.

"Don't I look fine?" She dropped two handfuls of bags onto the table. "I apologize." Roxie blew wispy strands of blue away from her heart-shaped lips. "Honestly, I haven't had a chance to wallow in my sorrows. After getting thrown from one crisis to another every bloomin' day."

"I know what you mean. What's your take on the kids' parents?" Jackson asked while Luna and Rogue were outside. "They seem prepared. For trouble. Wouldn't be surprised to find a nuclear fallout shelter built under the tranny."

Roxie laughed uneasily. "They're good people."

"So, they've been falsely accused?" Quite frankly, he had his doubts.

She didn't answer while Luna dropped an armful of wood blocks on the front bus step. After the accordion door swung closed, she continued in a low tone, "They've always been activists. A bit *too* radical, if you ask me. But for good causes, mind you. They certainly didn't start the forest fire the news blamed them for. That goes against every principle they stand for."

"You think they're responsible for those bombings?" Jackson asked seconds before Rogue hammily lugged in a bulging burlap bag toward them.

Roxie's fascinating, sparkling-blue eyes revealed no answers.

Looks like they weren't getting to Mt. Shasta that day after all. Which wasn't so bad since they were no longer in danger of the fires. Truth be told, he wouldn't mind if their adventuresome road trip lasted another day or two.

Or a lifetime.

Chapter 17

Luna Lewis checked the Grizzly woodstove, thankful for the heat. She despised the cold. The cubic mini kept the bus toasty on a thirty-to-forty-degree day, but it was much colder than that out there. So, they just kept stoking it to the max. Thank God, Dad had stocked compressed wood blocks, the efficient kind, which lasted longer and burned cleaner. But would they run out?

She was surprised Rogue hadn't ranted about how much CO2 they were releasing into the atmosphere. He must be cold. And scared. She worried about him; what sucky luck to be born a Gen Alpha. It had to be the absolute worst time to be a kid. What, with AI threatening to take over people's jobs, outrageous rents, humongous power bills, lab-grown foods . . . How could society continue to function? Normally. Even more concerning, how would her vulnerable brother survive this harsh toxic world? He needed to live in a cave or a commune.

People kept paying forward the clean-up to the next generation. Which meant, the future generations were totally screwed with taking on the karma of Humanity's suicidal actions—squandering Earth's resources. Unless by some freakish miracle, the corporations decided to do their part to save the planet's ecosystem by drastically reducing emissions, not just greenwashing the numbers so they looked good on a bogus spreadsheet.

Clearly, that was not going to happen.

Nothing escaped the toxicity spewed out by the corporations; and yet, the government blamed the people for the pollution, instead of enacting stricter regulations to stop the mega-polluters in the first place. Why? Government agencies like the EPA and FDA were bastardly incentivized to look the other way.

The unexpected image of the famous painting *The Scream* flashed in her mind. Only it was Earth's face screaming madly. Luna shook away the horrid thought with the realization that the planet's fragile atmosphere, correction, the delicate atmosphere Humanity *depended* upon, wouldn't survive another fifty years of abuse.

With every tap of the light switch, weekend binge shopping, eating out, and all those to-go coffees, Luna was as guilty as the rest of Western civilization. Sure, she drove an eco-friendly car in the pretense of doing her part. But in reality, EVs wouldn't put a dent in the energy crisis. But no one was talking about that on social media. They were more concerned with banning plastic straws and plastic bags. As if that were the solution.

Like a slap in the face, that "aha" moment hit her hard. Her constant craving for the city life's distractions was—the world she knew wouldn't survive another generation of abuse. The avenging ecosystem would see to that. She might as well live it up while she could.

"Can I heat my soup now?" Rogue's request jolted Luna from her unexpected revelation.

"Sure, hon," Roxie said.

Roxie was so cool, totally changing Luna's perception of older people, as in the Baby Boomers. The ones Luna worked with complained endlessly about their ailments or longed for the way things used to be, if they happened to corner her in the breakroom.

Roxie seldom complained and seemed to graciously take on life's challenges as an adventure. And Handyman Jack was a cool dude, always thinking of solutions instead of wallowing in defeat. The two of them had kept Luna upbeat over the past hellish days. She should adopt Roxie and Handyman Jack as grandparents. Was that even a thing? Sadly, she had lost her two remaining grandparents to the tripledemic.

Rogue peeled off the Amy's No Chicken Noodle soup label before setting the can on top of the Grizzly stove, just as they had done on their last winter camping trip. They had propane, but why waste it? The solar panels were basically useless until the sun reappeared; besides, the panels were coated with soot, and they had parked under a large awning. They had plenty of lighting with the strategically placed clip-on camping bulbs. Rogue had insisted on being in charge of keeping a set of bulbs charged on the Jackery portable power station.

After two days of no showers, they no longer needed to conserve water, once she and Rogue had set up the thirteen-gallon LifeStraw contraption. They simply purified the melted snow, and then filled the camping shower bladder with kettle-heated water which they warmed on the Grizzly. She had even started filling glass water bottles to restock what the guests had used. Handyman Jack said he'd fill-up the bus water tank as well as they purified more water.

She had to admit, Dad had the bus ready for a grid-down event. Which had her truly convinced her parents were planning on disappearing for a while. But expecting her and Rogue to give up their lives for Mom and Dad's ideologies was . . . unconscionable.

Handyman Jack blustered onto the bus along with a burst of ice-cold wind. "Boy howdy, that storm's a doozy." He hustled to the woodstove and rubbed his hands briskly over the radiating heat.

"You shouldn't stay out there so long," Roxie playfully scolded.

"I'm not an invalid just yet," he bantered back like they were a happy family caught in a snowstorm. "Just finished installing the chains on the rear tires. Good thing we parked under the awning. Or I'd be digging out the tires every hour on the hour."

"You should eat," Roxie said. "Pick out a soup from the cupboard."

"Don't mind if I do." Handyman Jack rummaged through the dozens of canned goods.

"You have to save the tuna for Pixie," Rogue reminded for the tenth time that day.

A new worry nagged at Luna. "Do you think it's too cold for the engine?" What if the battery died or the engine froze? Or the gasoline went bad. She had no idea of the possibilities.

"Naw, we'll be okay," Handyman Jack said. "Although it wouldn't be a bad idea to start the engine every couple of hours to keep everything from freezing up. It's only ten below last I checked. Vehicles can usually handle that."

"It's so cold, I think it broke the thermometer," Rogue exclaimed.

Handyman Jack appeared engrossed reading the minestrone label and ignored Rogue. Luna had wondered if the thermometer was broken as well, but she hadn't called out Handyman Jack on that one. She needed the reassurance, not trained in sub-zero weather survival. The one thing Dad had totally missed.

"Don't worry," Luna said, trying not to bask in all the possible things that could go wrong. "Amy's doesn't use BPA or have a plastic lining. So, you can heat the can on the Grizzly."

"Less dishes to wash," Roxie hinted.

"Good to know," Handyman Jack said. "When I was growin' up, we camped out in the backyard with a little campfire and heated cans of chili con carne in the coals. All those burnt roasted marshmallows . . . " He seemed lost in reminiscing. "Back then, cans were made of tin. Who knows what toxic chemicals they use in the manufacturing process nowadays? Other than aluminum."

"With all the aluminum we're exposed to, half the population will end up with Alzheimer's," Roxie bemoaned. "If we're lucky to live that long."

Rogue exhaled dramatically. "Boring. Hey, I know, let's play Monopoly."

No one responded. "Then please, please, let me help shovel the path to the road," Rogue blurted before shoving a cracker topped with noodles into his mouth.

"Need I remind you," Roxie interjected. "There's only one shovel."

"So, in the olden days they didn't have shovels," Rogue said defiantly. "I can, uh." He looked around. "Use that big pot on the stove."

"You hear that?" Roxie laughed. "We didn't have shovels," Roxie said pointedly to Handyman Jack.

"Yep, even worse, we had to rely on Morse code until they invented cell phones." Handyman Jack smirk.

Disappointment swept across Rogue's face, immediately dampening the mood.

"Come to think of it, I could use an extra pair of hands," Handyman Jack said. "If it's all right with the gals?" He winked at Roxie while Rogue obnoxiously slurped up another spoonful of noodles.

"Mind you, only fifteen minutes at a time," Roxie insisted. "Your parents won't be too happy with me if you come down with hypothermia."

"I know," Rogue said, perking up. "We can shovel for a few minutes, then come inside and warm up and play Monopoly, then shovel some more, then play—like all day. And all night."

Handyman Jack cocked an eyebrow. "You factor in any time for sleeping?"

Rogue shrugged. "Meh. Sleep's overrated."

"I'm in," Luna blurted, surprising herself. This was reminding her more and more of one of her rare, cherished, childhood memories, the ones before she had learned the world was screwed. Being "woke" sucked. She might as well indulge by enjoying the day vicariously through Rogue's zealous innocence. Because it wasn't lasting for long.

Luna had just cleared the latest three inches of snow from their bus-sized path to the highway. The powdery snow so light it was easier to shove aside than to shovel it. If the snow froze, it would be impossible to move with the wimpy plastic snow shovel. Stuck in the middle of freaking nowhere for the past three days with snow drifts taller than the bus in some places had her wondering if they'd ever get out of there.

So, they kept busy and played an ongoing Monopoly game when she and Handyman Jack weren't keeping the path clear to the main road. Although, they didn't shovel at night; they might freeze to death out there. Waiting for Caltrans to clear the roads was the hardest task of all. Patience had never been one of her strong points.

Rogue hadn't been helpful with clearing the path. Not after finding Dad's old camcorder. He had eagerly started his own docuseries, insisting it was vital to document their daily survival. He spent more time recording goofy experiments than their day-to-day lives. Like timing how long it took a bowl of ramen noodles to totally freeze with the spoon standing straight up. How long it took a pair of wet jeans to freeze standing up on their own. And his favorite, tossing a thermos of boiling water over his head and watching it vaporize over him like a miniature wispy cloud. He had bullied Roxie into recording that one over and over.

All Luna wanted was to get to SunFlower's and find out what the hell was going on with Mom and Dad. She was ready to rant about their selfish behavior. Or was she? Sadness seemed to be taking the edge off her anger. And she didn't understand where that was coming from. Like patience, compassion was a trait she hadn't bothered to cultivate. Maybe they weren't in her DNA.

A distant roaring interrupted her troubling thoughts. *Is it coming closer?* She listened intently. Yes!

She ran for the bus, slipping on an icy patch. She used the shovel as a trekking pole and regained her balance before falling. Luna cracked open the bus door and called out, "Someone's coming!"

Handyman Jack tugged on a coat. "Well, what d'ya know. Sounds like a snowplow."

"I wanna see," Rogue yelled.

"Young man," Roxie said, "you stay put."

"Precisely, one never knows what you might say," Handyman Jack added.

"Whatev." Rogue plopped onto the bench seat and pouted.

"I'll go flag down the plow before it passes us," Luna said.

"No hurry," Handyman Jack said. "It'll take it a while."

Luna rushed out of the bus with Handyman Jack on her heels, and they trampled down the cleared path to the road. At times it seemed as if they were stranded in the Arctic. Finally, they could leave. But the huge yellow tractor was still far off.

"Takes a while with all this snow," Handyman Jack said as his frosty breath disappeared into the thin cold air.

"How do they do that?" Luna was amazed at how high the plow piled the snow on both sides of the road.

"Definitely takes skill. Must be a good thirty-foot snow berm."

Luna stood there, mesmerized by the wave-like flow of snow as the plow pushed, scooped, and stacked piles of snow, higher and higher as it crept closer and closer.

"Say, Luna, we never had a chance"—Handyman Jack paused—"to talk things over."

Here it comes, she mused. "I get it. You think my parents are guilty. They probably are on some level. But they're not dangerous criminals. They would never intentionally start a forest fire."

"Then tell me, this is just a snowstorm. Not Armageddon. Why are you so damn uptight?" That hard look in his eye softened, as if he had known she had been silently freaking out since the snowstorm, despite her best efforts to hide it.

An arctic-like wind seemed to freeze her vocal cords as her chilling words admitted the dark truth, "It's scary out there. Last year over three thousand activists around the world—went missing. As in assassinated."

Handyman Jack squinted into the wind, as if thinking hard. "I wouldn't think you, of all people, would fall prey to such outlandish conspiracy theories."

"I'm dead serious. Some of these unscrupulous corporations will do *anything* to keep things business as usual," she emphasized, trying to explain the significance. "They know time is short. Squeezing out the last bits of coal and last drops of oil, so *they* can make us pay to the bitter end. Once our delicate climate goes nuclear and can no longer sustain farming, fishing. Or anything. Earth is going to look like the Dust Bowl era Roxie was talking about. While *they*," she denounced as scathingly as possible, "live in their posh bunkers, gorging on freeze-dried lobster and caviar."

"Really, is that what you think?" Handyman Jack was obviously taken aback.

Luna hadn't meant to sound like some hippy-chick from the sixties. But the imagery came flooding through her like a flashflood of knowing. Which used to happen to her as a child. Until she had learned to ignore it. SunFlower had started grooming Luna's psychic gifts until Dad had forbidden it, saying that kind of spirituality wouldn't save the planet and would get her killed. Still, her latent ability had boosted her career by predicting fashion trends.

Handyman Jack didn't seem to know what to say. His glazed-over eyes widened with a sudden knowing, as if he totally got her. "By God, Luna, you carry such a burden on your shoulders. I know this world's mucked up. I think we all know it, deep down. But don't let it tarnish you. Anything could happen. Who knows, they might re-invent free electricity, like that fella Nikola Tesla supposedly did back in the day. Before he was swindled out of his own invention."

She was impressed he was aware of that. "That's exactly what I mean. Those greedy a-holes have been screwing over the good guys forever." How did they keep getting away with it?

Moments later, all she could hear was the plow. Wait, there were two plows.

"Over here," they bellowed, waving and jumping like freaking idiots as the huge tractors inched closer.

The guy in the plow did a double-take when he finally saw them. He plowed closer and stopped a few feet away before climbing out of the tractor. "Son of a—how long you been here?"

"Three very long days," Handyman Jack drawled.

The guy wearing a huge parka and fur hat hiked toward their shoveled path.

"This snowstorm seemed to come out of nowhere," Handyman Jack said defensively. "You fellas with Caltrans?"

"Hell no. They won't make it up here 'til *after* the next storm. I already dug out six vehicles with people. Two of them, EVs. Those things should be outlawed in snow country."

Luna was well aware EVs used more electrons when using the heater or air conditioner, which resulted in lower mileage, which in turn often left oblivious drivers stranded. Including her, on her last birthday trip to Tahoe, granted her guy friend at the time had been driving his Tesla. They had simply called roadside assistance like any other clueless urbanite.

"Reminds me of an old saying. FORD, Found On Road Dead," Handyman Jack tried to joke.

The guy nodded. "Where's your car?"

"We're in a renovated school bus. Under that collapsing awning of what looks to be a defunct Chevron." Handyman Jack laughed it off. "How far are you plowing? Because we need to get down the mountain. As you can see, we're attempting to maintain a path to the road."

"That works," the guy said, briefly eyeballing Luna.

She smiled innocently with lowered lashes and shivered, deciding not to come off as a hard-ass since Handyman Jack apparently didn't need her help.

"I'm plowing down to the snow line. About five more miles. Looking for my sorry-ass brother-in-law," the guy said.

"Good to know there are still some decent folks around," Handyman Jack commended.

The guy lit a cigarette. "How'd you end up here in the middle of a ten-day blizzard?"

"The storm's not over?" Luna eyed the heavy opaque sky.

The guy shook his head long and hard. "We have two more back-to-back atmospheric rivers swooping across Northern California. It's not looking good for the Central Valley and the Bay Area. They're predicting major flooding for them. One minute they're losing their homes to the fires, and now they're worried about flooding."

"We were trying to bypass the fires," Handyman Jack explained. "Didn't see anything about a winter storm. The wifey's still giving me the evil eye. One can only take so much, shall I say, elevated estrogen." Handyman Jack winked. "If you know what I'm saying . . ."

Luna suppressed her laugh. *What a bullshitter.*

"I feel ya. That's why I'm out in this mutha of a storm. My sister wouldn't stop bitchin' when her el stupido husband went MIA. Not that I'm complaining. The snowpack was basically at zero percent. We're getting an entire season of snow in a matter of days."

Handyman Jack whistled through his teeth. "This weather whiplash seems to be the new normal."

"You can say that again." The guy took another long drag.

"Did it put out the fires in the L.A. area?" Luna asked.

The guy glanced around at the wintery landscape. "Nada, the storm's missing Southern California."

"I'd rather deal with snow than those damn fires," Handyman Jack said.

"Do you need medical help? There's a clinic in the next town," the guy said, walking their path to the bus.

"We're good. Been staying warm," Handyman Jack said as they kept the guy's pace.

The guy nodded. "Great, keep those chains on. They'll help with the icy trip down. Will the bus start?"

"No problem there," Handyman Jack said. "I take it you do snow removal for a living?"

"Sure do. We have contracts with the rural neighborhoods and businesses. I'd better get back to plowing. Here's the deal, pull in after the last of the vehicles following me. It'll be a slow trip down. See, I make a quick pass and stack the snow. Then my brother does a sweep with the snow blower. If you get stuck, I'll catch you on the rebound."

"Can't thank you enough." Handyman Jack pulled out his wallet. "Here's forty for your trouble. You dern near saved my marriage. And my life, for that matter." He chuckled.

"Keep your money." The guy shook his head adamantly, staring at a new wave of snow flurries that quickly morphed into fluffy flakes. "The weather report said it'll start snowing"—he looked at his watch—"in approximately two hours. As usual, they were wrong. They're saying another six feet tonight."

"That's insane," Luna muttered.

"This weather's apocalyptic." He took another hit off his cigarette. "One more thing, once you get below the snow line, I'd park it for a while. Traveling could get treacherous once you get below the snow level. And the rain hits. Billy-Bob's RV Park's in the next town. Good drainage there. It doesn't usually flood like the valleys do."

"Thanks again," Handyman Jack said before turning his back on the guy.

They busted butt to the bus. "The wifey?" Luna mimicked.

"Best not say a word to Roxie. I'll never own up to saying it," Handyman Jack said as if embarrassed.

Rogue was first to greet them at the bus step. "What did he say?"

"He's plowing a path down to the snow line," Handyman Jack said.

Luna met Roxie's grateful sigh of relief and quickly started warming up the bus.

"Did he ask where we're from?" Roxie asked.

"No, nothing," Luna said. "He probably thinks we're stupid tourists."

"Folks, we need to tighten down the hatches, ASAP," Jackson said. "He wants us to follow him down. More storms are comin' our way. Rogue, I take it you stopped checking the storm radio reports."

"Yeah, 'cause it just kept saying the same thing. Snow, snow, and more f'n snow. I thought they were looping the broadcast."

"Help me clean up," Roxie said, already putting away the Monopoly money.

"Hey," Rogue whined. "I was winning."

So much for their never-ending Monopoly game. Roxie always seemed to do something in the kitchen when one of them had been low on cash and landed on her Boardwalk and Park Place hotels. Handyman Jack always worked out payment plans with interest, which she and Rogue had started doing as well. It was like they were trying to see how long they could make the game last.

Rogue intermittently recorded his presumed win, only when someone landed on his railroads and purple and red monopolies. He planned to submit it to the Guinness World Records as the longest Monopoly game played in a snowstorm, in a bus, in Northern California.

Handyman Jack winked at Rogue. "We can always continue later with the same monopolies. With a brand-new pile of money and a clean slate to boot."

"Cool, and this time I'll put out a can of tuna fish and try to record Pixie zooming around like a crazy cat," Rogue declared like an obsessive movie director.

"That kooky cat is something else." Handyman Jack chuckled.

Yesterday, Roxie had left a can of tuna by the kitchen sink, hoping to lure the cat out of the back bedroom. Eventually, Pixie had made a rare appearance to gobble down the tuna just as Roxie had intended. Soon after, Rogue had gone into one of his tense outbursts, scaring Pixie. The psychotic cat had ended up jumping onto the Monopoly board, sending the game pieces flying.

Luna had never laughed so hard. They all had. She still couldn't get that comical scene out of her head as they scurried around securing loose items and constantly stole concerned looks out the windows.

"Hey, I see cars," Rogue blared. "They're leaving without us!"

"That's our cue." Handyman Jack quickly closed the overhead cupboards. "Get ready to drive through a tunnel of snow. Damn near thirty feet high on both sides of us."

"Awesome!" Rogue exclaimed.

Luna wasn't looking forward to driving the icy roads. The actual driving part was okay; it was the stopping part that grated her nerves. Or not being able to stop as visions of sliding off the road and disappearing down a snow-covered canyon plagued her. But with the snow berms so high, all she had to worry about was sliding into the vehicle in front of her.

"You want me to drive?" Handyman Jack offered, as if tuning into her thoughts.

Words from her management training appeared in her mind. Always appear confident. Never weak. "I'm good," she said.

"Well, you know the bus more than anyone." Handyman Jack clapped her shoulder. "It'll be okay, you'll see. The chains will make a much easier trek of it, albeit noisy as hell. Probably drive that kooky cat even more nuts than it already is. Once we get below the snow level, I'll remove the chains. And we'll make it to SunFlower's in no time."

Maybe that was why she was developing an old-guy crush on him. Handyman Jack made everything sound so easy, like everything was going to be all right. Then why couldn't she shake that doomsday feeling that life on Earth was never going to be the same. Again.

Chapter 18

SunFlower BlueStone raced along the rural Mississippi highway as fast as she dared, trying to make up lost time after purposely bypassing the major cities to avoid the bombardment of energies from millions of people. Chaotically charged energies of metropolitan areas required her total mental acuity; otherwise, she automatically reverted into a protective Merkaba meditation state.

She had been grateful for Prudy's warning to leave before the hurricane had made landfall in Florida, giving her time to cross into Georgia before the Florida governor had announced the entire state to evacuate or shelter in place.

Severe weather had created pandemonium in the Gulf states as well. Her trip had turned into a grueling journey stuck in hours of traffic congestion, causing a bedlam of road rage. For peace of mind, SunFlower had decided to take the less traveled roads, despite adding days to the trip.

Prudy had been right about ditching her EV for a combustion engine: charging stations were far too difficult to locate and wasted too much time. In the South, it wasn't uncommon to find charging stations vandalized by EV haters. Meanwhile, SunFlower struggled with the negative karma for spewing carbon into the atmosphere.

Something else plagued her super-consciousness, a pervasive disconcerting feeling Devin's New Pangea organization had been infiltrated. As if a malicious source monitored his progress. Rational thinking said she was merely giddy from being on the road for more than forty-eight hours with intermittent catnaps. She needed some serious REMs to rejuvenate her DNA. But every time she pulled over, Prudy warned it wasn't safe to stop.

"Ooh, there's the Love's!" She swerved, barely making the turnoff. She loved Love's, probably because of the name's positive connotation. The travel stop usually offered a decent selection of the healthier electrolyte drinks and trail mix snacks. She could use a bathroom break. More and more gas stations were closed, running out of gas of all things. She might as well get more gas.

By the time she turned off the ignition, Prudy hounded her once again. *"Have you not heard my warnings? You must not stop."*

"Ten minutes," SunFlower responded in her mind as she shut the door.

Her last stop at a gas station had been inundated with frantic travelers trying to get out of the hurricane's path. This place appeared empty except for the one clerk staring at the big screen TV monitor behind the register.

"Are you open?" SunFlower asked, worried the man might turn her away.

"Yes, ma'am. The boss ordered me to stay until we run out of gas," he grumbled, not taking his eyes off the TV he had to crane his neck to watch.

After relieving her bladder, she avoided her reflection in the mirror while washing her hands. She didn't want to be bothered with another one of those disconcerting, vanishing visions. She quickly scooped up the last of her favorite watermelon and pomegranate electrolyte drinks from the refrigerator section, stacked them on the counter, and went in search of organic snacks, like trail mix and granola bars.

By the time she returned to the counter, the young Hispanic man muttered, "Oh man, oh man, it's gonna get ugly." He made the sign of the cross with a shudder.

Quickly, she scanned his chakras. The poor man was entangled in fear. Strangling in it. A bitmap image of his wife, or was it his mother, came to mind. Along with two children. Oh, and that wind. Vicious and deadly.

SunFlower focused harder, scrying her super-consciousness for a clearer image. Something about a door—a cellar door to an old country house. But the woman couldn't open it. Not in the wind.

The words, "*The storm is coming for you! But there is nothing you can do*," invaded SunFlower's mind. She dropped her purse and grabbed her throat as if the words had stung her.

"*SunFlower*," Prudy streamed internally. "*Leave at once. We must not interfere with this soul's fate.*"

She understood fate, heartbreaking as it was. There were times when she must remain silent. Especially in the South, where to some bible-thumping fundamentalists, she was considered a heretic.

"Ma'am, where you going? Because it better be home. Look at that!" He pointed to the TV.

She ignored the television and retrieved her purse. "Fearmongering sells more advertising." For the most part, SunFlower avoided mainstream news, as it served as a platform to manipulate the population, telling people what to think and what to buy since the "powers that be" owned most of the news networks. Crystal and Prudy kept her informed of the *relevant* issues.

The clerk laughed nervously. "You want—all of this?"

"Plus, thirty dollars on pump three," she decided, based on a quick assessment. Now and then her random abilities helped with the mundane.

The clerk didn't seem too pleased as he laboriously scanned her haul of goodies. He'd rather get lost in the media hype, she mused.

"Guess you'll be needing a bag?"

Darn. She had left the reusable bags in her Tesla. "That would be great."

"One moment, please. I need to restock the bags." He exhaled heavily, shuffling to a closet, hardly taking his eyes off the TV.

"*You must not wait!*" Prudy demanded.

But SunFlower wasn't listening. Not after unintentionally catching a glance of the TV. Two sets of hurricane path spaghetti models—collided into one another. "Two hurricanes? And what are those other red lines on the map?" Sunflower asked as the clerk returned and dropped a bulky box on the floor.

"Yes, ma'am. It's not looking good. Those two hurricanes"—he pointed to the U.S. map covering the entire monitor—"the hurricane that swept over Florida and a new hurricane that spontaneously formed in the Gulf are colliding in the ninety-nine-degree waters of the Gulf of Mexico. Can you believe that?"

"What in the world?" A red banner scrolling along the top of the screen with the tagline *Category 6* had her flummoxed. "Is that possible—"

"They're calling it Megacane Bobby-Anne. Combining the names of the storms. And look over there, at those two hurricanes in the Atlantic. If they hit the East Coast . . ."

"*Prudy*," SunFlower scolded mentally, "*why didn't you tell me about this*?"

An alarm went off. The clerk grabbed his cell from under the counter.

His face went pallid. "A tornado warning—for my town." He looked around, as if waiting for someone to tell him what he should do. "My wife? My kids . . ."

"You should go to them," she found herself saying without thinking of the consequences of fate. "This second. Forget the gas. Just shut off the pumps and lock up."

The clerk made a phone call. "Oh shit, oh shit, oh shit, answer the damn phone. My boss, he never answers." The clerk set the phone down and looked at her helplessly.

"Go, in love and light. Help your wife and children get to safety," she said firmly. Even if it was against karmic rules.

"I just know I'm getting fired for this." He returned her thirty dollars before shutting down the pumps.

SunFlower grabbed her bag of treats and chanted a silent prayer for him and his family.

"Vaya con Dios," the clerk said as he hit the switch to the lights.

A sudden profound darkness descended within her. Something was happening, something unbeholden to cosmic law. But what? She ran back to the car, demanding Prudy explain why everything had gone wrong since she had begun the crucial mission of saving Devin's endangered climate activists.

But her ever-persnickety spirit guide had gone silent . . .

Chapter 19

Roxie Romero scampered to the convenience store gas station situated along a surprisingly deserted section of the rural highway, only to find it locked. *No*, she screamed inwardly.

Determined, she knocked on the double-glass doors. "Anybody home?" Roxie peered through the glass with hands cupped around the sides of her face.

A shadowy figure hovering by the cash register caught her attention. "Hellooo," she bellowed.

An older gentleman lumbered to the door. "Can't you read? The sign says *Closed*." The grumpy man donned in a blue and green plaid shirt pointed to the *CLOSED* sign that blended in with the collage of signage plastering the doors.

Since when did gas stations close in the afternoon? "Please, we're out of gas," she fibbed. They still had a quarter tank. Not enough to get them to Mt. Shasta. They had decided to avoid the always-busy chain gas stations, which were sure to use Wi-Fi surveillance cameras, after Rogue had adamantly warned government agencies could hack into wireless cameras, even the popular ones used by homeowners like Ring cameras.

The stocky Asian man seemed fit to be tied and stood there gawking at her through the glass, apparently contemplating to help. Pursing his lips even tighter, the man pulled out a ring of keys and painstakingly thumbed through the keys one by one with shaky hands until finally finding the right one.

Before opening the door, he eyed the bus suspiciously. And then her. "No bathrooms."

She must look a sight with blue hair, bright pink lipstick, and a tattered, hand-crocheted afghan draped around her shoulders like a shawl. She offered a cheery smile, far too wide for her liking while his glare hardened. "I didn't mean to pester you. We just need gas—or we'll be stuck right here," she pleaded, playing the damsel in distress.

"You cannot stay here." He continued glaring, as if she were begging for free gasoline. "The California Highway Patrol told us to shut down and get on home. You'd better make it quick. There's another one of those rivers in the sky about to hit. Since the Devil's Peak Fire last October, the ground can't take downpours. They closed the roads—" His glare turned into squinty-eyed suspicion. "Hey, how'd you get through?"

Roxie looked up at the cloud-laden sky and threw up her arms. "I guess we made a wrong turn somewhere. We're looking for that campground we used to go to. Did it burn down?" They had come across a road closure sign, but they had decided to continue since they hadn't had enough gas to make it back to Billy-Bob's RV Park the guy with the plow had told them about.

"Damn tourists." Finally, the clicking of the door revealed she had pulled off her desperate plea.

"Just a minute." He scowled at his phone, checking it for the third time. "Where are you?" he asked rather emphatically as if needing to say aloud what he was texting. Once done with his text, the man turned back to her. "Give me a minute to turn on the credit card ma-thingy."

Roxie pulled out a wad of bills, the last of their cash. "No need. Here's two hundred dollars."

She detected a slight smile hiding behind his perpetual frown when he retrieved it. "Pump two."

"Thank you so very much." Roxie scrambled to the bus.

Apparently, cash was still king in the rural areas of Northern California. According to several recent morning talk show debates, the U.S. government planned to outlaw all forms of cash in the not-so-distant future, thanks to the invention of digital currency. Modern technology at its worst.

Society had changed drastically since she had been born, turning dystopian in her lifetime. Those far-fetched Sci-Fi novels she had enjoyed during her college days, like *Fahrenheit 451, 1984*, and *Neuromancer* seemed to have been prophetic warnings for what was to come. Making her feel like the naive one.

Jackson slipped the tire pressure gauge into his rear pocket when he saw her. "Tires are good." They had decided Luna and Rogue should stay out of sight, thereby Roxie and Jackson could pose as a harmless retired couple on a road trip.

"Pump two," Roxie muttered as occasional fat drops plopped from the sky. "It took a while to convince the man running the place to open up."

Jackson flashed a devilish grin. "How could he resist?" He grabbed the nozzle. "Why the heck aren't they open?"

Roxie ignored his attempt at flirtation, too old for such shenanigans. "He said the CHP's closing the roads. This next storm must be really big." It had to be the third storm since the fires. In how many days? *Sheesh*, she had lost time; it must be close to a week since the fires.

Jackson eyed the sky warily. "What's a little rain after what we've been through? We'll make it to Mt. Shasta before dark."

She should be ecstatic with all the precipitation California was getting, despite the inconvenience. "Apparently, we're near the burn scar area of that humongous fire last year. The Devil's Peak Fire." One of her high school friends had lost everything in the devastating fire and had ended up moving to Florida.

Jackson kept his eye on the pump. "Ah, that one. So many fires . . . can't keep track."

"I'm glad it's not snow. Poor Luna, following the snowplow through those towering walls of snow—I thought that calm façade of hers might finally crack." Roxie laughed nervously, grateful Luna's white-knuckled drive down the icy mountainous highway had occurred without mishap. Although Roxie's nerves hadn't quite recovered.

Roxie nixed the chore of cleaning the windshield, since it was out of her reach. She tied the afghan blanket around her waist and jogged to the other side of the bus for a quick round of stretches to relieve her cramped legs and torso. She didn't normally sit for long periods.

When she wasn't volunteering for the community, she was tending her garden, seed-saving, canning, or making jellies to sell at the summer bazaar. *That's right*, she couldn't garden this year. Not after the thirty percent water restrictions had been enforced. Once again, reality cold-cocked her. She no longer had a home. Thus, no garden, water restrictions or not.

Well, she would just have to work on creating a perfect Italian meatball soup recipe to jar up. She had intended to add pressure-canned soups to her pantry for years but always seemed to run out of time. *Hmm, I could always make jellies with store-bought blackberries, strawberries, and raspberries, sacrilegious as it is.* It would keep her busy, she decided as she exercised back to Jackson just as the pump clicked off.

"That about does it." Jackson put the nozzle back in its holster. "Two hundred buckaroos don't get ya what it used to. Why, I remember when gas was under a dollar a gallon—"

The clouds suddenly burst. "Get inside," Roxie blared, covering her head with the afghan.

Once inside the bus, Jackson shook like a soaked mangy dog trying to dry off. "Oow-wee, that rain's downright brutal."

Roxie self-consciously toweled off with a hand-embroidered towel draped over the kitchen faucet. Luna's furrowed brows seemed deeper than usual as she rushed to the driver's seat. The girl needed to lighten up, or she would wind up with an ulcer by the time she was thirty. Who was Roxie kidding? They had lost their homes days ago and were now on the run from the FBI of all things. Perhaps, Roxie was the one who needed to take things more seriously. But it only hurt—when she thought about it.

Rogue resurfaced from his bunk and stared at them as if they had gone bonkers. "What happened to you guys?"

"It's raining cats and dogs out there," Jackson said with a shiver.

"Why do old people always say that?" Rogue whined.

Jackson gave Roxie the here-we-go-again side-eye. "Well, what would *you* call it?" Jackson pointed to the rapidly fogging windows.

"Duh, it's raining. Like a lot."

"Somehow, that does lose something in the translation," Roxie said dismissively.

Jackson nodded in silent agreement. "Sport, you mind checking the scuttlebutt on that storm radio?"

"I already told you, the cranking handle broke, and the solar batteries need recharging," Rogue scolded as if they were children. "And we can't recharge them because, like, it's raining. And the Jackery power station isn't holding a charge."

"Don't you have any *regular-folk* batteries," Jackson baited with a surly smile.

"Grrr . . ." Rogue stormed off and disappeared back into his bunk.

Roxie threw up her hands. "Don't mind him. He's having one of his moody fits."

Together, she and Jackson scrambled to the bench seat behind the cockpit. Luna started the engine, seemingly accepting the hard rain pinging off the bus as nothing abnormal. Luna flipped on the defroster full blast, and when a little patch on the windshield began to clear, she pulled onto the rural highway, undeterred.

"Rogue," Luna called, "I need the bottle of defogger for the windows."

Sheesh, how can she see? The wipers couldn't keep up with the bullet-like rain sandblasting the bus.

Jackson unfolded the crinkled map for the umpteenth time that day while Roxie wondered if they should wait out the downpour, despite everyone's desire to get to SunFlower's. Frankly, once making it below the snow line, she had stopped fussing over the weather as she had plenty of other things to worry about.

However, the intensifying deluge became exceedingly unnerving. Her stomach churned upon recalling the gas station clerk's almost eerie demeanor. He seemed to think this wasn't a normal storm. Rather, the storm of the century as her mom would have proclaimed. The kind the news media excitedly reported with fantastical live footage wreaking havoc on third-world countries, not modern civilization thanks to superior infrastructure and strict building codes.

Stop worrying. If the storm worsened, they would just have to pull over. After all, this was the United States of America. Extreme weather calamities, other than hurricanes and tornadoes, rarely resulted in much devastation beyond problematic flooding, downed limbs and power lines.

With the way things had been going, she needed to stop adhering to the glass half-full philosophy, always assuming things would work out in the long run with a little positive thinking and perseverance. Last year alone, a friend had lost a home to a fire, an aunt had lost her home to a Florida hurricane, and her uncle's home in Mississippi had been flooded out and had yet to be repaired due to legal issues with the insurance provider.

Pixie girl, where are you? Roxie called out in her mind, as if they were cosmically connected. She could use a comforting purr right about now. But for the most part, Pixie had remained burrowed under the covers in the back bedroom and only came out for a can of tuna.

The cold-hearted realization hit Roxie. *The Earth's turning on Humanity!* The sad part was they deserved it. Had asked for it, like bullies. A tiny voice inside her screamed, "*The shizzy is about to hit the fizzy.*" As in global warming, climate change, or whatever the politically correct term was this week. And it was happening now. *Today*! Not decades from now like the world leaders so boldly attested while touting their trillion-dollar, net-zero emission budgets.

It had to be the biggest sham of the century. Of humankind . . .

The usual jovial Jackson had gone silent. Roxie turned to him. "What's wrong?" True, she barely knew the man. Still, something was off.

"You said something about the CHP closing this stretch of the road . . ." He eyed the rolling hillsides.

From out of the blue, Roxie knew it like some inexplicable ESP moment she would never be able to explain. Or understand. "We shouldn't be here." The words seemed to clump in her throat.

"Wait, what?" Luna's eyes locked onto hers in the rearview mirror.

She didn't know how Luna could have overheard her with the roaring rain slamming the bus. But it was as if the three of them instantaneously had the same uncanny realization.

"Luna?" Jackson hesitated. "Think we ought to pull over for a while."

"It's just rain," Luna countered robotically.

Roxie wiped the foggy window with the afghan blanket with an ominous feeling bearing down on her chest. A graveyard of skeletal trees pierced the valley's steep hillside like charred remnants of a nuclear blast. They had reached the burn-scar area from last summer's fire, only in the ferocious downpour, it was like driving through someone's creepy nightmare.

Her vision went blurry. She wiped away the window's condensation again before realizing her vision wasn't going haywire. The trees were. Acre after acre of the rolling hillside seemed to ripple in unison, giving her an unexpected sensation of vertigo. She could not take her eyes off the quivering ground.

"Uh, uh, l-l-look—" Stuck in a stutter, Roxie tapped the window with one hand and grabbed Jackson's knee with the other.

"Holy Mother of God! Floor it!" Jackson yelled.

"Landslide," Roxie finally croaked out.

Luna didn't waste precious time questioning. Roxie and Jackson lurched backward once Luna stomped on the gas pedal. The bus glided into the opposing lane upon taking the curve in the road too fast, just as the rear of the bus took a hit. When the impact of the mudslide slammed into the rear of the bus, it sent them into a drainage ditch off the oncoming lane's shoulder. But it was the clamorous roar that scared her the most.

Rogue came tearing down toward them with bulging eyes. "I knew you were gonna crash!"

"Everyone all right?" Jackson asked first.

No one bothered to answer. Instead, Luna ran to the back of the bus with Jackson a close second. Roxie reclaimed her pounding heart and whispered a prayer, pleading the bus wasn't damaged. Their impromptu adventure would turn into a long night in jail once the authorities found them.

It was more than that. Quite honestly, she wasn't ready for her life to return to normal, fighting with the homeowner's insurance, the rebuilding, the endless boring day-to-day chores, the lost causes she seemed doomed to fight at the town hall. And the alone part. Like her life was basically over until the inevitable caught up to her: cancer, stroke, heart attack . . .

Roxie sat there paralyzed with ugly thoughts. Waiting for the verdict.

Rogue plopped down beside her and gently held her trembling hands. "Mrs. Romero, it's okay. Don't cry." The next thing Roxie knew, the boy cuddled up beside her, hugging her.

She hadn't realized she was crying. She gingerly brushed away the tears escaping the corners of her eyes. "I'm fine, hon." Still, she had truly needed a hug. "That scared the living daylights out of me."

"Haha!" Jackson whooped. "Near miss. From the looks of it, the mudslide merely clipped the bus." Jackson strode to the front of the bus while Roxie quickly composed herself. "Just need to dig out the rear tires. And pray damn hard no damage was done to the rear axle."

"See, Handyman Jack's awesome. He won't let us get hurt," Rogue whispered into her ear.

Roxie squeezed his shoulder. "He most certainly is." Her heart seemed to swell with bliss.

Luna didn't reveal any emotion as usual. It was almost as if the girl had been born to deal with calamities. She had been born in the right decade for that. The new children needed to be strong and hardy, as in the Great Depression era. Nature didn't have time to mollycoddle the oversensitive, immunocompromised, or just plain lazy bodies. That was the message screaming loud and clear in Roxie's mind. It must be nature's way of cleaning house.

An unknown voice chanted in her mind, *"Depopulation is the only way Humanity will survive."*

What in heavens? Roxie was used to plaguing thoughts invading her mind during stressful situations. But she would never think about *depopulation.* It was just another conspiracy theory touted by the far-right or was it the far-left? She never kept track of such folly. Then again, something had to give. It was becoming more evident that there was not enough electricity, gasoline, food, nor water for eight billion people.

Not in my lifetime, she screamed back in denial to her super-consciousness. Not after she had met this intriguing man . . .

Chapter 20

JACKSON JONES SLIPPED ON the grungy pair of yellowed-brown galoshes he confiscated from the storage compartment under the bus. Digging out the rear tires in the middle of a god-awful monsoon wasn't exactly one of his top-ten things to do. The crux of the matter was, if he hadn't seen Roxie's terror, more like sensed it, and if Luna hadn't gunned the bus at that precise moment—the mudslide would have wiped out the bus. Taking them with it. He tried blocking the horrifying thought from his mind, but it kept haunting him. Someone up there must be watching over them. Or had it in for them and somehow kept botching the job.

Behind the bus, a ten-foot-high pile of twisted, mud-coated debris completely blocked the rural highway. No one was getting past it for quite some time. With the shoddy snow shovel in hand, he dug away at the three feet of mud entrenching the rear tires while ferocious rain pelted him.

"Son of a—" Jackson muttered when Rogue skipped merrily toward him. "Sport, didn't I tell you to stay *inside* the bus?"

"But, I wanna help." The boy defiantly picked up a small muddy boulder. The boulder slipped out of his hands and landed inches from Jackson's foot.

Jackson gave the kid his best squinty evil eye. He didn't have the patience nor the time to deal with an unruly child, or whatever proper term society labeled disobedient kids. They had to get that bus out of there. Based on his unsettling flashes of vertigo triggered by the sporadic ground tremors, the rest of the burn-scarred hillside could give way any minute.

"Remember," Jackson practically growled, "there's only one shovel. Besides, you *are* helping." *By not pestering me*, he wanted to say. "By watching out the rear window for my thumbs-up signal."

Jackson scraped away a fresh pile of cascading mud and refused to give in to Rogue's persistence.

"Rogue?" Roxie yelled out the window. "Get your scrawny butt inside. This instant!"

Thank you, Roxie.

Rogue sulked away, walking as sluggishly as humanly possible. On a normal day, the kid's antics would have been comical.

The mud just kept sliding down the mudslide and to the tires faster than he could remove it. "Damn, damn, damn," Jackson spluttered with every scoop of sloppy-joe-colored slush he tossed. Should have known better than to trek across the fire-ravaged countryside during the first significant rainstorm of the season. Still, it hadn't been a top concern. Not with everything else happening.

Luna treaded carefully toward him with a steaming cup of . . . something. "Hey, you, Roxie said to take it easy. Here, she made you coffee."

He could use a breather. He glanced down defeatedly at the mud sliding down before leaning the shovel against the bus. A cup of coffee was precisely what he needed. "Roxie's great, isn't she?" He wiped away the beads of rain mixing with the sweat rolling down his forehead, despite the chill in the air, before eagerly accepting the caffeine offering.

Luna started shoveling before he could protest. "Sorry for my PIA brother. He's always getting in trouble for his drama-queen performances."

Jackson waved her off. "Kids will be kids . . ."

As if consumed by anger, Luna furiously tackled the growing pile of debris flow, removing the slosh faster than it slid down the hill. "I blame my parents. They leave him with aunts and uncles for weeks at a time to go on their protesting tours. His therapist says he has tons of issues. But honestly, I think Rogue just craves love and attention."

And maybe a normal childhood, Jackson wondered, savoring a sip of the dark roast coffee before saying, "Imagine that sort of upbringing causes a slew of insecurities." He'd never had children. So, he wasn't exactly well-versed in childrearing. "You seemed to pull through it okay." He admired her determined demeanor.

"I guess. This is going to sound awful." She flashed him a hard look. "My parents took me to their protests. And sort of used me"—she stalled—"as a prop. To gain media attention and social network followers. They even had GoFundMe campaigns that made tons of money. Capitalizing on my pathetically sad, chubby face."

"Oof." Jackson was flabbergasted. An image of a filthy crying child abandoned in a dried-out plastic-ridden riverbed toyed with his memory. That chilling futuristic scene of plastics taking over the waterways like some deadly pathogen had forever been ingrained in his memory. It clicked. "Naw, don't tell me? You're that infamous poster child. The one who was always in the news way back when." How time flew. "Must have been some twenty-odd years ago, back when Al Gore seemed to be on every damn channel, preaching about the planet's doom." Had the man been right about that?

She shoved the shovel in harder. "Yeah, I was sorta like a *muted* version of Greta Thunberg."

What a guilt trip to lay on a child. "Well, you had one helluva impact. Reminded me of the Crying Indian campaign back in the seventies. You're probably too young to know that one, the Native American with the tear?" Simple yet poignant.

"Yeah, we studied that campaign in college. They were liars way back then. That guy wasn't even an American Indian." She stopped shoveling for a moment. "Italian, I think. But he did make a super powerful meme."

"It's all about the marketing." Jackson recognized her tough façade disguised her pain. "From the sounds of it, you're still bitter, being exploited and all," he dared to say.

"Sometimes, but the donations poured in. My parents' foundation planted millions of trees. So, a lot of good came out of it."

Jackson wasn't buying it. Luna harbored deep-seated resentment for her parents. That explained her ambivalence toward them: one moment she seemed worried sick, the next, severely pissed.

A faint hint of apprehension seemed to sweep across her face. She cocked her head, eyeing the spongy hillside. "Did you hear that?" Based on their brief friendship, the young woman wasn't one to spook easily.

"Yep, been hearing quite a few debris flows based on the crackling of deadwood." It was more than disconcerting; it was downright deadly. They had to get out of there before another bogged-down hillside tumbled to the road.

Jackson relished the last swallow, already craving another cup, and eyed the pile approvingly as she uncovered the last tire. Although, he had taken care of the grunt work first, clearing out the myriad of limbs and boulders. "That just about does it. Why don't you go dry off while I check the undercarriage for damage. I'll signal Rogue when we're ready to give it a go."

Luna tugged the raincoat's hood farther over her forehead before handing the shovel back to him. "You think it's okay?"

"I'm sure it is." *It damn well better be.*

"I trust your judgment," she said before jogging off.

After he gave it a quick once-over, the undercarriage appeared undamaged, though he didn't waste time looking too hard as mud began seeping around the rear tires. With newfound energy, or perhaps trepidation of the unstable hillside, he made swift work of the slush, anxious to see if the tires could grip the road.

He chanced a look up at the rear window to find Rogue watching eagerly. Jackson gave the kid the thumbs-up signal to let him know it was time to skedaddle. He tossed the shovel into the storage compartment and then practically ran to the door. With one foot on the bus step, a disconcerting sensation seemed to paralyze him, causing him to collapse on the upper step.

Not wanting to look like an old feeble guy, he avoided eye contact and made like he had purposely plopped down on his butt in the pretense of yanking off the filthy galoshes. Which he did quickly, all the while struggling to fight back whatever the hell was gnawing at his gut.

Much to his relief, that odd sensation disappeared as quickly as it had come on, and he pulled himself up with the step railing just to make sure he was all right. A glance around revealed no one had appeared to notice his incident, with Luna arguing with the spinning tires, Rogue shouting a series of not-so-helpful tips, and Roxie wiping down the kitchen counter in the pretense of hiding her edginess.

Jackson caught his breath, relieved he was back to his normal, albeit aching, self. Unfortunately, the bus wasn't going anywhere just yet. And he sure as hell didn't want to dig out those tires again. "Luna, try backing up and going forward a few inches several times to compact the mud. Might help the tires get a grip." If need be, he could let out some air in the rear tires. An uncanny notion had him thinking they didn't have time for that.

Jackson clutched the railing and leaned out of the bus, standing on the lowest step to check the rear tires. Without warning, the right lane of the rural highway turned fluid. Buckling.

"Holy Mother of God!"

If the mudslide hadn't shoved the bus into the oncoming lane by several feet, the entire bus would have careened down the collapsing road. Finally, he turned to meet Luna's eyes, needing her to understand the imminent danger they faced, yet not wanting her to freeze up.

"What's happening?" Luna asked calmly. Nonetheless, she couldn't disguise the fear dancing in her eyes.

"Sinkhole!" Rogue bellowed over the rushing water before Jackson could respond. "We're gonna die!"

Roxie rushed to the kid, hopefully, to shut him up.

One quick peek at the rear of the bus revealed a new wave of muddy debris sloshing down the mudslide. It was now. Or never. "Luna, this is going to require some finesse. Now, nice and easy, give 'er some gas," Jackson said.

Bit by bit, the bus slid ahead. "Good, keep 'er steady—a little more gas." An unbearable swooshing inundated his concentration.

"Holy fuck!" Luna exclaimed. She stared at him as if he had spontaneously combusted.

He followed her wild-eye gaze. "Good God!"

The right lane morphed into a tumultuous river, rapidly flowing downhill a few feet away from the bus.

Luna downshifted. The bus gained yardage up the slight hill. If that sinkhole grew much wider—they were goners. He wanted to look at Roxie, to tell her it was going to be all right. But he couldn't. He had never been an outright liar.

Once more, Jackson took a firm stance on the bus step and precariously leaned out the door while clutching the metal pole to check the rear of the bus and the road. He must have clenched every muscle in his old body while willing the tires to gain traction on the mud-slicked road as the lane narrowed, crumbling into the newly formed river.

Jackson kept whiplashing from the road ahead to the adjacent growing river to the mudslide behind them. "You're doing good. Just keep moving." Not that anyone heard him over the water's rush.

He froze. *Is that a . . . car?* Careening down the muddy river toward the nose of the bus like a Tonka toy. Yards away, the wide-open silent scream of the woman behind the steering wheel sent the hackles on the back of his neck quivering.

The partially submerged sedan bobbled downhill toward them. In a moment of helplessness, he glanced back at Roxie's terrifying gaze, as if she could somehow say the right thing to resolve the situation. Because he couldn't.

Overruled by his nagging conscience, knowing he would most likely regret the impulsive decision for the rest of his numbered days, Jackson lunged out of the bus like a cavalier cowboy abandoning his trusty horse for a runaway stagecoach with a wobbly wheel—the precise moment the vehicle floated mere feet from the bus steps.

Why?

Because there was no one else to save the hapless woman.

Bam! He landed on the roof, then slid off. His fingers managed to find the roof rack, and he held on for dear life. Spitting out the waves of murky-brown water drenching him, he grappled for the door handle. *The damn door better not be locked.*

"Gotcha!" The door opened.

Bad move. The opened door served as a rudder and sent the car into a spin. All the while water spewed into the car. Shoving back his panic, he swung his torso inside the car and landed in the front passenger's seat. The young woman just sat there with that petrifying silent scream stuck to her face. She had no words for him. Instead, she twisted her head to the backseat with black bottle-cap eyes.

He followed her stare to find a baby in a car seat. "No . . ." This was going to be far more complicated. Water quickly flooded to the seats. He had a couple of minutes before the inundation drowned them all.

Maybe.

He forced the door shut to slow down the flooding. And spinning. To save that baby!

"Take off your seatbelt," he yelled impatiently to the woman, analyzing the situation.

The woman feebly tugged at her seatbelt. With no time to dicker around, Jackson drew the blade sheathed to his belt. A quick slash severed the seatbelt. He head-jerked to the backseat to find the water lapping at the baby's feet.

He scrambled into the back, cut away at the car seat harness strapping the baby, and nabbed the child. The woman held out her arms longingly. He obliged. The car was sinking fast. He had no intention of going down with it. None of them were. Not if he had any say in the matter.

The woman clutched the baby to her chest as if it were the last time she'd ever hold her child. He had to do something. As if in slow motion, he took in every detail: the pace of the rising water, their drift speed, the objects bobbing around like diapers, a pacifier, a sippy cup . . .

"Aha!" A tote with the familiar *YETI* label caught his eye.

He unzipped the soft backpack-style cooler and tossed out the ice packs and baby bottles. "Put your baby in this. Zip it up good." Jackson handed her the bag. "Practice taking deep breaths. And get ready."

Now for the tricky part. He grabbed the door handle. *Son of a bitch*! The door didn't budge. Even after repeatedly body-slamming it with his shoulder. The pressure of the water had apparently sealed it shut.

Ah, the windows. He tried the electric window button. Child-locked. "Roll down my window," he shouted over the chaos.

The woman shook her head.

"We're down to seconds. Try the damn windows. All of them!"

That seemed to knock sense into her. She furiously hit the buttons. Nothing happened. Precisely what he had feared after abruptly remembering an article he had once read: *more people drowned in their cars during flash floods than—*

Don't go there.

Then it came to him. "Hand me the cooler. Then climb into the back with me."

The woman silently heeded his request. He helped her into the backseat without struggle. "This had better work," he grumbled. Using both hands, Jackson forcibly pulled up the driver's headrest, thinking this better not be the type that required tools to remove. His fingers quickly found the mechanism's release buttons on each side of the headrest.

With a jarring swish, he pulled up the headrest. He eyed the two metal posts protruding from the headrest, trying to remember a trick he had seen on YouTube a while back. Would it work in real-time?

"Get ready to hold your breath. We're swimming out of here." There was no time to explain. He grabbed one of the headrest's metal posts and swung the other post at the window's corner. By the third bang. The window crackled. Luckily, it was tempered glass, not laminated.

He nabbed a packaged diaper floating by, bundled it around his hand, and broke away the protruding glass shards. As the water rose to their chests, the woman shook her head furiously. He grabbed the cooler backpack with the baby inside and slipped it onto his back.

"You first," he ordered as water gushed in.

"I, I, I can't—"

"Look at me!" Jackson peered deep into her terrified eyes. "Take a deep breath on one, two, three—"

The woman inhaled. He manhandled her through the broken window. After she wriggled through, he dove out the window. Praying the cooler kept the baby from drowning for the short time they were submerged.

The water swooshing into the car seemed to suspend him into a sort of animated yet motionless state, stuck between physical existence and a liquified state. Ah, but Jackson had always been a strong swimmer. He propelled his body with his legs and pushed up to the surface to find the woman thrashing and choking, barely keeping afloat.

He didn't risk unzipping the Yeti cooler to check on the baby while treading to stay afloat. Instead, he reconned the area. "There!" He pointed to the road sign protruding above the water-line just ahead. They were already drifting in that general direction. With a little effort, they could get there. And then, well, he would just have to figure out the next part. If they made it that far.

When—we make it there, he reiterated to himself.

He made it to the floundering woman. She reached for him. But she went under, taking in a mouthful of water. "Mila—" she choked out when her head resurfaced.

He finally realized she was calling for her child. "Mila's safe. Listen, stop fighting. Can you swim?" It was the obvious question he hadn't thought to ask earlier.

"Not really," she garbled.

"Anyone can dog paddle." He nabbed a branch drifting by. "Hold on to the branch. Like this. And kick your feet. But aim for that road sign." *Good, the current is slowing down.* "Mila will be safe on my back." He decided not to give her the cooler just yet. "Let's go." Before another sinkhole created a vacuum effect and devoured them.

Jackson propelled with his feet and used his arms to sweep away the debris, all the while muttering, "We'll get there. We'll get there . . ." For if the last thing he did as an overlooked senior citizen was to save a new soul, then by God, he was doing it.

Or he wouldn't be able to live with himself. End of story.

Chapter 21

Luna Lewis cautiously crept the bus up the slippery road's crest only inches away from the collapsing road. If they had left thirty seconds later . . .

She banished the frantic thoughts racing through her mind. Determined to get the bus out of there before the entire road collapsed.

"Nooo!" Roxie screamed.

Out of Luna's periphery, a flash of something white in the water caught her eye. But she remained fixated on keeping the bus from getting stuck again. Because in the rearview mirror, that huge debris pile spontaneously liquefied like a huge bowl of lumpy chocolate pancake batter flattening out as if it had been poured onto a gigantic griddle. And it was about to capsize the bus.

"Jackson?" Roxie wailed.

It took a moment to set in. "Oh, no, he didn't?" Luna couldn't believe her eyes.

Roxie's horrified stare in the rearview screamed louder than words. Handyman Jack had just jumped out of the bus on to some random car flailing along the river-like sinkhole. *That's insane.*

Rogue took over Handyman Jack's post, standing precariously close to the edge of the open door. "Get back!" Luna shouted.

Roxie was there, trying to move him to safety. Which wasn't working. At all. Rogue did what Rogue wanted. Most of the freaking time. Something she absolutely hated.

"Stop!" Rogue screeched, shaking Roxie away. "We can't just leave him."

Plagued by harrowing images of Handyman Jack struggling for his last breath, Luna had no intentions of abandoning him. But she had to get them away from that sinkhole. Before it consumed the bus.

"Just a few more yards," Luna gritted through clenched teeth, as if physically pushing the bus to gain yardage on the expanding sinkhole.

"Heavens, I don't see Jackson!" Roxie belted out.

"I'll find him!" Rogue ran to the back of the bus.

Luna slammed shut the door when Roxie plopped into the bench seat behind her and thumped her chest rapidly. She better not be having a heart attack. She couldn't save both of them. "Roxie, we're okay, just breathe."

"Don't you worry about me," Roxie's quivering voice ensured. "It's Jackson I'm worried about."

"I'm brainstorming." There had to be a way to save him. Right? Dad constantly preached there was a solution for *everything*. If one thought hard enough.

"There he is!" Rogue's yelp broke through her anxious thoughts.

Roxie scrambled to the back of the bus.

"He's saving someone," Rogue cried out.

"They need our help," Roxie yelled even louder.

That was the longest thirty seconds ever as she stopped at the top of the hill. "Rogue," Luna called out. "Take the wheel. If the sinkhole gets closer. Just drive—'til it's safe."

"But, but I wanna help save him."

Roxie determinedly plunked herself behind the steering wheel. "I'll do it. Don't look at me that way. I'm perfectly capable of driving the skoolie," Roxie stated calmly, regaining her composure.

Luna grabbed the other keychain, the one with the keys to the storage compartments. She hopped out into the pouring rain with the images of ropes highlighting her mind. *That's right*. Dad kept ropes and paracords with the tire chains. It was the only thing she could think of.

Luna rummaged through the supplies in the larger compartment under the bus. She grabbed a bundle of ropes. "Do you still see him?"

"Yeah, he's trying to swim. But the water is too crazy."

"Keep your eyes on him." Luna feverishly untangling the ropes, surprised her hands had automatically fashioned the longest rope into a lasso. One of the basic techniques she had aced in Apoc basic training summer camp.

As she and Rogue ran to the edge of the sinkhole, Luna practiced swinging the rope like a rodeo star, worried Handyman Jack was too far away.

Rogue waved madly to the two people clinging to a road sign. "We'll save you!"

Luna flung the lasso. Missing by ten feet. She got the swirl in the air despite the rain. And swung harder. By the fifth freaking time, she missed by maybe three feet. Just as she was about to snatch the rope back, Handyman Jack dove for the rope!

"Yee-ha!" Rogue whooped.

Handyman Jack slipped the looped rope over his head before tucking it under his arms. He swam back for the person clinging to the leaning street sign. Swoosh! The street sign went under. Along with the person, who might be a woman based on her small size. It was difficult to tell with all the mud plastering her.

Luna's heart jolted when Handyman Jack went under. But, he was probably searching for the woman. She kept the rope taut—giving him more yardage when it slipped through her fingers. She started a mental countdown, giving him thirty seconds—before she reeled him in.

Roxie came running toward her, shouting something. Probably because Rogue would not stop screaming. "Where's Jackson?"

Before Luna could answer, two heads popped up above the water's surface.

"Yes!" Rogue went berserk, jumping around and high-fiving the air.

"Stop acting like an idiot," Luna barked. She tugged harder, bracing her feet against a buckled edge of the muddy asphalt to keep from sliding into the water.

The asphalt collapsed beneath her feet. *Bam*! She was in the water. It wasn't as cold as she expected. But disgustingly slimy as she tried gripping the edge of the disintegrating road with the rope still in her hand.

"Lu-na?" Rogue's desperate plea seemed to reverberate through her head, due to her plugged ears.

Thankfully, Roxie was there. She tossed her the rope Luna had left on the road.

With two ropes in her hands, Luna let Roxie and Rogue pull her to the asphalt's jagged edge.

Rogue grabbed the ropes while Roxie helped drag Luna up by her jacket and onto the pavement.

"Wow." Luna struggled to stand on wobbly knees.

Rogue attempted to pull in Handyman Jack and the woman all on his own. Roxie rushed to help him while Luna fought back her weak knees. Finally, she caught her breath, and her legs started cooperating. Together, the three of them towed in Handyman Jack and the stranger.

"Boy-howdy, that was something else," Handyman Jack babbled as he slumped over the edge of pavement and gingerly took off a muddy pack from his back. "I'm good, take care of her first," he managed to say as he took in a series of shallow breaths.

"Rogue, don't let go of the rope yet," Luna warned. She and Roxie hurried to help the young woman, who stared blankly at them. Together, they hauled the woman out of the water.

Meanwhile, Handyman Jack had pulled himself out of the water and rested on his back, just breathing and shivering, even though it wasn't that cold.

"You poor thing." Roxie quickly shifted her attention from the woman to Handyman Jack. "You'll catch your death."

They were apparently in shock and needed warmth. Luna understood all too well. The short time she had been in the water had been traumatizing. Plus, the water was gross. She was a disgusting muddy mess. If they tracked in all that mud, it would take forever to clean the bus. "Rogue, get the water hose from storage. We need to hose off."

"The three of you need to warm up by the stove. Are you all right, hon?" Roxie asked the woman who fiercely struggled with the pack's zipper with shaky hands. Handyman Jack must have salvaged her go-bag from the car.

All Luna could think was the woman needed her meds or maybe a cell phone, so she helped unzip what she realized was an insulated cooler.

"What the—? A b-baby?" Well-versed in CPR, Luna checked out the infant.

"Heavens!" Roxie exclaimed.

The woman's quivering smile was a good sign. "Mila's breathing!" The woman gasped. "She's okay! Oh, thank you, thank you, thank you . . ."

"Guys, Handyman Jack's, uh, dead—" Rogue shouted as he ran toward them with the hose.

"For cryin' out loud, can't a fella take a break?" Handyman Jack made it to his knees. "I collided with a branch or something. Damn near knocked the breath out of me."

Roxie helped him to his feet. "Oh, you big baby." Roxie laughed nervously. "It would take more than a tree limb to get the best of you."

Rogue dropped the garden hose at Luna's feet. "I was so freaked. But I knew nothing could stop you, Handyman Jack! You're awesome," Rogue ranted.

"Rogue, you didn't attach the hose—" Luna shook her head.

"You didn't say that," he snarked with an exaggerated neckroll.

"It's called using your brain," Luna berated gently.

"Whatev." Rogue stomped off with one end of the hose.

"Okay, so, there's plenty of water in the water tank," Luna said, thinking out loud. "We should hose off before getting on the bus."

"Phew," Handyman Jack whistled. "You got that right."

"I'll get towels." Roxie bustled for the bus.

"It's on," Rogue shouted, skipping toward them.

"Ladies first." Handyman Jack gestured to their new guest.

"I'll do it." Luna's heart fluttered to her throat at the love exuding from the woman's face, despite her near-death experience. The fear she must have endured minutes ago, and now she calmly cooed and cuddled her child. Unconditional love—at its purist. Luna grimaced inwardly. Until the baby turned into a teenager. *Yikes*. Which was why she didn't want children.

Luna didn't wait for the woman to answer. She carefully trickled water over the woman's head and back while turning enough to avoid seeing Handyman Jack strip to his boxers. That was a visual she didn't need floating around her head.

Roxie returned with an armful of towels. "Oh, dear." Roxie averted her eyes briefly and tried not to look. But Luna swore she caught an intriguing gleam in the older woman's eyes. Roxie took the baby while the woman finished rinsing off.

"F-F-Folks," Handyman Jack said with chattering teeth. "Hate to be an alarmist. We need to get the hell off this damn road." He kept eyeballing the hillsides on both sides of the road.

The woman handed Luna the hose. "Your turn."

As Luna rinsed off, a paralyzing chill set in.

Roxie returned the baby to the woman. "Let's get you and your little one warmed up. Follow me."

Handyman Jack grabbed the hose. "Go ahead," he said to the woman. "I'll be there in a jiffy."

Luna had detected a hint of anxiety in Handyman Jack's tone. So unlike him. Not wanting to leave him alone while he rinsed off, Luna pretended to scope out the hillside when an otherworldly sound, a sound she couldn't place, seemed to rock her eardrums and her equilibrium. She braced her feet for balance when the sky burst. On them!

"Over there." Handyman Jack pointed with one hand on his stomach. She thought he was going to puke.

Uh, did the ground just tremble?

She followed his puzzling gaze. Just rain, she thought, ignoring the wave of nausea sweeping over her. His gaze turned into harrowing fear. And when she saw it, she stared at it like an idiot as well.

That can't be happening. The tips of the trees at the top of the hills seemingly vanished. And then the next level of trees that were in plain view disappeared, followed by the next level of trees, all slipping down the canyon toward the road like tall leafy dominoes.

"Run!" Handyman Jack yelled while she just stood there entranced by the approaching landslide. That was coming. For them!

Adrenaline kicked in.

They ran.

Rogue stood at the bus door, seemingly understanding something horrible was happening.

"Drive!" Luna ordered. Roxie had left the engine on. Right? She couldn't hear anything except the cascading hillside.

Her brother must have seen the fear on her face or heard it in her voice because it was one of the few times in his life he didn't question her. Although it could have been the rumbling earth or the earsplitting crashing of trees colliding into one another down the canyon.

She jumped onto the bus with Handyman on her heels. Once they both made it to the stairwell, Rogue sped off.

The roar of annihilation rattled her very soul as she stared out the windows at the landslide taking out the entire canyonside along with the road behind them . . . as if it had given them a head start—to escape.

The baby burst into a crying fit. Other than that, no one said a single word for the next few miles.

Roxie spoke first, insisting Handyman Jack get dressed in the bundle of Dad's clothes that she handed him. He still appeared disoriented. After all, he had lunged into a river-like sinkhole to save a mother and baby from drowning. Really, it was a miracle they had survived everything thrown at them the past week. It seemed like the fickle earth kept trying to kill them and then had a change of heart, saving them at the last second possible.

"Cora, drink this." Roxie handed their guest a steaming cup. "As for you, mister," Roxie lightly scolded. "Sit your li'l tushy down by that stove and warm up."

"Yes ma'am," Handyman Jack retorted.

"Rogue—" Luna stumbled down the aisle. "I should drive."

"He's fine." Roxie took her by surprise. "You look a bit shaken."

Was everyone crazy? "He shouldn't be driving—"

Handyman Jack waved her off. "Hell, he could be a toddler for all I care. He's the only one firing on all cylinders at this moment."

"Then we should pull over," Luna reasoned. She was perfectly capable. But something in the back of her mind told her to rest. Besides, she didn't want to lose a single second of driving time.

"Holy balls! My English teacher's never going to believe my next essay," Rogue hooted like an amped-up race car driver.

Fires, blizzards, sinkholes, and landslides . . . The past few days had been a matter of primal survival. The earth's vendetta didn't care if Rogue broke some silly law, like not having a driver's license. That was when the absurdity caught up with her. Luna broke out into hysterical laughter.

Everyone eyed her suspiciously. And then, one by one, the gang nervously joined in until the bus roared with tense laughter, as if releasing their mounting anxieties.

Her coo-coo brother had ended up saving them. "Rogue, you're my hero."

With a burst of intuition, she swore Rogue beamed with happiness. *Good, he needed to feel special.* Mom and Dad spent too much time saving the planet, not him. No wonder he was so messed up. How would he ever fit in if he spent his entire life engaged in social disobedience?

Couldn't Mom and Dad see it was useless fighting the system? It was broken beyond repair. And that was exactly what the New World Order would need. To take over.

Chapter 22

Roxie Romero dished out bowls of minestrone with a side of crackers while they waited for the unrelenting rain to let up. They had finally made it through the Sierra Nevada burn scar area several hours ago and were anxious to get off the rural roads after their precarious mudslide incident. It was a wonder they had made it through unharmed.

They had been several miles from Interstate 5, ready to risk a major thoroughfare, when the *floppity-flop-flop* warned of a flat tire. Roxie didn't want Jackson to change the tire in the deluge, not after his recent incident. The waiting was more nerve-racking than driving through the horrendous storm. Especially since they had only been able to pull over just beyond the road's shoulder, all the while images of another mudslide, sinkhole, and the possibility of more falling trees kept her in perpetual stress mode.

We'll be fine once we're on the interstate," Roxie kept telling herself.

Jackson seemed a bit unhinged, as well, always squinting out the foggy windows. As if expecting trouble to find them. But they hadn't come across many travelers attempting these narrow, winding roads in the nastiest storm of the season.

Luna had returned to her normal confident self. Roxie was starting to wonder if the young woman's tough exterior was merely a self-preservation method to protect her from the catastrophes plaguing this decade. Rogue was still just as unpredictable, a mish-mash of emotions, ready to explode or laugh at any given moment.

Cora, the young mother, and baby, Mila, seemed fine, despite their perilous ordeal. Cora reached for a bowl of piping-hot soup when the afghan blanket Roxie had lent her slipped off the young woman's shoulder. Roxie gasped at the barcode tattoo glaring back at her.

"You!" Rogue pointed at their guest accusingly. "You're an Immuno!" But the way he'd said it hit hard, as if Cora wasn't human.

Jackson lightly smacked the kid's hand down to the table. "Didn't your mama tell you it's rude to point?"

"But, but, she's a carrier," Rogue whispered hauntingly. "And, my parents don't believe in physical punishment. Like ever!"

"My apologies, it wasn't my place," Jackson said rather gravely. "Parenting has never been on my resume."

Luna glared down at Rogue with disdain-laden eyes. "Don't let Rogue guilt you. Grandma didn't think twice about smacking us. And she wasn't a bad person. Right, Rogue?"

"Yeah, sorry, Handyman Jack. I always get in trouble for being honest—I mean, for being rude," the boy quickly amended.

"A swat isn't the end of the world." Roxie spoke up before realizing it. Parenting had changed drastically since her childhood. Perhaps for the worst, based on the unruly behavior she regularly witnessed. Children blamed overbearing parents, and parents blamed the schools for their children's insubordination. No one took on the effort or responsibility, hence society seemed to be rearing a generation of degenerates.

Cora's flushed face revealed her embarrassment. She cleared her throat gently, as if she wanted to say something but decided against it.

Roxie immediately sympathized with their guest. She knew quite a few people her age and older who had been branded with what she referred to as the mark of the beast. The CDC had stated rather bluntly Immunos were possible carriers of mutant Coronavirus strains, since they couldn't fight off the variants, even with quarterly booster shots. Thereby, they were considered an existential threat to society. It was difficult for them to get jobs, reducing them to third-class citizens.

"I'm sorry." Cora quickly covered the tattoo. "I should have told you. Yesterday's COVID test was negative. Here, I'll show you—" Cora looked down helplessly. "Uh, my phone and purse . . . are in my car." Tears spilled down her cheeks.

"Those tests aren't worth the plastic pollution they create," Jackson grumbled. "By now most of the population has been exposed to COVID. I already had it once. How 'bout the rest of you?"

It was a loaded question. One Roxie wasn't prepared to answer. She nodded slightly, as if acknowledging his statement. She had lost good friends after getting tangled up in the myriad of conspiracy theories regarding the COVID-19 controversy. The polarization had since increased exponentially now that the excess deaths statistics and numerous other health issues such as heart attacks, bizarre-looking blood clots, and cancers were coming to light.

A friend of hers who had recently retired from the insurance industry had implied life insurance was about to go extinct for the average person, since apparently, excess deaths of working-age men and women had continued to rise long after the tripledemic had subsided.

Naturally, the mainstream media and their array of health experts denied excess deaths were linked to COVID-19 and/or the vaccines. She wasn't so sure. After all, once upon a time not so long ago, health experts had vehemently denied smoking tobacco caused harm. To this day, the ongoing tobacco epidemic killed millions each year. Yet people still refused to believe the irrefutable data . . .

"I'm not worried. I'm vaxxed," Luna said flippantly.

"Ew!" Rogue drawled. "That means you have these weird rectangular nanostructures growing in your body—"

"Sport, it's been a trying day." Jackson rubbed his temples gingerly. "You mind ratcheting down your opinions for five minutes."

Rogue stared at everyone around the table, as if they were the ones behaving ludicrously. "But, but the new law says Immunos have to disclose their weakness."

"Since when do you care about laws?" Luna huffed.

"After all, you've been driving the bus," Roxie gently reminded.

"Touché," Jackson quipped before sipping a spoonful of broth.

Cora cringed, as if she wanted to melt into the dinette booth's upholstery. It must be hard on her, branded like that. "Really, I would have said something. I totally forgot." Cora's spoon clanked to the table. "I have to wear this forever-stamp like I'm a pariah or something. I friggin' hate it." Her apologetic tone had quickly transformed into anger.

"At least they didn't stamp your hand," Luna said matter-of-factly. "That's the latest *punishment* for Immunos."

Next, Immunos will be forced into wearing yellow stars, Roxie mused. Wanting to change the subject, she asked, "Where can we drop you off?" They hadn't talked about that yet. After finding refuge on the bus and changing into dry clothes, Cora had dozed off by the Grizzly after breastfeeding the five-month-old. Roxie no longer worried they needed medical attention since ERs refused Immunos.

"I don't know." Cora blotted her tears. "I was on my way to my grandpa's. He's probably still waiting for me at the gas station. He is going to be sooo mad at me."

Aha. "Does your grandfather run that little country gas station?" Roxie asked. She turned to Jackson. "What was the name of that place?"

"Kim's One Stop Gas & Snacks," Luna said on cue.

"I knew you were Korean!" Rogue proclaimed, as if he had already forgotten his beef with her. "I could tell by your pretty eyes. Ooh, I love those marshmallowy choco pies. Do you have any?"

Obviously not, Cora had barely escaped with her life. Needless to say, everyone ignored Rogue.

"Your grandfather was doing just fine when we stopped for gas," Roxie assured. The young woman had gone through enough trauma without stressing over him. *Although, her grandfather must be worried sick about her and the little one.*

A torrent of horizontal rain pummeled the bus. Roxie fixated on the windows, afraid they might burst under the intense pressure. "This storm's relentless."

"After what we've been through the last few days," Jackson said. "I dare say our Goldilocks climate is on the verge of falling apart sooner than those so-called experts predicted. And there doesn't seem to be a damn thing our government can do about it."

"I'm hoping all this rain will end the drought," Roxie said, hoping to keep the conversation light.

"Not so much," Rogue spouted. "Did you know it takes decades to recharge aquifers? My science teacher, Mr. Carrington, he's way cool, said it would take like twenty atmospheric rivers to refill the super-low aquifers."

Jackson's brows knitted deeper. "Twenty?"

Rogue let his spoon plop back into the bowl with a splash. "Yeah, 'cause don't you know, most the water ends up going to the ocean. Or to those underground oceans in the earth's crust. They need to build more eco rain-capturing systems."

"I agree," Jackson said after slipping a knowing wink to Roxie.

"And, and did you know that AI—is the final invention?" Rogue quizzed, as if they had been talking about Artificial Intelligence. "Besides turning humans into slaves, AI's environmental footprint is crazy-bad. Like it consumes tons of freshwater and energy. More than the databases Mom and Dad—"

"Rogue!" Luna snapped, followed by a scuffling of feet under the table. "You're giving me a headache."

Thankfully, Luna shut up her uppity brother before he said something incriminating.

"Sorry. It just makes me so mad. See, capturing the rainwater could be the greatest invention since, uh?" Rogue seemed stuck on the proper comparison.

"Flushing toilets," Jackson finished.

"Definitely, cell phones," Luna added somewhat begrudgingly.

"Starbucks," Cora quipped with a shy giggle before covering her mouth.

Everyone turned to Roxie. "Polyester. I hated ironing." As a child, her most despised chore had been ironing everything from handkerchiefs to tablecloths to T-shirts, even jeans.

"Argh, wrong answer. Polyester's super toxic. And microfiber is deadly! It should be illegal. Did you know, we breathe in microfiber plastics like all the time? But don't worry, we don't allow it on our bus!"

"Rogue," Luna warned in a low tone.

Rogue glowered into his bowl, as if realizing nobody cared about his eco-unfriendly tirade.

"Say, Cora, did you happen to catch the weather forecast?" Jackson eyed the raging rain. "Beginning to wonder if it's ever letting up."

Cora shrugged. "It's supposed to rain for days. That's why I was going to my grandpa's. He storm-proofed and fireproofed his house after last year's fires. Even cut down all the trees around his house. Why are you guys taking a trip in this mega-storm?" Cora questioned.

Like idiots, was the tone Roxie discerned from the young mother. But it was a reasonable question. One Roxie wasn't sure how to answer. She certainly didn't want to embroil Cora and the baby in their FBI plight.

"Family emergency," Jackson announced off the cuff. "We're trying to get to Oregon."

"You must be lost then," Cora pointed out. "It'll take days to get to Oregon on the backroads. You need to get on Interstate 5."

Roxie almost choked on her soup. Luna went to the cupboard, as if thinking of what to say. Meanwhile, the conversation stalled while Rogue theatrically fidgeted with his cloth napkin, folding it this way and that, as if trying extremely hard to not look guilty.

"Yep," Jackson said. "We keep changing our itinerary, what with the fires and the rain. I wanted to see if my brother's house in Sacramento survived—"

"Oh, no," Cora exclaimed. "Sacramento's flooding now. The news said it was getting two years' worth of rain in the next few days."

"Yeah, that's why we changed our minds—to go to Oregon. To check on *Auntie Maddie*," Rogue added rather peculiarly. "The weather's crazy there too."

Jackson walked to the sink with a scowl on his face. They were obviously a bunch of terrible liars.

"Yeah, it's raining everywhere. Except Southern California," Cora said, lovingly cradling Mila in the crook of one arm, seemingly oblivious they were having a difficult time coming up with a cover story. "Did you hear about that megacane? It's like the biggest hurricane. Ever."

"Awesome! Is it coming here?" Rogue asked a bit too eagerly.

Sheesh, now we have megacanes? Roxie didn't know what to think. Of course, the girl was probably exaggerating.

"Texas, I think. Or maybe the East Coast," Cora said. "I wasn't paying attention to that with half of California on fire and the other half flooding. Besides, the Internet's been glitchy. It's hard to get a Wi-Fi signal since the fires started."

As if Roxie didn't have enough to worry about, now she had to worry about her brother in Delaware.

"Well, since you're going to Oregon, you could drop me off in Redding. If that's okay?" Cora's bright smile seemed to outshine her angst. "My best friend from high school's dying to see the baby. I'll text her. Ugh, I keep forgetting you guys lost your phones, too," Cora said incredulously.

They had better get their story straight. "We lost ours in the fire. The one in Gold Town," Roxie added, careful not to mention Valley Pines. She caught Jackson's silent approval when he returned to the table with a glass of water.

"So many fires. My grandma says she dreams about the Four Horsemen of the Apocalypse. Yeah, her dementia makes her say scary shit," Cora said dismissively. The baby woke herself up with a raspy cough. "It sucks without a phone. I can't keep track of the infant apps. Now I'm gonna get stuck paying penalties. By law, I'm required to log every single one of Mila's symptoms and vitals."

Roxie worried the poor little thing was catching a cold. Thankfully, Cora appeared too wrapped up in her own personal crisis to be suspicious of them, despite Rogue's especially peculiar behavior. Moreover, Jackson and Luna had saved her and the baby.

"Perfect, we'll drop you off in Redding," Luna said. "But someplace easy to get to. It's hard driving this in traffic."

"Best Buy is easy to get to. I need to buy a phone. Oh, I should make sure my debit card's still in my jean pocket."

"I'll go check for you." Rogue darted to the shower, where Cora's clothes were drying.

"O-kay?" Cora laughed. "He's funny. Thanks for letting me wear this cute summer dress. I so love these Betsey Johnson sandals. And thank you super much for saving us."

"You should keep them," Luna said.

"You guys are so nice. Hey, I know a shortcut to the interstate," Cora said, as if they were completely lost.

"Got it!" Rogue slapped the debit card onto the table. "Did you know, being phoneless is an actual disorder? Nomophobia, sorta like PTSD," Rogue said out of the blue.

It was all Roxie could do to keep a straight face, when the corners of Jackson's mouth quivered, as if holding back a chuckle.

"Well, okay then," Jackson said. "We can't sit here all day, waiting for the rain to subside. Luna, you mind holding the umbrella while I change that darn tire?"

"Sure," Luna said with a wistful sigh. "I'm so ready to get back to normal."

Roxie was sure they were all anxious to get back to normal. Whatever and wherever that was . . .

Chapter 23

SunFlower BlueStone muttered at the heavy-laden clouds in the distance. She should be used to it, after driving through storm after storm after storm the past few days.

"Prudy, are you there?" SunFlower called out. "I'm getting intense negative vibes. I think we should drive north for a while." The megacane was spawning sporadic thunderstorms all over the lower half of Texas. The dark clouds ahead were atrocious. The sky so ominous it gave her the screaming meemies.

"And you call yourself enlightened? Never, I repeat, never consent to fear," Prudy berated.

SunFlower exhaled deeply. *"There's a difference between fear and precaution,"* SunFlower rebutted internally. *"Fear, despite being a low-vibe attribute, serves a purpose. As in avoiding undertaking something incredibly foolish."*

"Then drive faster. You drive like a crone from the nineteenth century. Why do you presume I guided you to this specific vehicle?"

SunFlower waited for Prudy to answer her own question.

"Because it was the most effective escape vehicle in the locality of your 3-D world," Prudy prattled on.

"We'll get to Sedona if and when the Cosmic Collective Consciousness wills it." SunFlower had decided to spend a night in Sedona, since it was on the way back to California, if only to stop Prudy's incessant nagging.

Honestly, she didn't understand her spirit guide's urgent and unreasonable request to visit Sedona, when Luna and Rogue seemed to be in imminent danger. She had a sudden knowing those two had been added to the activist hit list, despite the illogic. Luna had forsaken activism, declaring it a waste of time, and Rogue, brilliant as he might be, was merely a child.

SunFlower listened intently to the faraway plea for help in her mind. Based on what she sensed, Crystal and Forest were in danger. Unfortunately, the storm's chaotic energies prevented her from connecting to their energies. Perhaps they were in hiding, shielding themselves.

"*Faster, you must go faster,*" Prudy chastised in the background.

A flash of fury swept over SunFlower. She stomped on the gas pedal just as the sky unleashed its wrath. The blinding rain bounced off the windshield in erratic waves, drenching the roads. Surprisingly, the car didn't hydroplane.

Unexpectedly, she found her chakras supercharged by the storm's ferociousness. Even her anxiousness disappeared as she became invigorated with the tempest's surging energies—becoming one with the storm. A scene of prehistoric Earth, a time when the dinosaurs ruled, exploded into her mind. Just as the creatures of that epoch had been predominantly larger, the weather had been ferociously fiercer.

A glimpse into the future showed that epoch was returning . . .

"*A preview of coming attractions.*" Prudy's laughter cackled in the furthest depths of her mind.

Intrigued, SunFlower longed for a clearer image of Earth's future, or had she revisited the past? Either way, it had been an intoxicating experience. She braked hard to pull over to the shoulder. This time she skidded to a stop into an adjacent barren field.

With partly closed eyes, she reverted to her astral body for a glimpse of Earth's future-self. Sometimes her willed visions appeared, but usually she only saw the pervasive baneful energies devouring Earth's aura, taking Humanity with it. At times she thought the endarkenment of Humanity would consume her soul, which was why she seldom went there.

As she ventured into the stifling, murky fog of nothingness, a thousand pinpricks warned her to turn back. Back to where a lightworker such as herself should be. She had no right venturing into the vast junkyard of mankind's invasive technologies, where thousands upon thousands of satellites swarmed Earth's orbit like a mechanical plague of locusts.

Still, she had to see what was occurring with the current timeline, for she sensed an apparent shift. SunFlower waded at the edge—awaiting a cosmic visual to reveal an explanation. Only to witness Humanity's precarious timelines collapsing into itself, one after another . . . the endless possibilities of the future vaporizing into oblivion. As if Humanity no longer existed.

That can't be right. Humanity still had a millennium left on this beloved planet, based on the Cosmic Collective Consciousness she and her fellow lightworkers tapped into.

She dared venture further, seeking the ultimate truth from the Akashic Records, which served as a cosmic library of Humanity's Past, Present, and Future. It was incapable of deception, unlike corrupt politicians, false leaders, and wayward activists with misplaced agendas swayed by their dogma.

All she encountered was a vast void of nothingness . . . And so, she pushed her ethereal self further still, until the molecules of her physical body seemed to dissolve into the etherworlds.

There was nothing to see.

"Sun-Flow-errr . . . I demand you, return!" It was the faintest of cries.

SunFlower tried to find her way back but seemed to drown in an endless void of nothingness, as if she herself no longer existed.

A forceful surge thrust her back into her physical body. Her head abruptly registered pain signals. All too real. *Thank the Goddess for that.*

"You have been verboten to traverse the etherworlds. Without me!"

"If you provided the assistance I desire, as is the purpose of one's spirit guide, I wouldn't have to take such risks." However, Sun-

Flower realized it was fruitless to blame Prudy. She had ventured too far.

"See how you are? No gratitude. After I disentangled you from the abyss of the Great Void."

The rear windshield glowed red. Then she heard the siren. "Now isn't that just great," SunFlower muttered. Quickly, she pulled out her wallet, found the car registration, and rolled down the window. Prepared.

"Ma'am, what the devil are you doing?" the Texas State Trooper berated. "Earlier, I clocked you at over one hun-erd. You got a death wish driving like that in this weather?"

"Sorry," she mumbled, more concerned about Humanity's disappearance than getting a traffic ticket.

He took a look at her license. "Aw, California. That explains it." He shook his head, clicking his tongue in a scolding manner. "In a convertible car rental," he said flatly. "Driving through the biggest hurricane to ever hit. Why, I ought to lock you up for plain lunacy. You're lucky I'm not scraping you off the pavement—"

SunFlower had to brush away the gory impression his crude statement brought to mind. Dying was the least of her concerns. She had been told by more than one spirit guide she was living to ninety-four. Which, didn't make much sense. Apparently, the planet didn't have that long. "I am truly sorry," she uttered again and smiled meekly. "I'm trying to get home."

"It's a little late for that. We're getting hit by the hurricane's outer bands. Wait here," he said before marching back to his patrol car.

She awaited her fate while he verified her driver's license. Had Devin provided her with an authentic forged driver's license? She no longer trusted anything. Current reality seemed to be a jumble of false flags—making it impossible to discern truth from mal-information. Everything she had believed in and had diligently worked toward, all for not. If what she had foreseen had been genuine, Humanity had no future.

Finally, the Texas State Trooper trudged back through the muddy field and gave her a piercing, long evil eye. "Missy, if it weren't that darn near half of Texas is shut down due to a state of emergency . . ." he spewed. "Anyhow, at this point, it's all about saving lives, not writing tickets. Lunacy—isn't my jurisdiction." He chuckled. "I'll let you go if you promise to keep it under eighty." He handed back the registration and driver's license. "Will she start?"

She turned the key, and the Mustang roared right up.

"Alrighty then, pull it to the shoulder. Wanna make sure you don't have any flats. Can't leave you stranded—we're gettin' dozens of reports of tornadas."

SunFlower obeyed, still in shock from her earth-shattering Akashic Record's vision quest.

The state trooper, capped in his iconic cowboy hat, which was covered with a silly clear plastic covering, walked around the car in the pouring rain. His aura revealed no malign energies. He was just a concerned soul committed to performing his job to the best of his abilities. Admirable. If the majority of people were like that, Humanity would not be on the brink.

"Everything looks a-okay. Now listen, you have two options. A," he said, tapping his pointer finger, "head up the road about twenty miles and knock on the door of the big old blue house. The Coopers have one of those water-tight storm shelters. Tell 'em Hal sent ya. B, take the Interstate 37 Junction north to San Antonio. And pray you make it there before the roads become impassable. Personally, if I were you, I'd get to SAT. The San Antonio International Airport has one of those sturdy multi-level parking garages. You can ride out the megacane on the *fourth* level. Officials are predicting 'unsurvivable' storm surge events."

"Sir, I was hoping to get to New Mexico tonight."

The state trooper shook his head. "Ma'am, excuse my French, but that's a *big* hell no. You don't have time for that. We ain't seen nothing yet. The National Weather Service predicts a whopping thirty to forty inches of rain by midnight. This is a Level Five weather event. The likes we've never seen. The only people driving around in this are storm chasers. Believe you me, I give those whackadoos a ticket every chance I get."

SunFlower was at a loss. She didn't know what to do. "I didn't realize it was this bad here. I was escaping the Florida hurricane . . ."

"Get to SAT, and you'll make it through this. The junction's about forty miles ahead. Of course, you're liable to run into some traffic with all the other evacuees."

"Thank you," SunFlower said, as if he were a million miles away.

"Alrighty then"—he tapped the Mustang's roof—"drive *responsibly*." He tipped his hat and walked off, muttering something about "those loco Californians."

Prudy's laughter inundated SunFlower's internal hearing. Under any other circumstances, she would be in hysterics as well.

"*Prudy, tell me the real reason you want to go to Sedona.*" SunFlower just remembered something Prudy had once said. Something about spirit guides preferred to be released at Earth's vortices or chakra points once their human departed. Sedona was Prudy's favorite.

Naturally, her obstinate spirit guide did not respond, leaving SunFlower's super-consciousness reeling with the shocking horror of a new unknown . . .

Chapter 24

Jackson Jones was reattaching his damp ponytail in the puny bathroom, when the bus lurched to the left. *Not again.* He certainly wasn't up to changing another tire in this blasted rain. It was like the biblical days of Noah out there.

From what he'd read from various periodicals, the planet's climate fluctuated throughout the centuries, as did the sun with its Solar Minimum and Solar Maximum cycles. Not to mention the climate patterns of El Niño and La Niña. That famous painting of George Washington crossing the frozen Delaware River during the American Revolution came to mind. Scientists had labeled that period as the Little Ice Age. Logically, the earth would also experience severe heat waves from time to time.

Nevertheless, this bout of weather whiplash had him rethinking his stance on the whole climate change kerfuffle. He didn't doubt human activity was most likely speeding up the warming process. But for the weather to abruptly go batshit crazy was mind-boggling. Environmentalists had cried wolf for so many decades he had become somewhat complacent and skeptical, convinced such dire environmental changes weren't occurring in his lifetime.

Was this merely a series of severe storms? Or the new normal? Either way troubled him.

This past week would read like *The National Enquirer* of catastrophic weather events. Come to think of it, his brother in Tennessee had lost not only his home but his entire town to a tornado the day before Christmas. And one of his high school buddies had lost his oceanside home in Santa Cruz last year after the cliffside had given way. Isolated incidences, until one looked at it closer. Albeit, with an open mind.

Meanwhile, any attempts to stifle global warming had curdled into a political brouhaha, polarizing the population: Democrats wanted to save the world with impossible laws that would bankrupt the regular Joe Schmo. On the flip side, some Republicans refused to acknowledge the problem existed by declaring it a hoax. Stalling legislative progress. Congress seemed to spend more time reversing policies and trying to oust one another than making progress on the critical issues Americans faced.

But for the love of God, if so-called "normal" weather was on the fritz to the extent of making everyday life damn near impossible, wouldn't people on all sides of the political spectrum finally agree to do what was deemed necessary? If not to preserve Humanity, then themselves?

Perhaps, having a front-row seat to the past week's events had him overthinking it. One thing was clear: the current climatic situation was turning downright *climactic*.

"Jackson?" Roxie's wavering call told him to hustle out of the bathroom.

Hmm, doesn't sound like a flat tire. As the bus ground to a halt, he steadied himself by groping the bunk beds, the dinette table, and the kitchen counter while scrambling to the front of the bus where everyone had gathered.

"What's going on?" Jackson asked before catching a glimpse out the windshield. "What the . . ." The stretch of road ahead was flooded.

Roxie's beleaguering eyes begged, *What should we do?*

Common sense warranted to sit tight and wait for the water to subside. But time wasn't exactly on their side. The FBI had no doubt widened their search perimeter and may have informed local law enforcement that fugitives driving a bus could be in the area. Despite his lame attempts to disguise the bus, he couldn't rule out they had not been spotted on the array of Interstate 5 traffic webcams monitoring the roads, especially in these inclement weather conditions. The sooner this monstrosity was off the road, the better.

"Can't we just drive through it?" Rogue asked.

"Maybe." Jackson was already formulating a plan. "But after that sinkhole—" Hell, he wasn't taking any chances. They were approaching the small town of Dunsmuir where the interstate wrapped up and down the mountainous terrain. Therefore, logically thinking, it was merely a flooded area in the valley, nothing more.

"The road could be washed out," Roxie warned in an unsettling tone.

"That's what I'm about to find out." Jackson darted back to the bathroom to grab the galoshes and the drenched windbreaker hanging in the shower. Not that the windbreaker would do much good. Still, the inner lining was fairly dry.

When he returned to the front of the bus, Luna stood by the door, donned in rain gear, always ready for a challenge.

Roxie gently clutched his arm as he stepped down the bus steps. "Do be careful."

He flashed Roxie a flirty wink that said, *Mr. Macho here will save the day*. But deep down, he was starting to wonder if they were ever getting to SunFlower's house, as if it were a mythical place in some never-ending dream.

"So, what's the plan?" Luna held the umbrella over him while he sat at the foot of the bus steps and tugged on those god-awful galoshes once again.

"Didn't I see a set of hiking poles in one of the storage compartments?" Jackson asked, thinking out loud.

"Perfect, I'll get the trekking poles." Luna darted to the storage compartment, leaving him in the rain.

He hurried to her as she pulled them out. "These just might do the trick." A neon-orange nylon rope caught his eye. It looked to be a good hundred feet or so. He quickly threaded the rope through his jean belt loops and knotted it tightly. "If I fall in—you know the drill."

"I got your back," Luna said as he handed her the other end of the rope, which she wrapped around her wrist.

They hurried to the edge of the flooded interstate. "Looks like it's rising fast." If they didn't make it through in the next few minutes, they'd be stuck. That meant backing up several miles until they came to a section in the meridian that wasn't blocked off by concrete traffic barriers or an off-ramp.

"Here goes." Jackson poked around with the hiking poles before stepping into the six-inch deep water. He ventured on, measuring the water with the poles before each step. No swooshing whirlpools were a good sign the water wasn't rushing into a sinkhole. Still, he cringed with every step.

He finally spotted the source of gushing water to his right. Water cascaded down a steep canyon wall, inundating the road. He busted butt to the far end of the flooded road, maybe fifty feet. "We're good to go," he shouted. Not that Luna could hear him over the downpour. He hurried back, scanning the flooded road for the telltale signs of the beginnings of a sinkhole.

Once within earshot, he yelled, "We need to get out of here!"

Luna ran back for the bus with the umbrella in one hand and the rope in the other. The water must have risen another two inches on his trek back. He ran back in splashing leaps, trying to match Luna's pace.

She was already shifting into gear when he hopped onto the bus, out of breath.

"Keep 'er in the middle of the road," he said as everyone remained abnormally quiet. "Go as fast as you think the bus can take it." What he didn't say as not to fluster her: a few inches more of water might stall the bus. Although the engine was pretty high up, the water was bound to wreak havoc with the brakes.

"You're doing fine," Roxie cooed as the underbelly of the bus seemed to gurgle in protest.

Jackson whistled through his teeth as they approached the deepest part. "Whatever you do. Don't stop, or we'll stall out."

Finally, after the world's longest minute, the bus made it through the flooded valley. "Good job!" Jackson said as Roxie handed him a fresh towel. He gladly took it after discarding the drenched jacket and galoshes into a reusable shopping bag.

"I'll hang up your jacket in the shower," Roxie said.

Jackson co-piloted anxiously from the bench seat, when the flickering of taillights caught his eye. "Is that a car up ahead?" Jackson asked.

"Yeah, I've been seeing vehicles off in the distance," Luna said. "They always disappear around these winding roads."

Roxie returned and sat beside him. "Sheesh, I'm glad we're not the only dummies driving in this mess."

Hmm, the fact they were catching up to traffic was not necessarily a good sign. Jackson checked his watch. Almost 3:00 p.m. They had dropped off Cora and the baby in Redding about an hour ago. "Suppose the locals who commute to Redding got off early, wanting to get to their homes in the outlying areas."

On the upside, they were going up in elevation, except for an occasional valley. Of course, all sorts of tributaries snaked down this mountainous region into the myriad of pristine lakes along with the Sacramento River. Could they support the deluge?

They should be all right once they climbed a few more hundred feet. Then again, this scenic section of Interstate 5, dubbed the Cascade Wonderland Scenic Highway, had been carved through the curvy canyons of the Cascade mountains and the Shasta-Trinity National Forest where the spectacular Mount Shasta played peekaboo with passersby before gobsmacking them in their faces with the volcano's bold magnificence.

Although, Mount Shasta wouldn't be saying hello to anyone due to the low cloud cover. Too bad. He would miss it along with the mystical peaks of Castle Crag, one of his favorite beauty marks etched into the earth that always had him imagining what the planet had looked like when it was young.

"Yay! We did it!" Rogue proclaimed, as if he had been driving.

"Now that we made it through that, I need a double shot of chamomile tea," Roxie said with an obvious bluster of relief.

Jackson wasn't so sure. Several sets of taillights flashed ahead before vanishing. "Might want to slow down. I do believe there are several vehicles around this next bend."

Luna eased up on the accelerator and swerved to avoid a green road sign lying in the road. As they rounded the bend, she slammed the brakes, sending the bus to the muddy shoulder. They careened into the banked side of the canyon with a thud.

"Everyone okay?" Luna's voice went husky.

"No worries," Jackson said more to himself.

Roxie's hands fell limply into her lap. "I'm glad I didn't start the tea kettle."

"Luna, just drive hella fast through the flooded road like you did last time," Rogue said.

Luna turned around and flashed her brother a well-deserved dirty look.

"If that were the case, that Jeep wouldn't be sittin' there," Jackson speculated. "Sport, hand me those binoculars."

Rogue begrudgingly handed over the heavy-duty set of Bushnells he had claimed from the supply closet. Jackson zoomed in on the scene beyond the dozen or so vehicles parked in the middle of the road. No matter how he adjusted the viewfinder, all he saw was a bunch of gray as the road, the water, and the darkening sky melded into one big misty blotch.

"What do you see?" Roxie craned closer to the windshield.

"A slew of vehicles and a lot of people catchin' up on their standing around." Jackson held up the binoculars expectedly until Rogue snatched them back. "Best I see what's goin' on," he grumbled, going back for the galoshes. Common sense told him the road was too flooded to cross.

Luna put on her rain gear once again, although it wasn't all that cold out there. Just wet, as if the air had liquefied. When Jackson walked by a frazzled-looking Roxie, he said, "Why don't you have that cup of tea while Luna and I get the scuttlebutt."

"Gladly," Roxie said, smoothing down her vixen-blue hair. "Putting on the kettle now."

"I'm coming, too," Rogue insisted, as if expecting to be refused.

No one told the kid no. Quite frankly, Jackson needed to save his energy for more important battles. The kid required too much energy. *No wonder his parents farmed him out to relatives and babysitters.*

The three of them set out for the people gathered several car lengths ahead. Jackson nosed to the edge of the crowd. Had he heard right? "Did someone just say the bridge is washed out?" Jackson yelled over the crowd.

The drenched woman next to him said, "It's completely gone! I was about to cross when rushing water from the creek came out of nowhere. And pulverized the bridge."

"Holy balls!" Rogue exclaimed.

"Wait—what?" Luna said, meeting Jackson's eyes.

Good thing they hadn't been the first ones on the scene. With this low visibility, what if Luna hadn't spotted the washed-out bridge? Perhaps luck was on their side. Despite all the catastrophes they had encountered, they had remained basically intact. Except for their nerves.

"Excuse me," Jackson said to the apparent ringleader, who was doing most of the talking. "We just pulled up. Is help on the way?"

That started an outburst from the crowd.

"Listen up," the ringleader said. "We need to turn around and go south."

Jackson pushed his way through the crowd and waved his arm in the air to get the ringleader's attention. "Afraid you won't get very far. We barely made it through the flooded road about a mile back," he said matter-of-factly.

The crowd went apeshit again.

"What did nine-one-one say?" Luna asked boldly.

"No damn cell service and no Wi-Fi. We're on our own," the ringleader said, trying to rein in the crowd.

"That SOS thing isn't working either," someone else said.

"The Coast Guard will save us," Rogue shouted defiantly, always eager to offer helpful suggestions.

"You crazy?" someone shouted back. "Helicopters can't fly in this."

"We'll be here for days . . ." a distressed voice from the crowd lamented.

Jackson and Luna exchanged pensive glances. Things just kept going from bad to worse.

"Someone will come for us. They have to," another voice assured.

"I need to make it home with the groceries my wife wanted," the ringleader said, throwing up his arms hopelessly. "Now I'm stranded. Ten more days of this rain . . ."

Damn! The snowplow fellow had been spot on. Jackson was surprised the storms were hitting this far north as well as the Sierras. "Must be one helluva atmospheric river."

"Yeah, atmospheric rivers are huge," Rogue drawled. "Think—a thousand-mile river of water in the sky."

"Then, we can't stay here." The flush-faced woman's vibrato revealed how close she was to a mental breakdown.

"My son needs his meds," a woman cried out.

Jackson, not ready to accept they were screwed, scanned the area methodically while the stranded travelers continued wallowing in their woes.

"Bingo," Jackson uttered under his breath. "Rogue, stay here with Luna."

"Hey, where you going?" Rogue called out behind him.

Jackson slushed and sloshed his way to the left side of the interstate with his focus on a rugged man who looked like he could have been raised by wolves. He was a hairy fellow, with one of those ZZ Top beards hanging down his chest. "You thinkin' what I'm thinkin'?" Jackson called him on it, no time for salutations.

The burly man rolled up his red and black checkered flannel sleeves and gave Jackson the once-over before answering. "Not stayin' chere with them shitheads." The man stared proudly at the pot of gold strapped to his truck rack.

Jackson followed the man's gaze to the small motorboat the man happened to be hauling. *Aw, Louisiana plates*. He thought he had detected a Cajun accent. "Great minds think alike. Question is, can we cross—in that?" Jackson head-jerked to the washed-out bridge.

"Safer than this shitshow." The man eyed the canyon's mountainside. "If da rocky hillside go, we be goners."

"You got that right. The hillside went on us earlier. Hell, my family and I barely escaped. And the road's flooded out a mile back," Jackson informed.

"Cain't be goin' back. Gots to get to Oregon. Gonna win that ten-thousand prize in da Annual Frostbite Open. Fishing tournament," he clarified. "Help get Crawdaddy in da water." The man clapped his hands expectantly as if Jackson were a hired hand.

"Sure thing." Jackson flashed Luna and Rogue a thumbs-up. *This better not be a colossal mistake*. He should get an idea of how rough the journey was before recommending it for Rogue and Roxie. Under normal circumstances, he'd wait for trained rescue personnel.

However, one thing was dead certain: these were not normal circumstances, despite the cockamamie scheme he had let himself become embroiled in; the earth seemed to be in the midst of a strategically orchestrated vendetta. What with fires in Southern California, floods in the north, and hurricanes. In February?

The ringleader's group must have caught on to their boat escape for the mob rushed over. "You can't be serious?" the would-be leader grilled.

"Ain't no one asked ya," the Cajun man clapped back.

"How 'bout a test run?" Jackson asked nonchalantly, not wanting to piss away their chance out of there.

"Who be first? Fifty bucks a pop?" the greedy Cajun man announced.

The grumbling crowd squabbled, not so discreetly questioning the Cajun man's sanity or lack thereof.

"You want us to *pay* fifty dollars to ride in *that*?" questioned a young man in Tom Cruise–style sunglasses. "That's just shitty."

The man whipped out his wallet all the same. The crowd quickly hushed. That was when Jackson spotted another group gathering at the opposite end of the washed-out interstate.

Jackson's plans were quickly falling by the wayside. They didn't have the fifty-dollar price-gouging fare. Their last fill-up had seen to that. One step at a time he told himself. "You might want to consider a spotter. There's an awful lot of debris," Jackson said as a six-foot branch bobbed across the flooded road.

The Cajun man's eyes narrowed to slits. He tugged at his beard a long moment as if contemplating. "I see what ya be doing. You be tryin' to grift me out of fifty bucks."

It was more like the other way around, but Jackson held his ground and said firmly, "Not at all. But I have a child, and two women with me. I want to test the waters so to speak."

The Cajun man nodded. "A-huh, you ain't got da cash."

Jackson let out a chuckle. "Hoping for a family discount. Besides, I have one of those nifty portable power stations. A Jackery," Jackson said, as if it were some new snazzy gadget.

The young man donning sunglasses, despite the sunless sky, sat in the boat, clinging to his laptop, while several others were already counting their cash. Jackson kept eyeballing the rising creek, as if sensing the forlorn energy—something was about to give, albeit the road or the mountainside.

The Cajun man kicked at the waves of water that had already extended a foot closer to the truck. "I be liken' da spotter idea. On da *first* run." He clapped his hands. "Let's get da show on da road."

Before Jackson had a chance to inform Luna and Rogue, who were coming his way, three passengers paid their fees and struggled for their balance into the rocking boat.

"Ya comin' or what?" the Cajun man pestered before starting the motor.

Jackson hesitated, only for an instant. He climbed into the boat just as Rogue started running and shouting toward him. "Be right back," Jackson hollered into the howling wind.

He sensed more than saw Roxie's devastation as she nearly jumped off the bus steps and sprinted toward the crowd. In that heart-wrenching moment, he felt more intensely drawn to that woman than anything he had ever experienced in his entire life. Something more profound than love.

The Cajun man handed him an oar as Jackson took a seat in the front of the boat. Bystanders on the north end of the interstate cheered as the boatload of passengers headed their way; all the while, Jackson drudged away branches along with a whole lot of mangled plastic sweeping across their path. It had him speculating if the flood had swept through the county dump. The paying passengers huddled with anxious faces as if not expecting to make it to the other side as the waves lapped into the small fishing boat.

Five minutes later, they crossed without incident. The crowd on the north end of the interstate pulled the boat up enough for the passengers to wade out to the pavement.

"Easy-peasy," the Cajun man declared.

A man in a suit and tie, still holding onto the edge of the boat said, "I'm next." Apparently, he wanted to cross to the other side.

The Cajun man did not hesitate. "Fifty dollars a pop!"

It was all Jackson could do to hide his contempt. "Now hold on just a minute. Southbound is flooded not more than a mile back. Unless you happen to know of a side road within the last mile." But Jackson didn't recall an exit.

Jackson seemed to feel the Cajun man's wrath wash over him for costing him the fifty-dollar toll.

"What? You mean we can't go south?" someone from the crowd howled.

"I-5's impassable northbound as well. Damn rockslide," someone said.

Jackson's stomach went acidic. They were stuck. "Any word on Caltrans?" Jackson asked feebly.

"Hell, it'll take days for them to get through. I heard on my CB, the National Guard's setting up a staging area right on the interstate. Near the Railroad Park exit," an older man said, probably the driver of the eighteen-wheeler that looked like it might tip over with the right side tires sinking into the soggy shoulder. "It's higher ground than this. At around two thousand feet."

"Why there?" Jackson was quick to ask.

"Apparently, they were ordered to evacuate campers and hikers in the vicinity," the trucker said.

"Only shitheads go hiking in a freak storm," the Cajun man remarked.

"Hey," someone yelled out defensively. "The Internet's been down for days up here in the State of Jefferson. California doesn't care about us. Half the time we don't get cell service."

Jackson chuckled inwardly. At one time folks around these parts had petitioned to create a new state. Some claimed to this day, that they lived in the fifty-first state of Jefferson. Needless to say, it was something an outsider didn't bring up unless they were ready for a heated debate.

"Seems to me we need to get to the National Guard 'til these damn roads get cleared." Jackson's statement was followed with groans.

"Cain't stay chere," the Cajun man said as he bailed out the pooling rainwater with a rusty tobacco can.

"Can I hitch a ride to Railroad Park with someone?" the fellow with the Tom Cruise sunglasses asked.

"I'll take you," a man with a collapsing umbrella that flopped in the wind said.

The Cajun man turned the boat around.

"If some of you don't mind waiting," Jackson said quickly. "Those folks on the other side need rides." The boat took off with Jackson before he heard a response.

The Cajun man sped back faster than he ought to. Then Jackson realized why. The swollen waters had breached the area where they had originally launched the boat. People scrambled to their vehicles and moved them to higher ground. Which was basically fruitless. Higher ground was only maybe a good three feet at most. With the way the rain was coming down, the river-like creek would breach that soon.

The rain blasted down harder as Jackson climbed out of the boat. The sky plunged into darkness. As if the sun had vaporized. He gawked at the harrowing sky when a tiny voice whispered in his ear, "Get out!"

"What the hell?" Jackson glanced around. No one was within earshot. He shook away the almost uncanny premonition, deciding he'd watched too many late-night scary movies as a kid. He calmed down a notch upon finding Roxie in the crowd. Her baby-blues latched onto his and didn't let go, giving him the courage to fight back his sudden apprehension.

As the boat scraped pavement, Rogue came huffing up to him with Luna. "I told them you wouldn't leave us. Huh."

"Sorry, didn't have time to get *permission*." Jackson winked at Roxie. "That SOB"—Jackson head-jerked to the loaded boat already making another run—"is charging fifty dollars per person to cross."

"A-hole!" Rogue berated.

"Tell me, how much does a Jackery go for on Amazon?" Jackson asked.

"I told you already, it's not holding a charge. I think the cold broke it," Rogue said.

Luna smiled long and hard. "He doesn't know that."

"That's cheating—" Rogue started in.

"That's *survival*," Jackson corrected.

"Rogue, hush now," Roxie scolded. "Do you want to be stuck here for days only to end up in juvenile hall? With the baaad kids?"

Rogue shrugged defeatedly. "Wait, we can't just leave the bus. I promised Dad I'd take care of it."

"This is one of those SHTF situations Dad trained us on," Luna said patiently.

"This is so not fair!" Rogue yelled to the sky. "Dad's gonna hate me forever."

"Then it's settled." Jackson eyed the growing line of people. "Sport, fetch the powerpack along with a backpack of clothes."

"Whatev."

"And don't dawdle," Roxie added sternly.

"What does that even mean?" Rogue babbled before running for the bus.

Roxie massaged Jackson's tense shoulders with one hand while she held an umbrella over them. "You're a good soul."

Jackson refrained from saying, "Don't thank me just yet." He didn't see how the entire lot of stranded travelers were getting out of the valley at the rate the rising water was taking over Interstate 5. But, dammit, he would do his best.

Not because he was a good soul, but because of his compelling desire to save the siblings. And Roxie.

Chapter 25

Luna Lewis stood at the edge of the flooded interstate with about a dozen other stranded travelers as the water crept higher, three inches higher, since the last time she had checked the slowly disappearing pothole. Once the water covered the pothole . . . it was time to freak.

Surprisingly, the travelers had amicably agreed to have one person from each vehicle draw straws, or in their case, pine needles, to decide the order. Something that wouldn't have gone down so smoothly in urban areas. Meanwhile, people constantly ran to their vehicles to grab something or move it to the top of the slight incline, which she had already done with the bus.

Rogue stumbled toward them, lugging a bulky backpack and the Jackery while Handyman Jack followed somberly with his duffel.

"You brought clothes, right?" Luna questioned.

"Duh," Rogue grunted.

After much deliberation, Luna had reluctantly left behind her coveted Bebe suitcase for her durable and practical rucksack, which she had packed with survival gear, even stuffing her camo cargo pants pockets with granola bars and two thermoses of water.

She wanted to remain as hands-free as possible. Always ready. For freaking anything. Because weird shit was happening. *Right now.* Since when did people get trapped between mudslides and washed-out bridges? On a major roadway. Maybe in some third-world country. But not in the United States.

She worried for Rogue and his delicate persona. Was this too intense for him? What about Roxie and Handyman Jack? They were old. Scratch that. "Old" was considered politically incorrect, according to the latest HR sensitivity seminar she had attended. They were required to say "olders" or "perennials." Which to her sounded even more offensive.

"Roxie, where's your bag?" Handyman Jack said as he caught up to them.

"Still on the bus," Roxie said solemnly.

"You're not taking Pixie?" Rogue chided as he goofed around, standing on one foot like a stork until he couldn't any longer and then restarted the countdown standing on the other foot.

"I have no intention of leaving my cat," Roxie countered.

"Rogue, since you have so much energy," Handyman Jack said, "why don't you help Roxie? We're up in two more boat runs. I want to stay here to stave off any trouble. If need be." His edgy tone revealed he wasn't liking their situation.

Rogue grabbed Roxie's hand. "This is crazy fun. Huh?"

"I emptied my mom's hiking backpack and left it on the bed," Luna said. "It'll be easier to carry than your suitcase. I also left out a smaller pack that will work for Pixie." Luckily, the cat was small. "Help yourself to anything you want in the closet and cupboards."

"Yep, dry clothes are a must," Handyman Jack said. "We can change once we get to the shelter."

"It would be nice to get one of Railroad Park's caboose rooms. But they're probably booked by now," Roxie said before speed-walking off to the bus with Rogue.

Luna had a sinking feeling Roxie might have to get used to wearing wet clothes. They all would. She followed Handyman Jack to the crowd as the boat loaded with the next five totally drenched passengers: a mom and her two teenage sons, and a young couple with an annoying poodle that barked incessantly at everyone and everything.

As if the poodle had eavesdropped into Luna's thoughts, Gigi went into a piercing high-pitched barking fit.

The burly boatman stood in the small motorboat with hands planted on his hips. "Ain't no yappy dogs on my Crawdaddy."

Great, here comes the altercation. It had been too easy. Too nice.

From out of nowhere, wooziness swooped over Luna, like she had just ridden one of those intolerable carnival spinning rides she loathed. She hunched over with hands on her knees to keep from passing out. *I must need a blast of carbs.* She forced herself to regroup by focusing on a spot on the road, waiting for the feeling to subside. That was when she noticed the pothole—had disappeared. Completely submerged.

She wanted to tell Handyman Jack as she struggled to stifle her nausea, but everyone was embroiled in a heated dispute with the boatman. She fought for control, unaccustomed to *not* being in control of every aspect of her life. Until the fire had decimated her childhood home.

Luna lost her balance. "Handyman Jack—" Her plea was lost to the escalating argument about the stupid dog. Instead of freaking out further, she pulled out a granola bar for a fast injection of carbs and focused on the argument.

"What the hell?" One of the men shoved the boatman into the water. A group of them flash-mobbed the boat and crammed inside.

"Hold on just a goddamned minute," Handyman Jack intervened. "Use some common sense, the boat can't take more than six."

She had never seen Handyman Jack so pissed. The boat spluttered off with the boatman swimming after it. All the mud and limbs in the water must have changed the boatman's mind. By the time Handyman Jack looked her way, she had recovered from her embarrassing episode of weakness.

Handyman Jack shook his head fiercely. "Can you believe that?" He didn't wait for her reply and turned to help the boatman out of the water.

"I'll get them shitheads," the red-faced boatman shrieked before stomping off to his truck where the water had breached the tires.

"Luna, you all right? You're lookin' a 'lil peaked." Handyman Jack had finally noticed.

"Sure," she uttered, munching her last bite slowly, forcing herself back to normal, even if it was only mind over matter.

Meanwhile, the two of them stood at the edge of the waterline and watched the boat flail across the rapid-like waters.

"Any ideas?" Handyman Jack asked gravely, as if delving into her brain.

Then it hit her. "Fuuuck, who's bringing back the boat?"

The rest of the crowd went from applauding the boat-jackers to hysterical yelling.

"Please, oh please," Luna implored. "Bring back the boat."

The crowd began an eerie chant, "Bring back the boat. Bring back the boat. Bring back the boat . . ."

When the boat made it to the north end of the interstate, the boat pirates hopped out. And ran for a white truck. They jumped into the back of the truck and had the nerve to wave back at them as the truck raced off, abandoning the boat along with everyone stuck on the south end of the washed-out bridge.

A gasp from behind sent Luna spinning around to find a wide-eyed Roxie in a pair of Mom's skinny jeans and Peruvian poncho—staring in apparent disbelief.

Roxie clutched the smaller backpack to her chest. "What's happening?"

"Those SOBs mobbed the damn boat," Handyman Jack huffed.

"They just left us? You fuckeroos!" Rogue wailed with brandished fists punching the sky.

Another dizzy episode attacked Luna and seemed to set her belly on fire. She sort of bobble-headed around. "Uh, earthquake?" But nobody was paying attention to her. Weird, it was like a shimmering translucent cloud of billowing toxic energy hovered around them. The image reminded her of those heat-like waves of a highway mirage wavering over the road in the distance on a hot day.

Had she caught something when falling into the muddy water earlier? No. It was too soon for that. Right? She hadn't been sick since that mild breakthrough Coronavirus case she had been diagnosed with years ago. Now the news hinted the H5N2 bird flu could be the next super-spreader: as in Disease X. She certainly didn't have time to get sick. Not in this crazy weather, not with the most important job interview of her life . . .

She might as well be honest with herself. There would be no interview. The FBI was looking for her. Despite her parents' overzealous activism, they were good people. Trying to do the right thing. It was the rest of society whom she blamed. For being idiots! For not giving a shit about the planet. If the corporations and government officials had made the wise decisions, people like her parents wouldn't have to risk everything. Why shame people for not buying eco-friendly products when non-eco-friendly products should be banned. Period.

Frustration strangled her throat. Luna wanted to scream at everyone for not doing their part to save the climate. Earth. Humanity! But, after that crazy surreal dream years ago, she had realized saving the planet was pointless. They had surpassed the tipping point. Still, the climate collapse wasn't supposed to happen for a while.

Not this week.

The boatman tapped his horn before jumping out of his truck. He motioned to Handyman Jack. "Over chere."

"What do you think he wants?" Luna muttered.

"'Bout to find out." Handyman Jack strutted for the truck.

Luna kept his pace, feeling back to normal. When they reached the truck, the boatman was digging through a large toolbox in the bed of the truck. He pulled out one of those atrocious orange lifejackets that had to be from the last century.

"Aw, I know what you have in mind," Handyman Jack said. "You're gonna need a longer rope."

"Wait, you're swimming across?" Luna was dumbstruck. "That's so stupid . . ."

"Cher, if I wanted me a nagging wife, I woulda done been hitched by now." The boatman strapped on the cumbersome life-jacket. "All I need is my Crawdaddy!"

"In case you haven't noticed," Luna said to no one in particular, "the water's risen a foot in the past fifteen minutes."

Handyman Jack flashed her a "zip-it" scowl.

I get it. The boat was their only opportunity out of there. In a few minutes, they'd have to retreat to the bus. And probably camp on the roof. What if the flooding swept the bus away? She shook away the illogical thought.

Roxie and Rogue walked hand and hand toward them. Rogue was a sweetie when he wasn't stuck trying to fix all the wrongs of this cruel world. Luna smiled inwardly, unexpectedly missing the good times they used to have. Before the world had gone insane in every way possible.

The beardy boatman tossed a rope down to Handyman Jack.

"If I help you," Handyman Jack said, unwinding the rope. "I have to know you're coming back for us. With Crawdaddy." Handyman Jack's stare seemed to hold the outraged man in check.

Luna understood the boatman's anger; she'd be hella pissed, if a mob had stolen her boat during a life-or-death situation.

"Hey, I may be a greedy sonuvabitch. But I ain't leavin' no-body to drown." He jumped off the tailgate and splashed into the water-covered road. It had flooded several more inches. But the rain had stopped. The water must be flowing down the canyon's intricate network of streams.

"Well, then, let's do this the safest way possible." Handyman Jack looped one end of the rope through the man's belt loops.

Without a word, they trekked through the water-covered interstate until the water reached their knees.

"I'm not liking the current," Handyman Jack grumbled.

"Hey, look! The boat's escaping." Rogue was the first to notice.

The boatman plunged in and swam for his boat. Handyman Jack went farther into the rising waters, giving the boatman more line. But Luna was pretty sure the rope wasn't long enough.

"Heavens," Roxie pleaded to the sky, "please help that crazy man."

The current swept the boatman and the boat sideways—westwardly across the road. Then, the boatman ran out of tether. Missing the boat by a few meters. He turned to them and yelled something.

With questioning, tortured eyes, Handyman Jack asked what he should do.

The boatman held up a large knife. He must have cut the rope, for the boatman disappeared into the water.

"We gotta do—something!" Rogue yelled.

"For cryin' out loud, stop your blathering," Handyman Jack said. "I wouldn't count him out just yet."

Roxie laughed. "That man's too ornery to drown."

And so, they stood there, in knee-deep water that soon breached their waists. By the time it reached Rogue's neck, it was time to make a hard decision. Because there was no sign of the boatman.

"We should go to the bus." Luna's monotone voice hid her despair. "We can hang out on the roof under umbrellas if we have to. We have a pup tent—"

A high-pitched whine seemed to pierce her ears. *Is that a motor?*

They turned around in unison to see the boat heading toward them with the boatman waving like a lunatic.

"That lucky SOB!" Handyman Jack shouted. He did a little jig before bear-hugging Roxie, which must have taken his wannabe girlfriend by surprise based on her flushed cheeks.

They sloshed as far into the rising waters as they could walk and waited for the boat while the remaining travelers who had retreated to their vehicles rushed to the boat launch area.

"Hot damn!" The hairy boatman wrung out his crazy-long beard. "Told ya I ain't leavin' without my Crawdaddy."

But the others were coming their way. Luna didn't want to wait another second, even though technically it wasn't their turn. Or was it? Well, they were there, next to the boat. The others stood at the ever-rising waterline.

Handyman Jack didn't waste any time talking. He helped Roxie and Pixie in first while Rogue tumbled into the boat headfirst. The boatman helped Luna in, and then they all helped an exhausted Handyman Jack into the boat.

"What did you say your name was?" Handyman Jack asked.

"Leroy LaFleur. Captain of my own personal Cajun Navy."

"Captain LaFleur"—Handyman Jack clapped his back—"one day, let's you and me reminisce about this over a round, hell, a pitcher of beer. And a steak dinner to boot. On me."

"I'm a holdin' ya to it." Leroy LaFleur whooped to the sky when it started raining. Again.

"I left the Jackery in the backseat of your truck," Rogue wailed into the wind. But nobody seemed to notice or care.

The raging creek was dangerous to navigate in such a small boat. Leroy managed to keep the boat pointed in the right direction. A low-frequency rumbling resonated within Luna's chest. That strange wooziness befell her again. But this time, they all must have noticed the rumbling when everyone including Leroy exchanged harried glances.

The boat rocked from side to side, waves splashing into the boat.

"Another mudslide?" Roxie bellowed.

"Over there." Rogue pointed to a wall of muddy debris cascading down the eastern canyonside. Rushing straight toward them.

"Captain, can't you make this thing go faster?" Handyman Jack's wavering shout had everyone staring at the inundation barreling closer as it took down the innocent trees in its path.

"Hell yeah." Captain LaFleur revved the engine.

A wave of debris burst into the water, staining it putrid-brown. Handyman Jack quickly brushed aside a massive log with the oar. But there was only one oar.

"Get yo-selves ready to jump on out," Captain LaFleur shouted, bearing straight for the north end of the interstate. "I be riding in hot, beaching it."

Luna tried gauging the rate of the landslide with the boat's speed. But the landslide was winning, looming larger. Toward them.

"Faster!" Rogue roared.

Roxie kept her head down and seemed to be praying. Luna struggled with her nausea when realizing the landslide must be affecting her equilibrium. Odd, but possible. She'd pay more attention if it happened again.

"Watch out!" Handyman Jack yelled as a treetop sideswiped the boat. Knocking the boat's helm so that it pointed west.

"C'mon, Crawdaddy," the boatman bellowed. Captain LaFleur let out a string of French-sounding curse words and defied the laws of physics as he forced the boat in a northeasterly direction.

A honking horn had them looking at the other side of the washed-out bridge. The guy with the white truck had returned. For them!

Miracles really did happen.

But they hadn't reached safety yet. The current was stronger than the boat's small engine could handle. They veered westbound sideways in a raging river littered with dangerous sharp branches. They couldn't jump out and swim for the shore. Not in all that crud. And the wall of mud and trees continued tumbling and rumbling toward them.

The guy with the truck was hollering something. So close, but too far. He pulled out a board, like a two-by-four from the truck's top rack and stepped to the edge of the water. Then he tossed it toward the boat.

Instinctively, Luna grabbed the board.

"Good thinking, use it to turn us in the right direction," Handyman Jack said.

She leaned over the edge with Roxie and Rogue hanging on to her legs. She used the board as a rudder, taking them out of their westward drift. Between her, Captain LaFleur, and Handyman Jack, they forced the boat to the other side of the impromptu river.

"When da boat hits pavement, jump on out before da wall of mud takes us out," Captain LaFleur grunted in a gritty voice, a voice that totally fit his ruggedness.

"You heard the man. Jump out and swim. Or run. Whatever you can do. To get to that truck," Handyman Jack demanded.

What about Roxie; she couldn't exactly run. Not with her cat. "Roxie, give me the pack with Pixie. I'll stuff it inside my jacket. Rogue, just freakin' run. And don't look back. I'm serious!" Luna would never forgive herself if something happened to him.

"Yeah, okay." His solemn compliance revealed his terror.

"Roxie, dear," Handyman Jack seemed to say earnestly, "don't you worry none. I gotcha."

A spark of energy seemed to flash between Roxie and Handyman Jack. Or had it been merely a spark from an optical migraine? Reality had lost all boundaries.

"Ohhh," Roxie groaned. "Thank heavens, we dropped off Cora and the baby in Redding."

"Aw shee-it, it's a gainin' on us," Captain LaFleur shrieked.

The wall of mud loomed feet away. But dry land was seconds away. The boat jolted upon contact with the road, sliding roughly to a stop. They jumped out like adrenaline junkies on a survivalist show.

The guy with the truck grabbed Rogue, who was the fastest, even with his bulky go-bag. Luna and the cat were a fast second. She turned around to find Handyman Jack and Roxie several feet behind. The determination etched on their faces belied their ages: not feeble as society mocked. Perhaps condemning perennials for no longer providing value to society was yet another big ugly lie of the times—for Luna recognized their lust for life.

Luna planted her feet on the road and reached out to Roxie as Handyman Jack helped Roxie to the road. The crazy captain was back in the water, apparently trying to remove a mangled tree limb wedged in the motor.

"Leroyyy!" Rogue screeched. "Watch out . . ."

Captain LaFleur vanished. The massive debris flow devoured him and the boat seconds before the edge of the landslide knocked Luna, Roxie, and Handyman Jack to their knees.

With shaky knees, Luna forced herself to her feet. Finally, the three of them, with Roxie in the middle, sloshed to the truck. Totally drenched. All Luna wanted was to take a long, hot shower to wash away the itchy mud already caking to her skin.

"Is everyone okay?" the man with the truck called out.

"I've been better," Handyman Jack retorted. "If you don't mind, let's wait a few minutes for the Captain, God rest his soul."

No one said a word. Not even the loco cat stuffed inside her jacket made a sound.

Time seemed to stand still as Luna tried to make sense of the extreme weather events they had somehow endured the last week. It was truly a miracle they had survived. But her heart guilted over losing Captain LaFleur like that. Even if he was a jerk—had been. The man had saved their lives.

She empathized with the people waiting for the next boat trip . . . Well, she hadn't locked the bus. They'd figure it out. There was still food in the cupboards. And plenty of water.

The rain just kept pouring down on them.

"We'd better get to shelter," Handyman Jack eventually said. "Captain LaFleur is probably halfway to Redding by now by way of the Sacramento River. Looking for that damn boat."

Before Luna realized it, the truck stopped on Interstate 5, where several huge military tents had been erected in the middle of the freaking interstate. She panned the horizon just as a break in the low clouds revealed a glimpse of a rocky spiral-like structure.

That's Castle Crags. I know exactly where we are. She mentally prepared her next plan of action.

Chapter 26

SunFlower BlueStone squinted tighter in an attempt to distinguish the road ahead from the darkening sky. If not for the dashboard's LED clock glaring 2:00 p.m., she would've thought it was early evening. Meanwhile, she was stuck in stop-and-go traffic with thousands of other vehicles apparently fleeing north. Even the southbound side of Interstate 37 had two coned-off lanes of traffic going north.

Curious to verify the time, she grabbed the cell phone from the Faraday pouch. The phone immediately rang, giving her heart chakra a jolt. Who was calling on the burner phone Devin had given her for this impossible mission?

"Hello?" she questioned.

"Where are you?" asked the panicky voice.

It definitely wasn't Devin. It must be one of the activists she had failed to connect with. "I think you have the wrong number." SunFlower breathlessly awaited the code message response.

"This is Starlite Summers. You didn't pick me up in Cassadaga."

"Sorry, the weather—" An excruciating headache descended upon SunFlower. The visual of a crime scene map dotted with an array of red push pins filled her mind. The pain in her head intensified, as if the push pins pierced into her brain.

Crap. The woman hadn't said the correct code phrase. *A trap!* Quickly, she shut off the phone and put it back inside the pouch. According to the always-paranoid Devin, the Faraday pouch blocked cell and Wi-Fi signals, preventing anyone from tracking her. Until she had removed it . . .

The proverbial "they" were on to her. She would have made an awful spy. Surely, no one could find her now, not amongst the evacuation. Not in this horrific weather.

She inched up another two feet to the rear bumper of the car in front of her and then pulled out the folder crammed with documents from under the seat. Starlite Summers was not on the list.

Once again, all lanes were at a standstill. And the gas tank needle hovered over the quarter tank mark. At this rate, she wasn't making it to the airport or a hotel, as the interstate seemed to sink based on the rising waters lapping at the tires of the vehicles around her. How long until the vehicles started stalling?

"Where in the Goddess are you, Prudy?" SunFlower cried out. "I need your help . . ." Her spirit guide seemed to have abandoned her.

SunFlower forced back her tears. She would get through this. At the very worst, she'd be stuck at an evacuation center for a few days awaiting the flood waters to recede. That was all. *Think positive thoughts.*

"*SunFlower?*" Prudy's voice finally found her.

"Where have you been?"

"*I was summoned elsewhere,*" Prudy said.

"Can't you see the situation I'm in? I'd say my predicament takes priority over whatever you've been doing," SunFlower chastised. "What are my options? The road's flooding. I'm never making it to higher ground. Not with all these people in my way."

SunFlower didn't like the way that approaching stormfront looked. "Prudy, are you still here? I demand you, advise my best option."

"*SunFlower, I regret to inform you . . .*" There was a long pause. "*First and foremost, I apologize for not being the most amicable spirit guide.*"

That was the understatement of the century. Odd, Prudy never apologized for anything.

"Very well. Should I continue to the airport or try to go west or what?"

"*'Tis not for me to say. The timeline we were devoted to no longer exists.*"

"What are you talking about?" She pulled up another foot. But the sky was so dark. "Should I take the next exit and go west?" Why had the state trooper told her to go north? Evidently, Interstate 37 served as a major hurricane evacuation route. She'd much prefer the country roads. It took longer, but she didn't have to deal with the traffic. She couldn't think straight with all the confusion and fear the evacuees harbored. "Prudy, are you listening?"

"*All I am allowed to disclose—our mission has been nullified.*"

"I know that. I'll tell Devin I'm simply not suitable for such clandestine undertakings. He'll have to send someone else to secure his endangered activists."

Whoa, can the sky get any darker? People were getting out of their cars, staring at the sky, taking pictures or videos like they were having a block party in the middle of the road, despite the rising waters.

"*To be more precise,*" Prudy said, "*our cosmic mission has come to an abrupt termination. The global leaders, including the last president of your united territories, have detrimentally altered the timeline.*"

The last president? Last, as in the previous president? Or last, as in there would be no more American presidents? Her body broke out in a cold sweat. *No-no-no.* Prudy was messing with her again.

Struggling to regain control of her body, mind, and soul, Sun-Flower sluggishly placed heavy arms on the steering wheel, as if they weighed a hundred pounds. The jabbing of pins assaulted her third eye again and seemed to burrow into her head, scrying for information. Information she refused to provide. She'd never reveal Devin's network, cultish or not, for together they had saved hundreds of activists and lightworkers.

"Prudy, what's happening…" But the words stuck in her throat. She couldn't even summon Prudy in her mind. As if the unwelcomed force had taken control of her.

Mentally, she kept fighting back the intruder. "Prudy, help?" SunFlower finally squeaked out.

"*Your lifetime has served its purpose,*" a familiar voice whispered into her mind. "*The Cosmic Collective Consciousness is grateful for your noble contribution.*"

SunFlower refused to accept the hostile message.

"*As the natives say—game over,*" her cocky spirit guide blurted.

"Prudy, what's wrong with you? Did the storm's intensity make you go mad?" It was the only thing SunFlower could think of. Sure, Prudy could be selfish, impetuous, and overbearing, but not psycho.

"Holy crap!" The sky turned a bizarre greenish hue. The image of a ginormous vortex filled her vision. Prudy did have an annoying habit of messing with her head when she didn't get her way. Maybe she should have driven straight to Sedona, instead of seeking refuge in San Antonio. Had SunFlower unwittingly altered the timeline by failing her mission?

"Prudy, explain exactly what you mean." SunFlower's eyes flung open despite the centrifugal force that seemed to force down her eyelids. Aw, but the vortex loomed ahead. Spinning larger and larger.

Despite her distress, an unexpected wave of peacefulness swept over her.

"*SunFlower, 'tis I, Saint Germain. We are grateful for your dedication. Nonetheless, you are being summoned to rebegin your Earthling soul-journey.*"

Anger melted into confusion. Saint Germain had only visited her on rare monumental occasions, she pondered with eyes glued to the funnel cloud traveling alongside the interstate maybe a hundred miles away. Or was it twenty? It was impossible to tell. Moreover, she rationalized this was merely a lucid cosmic vision. Until her solar plexus started convulsing.

"*Do not resist. We wish to comfort you in your passing,*" the voice claiming to be Saint Germain consoled.

"Prudy, shut your mouth. Or I'm disowning you," SunFlower warned before regaining composure. Although, she doubted canceling one's spirit guide was as easy as canceling a frenemy in the Metaverse.

"*That is not me,*" Prudy cackled.

SunFlower's heart sank.

"*SunFlower, precious lightworker of All That Is, listen carefully. 'Tis time to release this lifetime . . .*"

"I will do no such thing. I'll have you know, I've been told by several benevolent beings I'm living to ninety-four. So, go away, whoever you are."

Constant lightning flashes accosted the sky, ripping the sky into jagged fragments—revealing the approaching horror. Was that humongous tornado coming her way?

"*The Cosmic Collective Consciousness regrets to inform your soul-contract has been, shall I say, renegotiated.*"

"*You have been deactivated. I am free at last,*" Prudy prattled.

"It doesn't work like that. I have some say in the matter . . ." SunFlower dared to argue, Saint Germain or not. She had the karmic right to understand what was happening. Her body tried to float to the car's ceiling, but she fought it, squeezing her root chakra with all her will. "I have not completed my soul-mission. Furthermore, I do not consent to this—this trickery."

"*I shall provide a brief explanation, dear one. Our timeline has been meddled with. We need our faithful lightworkers for one final attempt to rescue Humanity from—itself.*"

SunFlower wondered if this was some sort of a hallucination, because that tornado was certainly getting closer, and this vision couldn't possibly be real. "I no longer wish to continue this conversation." There, she said it. She would simply deny its existence, whomever or whatever was communicating with her.

Saint Germain's enthralling voice boomed into her mind, "*As we speak, We are recruiting our veteran spiritual warriors for the final battle. To save Humanity.*"

The normally calm and collected SunFlower couldn't steer the car as her hands evaporated in front of her very eyes. As in gone. Yet there was no blood. No pain. Just an unstoppable pressure pulling her up to the car's ceiling.

"No! I won't go like this. I tried so hard. To do all that is asked, sacrificing—everything! For a benevolent Humanity on Earth."

"*This We know, dear SunFlower. You have sacrificed greatly. 'Tis with our deepest sympathies We require your help once again for Humanity's future-self reveals We lost this round.*"

"How could we lose?"

"*We shall be better equipped this time,*" the voice said. "*We have gained pivotal allies and rooted out cosmic traitors. Prepared to re-embark our arduous mission.*"

It hit her like an anvil. "You mean, I have to be reborn? It took me a flippin' thirty-six years to figure out I was even on a spiritual quest. Because you realize, by not permitting lightworkers to remember our said soul-contracts and prior lives, we spend most of our 3D lives on this plane trying to find ourselves. You really should do something about that." No wonder the good guys always lost. When they were required to follow the impossible code of cosmic law, whereas the bad guys did whatever the hell they wanted. "Malevolent beings don't have a conscience. Hasn't the Cosmic Collective Consciousness figured that one out by now?"

"*Yes, yes, We understand. Nevertheless, We remain bound by Cosmic Law. This time, our lightworkers shall be fast-tracked, if you will, with full disclosure of what is expected along with the prophesied outcomes. If We prevail, the healing starts with Generation Beta, as in a second chance.*"

SunFlower didn't know quite what to think, but she was more concerned with evaporating into the ceiling and, *holy crap*—that tornado was barreling straight toward the crammed interstate. Panic ensued. The evacuees trapped on the road created impromptu lanes. Getting stuck in the flood waters.

The power transformers off in the distance lit up the skyline like humongous sparklers, revealing the proximity of the tornado. Swarms of people abandoned their vehicles and ran for an Exxon gas station on the frontage road paralleling the interstate. Women carrying babies, mothers and fathers hurrying their children, older people—all running for shelter.

Tennis-ball-sized hail pummeled them. They weren't making it to shelter, she envisioned. The scene so soul-shattering she had to turn away from it.

"If I may be so bold," SunFlower faltered, "I have a request."

"*State your demand quickly*," the annoyed voice said.

SunFlower swallowed hard. "I demand to renegotiate my soul-contract. I wish to reincarnate on a benevolent planet in an enlightened society. I refuse to return to the ugly hate of Humanity!"

Prudy's hideous laughter sent SunFlower into an uncontrollable giggling fit. At least it would be written in the Akashic Records that she had died laughing as her backside dissolved into the ceiling.

The entire sky seemed to rotate above her. Breathtakingly deadly. A whirling rush of wind sent the Mustang airborne, along with what had to be hundreds of other vehicles caught in the vortex of the mile-wide tornado. Pleas from the thousands of hapless souls seem to swirl around her, not finding her, not soul-crushing her. Ameliorated with an unknown serenity, SunFlower became one with the fantastical whirlwind, as if aware of each and every molecule of her body becoming one with the storm. No longer fighting it, she allowed herself to soar to the heavens.

Ah, the peacefulness. Where she longed to exist. For eternity. Until a sudden vision of a crashing helicopter took over her mind.

A vivid image of Rogue's despondency mortified her. *Damn,* was it the Cosmic Collective Consciousness's attempt to man-ipulate her into returning to this hateful planet?

But she had too much love in her heart to abandon Rogue.

That was when she made the rash decision. "*Wait*!" She had lost her voice, and so she pleaded mentally, "*I wish to be Rogue's spirit guide—is that possible*?" What if she had offended Saint Germain?

"*Well chosen.*" Saint Germain's loving face replaced Rogue's. "*The Cosmic Collective Consciousness shall consider your final re-quest.*"

Had SunFlower just made an irrevocable mistake? She couldn't fathom how her heart could endure another tormenting lifetime on Earth. Even as a spirit guide. But even more unfathomable was deserting such a gentle soul as Rogue to the harsh reality of Earth's tenuous future.

Chapter 27

Roxie Ramirez ignored Jackson when he fussed with helping her out of the back of the pickup truck as she gawked at the rather intimidating military tents perched in the middle of the interstate. Not that the tents scared her; it was the overall implications they signified.

Three men in military fatigues scurried toward them with a stretcher. "Who's in need of medical attention?" the man with lieutenant bars on his cap asked.

The men, apparently soldiers, seemed to think she was the one hurt. Roxie shooed them away. "I'm fine." Her wavering voice belied her confidence. Naturally, she was rather shaken from that perilous boat ride and hadn't been able to stop fretting over the captain's fate. But, seeing the military scuttering around had her concerned that something other than the severe weather was amiss.

Did the FBI sic the National Guard on them? Paranoia at its worst, Roxie mused, dismissing the absurd thought. They wouldn't need tents for that.

"Don't go stubborn on me," Jackson started in. "All of us should get checked over, blood pressure and whatnot. Any scratches could get infected."

Roxie shrugged. He was probably right. "I will if you will. Mind you, I'm perfectly capable of walking. Without any help," she rattled off, calling rank on him and the soldiers.

"This way, ma'am," one of the soldiers said with a smirk.

"Hold up," the lieutenant ordered. "Any weapons?"

Thank goodness Luna had left the rifle. "Just my poor cat." Roxie pointed to the roving pack slung over her shoulder. That didn't make any sense. They must think she had gone bonkers.

"Not an issue. As long as you keep it contained. As in out of sight," the lieutenant clarified. "We don't have any kennels."

"Before we forget," Jackson said, stroking his shaved-off mustache. "There're still some people stuck on the other side of Interstate 5 a few miles back. It was flooding fast when we caught the last boat ride out of there."

"We are aware of the stranded civilians," the lieutenant said. "Once our high-water vehicles return, we'll deploy a team there."

"I can't believe the Army National Guard's like right here." Rogue ogled. "I wanna take a selfie with that dude over there with the huge gun—"

"Rogue," Roxie said sternly, "don't you go pestering them. They have a job to do." *Heavens, why do they have their guns out?*

"See the sign?" The lieutenant pointed to a tiny sign on the tent. "No selfies!"

Rogue kicked at a lone pebble on the road. "I don't have a phone anyway," he muttered.

"Surprised they activated the National Guard so quickly," Jackson said. "Woulda thought the California State Guard handled this sort of thing."

"Yeah, for a rainstorm?" Luna questioned.

"This is no ordinary rainstorm," the lieutenant said. "According to the National Weather Service, we're in for an unknown number of severe storms lined up to slam the Pacific Northwest in what we're calling Storm X."

"Thank heavens. It'll put out the fires in Southern California," Roxie said, finally glad to find someone with information.

"No, ma'am," the lieutenant said, "with zero containment and over ten million acres burned—"

"But Palm Springs is fine," Roxie said.

"Ma'am, I regret to inform the inland areas, including Palm Springs, were devastated," he said without the slightest hint of emotion.

Roxie's heart wrenched. All she could do was hold on to the hope her dear sister, Rosa, had made it out in time.

Jackson put a comforting arm around her shoulder. "No doubt, the Guard's helping out there as well."

"Due to the catastrophic weather events inundating our country at present, the Army National Guard has been activated in all fifty states."

"How's that?" a befuddled Jackson quizzed.

"We've got hurricanes in the east and south, which is spurring unprecedented tornado outbreaks and tremendous flooding. Emergency personnel are overtaxed. Basically, everyone has been ordered to shelter in place or evacuate if in a fire or flood zone."

"Whoa, the Monster-storm of the Millennium is finally here. And I left the f'n camcorder on the bus," Rogue blurted as if impressed and deflated at the same time.

"But, what are you guys doing *here*?" Luna pressed.

The lieutenant gave Luna a disapproving once-over before answering. "Just following orders, ma'am."

Luna, Rogue, Jackson, and Roxie stopped in mid-step. That time, the lieutenant hadn't sounded so convincing. Of course, the military wasn't required to disclose the truth to civilians.

"In all actuality," the lieutenant said after the awkward moment, "due to the extreme weather events, we're conducting a multi-branch training exercise. Taking advantage of the—situation. To test new equipment and the newbies."

There it was again; the untruth in the lieutenant's voice resonated within her. Something was off. And she didn't know what. Never in her sixty-something years had she witnessed a military command post commandeer a major roadway. Perhaps they were expecting civil unrest. Like looting. Not that anyone would be able to get very far.

"So, we get to stay in an awesome tent?" Rogue exclaimed. The harsh reality hadn't sunk in for the boy. They only called in the Army National Guard when things were beyond bad.

"For one night. According to the forecast, there's a break in the band of storms. Giving us the green light to airlift civilians to a designated shelter on higher ground. The evac's scheduled for zero nine hundred, depending on tomorrow's forecast. However, the situation remains fluid. Stay sharp. Be ready to evac at a moment's notice."

"You takin' us to Redding?" Jackson inquired.

"That info is not available at this time. The Sacramento River is already flooding its banks in the valleys like Redding and Sacramento. Several dams are at critical flood stage."

"This is so crazy," Rogue rambled. "Do we get to eat real MREs?"

The lieutenant barely smiled. "The mobile mess hall didn't make it. So, MREs, granola bars, and fruit are all we have."

Roxie instantly lost her appetite at the thought of eating an MRE.

"Here we are." The lieutenant stopped in front of a tent with the familiar emblem of a red cross on a white background. "Sergeant Thompson will take care of you," the lieutenant said briskly, as if relieved to hand them off to the medical unit. And he marched off.

Roxie quickly scanned the rectangular medical tent. She recognized several people from the interstate getting examined. An older man was having an EKG from what she could tell with the mess of censors taped to his body. Another person apparently had a broken arm. A middle-aged woman with two bawling kids seemed to be in the middle of a full-blown anxiety attack requiring oodles of attention.

A female nurse or medic with an armful of clipboards approached. "Please disclose your injuries, medical conditions, medications. . ." she said in a robotic voice.

Roxie, Jackson, Luna, and Rogue shook their heads no. They were a healthy lot.

"Outstanding. However, we're required to document your vitals. If you will just complete these release forms." The medic handed out the clipboards. "I'll take you now. If you give me verbal permission?" she said to Roxie.

"Heavens, do I look that bad?" *I must look like a drowned rat with blue hair*, Roxie mused.

The medic barely cracked a smile. "I need to process your group before they arrive with the campers."

"Campers?" Jackson asked.

"We're waiting for the high-water convoy to return from Happy Camp. Hundreds of civilians in the outlying areas are trapped."

The medic's no-nonsense attitude made Roxie more tense. The gravity of the current weather situation hit her again. Roxie sat down in the appointed chair and resigned to being "processed" while the not-so-gentle medic wrapped the blood pressure cuff around her upper arm.

Roxie spent more time worrying what name to write on the release form than her blood pressure. She glanced back uncertainly at Jackson and Luna.

"One thirty-seven over seventy-seven," the medic informed.

"That's great, considering. Sheesh, we barely made it. A landslide nearly took us out—" Roxie stopped. It was apparent the medic didn't have time to chat.

The medic grabbed Roxie's clipboard and filled out the vitals chart, including blood pressure, heart rate, oxygen rate, and temperature, and then handed it back to her. "Don't forget to include any allergies and return the forms here." She pointed to a makeshift desk overflowing with folders and paperwork.

"Oh," Roxie started, before the medic turned away. "I heard there was a hurricane on the east coast. Is it near Delaware?"

"I'm not authorized to disclose such information." The medic's lips hardened.

Tears pricked the corners of Roxie's eyes. "Excuse me," Roxie said harsher than intended. "I need to know." She wiped away a stray tear. "My brother lives there. I just found out my sister, who lives in Palm Springs, is probably—" She couldn't say "dead."

"I understand your concern. My husband's stationed at Dover AFB where the elevation is around twenty-nine feet. Yesterday they were scrambling to relocate everything they could," the medic whispered. "The last update I saw, two Cat 5s were spinning towards the eastern coastline. These hurricanes are so power-ful—they aborted the evac. It's like a weather warzone out there. Be grateful you made it here with your family. You're the lucky ones."

"Oh, I didn't realize all this was happening as well." Roxie reached out to pat her hand, noting the woman's wedding band. What if the medic had been ordered to leave her children to help others instead of her own family? It must be difficult.

"Next . . ." The medic motioned toward Jackson, Luna, and Rogue.

"That'll be me," Jackson said, rushing over.

That man had too much energy for his own good.

Rogue darted to Roxie with cockeyed brows. "So, you don't need special medical help?"

"Just because I'm—never mind. I have an awful lot of bruises. Other than that, I'm fine," Roxie insisted. Although, she could use a hot cup of coffee. Or a long nap. Either would suffice.

Luna grabbed Roxie's clipboard. "Good, you didn't complete it yet. Use an alias."

Roxie wanted to say *I'm not a complete nitwit* but held her tongue. She tried to remember if they had said anything incrim-inating. Hmm, Rogue had mentioned the bus. That wasn't good. "Damn, damn, damn, I said Rogue's name earlier."

"Fuuuck," Luna murmured.

"Did you know my name's illegal in New Zealand," Rogue butted in, "like for parents to officially name their kids?"

"How's that relevant to our situation?" Roxie snapped, rubbing her head.

"It's okay," Luna said. "Let's use similar names. Like Rosie, instead of Roxie. And I can be Lula."

"That works," Roxie said, thinking out loud. "Jackson can go by Jason. And Rogue—"

"I wanna be Ronin," he pleaded.

"It has the same scalawag ring to it," Roxie remarked playfully. "We can go by common surnames like Smith or Davis."

They quickly completed the forms. It was alarming knowing the Army National Guard might put two and two together and figure out the four of them were wanted by the FBI. Still, from the looks of it, they were inundated with rescues. With more on the way.

By the time they had all been given a clean bill of health, Jackson had claimed a section in the civilian-designated tent that was partitioned into sections, creating several rooms with symmetrically placed rows of cots topped with blankets and pillows. There had to be more than a hundred stranded people, sitting and standing around with forlorn faces, waiting. For what, she wasn't sure.

Luna was out there mingling, prying hapless soldiers for information. The young woman had even changed into rather tight jeans and a low-cut sweater while Roxie and Jackson pretended to enjoy endless rounds of Crazy Eights that Rogue had insisted on playing the past two hours. It served as a much-needed distraction.

Roxie had changed into comfy-cozy sweatpants while her two pairs of jeans dried. She couldn't wait to call it a night. Despite the constant chatter, she could sleep through anything, but she wanted to stay alert for a while. She longed to get to SunFlower's. Away from prying eyes. According to Luna, they were only about ten miles away. Close enough to walk, if only it wasn't storming.

Rogue yelled, "Over here," to Luna, who sashayed over to another soldier.

"Is she flirting with that rugged-looking soldier?" Roxie wondered aloud. It was rather odd seeing the serious young woman giggling and acting demure.

"Yuck." Rogue gagged theatrically before pantomiming a kissing session complete with exaggerated sound effects.

"Does *Lula* have a boyfriend?" Roxie asked.

Rogue shrugged. "Meh, I think she's asexual."

Jackson waved the boy off. "I'm not on a need-to-know basis."

Roxie couldn't recall what had happened to Luna's high school boyfriend. They had planned to save the world and join Greenpeace. *We all have our dreams—until real life smacks us in the face.*

"Yes! I win again!" Rogue slapped down the last card in his hand, clearly uninterested in the conversation. He kept eyeing Roxie inquisitively, like he wanted to say something.

"Rox—*Rosie*," he quickly corrected. "You never told us what happened. You know, at Walmart."

"And I don't plan to. I'm sure you can watch it all on YouTube. Eventually."

"But, but, I wanna know if you saw any—dead people. It must have been super scary."

"Sport, can't you take a hint?" Jackson rushed to her defense. "Zip it."

Roxie couldn't think about the shooting; it had been too horrific. Especially with all the events that had transpired the past week. All she could do was take it day by day and focus on her goals. Otherwise, she was sure to go off the deep end.

"Okay, let's play for money this time," Rogue decided. "You can give me IOUs until you guys can go to the bank."

Jackson rolled his eyes at her as Rogue enthusiastically gathered the cards. "Sport, I'm about played out for now. Let's see if *Lula* has any news for us."

Luna hurried toward them with a green duffel bag.

"I saw you acting all slutty with that soldier guy," Rogue berated. "Can't believe you're trying to get laid."

"Hush." Roxie was quick to reprimand.

A slight smile flickered around the corners of Luna's mouth. "He wasn't that cute. But!" She opened the duffel wide enough for them to see inside. "I snagged the forms we filled out."

"You little vixen." Roxie had to admit, Luna had the gall and the curves to succeed in such chicanery.

"Excellent," Jackson said with obvious relief.

"The newbs can't log into the database," Luna explained. "It's like their equipment's malfunctioning, or they don't know what the hell they're doing. Which means, they didn't log our info yet."

"Eventually, they'll figure out their count is off," Jackson said.

"Yeah, but it will buy us time," Luna said. "We just need to play it cool until we get out of here. Just in case they have BOLOs on us."

"BOLOs?" Roxie repeated.

"You know, be on the lookout—for fugitives," Rogue declared emphatically. "Don't you watch *NCIS*?"

"What worries me," Luna said, "I couldn't find out where they're taking us. It's like they don't know—anything. Don't take this the wrong way, but I'm hooking up with the radio guy tonight. He should have some intel."

"Slut," Rogue uttered under his breath.

"Careful," Jackson said to Rogue. "That goes for you as well, *Lula*."

"I can take care of myself," Luna carped.

"The staff sergeant monitoring the entrance, asked us for our IDs twice," Jackson said in a troubled tone. "Told him we lost them on the boat ride. But, the truth of the matter is, once they find the bus, which could be as soon as tomorrow morning, they'll likely ID it by the VIN. Vehicle Identification Number. Then, our cover's blown."

That had Roxie thinking. "They're looking for a brother and sister and two seniors . . ." Roxie pondered out loud. "What if we split up? Girls with the girls and the boys with the boys. That might help for a bit."

"But the lieutenant guy knows we're together," Rogue said.

"He knows we arrived in the truck together. However, he doesn't know we were *traveling* together," Jackson said. "And with all the chaos, it might throw off the authorities. Just long enough."

"Perfect!" Luna was the first to agree.

"What else did you get?" Rogue grabbed her duffel.

Luna snatched it back. "MREs." She quickly handed out several pouches.

"Cool." That shut up the ever-inquisitive boy while he scrutinized the MRE labels, telling them how bad the ingredients were, and how he couldn't wait to try one.

If they were leaving in the morning, they didn't need that many MREs. Then again, Luna was more tight-lipped than usual.

They gathered their belongings and separated into different partitioned sections. Poor Pixie. Once she and Luna had claimed their cots, Roxie took Pixie outside to take care of her business in a patch of weeds next to the interstate's shoulder. Despite the late hour, the area was lit up with huge portable lights. Probably for security.

A strange compelling sensation overtook her as if warning something wasn't right. With the world . . .

Chapter 28

Jackson Jones awoke to the reverberating thuds of a helicopter. *Is the evac underway so soon*? Discombobulated, he gently smacked his cheeks in an attempt to awaken from an extraordinary bout of deep sleep. Come to think of it, he hadn't slept so soundly in ages. Years. His body must have been recovering from yesterday's traumatic events.

It was ten minutes shy of 6:00 a.m. He did a quick scan of the tent to find it abuzz with startled faces as people ascended from their military-issued cots.

A sleepy-eyed Rogue popped up from under his blanket. "Now what?"

"Think our ride's here." Jackson craned for a glimpse of Roxie and Luna in their sleeping quarters on the south side of the tent. His searching eyes finally found Roxie's. And he did not like her open-mouthed, wide-eyed, beleaguering expression as she swiveled frantically from side to side.

Don't tell me that kooky cat's on the loose? In all actuality, Jackson had been surprised the stern-faced lieutenant allowed pets in the first place. Fortunately, the soldiers hadn't bothered to frisk them for weapons; they must have looked harmless. Jackson had not disclosed his revolver was stashed in a pair of dirty underwear. Having a gun might rouse suspicion, although this was one of the more conservative areas of California.

He quickly slipped on his rugged, waterproof logger boots. "Sport, why don't you get dressed and pack your belongings while I find out what's going on."

He cast another look at Roxie, torn by her silent pleas, which seemed to scream, "Something is wrong," as if he connected with her on some inexplicable level. He scrambled to the gathering crowd outside in time to see two men in suits hop off a small black helicopter. Definitely too small for a rescue helicopter. Not that he knew much on the subject.

Jackson moseyed through the crowd, watching for clues, trying to read into the situation. His nerves went into overdrive when someone exclaimed, "What's Homeland Security doing here?" Self-consciously, he flipped out the ponytail that kept getting caught under the back of his vest and quickly did an about-face.

He caught Roxie's eye as he walked to the refreshment table loaded with water bottles, fruit, and granola bars. He was busy pretending to read the granola bar wrapper when she nudged next to him and slipped him a note.

Jackson reread the note with a burst of anger. "Why would she just up and go?" The young woman was too sensible to do a boneheaded thing like that.

"She's gone," Roxie insisted. "Now *I'm* responsible for Rogue." Roxie thrust two water bottles into her backpack and then grabbed a handful of granola bars.

To say he was taken aback and outraged by Luna's blatant selfishness was an understatement. "When—"

"People, may we have your attention," a loudspeaker blared. "The evac will commence shortly. Dress quickly. And line up for roll call outside."

Hmm, that did not sound right.

Roxie threw up her hands. "I thought we weren't leaving until nine."

He hated adding to Roxie's distress, but she needed to know. "The lieutenant also mentioned to be ready at a moment's notice.

However, that's not an evac helicopter. They could be on to us." The roll call was probably to figure out the unaccounted for.

"What are we going to do?" Roxie's voice cracked.

All he could do was offer her a reassuring smile. The only thing in their favor: civilians didn't follow orders so well, as people rushed the bathrooms and snack bar. Civilians weren't used to the military's hurry-up-and-wait style. He might as well take advantage of the chaos.

Rogue hurried to the snack bar with his pack. "Someone said Homeland Security's here. Like now!" The boy blabbed louder than he should have. "Something really, really bad's about to happen. I just know it."

"Sport, I'm well aware of that," Jackson said. "We have another problem. Your sister went solo on us. Says she doesn't want to involve us any further in the situation." It was a little late for that. "She thinks she can hike to Mt. Shasta."

"Awesome!" Rogue snatched the note.

"No, it's not," Roxie scoffed. "She can't hike in this monsoon-like weather."

"You guys don't get it," Rogue said. "There's a hiking trail around here—The Pacific Crest Trail or something like that."

"Too dangerous." Roxie's words disappeared into the escalating excitement taking over the tent.

"She's an expert hiker," Rogue nattered on. "She used to hike from Castle Crags to Mount Shasta with her survivalist club every summer until she moved to Sacramento. And get this, Castle Crags is only like a mile away."

"Yes, I'm familiar with the area." Jackson nodded, trying to tug on his mustache. He kept forgetting he had shaved it off.

"Attention: we need everyone to form two orderly lines outside," the loudspeaker blared once again. "All non-military personnel report outside. Immediately."

"What should we do?" Roxie's beautiful eyes begged.

"Suppose we let this play out and whatever happens, happens. Luna has to do what she needs to do." What could they accomplish? Hell, he didn't even know what Luna's true objective was. "After all, we are not exactly criminals."

"What?" Rogue's high-pitched disapproval was drowned out by the remaining people ransacking the snack table. "You're gonna give up? On me and Luna?"

"I'm sure we can explain the entire situation as a misunderstanding of sorts," Jackson said, thinking out loud. "Initially, we were just trying to survive. And then we were caught up in the thrill of it all. Besides, you're still a kid. After the questioning—"

"Guys, guys, don't you see? 'They,'" the boy said with air quotes, "terminate the *effective* activists," Rogue whispered hauntingly. "As in murder them. 'Cause that's what they f'n do to the people they can't control. The huge corporation CEOs don't want us revealing the *inconvenient truth*."

Luna had been concerned about that as well. It must be a heavy burden for a child to cope with. "Mr. Gore, surely, you exaggerate," Jackson said lightly, keeping his eyes on the commotion at the tent's entrance. Soon, the soldiers would herd out the stragglers meandering inside the tent. But there were still several groups of people getting dressed while the bathroom lines gradually dwindled.

"For real, cross my heart, swear to die." Rogue pantomimed.

The boom of a gunshot shattered Jackson's phony persona of calmness. Screams followed.

All Jackson said as he sprinted to the tent's crowded entrance was, "Stay here. And get your packs ready." Three soldiers aimed their weapons at a man pinned to the interstate's pavement. The two Homeland Security agents were quick to respond. Perhaps the authorities had been after the man the entire time. But why not arrest the man from the get-go? Unless it was a jurisdiction issue.

"People, remain calm. Form two orderly lines," a soldier announced through a bullhorn while the unlucky evacuee was patted down and handcuffed.

A strange doomsday-like gloom descended over Jackson. As if he were being forewarned. Rogue was right. Something was happening. For one of the first times in his life, he didn't know whom he should trust. He headed back for Roxie and Rogue huddled in the far back of the tent while a dozen or so slowpokes scrambled about from the bathrooms to the snack bar and flagrantly ignored the mandatory roll call.

"Looks like they found who they were looking for," Jackson said, trying to convince himself that was the end of it.

"That means we're next! And, and, when they find us, they'll take us someplace. Like Gitmo. Torturing us to reveal the secret network of activists. That's how it works. And if we don't talk. We're—" Rogue theatrically slashed his throat, followed by gagging. Or had it been an over-the-top blood-spurting sound effect?

Jackson crossed his arms firmly against his chest. "Sport, how many of these activists do you actually know?" The kid was turning this into some Cold War spy novel.

"Uh, uh . . . I can't reveal their names. Or I'd have to eliminate you," Rogue shot back snidely.

"For Christ's sake." Jackson turned to Roxie. "What do *you* think we should do?" She could settle this once and for all. For deep down, he knew, he'd follow her to the ends of the earth.

"Jackson, this is more serious than you realize. Back when Luna was in college, I used to proofread her rather radical essay blogs before she posted them. God knows what subversive groups she associated with back then. But the things she wrote about"—she paused—"Orwellian," Roxie whispered.

"Oh, yeah, she used to blog for this underground site. Under a pen name. She gave updates on the latest activism activities. Dad was super pissed when she gave that up a few years ago. She used to be so woke. I don't understand why she stopped giving a shit . . ." Rogue said wistfully.

"I see. So, she really is considered a person of interest." It was not what Jackson wanted to hear.

The swooshing of helicopter blades filled the void of the conversation.

"So, what do you want to do?" Jackson asked Roxie point-blank.

Roxie sighed long and hard. "I guess, we can try to get out of here. Unnoticed. Mt. Shasta is only about a ten minute drive." Surely, she could handle the hike.

"Yes!" Rogue hugged her tightly.

"Well, okay then, we do it as safely as possible. Which means, no hiking through the wilderness. We couldn't even last on a bus. And when this next storm hits, we take shelter in the first place we find until it's safe to move on. Understand?" Jackson said pointedly to a grimacing Rogue.

"Last call! All civilians report outside immediately," the soldier yelled in the exasperated tone of a cat herder.

"Really wish Luna had given us an update on the weather," Jackson grumbled.

"So, are we going to find her or what?" Rogue spouted to the tent's ceiling.

"You think you can handle hiking in this brutal weather?" Jackson said to Roxie. "Until we find shelter?"

Roxie punched him in the arm. "Mister, I'm not over the hill yet. Mind you, I take daily walks on the river. Used to. I'd rather walk through a thunderstorm than get on that helicopter. Besides, where do you think they're taking everyone?"

"This is weird," Rogue butted in. "Last night I had this freaky dream. The helicopter sorta crashed—but we weren't on it."

Jackson didn't have time to talk about a silly dream. He wished he knew if Luna had pried any info from the radio man. Did she know something they didn't? Something crucial.

"So?" Rogue said impatiently.

Jackson had lived long enough to know there was no use arguing with a headstrong dame and a delusional child. "Lord, help us." Jackson pulled out his handy-dandy Buck knife. "Wait here. I'll see what's going on out back."

He slashed a gash in the tent large enough to get a view outside the back to find nothing but a convoy of parked military vehicles. No signs of any soldiers patrolling the area. Could they simply sneak down the interstate to the first exit they came to? The string of parked vehicles would provide some cover if they snuck from vehicle to vehicle. As he recalled the Railroad Park exit wasn't far off, although two exits back had been totally flooded.

Roll call had started. He didn't have time to waste hashing out the details. Because, if he used the common sense God had given him, he'd never attempt such a foolhardy escape.

Jackson slashed a longer slit in the tent and peeked outside again. "The coast is clear." *Damn, can't believe I just said that.* He spied the cat roving inside Roxie's borrowed backpack. "I'll take that off your hands."

Roxie held up her hand. "She's my cat."

"Then, we'll take turns," Jackson stated firmly. "Rogue, lead the way."

"Yes, sir!" Rogue proclaimed with the gusto of a hardcore Marine.

Jackson figured they wouldn't shoot a kid if they were busted within the first minutes of their dicey escape attempt. Hypothetically, they weren't prisoners as of yet, merely evacuees. "Sneak to that first cargo truck. Stay on the shoulder between the vehicles and the road. And stay down. Then, just go from vehicle to vehicle. In stealth mode."

Jackson swore he heard his own heart thudding over the helicopter, or was it Roxie's, as Rogue tiptoed to the interstate's shoulder.

From vehicle to vehicle.

As he and Roxie shadowed the kid's footsteps . . .

Chapter 29

Luna Lewis ran for cover under a huge sprawling, umbrella-shaped Madrone when the rumbling of a helicopter broke her concentration. She glanced at her waterproof sports watch, complete with compass and altimeter. It was the one prepper item she always carried in her purse. Just in case the shit really did hit the fan one day, and she had to hike to Mom and Dad's, using the backroads. She wasn't going to be one of those clueless urbanites stuck in the city. In that way, she had never truly forsaken her survivalist upbringing.

It's too early for the evacuation.

She pulled out the map she had swiped from a soldier's workstation while shamelessly toying with him. She needed to verify her coordinates after the risky dawn hike down the interstate off-ramp into the sporadically flooded streets of a rural neighborhood. After walking past the Railroad Park Resort entrance, she had hiked north on Crag View Drive located on the edge of the small town of Dunsmuir.

There, she tapped the map. First Street crossed the railroad tracks, and it should be up ahead. She had tried a gravelly dirt road earlier but had ended up in six inches of mud. Luna pressed her back against the Madrone, assuming the helicopter was landing at the base camp. She didn't really think the Army National Guard unit had caught on to them. Except for maybe the lieutenant, the inexperienced weekend warriors didn't seem to know what the heck they were doing. This extreme real-life weather event would give them valuable training.

She felt bad. Roxie and Handyman Jack would have to endure Rogue's ranting when he found out she had deserted him. A flirtatious conversation with an E-1 private fresh out of boot camp told her civilians were getting evacuated to Travis Air Force Base, if the base wasn't in danger of flooding. Once the civilians arrived at the military base, they would essentially be trapped there. From what she had overheard, all military bases were in lockdown. Which seemed odd for a weather event.

Yesterday evening, she had purposely caught up to Rogue and had casually reminisced about her hikes along the Pacific Crest Trail, to throw him off. Knowing Handyman Jack and Roxie wouldn't attempt following her. Realistically, *nobody* could hike those trails in what was predicted to be the severest series of storms ever to hit California in recorded history, according to the cute telecommunications guy.

If she was fast, she could hike to SunFlower's farmhouse in a few hours. Rogue, Roxie, and Handyman Jack would only slow her down. Moreover, she told herself that abandoning them was for their safety, despite wanting to confront her parents on her own terms. That meant not being so nice. Once she found out they were okay, well, she planned to stay with SunFlower until she figured out what to do with her life.

Still, she worried for Roxie and Handyman Jack. Those two had been incredibly selfless, helping without knowing what was really going on. Would they be prosecuted for aiding and abetting? As for Rogue, she didn't think the FBI or Homeland Security would prosecute a kid.

Or would they?

Luna hadn't realized how radical her parents' activism had turned. Her parents were getting older, and she had assumed they had reverted to low-key marches and lame acts of disobedience like dying water fountains blood-red or splattering renowned works of art with soup. Stupid stuff that only seemed to bring out the haters—not the actual planet lovers.

However, if for some remote reason Mom and Dad were guilty, something far more drastic than losing their homeowner's insurance must have occurred. Dad always said, "Drastic times call for drastic measures." Was civilization really that close to falling apart? Or had her parents fallen down the dystopian rabbit hole?

All she knew, like some innate sense, was the compelling need to connect with Mom and Dad. They had disappeared on her during eighth grade for two terrifying weeks. She remembered thinking it had been the end of the world back then. That they had been murdered, and she would be the next target on the hit list.

Luna studied the sky and concentrated on her hearing. There had been no signs of the helicopter for the past ten minutes. Time to trek some miles. It would help to stop thinking about those traumatic days when she had thought Mom and Dad had been murdered. When her parents had finally been released from imprisonment, looking like abused POWs, they had refused to talk about it, stating they had been forced to sign non-disclosure agreements.

According to SunFlower, Luna's social media blitz, along with her influencer friends and followers, had saved their activist-asses. But she probably couldn't save their reputations this time. Not if her parents were in any way affiliated with the data plant attacks.

Yes, there's First Street. The water didn't quite reach the top of her boots as it flowed down the canyon-lined embankment of Interstate 5 to the rural roads down to the Sacramento River. Not that the river or train tracks were visible with all the gorgeous trees lining the road. At least the trees provided cover—until she was on the tracks. Then she would be an easy target from the air.

She strutted along at an easy pace when all she wanted to do was run. Run like hell. However, running would call attention to her in the quiet neighborhood. She simply made like she belonged, disguised as a genderless resident taking a walk to scope out the storm damage. Stupid but not implausible.

The faraway echo of a gunshot sent the back of her neck quivering. "Shit!" Had they discovered her friends' identities? Once again, she took refuge against a tree trunk and listened carefully, watching for anything and everything.

A series of splashing thumps caught her attention. She panned the area with the binoculars strung around her neck. A man in a yellow slicker stacked sandbags around his porch, probably in a last-ditch effort to keep his home from flooding. Those sandbags wouldn't hold for long, not if that NOAA Severe Weather Alert she had seen was accurate.

A sudden wind whistled through the mile-high conifers, leaving the trees to sway at its mercy. The sprinkles turned into rain earlier than forecasted. Time to get to the elevated train tracks before she had to swim there. All she had to do was simply follow the tracks north. Eventually, she'd get to Mt. Shasta.

But in this wild weather and a BOLO with her picture on it, things could go screwy. Any second.

"Yes," she murmured with expectant success when two sets of railroad tracks came into view. She checked the compass bearing on the watch once again. With the low-hanging clouds and the narrow canyons, she had no landmarks to pinpoint her direction.

"What the—" Luna tromped through the partially submerged street to find a truck driving on the tracks, heading southbound several meters away. Thankfully, it had already passed the intersection. She retreated behind a utility building and spied from there, waiting for it to leave.

The truck stopped on the tracks, and a man stepped out. He appeared to be scanning a section of the tracks with a device. Must be maintenance personnel monitoring the tracks for damage. There had been an incredible amount of train derailments over the past few months. It had her wondering if it had been another activist plot. Or something more nefarious.

The whirring of a helicopter told her the evac was on. *Sorry, Rogue, Roxie, and Handyman Jack for crapping out on you guys.* Once again, she was furious with her parents for putting her in this situation. What was wrong with them? They would rather risk imprisonment for their actions. And what, leave Rogue for her to raise? This was—had been—Luna's time to live it up before the world leaders screwed over the planet. Permanently.

That's it. SunFlower will just have to raise Rogue, Luna decided. Her mother's soul-sister would make an amazing mother.

"Fuuuck!" She stopped ranting when a low-flying helicopter made its presence known. Searching for someone? If it had thermal imaging equipment, it would spot her infrared heat signature. While the guy on the tracks stared up at the helo, she sprinted to a budding oak tree. Trees disguised one's heat signature somewhat. But not enough.

She remembered the emergency blanket pre-packed in her ever-ready rucksack. She managed to unfold the mylar blanket just as the man on the tracks waved to the circling helo. Were they really searching for her so soon? Well, they wouldn't detect her heat signature under the mylar blanket.

As the helicopter circled lower, she crouched smaller against the oak with a case of buyer's remorse. She should have purchased the mylar blanket from a bona fide prepper store, like the Canadian Prepper dude. The so-called mylar blanket might not be authentic. Online sellers were riddled with fake reviews, making it hard to believe anything.

Whoosh!

The sky fell.

On her.

Rain assaulted the earth like some lethal primordial storm on an alien planet. The helicopter couldn't fly in it. She pivoted, listening. Only hearing the rain. She couldn't hike in a microburst. Sure, she could be overconfident at times, even cocky. *But I'm not a freakin' idiot.* The dilapidated house she had passed minutes ago seemed to call to her.

Desperate for shelter, she jogged toward the building, no longer worried about the guy on the tracks—instead, wondering why people lived so close to the train tracks as the apocalyptic-like rain hammered down. She hoped Rogue, Roxie, and Handyman Jack had taken the first helo ride out of there. Because there was no way in hell those tents could withstand the purplish-black mass she had seen on the Doppler radar weather map. Even the soldier she had flirted with had seemed spooked by the approaching storm's satellite image.

Blinded by the rain, Luna made it up the cracked cement steps to a dilapidated porch of a house that must have been built a hundred years ago based on the tiny outhouse building complete with sun and moon cutouts. After a quick recon, the boarded-over front door and windows were impassable without a crowbar.

However, one corner of the covered porch remained partially attached. Just wide enough for her to take shelter from the rain. She leaned heavily against the wall, slid down until her butt hit the concrete, and huddled into a ball, making herself as small as possible.

There, she waited, for the damn rain to subside—enough to continue her hike to SunFlower's farmhouse.

Chapter 30

Roxie Romero tucked the bottoms of her borrowed green cargo pants into the borrowed hiking boots, which were a tad too roomy, before sneaking down the Railroad Park exit; all the while her heart raced like a thoroughbred. Why in heavens did she think the three of them could delude the FBI and possibly even Homeland Security in the midst of these dreadful storms?

But she had an inkling as to why. She hadn't been able to endure Rogue's heartbreaking disappointment when he had thought they were giving up on him. Or perhaps, she wasn't quite ready for this fantastical misadventure, the adventure of her lifetime, to come to an end. Whatever her true motive, her aching joints weren't about to forgive her tomfoolery as she followed a restless Jackson and determined Rogue.

She cooed a lullaby to Pixie secured inside the backpack snuggly strapped to her back, expecting to run into an armed soldier any moment. The lieutenant must have realized they were missing by now, unless they were as disorganized as Luna had advised.

They had just hiked past an interstate overpass when the not-so-far-away *whup-whup-whup* of a helicopter drowned out her anxious thoughts. Jackson swung around and motioned to go back. Under the overpass she presumed, for that was the only place to hide.

They trudged back through the rising water. This was getting old. Really fast. The helicopter thudded closer as they scurried for cover. They waited on the road's shoulder beside the overpass's cemented slope and glanced around, wondering what to do. The military command post wasn't much farther down the interstate, too close for comfort.

Jackson eyed her questionably. "They might send out a search party. Think we ought to climb up and hide under the overpass beams."

"I don't see that happening," Roxie muttered under her breath. How could she climb up the cemented slope? Twenty minutes into the hike and she was already regretting her irrational decision.

"Give me the pack with Pixie," Jackson said without acknowledging her refusal. "I'll nudge you up."

She just kept shaking her head as Rogue effortlessly scaled the concrete slope. But when the roar of approaching vehicles blared louder than the helicopter, with a little help from Jackson, she found herself sitting next to a large beam covered with a flock of pigeons riding out the storm as a convoy of three military trucks slushed through the flooded road below.

The helicopter hovered next to the overpass a little too long for her liking, transforming the road into rippling waves. "Do you think they saw us?" Roxie wondered out loud.

"We'll know soon enough," Jackson grumbled.

Finally, the roar faded off.

"That's a good sign," Jackson husked. "Doubt those trucks were looking for us. Most likely the search and rescue team. Nonetheless, we better wait for those high-water trucks to return."

"Don't worry, Mrs. Romero," an excitable Rogue said. "This one super-nice soldier told me they were waiting for those super cool high-water trucks to get back."

"That's right," Roxie said. "The medic mentioned they needed to rescue stranded campers."

She wasn't looking forward to climbing down, more like sliding down on her tushy. Funny, how she ended up by the Railroad Park Resort. She and her late husband used to celebrate his birthday there every year, booking a one-night stay in one of the renovated cabooses and visiting the train museum and shops in town.

The idea popped into her mind like a proverbial light bulb above her head. "I know where Luna's going," Roxie blurted.

"Go on," Jackson encouraged.

"The railroad tracks."

"What makes you think that?" Jackson asked.

Familiar with the quaint town, Roxie explained, "Dunsmuir is Amtrak's last stop in Northern California. I should know. My late husband and I took the Coast Starlight trip numerous times. He was a train nut."

Rogue shook his head defiantly. "So . . ."

"The tracks head north to Mt. Shasta or south to Redding," Roxie shot back, matching Rogue's incredulous tone.

"Bingo," Jackson chimed in. "I assume these tracks are on an embankment, as in not at ground level?"

"For the most part," Roxie said, trying to remember.

"We're supposed to take the Pacific Crest Trail. No one will ever, ever find us there," Rogue continued, championing his cause.

"Precisely," Jackson jabbed. "All it takes is one mishap, like a mudslide. A sprained ankle . . . And we'd be stuck for days. If not worse."

"That trail," she said directly to Rogue, "is extremely difficult. I know, because I barely made it to Castle Crags some ten years ago. I wouldn't last long on the Pacific Crest Trail in this lousy weather."

"Blah-blah-blah," Rogue retorted. "You said you would—now you don't even want to try."

"Zip it!" Jackson said rather sternly. "Roxie, ol' gal, you've got me convinced. The tracks must be nearby." He rifled through his duffel. "Damn, left the map on the bus."

"The railroad tracks shouldn't be hard to find. The interstate, Sacramento River, and the rail line run through this narrow valley. If I remember correctly"—she paused to recollect—"after this off-ramp we turn left. Or is it right?"

"Logic says to head north and look for a cross street," Jackson said. "If we're lucky, we'll come across the railroad tracks."

The reapproaching helicopter sent her heart reeling.

"It's coming back for us," Rogue shouted as they crouched in a cranny under huge support beams.

Jackson cocked his head and cupped his ear. "Nope, that's a different helicopter. The rhythm's different. They must be starting the airlift. Last chance, should anyone change their mind. I won't hold it against you."

Rogue turned to her. She couldn't let him down. "I'm in this to the bitter end," she said more firmly than she felt.

"Then why are we just sitting here?" Rogue nagged.

"Not so fast," Jackson said. "Let's give those National Guard trucks time to get back."

"Whatev," Rogue spouted vehemently to the pigeons pecking at one another.

Jackson reshouldered the pack that Pixie was in. "Let's work out a plan."

Rogue rolled his eyes dramatically. "Ugh, always planning."

"Once we start out again, sport, you're in charge of combing the area for the railroad tracks with those nifty binoculars," Jackson stated with enthusiasm.

"Cool, these are Dad's super-expensive ones. He hardly ever lets me use them."

That seemed to jolt Rogue out of his grumpiness. Roxie nodded with feigned interest while the kid chattered on about the binoculars. Better to have him hyper-excited than cranky, she decided. Either way required too much energy, and she needed to conserve hers if she was walking to the city of Mt. Shasta.

Her stomach let out a loud gurgle. Jackson didn't bother stifling his laugh much to her embarrassment.

"Excuse me." Roxie patted down her pants pockets until she found the granola bars she had grabbed. "We should eat something." Hopefully it tasted better than last night's MRE.

Rogue gagged dramatically. "Those ones taste like doggy biscuits."

"We could do without the commentary," Jackson said. "Just eat it. Your stomach will thank you later."

They munched away on their bland breakfast and listened for helicopters and for the trucks to return to base camp. Meanwhile, the wind picked up considerably, blowing debris from the interstate over the overpass into the rising waters below them.

"Do you think the military will send more trucks?" Roxie worried.

"Doubt that," Jackson said after taking a swig from his water bottle. "They need to get those folks airlifted to safety. It could get ugly. Remember the snowstorm we were stuck in? I was chatting up one of the soldiers. He said the higher elevations around here got damn near thirty feet of snow."

"So?" Rogue spat out his food. "Sorry, raisins are gross."

"Well," Jackson enunciated in a trying voice, "this warmer storm will melt the snowpack. As in exponentially. No doubt, the creeks and streams flowing down the canyons and mountainsides will get inundated. The Sacramento River will be pushed to its limits. As in major flood-stage. Frankly, this is more dangerous than I anticipated." Jackson quickly dropped eye contact with her.

Did Jackson suddenly realize their folly was a huge mistake?

An eerie whooshing wind whipped through, sending the jittery pigeons into a tizzy. They babbled about with ruffled feathers as if blaming each other for the disturbance. Without warning, torrents of rain assaulted the road in a commotion so loud, it was as if she had a sudden bout of roaring tinnitus.

Roxie stared in awe, barely able to catch her breath at the sheets of water gushing down both sides of the interstate above, encasing them inside a magnificent waterfall. Even more spellbinding was how the sporadic winds sent the waterfalls into rippling wavy cascades.

"Awesome," Rogue exclaimed. "It's like we're inside a waterfall."

"Mystical," Roxie said dreamily.

Jackson let out a long whistle. "Sure hope those helicopters got everyone out. This wind is something else."

"I'm glad we weren't walking when this hit," Roxie muttered.

Rogue's eyes widened under the glow of his flashlight. "Oh, no, what about Luna? Do you think that helicopter found her?"

Roxie rubbed his tensing shoulders. "If we heard the helicopters, she did too. I'm sure she hid."

"Yeah, she's pretty smart. With things like that," Rogue quickly added. "Hey, what's that?"

They sat there with cocked heads, listening. Roxie didn't hear the military convoy until it splashed through the waterfall. She hoped it hadn't found Luna.

"Let's wait out this rain a little longer," Jackson said. "Although, we can't be afraid to get our feet wet, or we'll be pigeonholed with these damn pigeons for days." He chuckled at his silly joke.

"Just say when," Roxie burst with unfelt enthusiasm.

"When?" Rogue asked with puzzled brows. "Ooh, I just remembered. I brought the rain ponchos from the closet. Dad always kept a bunch. I even brought LifeStraws and bunches of survival stuff. And I have the MREs Luna gave me. We can hike for days."

Rogue's exuberance was completely lost on her. What in the world were LifeStraws? She had a feeling she would find out sooner than she wanted.

"Well okay then," Jackson said, "let's get organized. If this rain doesn't let up in fifteen minutes, we'd better get moving. Don't want to spend the night here." Jackson ripped open one of the camouflage rain poncho packages. "Sport, once we make it to the city, do you know your way to SunFlower's house?"

Rogue dug through his pack. "Sure. It's pretty simple. Her house is down a long dirt road."

"According to the bus registration—" *Sheesh*, she couldn't remember the street number. "It's on Shambala Way. The cross street would be helpful," Roxie carefully suggested.

She was answered by a nonchalant shrug of the shoulders as Rogue held up a compass triumphantly. "Meh, she lives in the woods. I'll know the way when I see it."

"You better," Jackson started in. "The three of us can't be traipsing around, looking like a bunch of vagabonds. Someone might call the police on us."

"You worry wayyy too much," Rogue exaggerated. "We just take the main street, then walk toward the mountain, past the school. Honest, I know the way."

Roxie rubbed his shoulders. "I'm sure you do." There was no point in grilling him.

"Okay then," Jackson said, "how's 'bout we go through our packs and get out our rain gear? The drier we are, less chance of catching pneumonia."

"What about Pixie?" Rogue asked. "She's gonna poop in the backpack."

"Ahh, she's a good girl." Roxie slipped her hand through the narrow opening and petted her reassuringly. She was not leaving Pixie behind. No matter what anyone said. She would let her cat out once they found a suitable area. Meanwhile, Pixie was probably drooling over the squawking pigeons.

"Is she even breathing?" Rogue asked.

"She's fine," Roxie clapped back. Their adventure better not get the best of Pixie.

Jackson smiled reassuringly. "That kooky cat will most likely weather through this better than any of us."

Instantly, Roxie's mounting tension eased when Jackson wrapped his arm around her shoulder. She let the rain wash away her worries, and veiled by the waterfalls, a false sense of security enveloped her. For this one moment, she indulged in the unabashed pleasure of snuggling against his comforting warm body.

As if everything she had been through her entire life had waited for that precise moment. Of simple bliss.

Chapter 31

Jackson Jones cinched the rain poncho's hood tighter. Utterly pointless. Nothing was keeping out that blasted rain. The prepper stormproof umbrella, the one Rogue had raved on and on about not more than ten minutes ago, had just succumbed to a brutal wind gust that must have been close to hurricane-strength. Roxie had the only working umbrella, which she used more as a walking stick and only opened it when they sat down for a quick break.

The intensifying storm, with its erratic winds and pelting rain, reminded him of the time he and his friends had braved hellacious waves at Melbourne beach during a Florida hurricane. Albeit, with the help of a twelve-pack of Pabst Blue Ribbon. His only excuse: he had been in his invincible twenties.

Now that Jackson was considerably older and presumably wiser, he chastised himself for thinking they could trek the train tracks during what Rogue had dubbed *Stormageddon*. While the kid was stoked about the journey, Jackson wasn't so sure this was the brightest of ideas where Roxie and that kooky cat of hers were concerned. On the upside, it wasn't a cold rain.

He tromped on and kept his eye on the raging rapids of the swollen Sacramento River meandering beyond the right side of the tracks along its circuitous route from the Klamath Mountains to the Central Valley, eventually finding its way to the delta. No doubt already breaching its banks in low-lying towns along the way, like Redding and Sacramento. It had him wondering if Captain Leroy LaFleur had ever found his beloved boat. *Poor fella.*

The three of them constantly watched for trains. With any luck, train activity had been grounded due to the volatile weather. Every now and then, he swore a lone figure in the distance briefly appeared and vanished like a wraith frolicking in the mists. Common sense told him it had to be Luna, even though Rogue hadn't been able to confirm it with the binoculars due to the rain.

Several sets of train tracks came into view. Up ahead, a brown blurry blob made him wipe his eyes for the zillionth time. Boxcars or a stranded train? He pointed it out to Roxie.

"We must be getting close to the Dunsmuir Train Station," she shouted, her words contorted by the windy rain.

"Making progress." Jackson hustled to catch up to Rogue and tugged on the back of his poncho. No matter what he said, the kid had to lead the way. Jackson signaled them for a quick word. "Be on the lookout for people." He had spotted homes in the distance, but due to the storm's low-visibility, no one would likely notice them, nor have the gumption to confront a group of down-on-their-luck drifters walking the tracks.

Together, they approached what looked more like a railyard than a train station based on the string of engineless boxcars and unattached locomotive engines. "The train station must be further up," Jackson said.

A blustery north wind nearly knocked them off their feet. On instinct, he knelt down, yanking them down with him, and held them in a tight huddle.

And then—the sirens went off. Sounding exactly like those spine-tingling sirens that used to scare the bejesus out of him that long, hot, miserable summer he had spent with his memaw in Florida.

Rogue's hands flew to his ears while that cat of Roxie's bounced around in the backpack like it was having a catfight with itself.

A wide-eyed haunting expression took over Roxie's normally cheerful face. "A tornado? Here?"

"Can't be," Jackson grumbled. He sure didn't like the look of those tumultuous clouds, the way they swirled around. But when the whistling winds morphed into horrific howling, he wasn't so sure. The tops of the evergreens shimmied faster and faster. Bits of limbs, tree bark, pinecones, and whatnot whirled above every which way.

He convinced himself it couldn't possibly be a tornado. They had already witnessed enough flukes of nature to last a lifetime. It didn't seem feasible for a tornado to touch down there, between the fairly narrow canyons of Dunsmuir. But if it started hailing . . .

"Sport, please tell me that's the Saturday noonday whistle." As he recalled, it wasn't unusual for rural communities to test emergency sirens on occasion.

"Duh, it's not f'n Saturday," the kid sputtered.

Hell, Jackson didn't know what day it was. All he knew—they had to take cover. ASAP! "Obviously, the siren's a warning." He scanned the area for danger.

"What should we do?" Roxie fretted, glancing from side to side.

The fear emanating from her hypnotic blue eyes needled at his own fear. "Let's get to those boxcars." Jackson pulled Roxie to her feet. "With any luck, we can ride out the storm in one."

"I'll find one!" Rogue charged off before Jackson could stop the whippersnapper.

Gritting his teeth at the swarms of pine needles smacking his face, Jackson pushed on, clutching Roxie's shoulder while she covered her face with her hands. A bizarre notion warned if he didn't hold on tight enough, the next gust might whisk the slender gal away.

Step-by-step, they lumbered on like doomed cartoon characters escaping for their lives via slow-motion. To say he was relieved when he looked up to find Rogue waving madly at them was an understatement. "Looks like he found one," he shouted into Roxie's ear.

Roxie attempted to run, tripping on a railroad tie. A windshear-like gust slowed her fall, and he caught her in his arms in what would have been a sweet romantic moment. Well, maybe if he were twenty years younger. But at that point, it was all about survival. They faltered, fumbling for their balance. And composure. And marched on.

Rogue kept shouting something or other from the boxcar like a hysterical nutcase. By the time they stumbled to the boxcar, they were both exhausted. He had to lift and shove Roxie up into the boxcar all the while Rogue cheered them on without bothering to help.

Finally, the sirens stopped.

Once inside the empty boxcar, Jackson plopped to the floor onto his butt. "That wind—never seen anything like it," he choked out as he fumbled around for his water bottle.

"Heaven only knows how we made it," Roxie blustered breathlessly.

Jackson and Roxie both guzzled their waters while Rogue struggled to close the boxcar's door. Still, that ferocious wind had electrified the hairs on his arms and legs with an unnerving tingling sensation, as if his limbs were on the verge of going numb. He rubbed down his arms and legs and Roxie followed suit.

Rogue eyed them suspiciously. "You guys are way weird."

"Wouldn't exactly call you *normal*," Jackson zinged.

They all started laughing, relieving his angst. To be honest, Jackson had found those last few minutes on the tracks downright touch-and-go.

"I'm so grateful those lousy sirens stopped. The worst part of the storm must be over," Roxie said once she contained her laughter.

"I wish I could have recorded that," Rogue exclaimed. "You guys were in the 'suck zone' of a mini tornado."

"Naw, more like one of those—day-ray-chos," he pronounced phonetically, trying to remember how to say the darn word. It was a new one for his vocabulary. "Matter of fact, that's why I happened on the bunch of you that fateful day. A derecho ripped through my buddy's property. I was on my way to Medford to help Chip clean up the mess . . ." *Certainly hope Chip doesn't think I died in the fire.*

"Guys, I'm serious. That was a f'n tornado. Like an EF Zero," Rogue said firmly.

Roxie fiddled with the backpack's temperamental zipper. "Whatever it was, I'm glad it's over." Pixie practically leaped to the ceiling before she finished unzipping the pack. The cat zoomed around like it had OD'd on expresso-bean-laced catnip.

Rogue made several attempts to catch the distraught cat, running around as wildly as the cat.

"Sport, a man knows when he's bested," Jackson hinted.

"Give Pixie her space," Roxie said, still not moving from her seat. "She probably needs the cat box."

A gale-force wind battered the boxcar, causing their shelter to lurch.

"Hey!" Rogue shouted. "The trains, uh, uh . . ."

"Moving," Roxie whispered.

Roxie's round-eyed stare told him to downplay their situation. "The boxcar's not attached to an engine. Just grin and bear it," he said. Still, what if the winds sent the boxcar careening southwardly downhill, all the way to Redding? *Implausible, not impossible* that anxious voice in the back of his mind nettled.

"What about Luna?" Rogue asked.

"She's tough and smart," Roxie reminded.

"Yeah," Rogue said rather meekly.

"The good news," Jackson chimed in, "those helicopters must be long gone by now. They can't fly in these winds."

Roxie let out a long yawn. "Do you mind if I close my eyes for a bit? My nerves are completely shot."

"Go right ahead," Jackson said. "I might as well get in a few winks myself."

"You guys want to sleep. Now?" Rogue couldn't have possibly rolled his eyes any louder. "Boring."

They ignored the eternally hyper kid. He and Roxie created separate niches in opposite corners on the fairly clean boxcar floor, using their packs as pillows.

And the sirens started once again.

Boom! The boxcar went airborne if only for a few seconds. Roxie gasped and parked herself into the corner walls. The boxcar landed at an angle with a jerking crash—as if it hadn't landed precisely on the rails.

"This is insane!" Rogue's panicky cry revealed his terror.

Jackson slid open the boxcar door just enough to get a peek at the tracks. "Wouldn't you know, that blasted wind lifted us off the rails. Could be a good thing. It ought to keep us from moving much."

"Unless we go flying into the f'n river!" Rogue cried out.

"Stop with the swearing," Roxie scolded. She must be as tired of it as he was.

"Mom and Dad *want* me to express my true feelings."

"Well, express them—silently," Jackson warned through clenched teeth as another wind gust rippled the sides of the boxcar. This time he leaned into a corner like Roxie, wondering if this nightmarish storm was ever ending.

Boom!

So much for resting. They exchanged harried glances as the boxcar shuddered from the impact of something . . .

Boom!

Roxie and Rogue crawled to Jackson, no doubt seeking comfort that everything was going to be all right. How could he promise that when the world he had known these past sixty-odd years was changing in practically every way possible?

Boom!

Roxie and Rogue nestled closer to him. "What the hell's going on out there?" Jackson uttered.

"Another landslide?" Roxie's widening eyes questioned.

Jackson shook his head. His gut instinct warned it was something far more perilous than a landslide. And he just had to pray mighty damn hard they weren't in the trajectory of one of those huge evergreen trees—when it landed. "I'm afraid to say." He stopped as if buying more time. He could be wrong.

The boxcar rattled again from another sonic boom–like crash.

"From the sounds of it, these derecho-like winds are taking out the trees. Most likely the weak and diseased ones. One by one." Jackson forced himself to hold back his shudder at the thought of the majestic forest crashing down on them from all directions. This area was jam-packed with trees that had to be over a hundred feet tall. *How does one outrun that*? There was no place to hide, except for an underground shelter.

"Are you kidding me, the trees are . . . falling?" Roxie's trembling voice revealed her horror. "It was bad enough in the fire."

"Someone, please make it stop!" Rogue wailed louder than the next gust. "The trees are the only thing saving our planet. Don't you know, trees store like a hundred years' worth of CO_2? But when they die, the CO_2 is released. And with all the trees dying. From the fires, and, and the winds, it'll take way longer to heal the planet."

"You don't need to worry 'bout that right now," Jackson consoled, attempting to comfort everyone. Including himself.

They huddled closer. That horrible earth-shattering felling of a tree, possibly a hundred years old, succumbing to the forces of nature reminded him of an old commercial ingrained in his memories: "It's not nice to fool Mother Nature." Jackson was starting to understand Rogue's obsessive anger. Humans had really jacked up the planet.

The world he had known, depended on, and revered. Was going to hell in a handbasket. Even without this weather whiplash, the economy was mucked-up with no signs of recovering, thanks to obscenely high interest rates. Nowadays, who could afford to raise a family? The grand ole U.S. of A. and its capitalist glory days seemed to be going supernova on them. Thing was, he didn't much like the other options, like socialism and communism. Perhaps it took a carefully orchestrated combination to run the globe. It was just plain scary with all that power in the hands of the greedy one-percenters who wanted to play God.

Boom!

Their boxcar rocked. That kooky cat went berserk again.

"That one must have landed on the tracks," Jackson contemplated out loud as the reverberation gradually abated.

"We're moving again," Rogue's panicky tone warned.

"We can't go far," Jackson assured as the boxcar skidded completely off the tracks.

"Pixie girl." Roxie tapped her lap until the black-eyed cat slinked to her with lowered flickering ears. "That's a sweet girl." She clutched Pixie to her chest and showered her with pets.

"So, are we gonna just wimp out in here and wait for the trees to, to, to squash us?" Rogue always seemed ready to ignite an already volatile situation.

"All in good time. We should wait for this god-forsaken wind to die down," Jackson said plain and simple. "But, hey, I'm not your dad. If you want to go solo . . ." No sense in arguing with the kid.

Roxie's lip quivered, as if holding back a smile.

"Whatev." Rogue leaned against the boxcar with a thud.

Roxie went about dumping her backpack and neatly repacked it for the second time since they had started off. She sure did tidy up when she was nervous. A useful habit, he mused.

"What *is* that?" Rogue whispered with the most befuddled, kooky-eyed expression.

Jackson cocked his head, trying to make out if the distant roar was another approaching cloudburst. "Sounds like it's raining pretty hard—"

Bam! They were blindsided, as if the boxcar had been transported into the middle of a battlefield. Although it sounded more like thousands of rocks pulverizing the boxcar. "That's one helluva hailstorm," Jackson tried to shout above the deafening roar. The boxcar could take it—but could they? It was nerve-rattling, to say the very least.

Once again, they huddled together.

Good thing they hadn't started hiking again. Nonetheless, the kid was right; they needed to start putting the miles behind them and get to where they were going. Before all of Northern California was declared a federal disaster zone.

Chapter 32

Luna Lewis pushed on against the vicious wind, out of sheer spite, as it threatened to derail her off the train tracks. So much for making good time. It didn't help that the train track's northern route curved around the mountainous terrain, often hugging the raging Sacramento River. Depending on the weight of her pack, she typically averaged one mile every fifteen to twenty minutes. Not in this weather.

She would have made it to the city of Mt. Shasta by now if she had taken Interstate 5. That hadn't been an option. Not with several rescue units scheduled to return from the California/Oregon border throughout the day. From what the telecommunications guy had said, all high-water vehicles were preparing for deployment to the flood zones from Redding to the greater Sacramento area due to probable mass casualty events. Based on the last weather update she had seen, some areas in the Central Valley and Northern California were predicted to receive four-to-five inches of rain. Per hour!

That had to be a computer glitch. Right?

Despite the roaring white-capped river that had meandered to the left side of the tracks after the train bridge, it served as a comforting guide. Reminding that she wasn't lost. She clearly recalled waiting for an annoying long train on her last visit to SunFlower's farm. On West Lake Street. Despite the low visibility, the West Lake Street/train track intersection should be easy to identify, since it was near a Starbucks.

From there, she would have to hike through the small town for a few miles before reaching Shambala Way. Although she didn't recall the street names, she knew her way to SunFlower's. The train tracks would get her there eventually. Unless this was a completely different train route? *Damn*, she hadn't thought of that. She couldn't even rely on the majestic views of Mount Shasta and Shastina as a compass, since the volcanic mountains were shrouded by storm clouds.

Rogue, Roxie, and Handyman Jack were probably enjoying a comfy room at a military base by now. Yeah right, if they weren't being interrogated. It wasn't like they had any info to divulge. Realistically, the four of them couldn't escape the FBI forever.

She realized that pivotal moment of no return had occurred once they had left the lodge at Granite Hill Lookout. The FBI had undoubtedly contacted her employer by now, or worse, shown up at her workplace. Had she been terminated? The lifestyle she had so meticulously curated to fulfill her dreams. Was over. As in totally screwed.

At this point, Luna had nothing more to lose. Well, except her life, if she fell into the river, or died from exposure if she injured her leg and couldn't walk. The ex-adrenaline junkie in her wasn't letting that happen. That same deep-driven competitiveness was what made her so successful in the cutthroat fashion industry.

Once she confirmed Mom and Dad were okay, she planned to take that boring activewear buyer position an old boyfriend in Australia kept begging her to accept. Maybe they'd let her design a sexy line of non-toxic, eco-chic activewear. She still had designs saved on the cloud. It wasn't designer shoes, but it would be better than living off-grid. Waiting for the FBI to find her. Sure, she could claim her innocence, but she didn't want to be the patsy.

She just had to get to Australia. With a new identity. *Hmm . . .* She allowed herself to daydream about the possibility. It was doable after what she had stumbled upon zipped away in her rucksack:

a tattered notebook of old contacts from her activist days. People who owed her favors.

If her contacts were still alive.

The Sacramento River thundered into her thoughts, begging for attention, so it seemed. It had breached its banks and had swollen wider, higher, and fiercer. She stopped for a second and stared up at the sinister sky and envisioned herself, right there, as seen from Google Earth—a mere speck amongst the humongous trees lining the river and train tracks. Totally insignificant.

A bizarre hissing-like whistle blustered through the erratically swaying treetops. *How can those trees bend like that?* For an instant, she worried the wind might snap them as effortlessly as those tall match sticks Mom kept on the fireplace hearth. She hunched her head down and braced for the wind. And continued on. But the wind didn't find her this time. The wind must be higher up.

Wait. "That's not normal." Luna stopped dead on the tracks at the unnerving crackling taking over the forest—as if the entire forest was trying to wake up from a deep freeze.

After a three-sixty scan, she knew what it was.

Bam! That horrid crash . . . of a tree. Sent her cringing.

But it was more than one downed tree. The booms echoed through the forest, announcing their deaths. All around her. There must have been a hundred of them—trees—crashing to the earth. Only the forest was so dense she didn't see where any had fallen.

The town's emergency siren added to the pandemonium. The siren gave her the shivers, reminding her of the worthless nuclear bomb drills she used to train for. Really, if a nuke was hitting that close, people would get vaporized before they made it to a shelter. Especially in modern-day traffic.

Clearly, the sirens warned the community to shelter from the severe weather. She had no plans of wimping out and stopping again, despite this being the most brutal storm she had ever encountered. Still, the tops of the trees swayed like ginormous feather dusters.

That peculiar gut-wrenching spasm attacked her solar plexus seconds before another series of thunder-like crackling splintered her ears, this time even louder.

Closer?

"Seek shelter!" Dad's voice barged into her mind. His constant Shit-Hits-The-Fan rhetoric had been a part of her everyday life for so long, it was often second nature. After living on her own, she had stopped catastrophizing that every minuscule incident was a prelude to world disorder. Since the fires, she had to admit, worries of a national crisis or black swan event had infiltrated her rational side.

The outer edges of a lengthy horizontal roll cloud loomed toward her at fast-forward speed. "That's definitely not a normal cloud." Like a character out of *The Day After Tomorrow*, she couldn't believe a surreal cloud like that actually existed. Staring her in the face.

Luna skipped over railroad ties, scanning the forested side for a building or vehicle. Anything. Reining in her paranoia, she realized she was out of range of any falling trees. Probably. But looking up at those amazingly tall trees . . . she wasn't so sure.

The spooky Photoshop-like cloud blotted out the remaining sunlight filtering through gaps of the storm clouds. Turning day into twilight. A gust of wind finally found her and battered her until she lost her balance. She fell on her back with the rucksack taking the brunt of it.

She couldn't get up. Not with the wind lashing at her. She curled into a tight ball, right there on the tracks, and shielded her body from the debris pummeling her. The one thing she didn't have to watch for were trains; according to the telecommunications guy, all train activity had been halted.

Finally, the crazy wind blast subsided. She pitied whoever hadn't taken shelter. Sitting on a railroad tie, she dared to stare straight up at those menacing clouds. Until a chunk of ice shattered on the rail inches from her. Now she understood Dad's warning; it was her conscious telling her to seek shelter. Wind and rain she could push through. Not a hailstorm, not if the hail was as relentless as the wind and rain.

She spied the forested side of the train tracks, section-by-section, for shelter. Nothing but a dirt road. She squinted for a clearer look. Off in the distance, she eyed a small gray building adjacent to the dirt road paralleling the tracks, which was surrounded by the same whitest-gray gravel-like rock used on the tracks. She had passed several along the way. They must be maintenance buildings for the railway or power company. Well, it was something.

Unable to get to her feet, she struggled with the rucksack and her stiffening muscles. The rucksack had somehow caught onto a wooden railroad tie. And she couldn't turn around enough to see where it was stuck. Quickly, she unharnessed the rucksack and finally succeeded in hacking off the splintered railroad tie with her survival knife.

Another chunk of ice landed inches away, scaring the crap out of her.

She forced back the panic seeping into her veins when the tree-tops started going all bendy again. Another one of those wild wind gusts was coming. She made it to the roughly six-by-six-foot building. Locked building. She rummaged through the rucksack for the survivalist credit card–sized lock-picking tool Rogue had been messing with. "Shit, he didn't put it back."

Baby hail hammered down from the sky. It was coming. Now! And it was going to get bad. She banged the lock, but it was digital, and she had damaged the locking device. She wasn't getting inside. Willing in practicality, Luna leaned against the south side of the building, which thankfully sheltered her from the hateful wind just as globular balls of ice plummeted to the ground.

Bam! Bam! Bam!

What the hell? A blob of ice the size of a grapefruit landed inches from her foot. More clanged against the metal maintenance building with a vengeance. Adrenaline junkie or not, she wouldn't survive a fierce hailstorm. In this insane weather, she must expect the worst.

Quickly, she removed the rolled sleeping pad attached to the bottom of the rucksack, and then covered the rucksack with the mylar blanket. She gently balanced the rucksack on her head before snatching the four corners of the blanket to secure the rucksack. She tied the blanket ends around her waist and sat on the pad, praying the amateurish shelter protected her from the bombardment.

Just her shitty luck to get caught in a freaky storm with apocalyptic hail and winds. With the way the wind rumbled through the trees, she wasn't going anywhere. She shuffled around with the mylar blanket and the rucksack until finding a comfortable position.

Rambling worries drifted through her mind. Rogue must hate her for leaving him. Was Roxie disappointed in her? Her ex-babysitter had always been so good to her family. She convinced herself Handyman Jack would keep them safe.

She blocked out her anxiousness, the rain, the wind, and the clattering hail using a meditative technique SunFlower had once taught her. Gradually, she found herself decompressing. After a restless night working out her escape plan, she was ready for a power nap.

Boom! The ground quaked.

"What the hell is that?" Luna struggled to wake up, fighting with the mylar blanket.

"Another tree, you idiot," she grumbled as her memory returned. The rain and hail had stopped. The wind hadn't. "Damn!" It was after two in the afternoon. And it was so dark. There was no way she was making it to SunFlower's today.

She hurried to the tracks to check the river. "Oh, yeah." It had practically doubled in width, encompassing a swath of trees in its path. Would it breach the tracks? The river reminded her bladder it was time to pee. *Ugh, not here—out in the open.* What if remote trail cameras monitored the tracks for wildlife? She didn't want to be caught with her pants down in a viral moment.

She hurried past the utility building to the saturated forested area beyond, until she found a niche between three large trees. "Please, don't fall on me."

She had successfully completed her task, when the wind shrieked above. Not again.

Blindsided with excruciating pain, she instinctively patted her head.

"Blood?"

A huge pinecone rolled next to her foot. Queasiness overtook her. "Really? This is how it ends? A freakin' pinecone takes me out?"

She struggled to maintain her balance. As her legs buckled . . .

Chapter 33

Roxie Ramirez nonchalantly reshouldered her pack, hoping Jackson didn't notice. Otherwise, the gentleman that he was, would offer to carry Pixie again. He'd already burdened himself with his duffel and the pack she had borrowed from the bus filled with her purse, clothes, and other essentials.

"You need to rest a spell?" Jackson inquired good-naturedly.

Sheesh, he must have spotted her discomfort. Walking, she could do all day long. But her old bones didn't like the backpack.

Rogue, who maintained a steady ten-foot lead, spun around toward them. "Guys, we can't keep stopping. Or we'll never catch up to Luna."

Roxie and Jackson exchanged knowing glances.

It was the wet clothes she found most annoying, despite changing into dry jeans earlier. "I'm fine," Roxie murmured. The rain seemed anticlimactic after that traumatizing hour stuck in the boxcar with the clamoring hail clobbering them.

Jackson kept scowling at the tumultuous sky. "Those clouds look like they're about to let loose again. We need to find someplace to hole up. Don't suppose you have an ETA on our destination?"

"Oh, no!" Roxie clasped a hand over her mouth, momentarily mortified. "I completely forgot about Cantara Loop. And Sawmill Curve." Hank used to tell her about the train derailment accident every time they had chugged through Cantara Loop's horseshoe curve. It had been the largest chemical spill in California's history, at the time. A tank car had jumped the tracks, dumping something like nineteen thousand gallons of herbicide into the Sacramento River, polluting over forty miles and killing practically all the fish and wildlife in its path from what he had said.

"Say again?" Jackson frowned with concern.

"The Union Pacific tracks snake up and down and around the canyons and mountains. Taking us completely out of our way. It could add a day or two to our hike in this lousy weather."

"Phew." Jackson let out a long sigh. "Here I thought we'd be where we were gettin' to by now. No worries. We just need to head east at the first main road crossing we come to."

"We should be coming to the train trestle soon. As I recall, that's where the river crosses to the left side of the tracks."

"Good to know," Jackson said. "In all actuality, taking the tracks was the wisest of decisions at the time. In retrospect, do you still think the hike was better than taking the helicopter?" He laughed.

"Don't rub it in," she jabbed back.

"No harm done," Jackson said in his soothing, carefree tone, the one she loved. "We made it. And we found that boxcar in the nick of time. Never seen hail like that."

"Get used to it," Rogue shouted back. "It's called Godzilla hail. The new normal."

Roxie didn't know what to think about all these new severe weather terminologies. However, "hailstorm" didn't quite capture the severity of the storm they had endured. Hell-storm was more like it.

"How often did you say you took the train?" Jackson asked.

An unexpected wave of nostalgia had her missing Hank. "We took Amtrak's Coast Starlight to Washington about four times a year to visit Hank's brother and sister-in-law. Hank, bless his soul, always had to take the train. He was such a train nut." She hadn't minded so much. It was a lovely, scenic trip, without the stress of driving.

"Do you still visit them?" Jackson asked, as if wanting small talk.

"Sadly no. They didn't survive the pandemic."

"Afraid I lost several older relatives as well. The whole Coronavirus thing—Darwin's waiting room. Thinning out the herd for those burdening the system. Collecting Social Security and whatnot," Jackson said surprisingly.

"You think?" Roxie was taken aback by his blatant statement. He didn't seem like the conspiracy theorist type. More like an open-minded Republican.

He didn't answer for a bit, as if choosing his words carefully. "Try as I might, I never made sense of all the data. The way the CDC pushed those vaccines before completely vetting them. I mean, a pandemic in general is understandable. It's bound to occur every now and again. It's the way those in charge vehemently denied the possibility of the Wuhan Lab leak from the get-go. That's what convinced me those swindlers were lying through their teeth."

She was glad they were on the same page. "I did think *that* was peculiar. It seems like the CDC should have seriously considered all possibilities. Especially, a lab leak." The government's adamant denial had appeared as juvenile as a toddler caught with his hand in the cookie jar.

"I apologize for getting all fired up. It still has me fuming." Jackson kicked a lava-like rock so hard it flew past Rogue.

Roxie should learn to keep her trap shut. For even now, the tripledemic's lousy vaccines, unbearable masks, impossible vaccine passports, and lockdowns remained trigger topics. Probably because so many people had lost their loved ones, jobs, and homes. Many of her favorite products from the pre-pandemic days had completely disappeared from the shelves, making her wonder if a lot of the smaller companies had gone out of business. The supply chain still hadn't returned to normal, and inflation was through the roof. Her new oven had been on backorder for months. *That reminds me, cancel the order when I get a bloomin' phone.*

Perhaps the tripledemic's greatest travesty, besides the millions of lost lives along with the countless vaccine injuries, was how it had been politically weaponized, creating a huge divide in the nation . . . that hadn't abated to this day. This used to be a free country, one where people had not been ostracized or brutally bullied for believing something different than their neighbor. It reminded her of the sixties and the whole Vietnam War controversy.

A lightning bolt blinded her. She stopped and counted aloud, "One Mississippi, two Mississippi, three Mississippi, four Mississippi, five—"

Thunder blasted the sky.

"Damn," Jackson said, "better find cover. Before those clouds let loose. Sport, why don't you kick it up a notch and scout for shelter."

"On it." Rogue shot ahead.

"Those are ferocious-looking clouds," Roxie babbled to herself. She did not want to get stuck in another downpour. Poor Pixie was already going to be traumatized for weeks. "It's okay, Pixie girl," she whispered into the pack, still thanking her lucky stars she had caught the frantic cat before escaping her burning home. Pixie, her purse, her mother's pillowcase, and a backpack with basic travel essentials were all she had left. She didn't even have a car. *Oh, I need to call my car insurance guy.* She wasn't looking forward to going through the rigmarole of buying a new car.

Another lightning bolt accosted the sky. She only made it to four Mississippi that time. Rogue started jumping up and down, pinwheeling his arms and shouting.

Jackson gave her a quizzical look. "You think he found something?"

"Discretion isn't exactly one of his talents," Roxie said. "I think he found the trestle." All Roxie had made out was the word "bridge." Although, she couldn't make out a bridge in the descending grayness of the plummeting sky.

She trekked on faster, adrenaline already giving her the energy surge to boost her along.

"Well, I'll be darned. I see the train trestle you were talking about," Jackson said, pleased as punch. "I'll see if there's a spot to wait out the storm." Jackson hurried off, leaving her behind.

Finding the train trestle was a good sign, reminding her they had made a bit of progress. Ah, but the river was flooding. Fast. And the lightning was at three Mississippi. It was a fast-moving storm. Why wasn't that surprising? Nothing was normal these days.

Jackson waved her on. The sky exploded when a piercing lightning bolt zapped her retinas, leaving an after-burn image imprinted with eyes wide open. She froze. Not exactly sure where the next railroad tie was, and she didn't want to risk falling.

She stood there and braced for the thunder. Not even making it to two Mississippi. Even so, she hadn't been ready for what had to be the loudest thunder she had ever heard in her entire life. Even the earth juddered. And there she stood: stupefied, straddled by the metal rails. Jackson and Rogue must be thinking she was a nitwit.

Ah, but then Jackson was there, by her side, guiding her along the tracks, step-by-step, toward the trestle. "There's a nook under the foot of the trestle where we can ride out this god-awful lightning. But we need to watch our footing. The river's looking mighty treacherous."

Finally, her vision returned to normal, allowing her to see the narrow ledge. "Uh—"

"It's easier than it looks. The ground is packed down pretty darn hard there," Jackson said, taking the liberty of unharnessing the pack with Pixie. "All you need to do is inch across and lean into the embankment, like so."

Jackson scooted across seamlessly, taking little side steps as he leaned into the earthen embankment under the trestle's support beams, bracing his body with his hands.

"Don't worry, it's not too scary," Rogue said.

She wasn't too sure about it. Until that next lightning bolt lit up the sky like huge skeletal fingers clutching for the earth. A long series of booming thunder instantly followed. At that point, she was ready to risk the narrow ledge.

"The bridge is all metal," Rogue blurted. "If it gets zapped, we'll get fried."

"Zip it," Jackson shot back.

Roxie had to force the image of getting electrocuted out of her mind. Jackson came back for her once again and gently nudged her along. She just wanted to get to that nook under the foot of the bridge before the next lightning bolt hit. She leaned into the dirt embankment under the base of the bridge and skirted toward Rogue.

"See," Rogue spouted, "it's super easy."

Roxie smiled faintly as she nestled into the spot next to Rogue while Jackson quickly snuggled next to her. She finally caught her breath. Still, she avoided looking over the narrow ledge where the river raged with rapids. Images of Luna caught in the storm haunted her. *I do hope Luna's someplace safe.* She said a quick prayer.

Another bolt of lightning assaulted the earth—so loud the bridge seemed to squawk back in retaliation. She could not stop shuddering with every lightning strike.

Jackson's lips grazed her neck when he whispered into her ear, "That one was a doozy."

This isn't so bad, she decided. Apparently, she didn't mind being the one mollycoddled for once. Hank hadn't been all that affectionate. She had always been the caregiver, for her family, and then her community. As it had been expected of her, she presumed. However, being on the receiving side of kindhearted compassion—was quite pleasant, despite the circumstances.

The fierce lightning storm had only lasted about twenty minutes. And then, they had started out again, anxious to find a road intersection. Roxie didn't want to be walking the tracks once the sun slipped below the canyons. That could get dangerous as well. No telling what wild animals might find them. Jackson had already loaded his gun, as if expecting trouble after Rogue had gone on and on about how they could get attacked by zombie deer. She didn't know if the boy had made it up or if it was from a horror movie. These days, she no longer automatically dismissed such outlandish possibilities; anything could happen at any given moment.

Jackson seemed unusually quiet. She wasn't ready for her pleasant mood to dissipate just yet, so instead of worrying about the possible dangers lurking around the next bend or rebuilding her home or the mementos she had lost in the fire, she daydreamed of all things, her vast collection of Yahoo emails.

Since she still used the same email address from the nineties, she had thousands of saved emails tucked away in well-organized folders, precious emails from her mother, her children, and siblings. She better not mention that to Rogue, or she'd have to endure a tedious rant about how un-eco-friendly the cloud was.

She couldn't wait to check her folders and sent emails to find what jewels awaited. All those photos . . . That would be her next project, creating a series of scrapbooks, a retelling of her life. Only the tangible scrapbooks—the kind she could hold and thumb through during the difficult process of rebuilding her home. Digital scrapbooks didn't seem to capture the nostalgia, which was the purpose of a scrapbook. Of course, that was more than likely a generation preference.

The thought of not having homeowner's insurance needled at her again. If that were the case, she should have enough money saved for a down payment for one of those cute tiny homes on wheels. She could live in a THOW community. Maybe in Oregon. But she needed a place where she could have a nice-sized garden. She wasn't so sure she wanted to go back to the same old life she had. Something inside of her had changed. Something she couldn't quite place.

Her indulgent daydreaming was spoiled when Rogue started shouting. This time Jackson jogged off for him. She speed-walked, careful of her footing. By the time she reached them, tears streamed down Rogue's rosy cheeks.

The boy meekly held up a dangerous-looking knife with a wide curvy blade. "It's the APO-1T knife Dad bought Luna. Designed by that survival chick, you know, Survival Lilly? See, Luna's initials, LL." Rogue traced the initials carved into the handle. "Luna would never, *ever* leave it. Something's hella wrong . . ."

Jackson picked up the sheath a few railroad ties down. "Give me that thing before someone gets hurt."

The kid pivoted from side to side. "Do you think a zombie dear, or coyotes, or, or a mountain lion got her . . ."

Roxie gave Rogue a long comforting hug before he went hysterical on them. "I'm sure she's fine."

Jackson carefully sheathed the knife. "Don't see any sign of a scuffle. Luna must have dropped it."

"You don't get it," Rogue lashed out. "Luna doesn't make lame-ass mistakes. She's an *expert*."

"Okay, okay, we'll investigate," Jackson added quickly, eyeing their surroundings.

"Hey"—Rogue pointed—"a building!"

They had walked past several of those small gray buildings that looked more like large metal utility boxes.

A lightning bolt accosted the sky. Roxie barely made it to the end of two Mississippi. The sky retaliated with a series of strobe-like flashes. *Sheesh, not another storm.* Feeling like a lame-ass, as Rogue had so vehemently accused, she gave up keeping up with them. It didn't help that poor Pixie was going bonkers, thrashing around in the backpack. Luckily, the backpack protected her from frantic cat claws.

Jackson waited for her to catch up with him rather impatiently by the way he kept glancing around. Rogue darted down the train track's gravelly slope and to the utility box.

"Hey," Rogue bellowed. "There's a b-b-body."

On that note, Jackson rushed off. "Sport, hold on just a minute."

What a ridiculous request—asking Rogue to wait. Carefully, Roxie traversed down the track's incline, all the while hoping Rogue had been exaggerating, and that there wasn't a body. Of a person. Maybe a deer or a fox, she decided.

But the way Rogue and Jackson rushed around had her worried it was Luna. "Heavens, please let the girl be all right."

Jackson shouted something to her from the tree line as Roxie scurried past the utility box. She recognized Luna's heavy-duty rucksack. And she knew . . .

Rogue waved bloody palms in the air. "She's dead! She's dead!"

"Stop your caterwaulin'—" Jackson stopped and cocked his head at the foreboding sky.

Roxie rushed to Luna with an unexpected burst of energy. Quickly, she knelt beside her limp body to check for a pulse.

"Hear that?" Jackson whispered. He seemed more concerned with the storm than Luna.

"Thank heavens!" Roxie cried out. "I have a pulse." Based on her bloodied forehead, Luna needed medical attention. She must have taken a tumble.

Rogue flashed Roxie a heartfelt yet baffling frown. "You mean, my sister's *not* dead?"

Jackson still hadn't seemed to register that Luna was alive. He cupped his ear with his hand, as if listening intently. All Roxie heard was that ungodly wind. The three of them looked up at the same time as the evergreen trees billowed above. And then, the sirens went off.

"Not again!" Rogue moaned.

"My sentiments exactly," Roxie exclaimed. There was no place to take cover.

"Must be another one of those derechos," Jackson shouted. "We need to get away from these trees."

The last time the sirens had gone off, the maniacal winds had toppled hundreds of trees, based on the continuous booms they had endured while taking cover in the boxcar. It made her wonder how many trees had been uprooted. "What about the utility box?" Roxie pointed. Although, it was rather small for four people and was most likely crammed with electrical components.

"Right, I'll check it out. You two stay with Luna." Jackson headed for the utility box.

Roxie gingerly smoothed back Luna's hair before wiping away the blood smeared to her temple. "The blood congealed," she said, but Rogue wasn't listening. He was too busy jumping around like a miniature madman, shouting to the forest that Luna *wasn't* dead.

The wind wreaked havoc with the treetops. Roxie walked around a humongous pine tree to find the spot with the least wind. Much better. She maneuvered Luna to the opposite side of the tree, and then nestled against the tree trunk with Luna's head in her lap and gently rocked her, all the while praying the young woman wasn't suffering from a life-threatening concussion.

A rather large pinecone walloped the ground several feet from her. If only that maddening siren would stop. She needed to clear her head. Roxie leaned back against the tree and acutely focused on the myriad of trees, as if seeking a path through a magnificent, forested maze. A euphoric sensation befell her. And she basked in the tranquility of it.

It dawned on her that Jackson should be back by now. But, she wasn't moving—transfixed in a sort of blissful state, entranced by nature's glory. Meanwhile, the storm's chaos seemed to spin around her, safeguarding her from nature's fury.

She happened to look up to find Jackson standing above her with defeat stamped across his well-creased forehead. She realized the sirens had stopped at some point; that was how blissed-out she was.

"*Everything will be fine,*" Roxie attempted to say, but her mouth refused to move.

"Oh, no, Roxie's dying too!" Rogue proclaimed. "This must be like a, a *Blair Witch* forest!"

"Sport, stop this nonsense. No one's dying today!" Jackson said a bit sternly. "Not on my watch."

I better snap out of this peculiar euphoria before Jackson has a conniption fit and Rogue has an aneurysm. But Roxie had no control of her body. Perhaps because she didn't want to return to the chaos. This was entirely too peaceful.

A glimmer of something metallic shimmered in the distance, as if calling out to her. *Interesting.*

"Don't die!" Rogue's voice faded away.

The next thing she knew, Jackson was kneeling beside her and patting her face with gentle smacks. That did it. She was back to the harsh reality as the wind took umbrage with the trees.

"I'm fine," Roxie finally said aloud once and for all after gaining control of her physical body.

Jackson flashed her the oddest look of quizzical admiration. "No dice with the metal building. With Luna indisposed, we should hunker down right here." He set down Luna's rucksack.

"We can make a tent shelter with our rain ponchos," Rogue announced.

"What's going on?" Luna sprang from Roxie's lap, scaring the living daylights out of everyone, based on their gasps.

"Luna!" Rogue hugged her first.

"Easy does it," Jackson said, practically tearing him from her.

Luna pulled herself up. "Why is everyone looking at me like I spontaneously reanimated into a zombie or something?"

"Hahaha, you're so funny! Wait." Rogue backed away. "Are you—a zombie?"

"Grrr . . ." Luna said with claw-like hands.

Poor Rogue, he could have had a heart attack right there. He needed to do something about his fascination with zombies and dead people.

"You guys are freaking me out." Luna gingerly patted her head. "Where are we? Wait, I remember. A pinecone nearly killed me."

Jackson picked up a huge pinecone that had to be over a foot long. "These things are like mini torpedoes."

Roxie patted her heart. "Hon, you had us worried."

"I am so freakin' confused," Luna said with crossed brows. "How did you guys find me? You were supposed to take the helicopter—"

"Good to have you back," Jackson said a bit gruffly. "Hate to spoil the reunion and all. We need to ready ourselves for this new stormfront."

It started sprinkling right on cue.

"Can you believe this wind?" Roxie rambled as déjà vu took over her senses. "Just a moment." She paused, racking her brain, as if she had forgotten crucial information. Then it came to her. "I saw a street sign beyond those trees back when I was zoning out. I think it said Mott Road. Is that around here?" Or had she been hallucinating?

"Roxie, you're amazing," Luna gushed. "I know Mott Road!"

"You know where we are?" Jackson seemed aghast, staring up at the trees and then back to Roxie.

"I think so," Luna said, trying to stand up.

Roxie ignored Jackson's befuddled frown. "No, I have not gone bonkers." Although, she wasn't so sure. It was a topsy-turvy kind of day. Moreover, had been a topsy-turvy week. However long it had been since the fires had started. Her life had been upended in practically every possible way. But at least she still had her Pixie cat. For as silly as it was, Pixie remained her primary purpose: to have a purpose.

Roxie strode into the forest with her feet sinking into the ground. She soon became lost in the labyrinth of towering trees. She wasn't too surprised when encountering a patch where several trees had been uprooted and had collapsed into one another like the makings of a giant teepee without a covering. Despite the higher elevation, the mushy, saturated ground had started to flood. With the inundation, the ground could only absorb so much.

There it was again, a flash of metal standing out between the dark mass of tree bark. "There." Roxie pointed. She turned to find Jackson had followed her.

"Why, Roxie, I do believe I see it," Jackson said excitedly. "How the heck did you see it from back there?"

All Roxie could do was shake her head, unable to explain her out-of-body-like moment.

"Hey, wait for me. What do you see?" Rogue wasn't one to be left behind for long.

"Now hold on," Jackson snapped. "We can't just leave your sister after finally finding her."

"Oh yeah," Rogue uttered.

They hurried back to Luna. And Pixie.

Luna was already on her feet, doing a round of stretches, when they reached her. Although a bit pale, she appeared all right. Just not as full of oomph as usual. "Well?"

"Mott Road's about four hundred yards or so to the east," Jackson answered. "You up to walking?"

"Sure," Luna said, slipping on her rucksack. "We can't stay here. Hear that?" She cocked her head to the sky.

The not-so-faraway roaring gush of a cloudburst splattering the treetops grew louder and louder. Seconds later, the microburst found them. They ran, ignoring the ferocious wind whispering their impending doom as the forest pelted them with pine needles, leaves, limbs . . .

Rogue shot off past them, taking the lead once again. He stopped when reaching the road and turned to them with his finger to his lips. They continued cautiously when Roxie spotted what looked to be a warehouse across the street.

"You think we ought to see if anyone's there?" Jackson asked. "Could be a great spot to wait out this downpour."

"Yes, please," Roxie muttered. If a pinecone had taken out Luna, no telling what damage all this flying debris could do.

"I'll do a quick recon," Jackson said.

"I'm coming with you."

It took a second for Luna's faint voice to register. Roxie grabbed the girl's arm. "Please, stay with me. I'm still feeling a bit out of it," Roxie said, knowing all too well, Luna wouldn't tolerate being treated fragilely.

"Luna, are you sure you know *precisely* where we are?" Jackson questioned.

"Pretty much," Luna said in a half-dazed state. "Mott Road's near the Dunsmuir Airport. I gave SunFlower a ride there once." She looked at her watch. "My hiking watch says the elevation here is three thousand two hundred feet. So, if the rains keep flowing downhill, we should be able to walk to SunFlower's, despite the flooding. Taking the tracks is a time-suck." She fell to her knees without any warning. She tried to get up and stumbled back down to the ground.

Jackson was by her side.

Luna brushed him away. "I just need a second. I'm still woozy."

"No hurry. We'll wait here as long as you need," Jackson said.

The sirens started again.

Luna squinted up at the sky, using her hands as a shield. "No. I don't want to be out in another insane microburst. If I pass out again, drag me on this." Luna held out one of those shiny silver emergency blankets.

"Seriously?" Rogue yelped.

"We can't stay here—with killer pinecones." Luna's voice faded into the wind.

"Agreed. I'll carry your rucksack," Rogue said in a wise old voice.

"Now you're thinking," Jackson said. "Hang back, while I check out the building." A determined Jackson plodded off, leaving them behind.

"Be careful . . ." Roxie cried out after him. It was a pointless statement—with everything happening around them.

Chapter 34

Jackson Jones leaned into the blustering wind with a flimsy rain poncho as his only protection from the sudden torrential downpour. No matter, he had been thoroughly soaked since they had started this morning's ill-fated escapade. He wasn't letting that stop him. Not after everything else they had been through. Especially since they were so close to their destination.

The clouds seemed to descend lower and lower, turning the late afternoon into dusk. They needed shelter. ASAP. He stopped under a tree to scout out the self-storage facility they had stumbled upon. He panned the area before venturing farther, checking for cameras. Nowadays, everyone and their dog seemed to have a Wi-Fi security system. He had absolutely no idea how to bypass those contraptions.

With any luck, the Internet was down, and no one was remotely viewing his not-so-stealthy intrusion as he sloshed through the partially flooded entrance. A mass of flying objects accosted him. He ducked, dodging a barrage of bulging black garbage bags hurtling straight for him. He wasn't prepared for the peculiar sensation of the wind holding him hostage, despite his best efforts to get the hell out of there.

Jackson finally found the strength to burst through the wind-shear sensation at the precise moment the airborne garbage bags plopped to the flooded entrance in unison. They glided along the rising water until the wind found them once again. This time, he barreled through. With no intention of stopping.

After a quick once-over, Jackson took note of the empty parking lot. He tried the building's front entrance. Locked. He pressed his face against the foggy window. No lights. He wouldn't be surprised if the power was out, thanks to the hellacious winds. The place appeared closed, no doubt due to the inclement weather. Still, he didn't fancy breaking into the building. As of yet, he hadn't committed any serious crimes. *Yeah, keep telling yourself that.* Aiding and abetting fugitives wasn't exactly a slap on the wrist.

Hoping to find an outbuilding, hell, anything, Jackson jogged around the corner to the first row of storage units. With one hand blocking the gusty rain from his face, he scanned the roll-up doors on the off chance one of the units wasn't padlocked.

That was a big fat no. He scurried to the next row, and then the next. All locked. Jackson peeked around the corner to the next row of storage units. Wait a minute. The front of a truck caught his eye. He jogged on to find a T-shape row of units. An older moving truck with the Penske Truck Rental name showing through a faded white coat of paint had backed to the roll-up door.

Apparently, someone had been in the process of moving when the storm hit. What a time to move. Perhaps the sirens had scared the movers away? This might just be the lucky break he was looking for. He peered between the back of the truck and the roll-up door. Yep, no padlock. But he couldn't squeeze through to open the roll-up door. And naturally, the damn truck doors were locked.

Nothing a little MacGyvering can't fix.

Jackson quickly sifted through his duffel for the small spool of wire he had taken from his storage shed. A great catch-all for repairs. That and duct tape. As the saying went, "If you can't fix it with duct tape, then you ain't using enough duct tape."

He snipped off a piece of wire with his handy-dandy plyers and quickly fashioned one end into a small loop. He pulled back the deteriorating weather stripping from the truck's driver's side window and then jammed the wire hook down into the door's locking mechanism. Until finally catching it in just the right spot. *Bingo*!

Quickly, Jackson put the truck in neutral and coasted down the slight decline a good two feet from the door. Too bad they wouldn't all fit inside the truck's cab. Well, it would be a good lookout spot. They could take turns on guard and monitor the storm. He rolled up the storage unit's garage-like door to find the room half-full of moving boxes and outdated furniture. He couldn't help but hope the movers had found a place to hang tight during the storm.

He had left Roxie and the gang at the tree line while he scoped out the facility. No doubt they were getting antsy. He hurried back, dodging a hodgepodge of random items blowing about. Rogue waved frantically when he saw Jackson. Jackson motioned them over. It was time to hunker down. The wind was downright deadly. All it would take was a freak accident. *Like a random pinecone.* That one still had him baffled. *What were the odds on that?*

Rogue took off for him, leaving Roxie with her two backpacks. Luna trudged on, seemingly oblivious to their treacherous environment. Jackson shook his head and made a beeline for Roxie while mentally bracing for impact and shielding his eyes with flared fingers so he could see.

He shortstopped Rogue. "Go back and help your sister." Brilliant as the kid was, at times he had the common sense of a tree stump.

Roxie was still floundering with her two backpacks when he made it to her. He strapped one over each of his shoulders, and with one arm around Roxie's slender body, they pushed through the brutal wind. "Just lean into the wind," he shouted into her ear. It was really all they could do.

A sheet of corrugated roofing flew past them a good twenty feet away. Too close for comfort as Roxie's shuddering body revealed. Nonetheless, they forged through the battering winds.

Finally, they made it inside the storage unit just as the winds escalated further. Another one of those supposedly "rare" derechos? In all of Jackson's sixty-plus years, he had never witnessed such whacked-out weather as he had lived through the past week.

"Heavens," Roxie belted out. "It's like a hurricane out there."

"Told you climate change is for real." Rogue had the gall to smart-mouth.

Jackson resisted an eye-roll urge while quickly tossing aside several boxes off the raggedy brown, corduroy couch. "Roxie, Luna, take a seat before you gals conk out on me." He didn't think he could handle one more calamity. Not today. Not tomorrow. He'd had his share for the decade.

"What I don't understand"—Roxie grappled the armrest and gingerly sat down—"every bloomin' day I see articles warning we need to decarbonize by 2035. Or is it 2050? What good's that if all this crazy weather is happening? Now!" Roxie rattled off, taking Rogue's bait.

"2050 is the Paris Agreement. But California wants to go all-electric by 2035," Rogue said in the tone of an aggravated schoolteacher.

"At this rate," Jackson groused, "we won't make it to 2035. End of story!"

"It's not my fault those jerk-offs, you know, the people *really* in charge, don't care," Rogue sniped. "Like, we should have gone green decades ago."

"I'm starting to think this is the climate scientists' fault," Roxie went on, "by harping on the one-point-five degrees—"

"Celsius—not Fahrenheit," Rogue blurted. "Which translates to two-point-seven degrees Fahrenheit."

Roxie waved him off. "But they made the one-point-five *Celsius* sound so minuscule. What's a few more degrees? Sheesh, we can handle two to three degrees of warmer weather. I never read a thing about thirty to forty degrees of hotter temperatures. And this is still winter. What will summer bring? I'm just saying, *they* didn't clearly explain the consequences."

"Yeah, they did—but nobody was listening," Rogue complained to the ceiling.

Luna had plopped onto the opposite end of the couch and proceeded to organize her pack, staying out of the conversation.

A surge of unexpected anger swept over Jackson. "With all these weather calamities, the insurance companies will go bust. Eventually, only the rich will be able to afford homes," Jackson said. It clicked. If the climate tweaked out enough to interfere with the farmers, they were screwed.

"That's why we have to overcome our substance abuse of—fossil fuels," the kid enunciated slowly.

"Don't see that happening," Jackson said. "Hell, the U.S. is constantly riddled with brownouts in the summers and winters as it is. How do they expect to fuel millions of EVs when they can't even meet the current household demands?"

"My electric bill has doubled in the past two years," Roxie chipped in.

"Guys, guys," Rogue blurted, "there's solar and wind and—"

"Not doable for most folks," Jackson cut in. First of all, he had too many trees. "A buddy of mine installed solar. Spent damn near forty thousand on a shoddy system that doesn't keep them cool in the summer or warm in the winter." On top of that, his friend's homeowner's insurance had canceled him, stating they didn't cover solar.

"Sheesh, who can afford solar?" Roxie's tone escalated.

"Duh," Rogue drawled sarcastically. "There's tons of government programs—"

Roxie cut him off. "Funny, I didn't qualify for a single one."

"It's the same old shit, a transference of power from Big Oil to the Electric Grid Moguls," Jackson said. "Either way, they're bleeding us dry. And I dare say, not for the planet's best interest but for those greedy SOBs." *Oops*, might have gone too far, he mused as the kid's face turned redder and redder.

"It's climate deniers like you—" Rogue erupted like a pyroclastic volcano.

"Aw, I see it plain as day," Jackson clapped back. There was no denying climate chaos wasn't real after the past few days. "Thing is, Americans can't afford the changes they're proposing." At this rate, he might end up living in a school bus like a modern-day nomad. "Say, whatever happened to that planet savior, Al Gore?" Jackson muttered as he removed the stack of boxes from a recliner.

"He didn't get to be the president because people like *you*," Rogue berated, "didn't vote for him."

Jackson let the box of books he was about to set on a shelf fall to the floor. He didn't appreciate being blamed for corporations' greed.

"See," Rogue said, "Gore invented this awesome carbon credit system . . ."

Based on an article Jackson had pondered over in *The Guardian*, the Carbon Cowboy Credit system wouldn't resolve the energy crisis. It merely justified the richies to squander energy usage since they could afford more.

"Luna, hon, what's your view on the subject?" Roxie asked as Luna massaged her head. "Oh, I'm sorry, we're getting too loud for you."

"Forget her. Luna doesn't believe in the Climate Crisis anymore," Rogue chided.

"Huh!" Luna glared at Rogue. "Your *ego*-prophet hero, sold us out. Didn't Mom and Dad tell you about the Blood and Gore carbon credit Ponzi scheme? It will make him a trillionaire while enslaving the middle class."

"Traitor," Rogue sing-songed over and over and covered his hands with his ears. "That's urban legend shit!"

Roxie sighed. "Who knows what to believe these days."

"Rogue, don't you see?" Luna jumped to her feet. "I'm sorry to be the one to tell you the actual truth. It's too late. We fucked up our planet! Deal with it! It'll take hundreds of years to repair the damage humans caused. We can't just fix it with farty EVs, shitty windmills, and crappy solar panels. I mean, those things require an *insane* amount of CO_2 emissions to create. Solar panels are made from glass, which is made from sand. Which is going extinct. And before you say it," Luna continued, "mining lithium, or practically anything, emits enormous amounts of CO_2. Just from another country. So, on a spreadsheet, the U.S. appears to be emitting less CO_2. But it's just creative accounting." Finally, Luna stopped.

"But, but, they're coming up with awesome new ideas all the time." Rogue wasn't ready to let go. "You know, like those big-ass machines that suck up CO_2 from the atmosphere and store it underground. Or those electric roads in Sweden that charge EVs while driving."

It was Jackson's turn to play devil's advocate. "If there's one thing I've learned, for every action, there's a reaction. Think about it. What d'you suppose the long-term effects of storing carbon in the ground will cause?" From what he had read, carbon capture and storage required an enormous amount of energy as well. Not to mention, piping out the CO_2 was highly explosive and expensive.

"The constant exposure to electric roads bothers me," Roxie said. "Think of all the cancers and nerve issues that's going to cause. And storing carbon in the ground makes me think an increase in earthquake activity."

"It's totally natural for carbon to be in the ground," Rogue defended with gusto.

"But, an entire atmosphere of it? That's just robbing Peter to pay Paul," Jackson quipped.

"What does that even mean?" Rogue whined.

"History has a way of repeating itself." Jackson couldn't stop himself. "Back in the day, those so-called 'experts' said the same thing about nuclear waste. Just store it underground or heck, dump it in the ocean. No one's the wiser. We're still paying for that one."

"You can't believe every conspiracy theory you hear," Rogue said, slathered with sarcasm.

"Case in point," Jackson said, "in the early nineties, a buddy of mine had the opportunity to buy some cheap acreage in the boonies of New Mexico. He wanted to start a cattle ranch. Until he heard the scuttlebutt from the locals warning the government had buried nuclear waste from all those White Sand's missile tests during WWII. After a little testing, we discovered sections were, indeed, still radioactive. Not much, mind you. But who'd want to have a cattle ranch out there? Moreover, who in hell would want to consume the meat?"

"Ew, that can't be true," Rogue said.

"Afraid the Geiger counter differs with you. The point of my story is: we don't always know the damage our actions will cause further down the road." Such as fossil fuels destroying the climate. Ah, but Jackson didn't say that out loud.

"So, if you know so much, how do you think we can get to net zero?" Rogue huffed.

Jackson winked at Roxie before turning to a hotheaded Rogue. "Suppose the tried-and-true *Gilligan's Island* method of pedaling a stationary bike for energy would do the trick. It would make people take note of how much energy they use. Eliminate waste-fulness."

"Whatev," Rogue spouted. "Are you a climate change denier or what?"

"Who says one has to be on a particular side," Jackson theorized. "The more outspokenly rigid people become with their beliefs, the more divided our country becomes. Stalling progress for all of us. Including the planet." He left it at that.

Luna opened the storage unit's door, letting in a surprisingly warm blast of air. "I'm sitting in the truck."

"Now hold on just a minute," Jackson said a little harsher than intended. "We should monitor you—"

"And do what? It's not like I can go to the hospital." Luna ambled to the truck.

"Rogue, go with your sister." The chill in Roxie's sharp tone left no room for rebuttal.

Rogue stood there, wavering.

"Young man," Roxie started, "go. And be nice to your sister."

Rogue stomped off.

"Let me know when the weather breaks," Jackson hollered as the door rolled down and hit the concrete floor.

"Pardon me," Jackson said. "I apologize for letting the conversation go awry." He was ashamed of himself. "I don't need some twerp telling me the world's going to hell." He supposed the climate change debate with Rogue was a long time coming.

Roxie nodded knowingly. "That's just Rogue's way of coping. From his viewpoint, he has a right to be angry. With everything. His entire generation is basically rooked. Realistically, what kind of future do they have? Everything's a mess, from the economy—to this cursed weather."

It caused Jackson to pause in reflection.

"In our day," Roxie continued, "we believed the great American Dream was within our reach. All we had to do was work hard. Maybe go to college, get a decent paying job. Get married, have kids, buy a house, a new car every few years, take fancy vacations . . ."

Jackson found himself tapping his lip in agreement. "You're right. These next generations are screwed up the yin-yang. Folks are having a hard enough time just putting food on the table."

"Sad but true." Roxie let down her damp curly hair, which had been bound up in a bun. It cupped her face in a fairytale princess sort of way.

"Now I really feel like an ass," Jackson confessed.

"Don't be so hard on yourself. Rogue is—rather challenging. Lashing out and wanting attention. However, my circle of friends' grandchildren exhibits similar behavior. It must be a byproduct of these uncertain times we live in. On top of that, there's the whole social media thing. And the gender thing. All this stress takes a mental toll. Well, that's my humble opinion."

"Don't get me started on the social media debacle. A bunch of braggarts and liars and con artists. That's how I see it," Jackson said. "You seem privy to the times. Can you help me comprehend this gender conflict issue young people seem to be going through nowadays? Rogue said he was nonbinary."

"Oh, last month he was bigender."

"Which one is that?" Jackson asked. He had read up on the topic but was still dumbfounded by it all. Was he afraid to understand it?

"Bigenders identify as both male and female. Or as female and agender as I recall. Interesting, that now he doesn't identify to being male or female. I wouldn't be surprised if he changed his mind again. And that's probably another category . . ."

"How do you know so much about the subject?" Jackson asked.

"My community center requires volunteers to attend annual gender diversity seminars. To avoid lawsuits. When we're volunteering, we're not even allowed to mention gender. Honestly, I don't understand the gender confusion. But I don't deny gender identity is a real issue. I am, however, at a loss why younger generations get so mad with my generation for not understanding. After all, young people don't understand half the things we went through in our day."

"Precisely," Jackson said. "They couldn't care less. As if seniors don't matter."

"And yet, we're the ones getting called out for being ignorant and insensitive." Roxie waved it off. "Well, we don't have to understand the 'why.' Just know the issue exists. I'm a firm believer we should not be judgmental regarding other's life choices. After all, we live in a free country."

"You're absolutely right," Jackson said. "I've always prided myself on believing in the 'to each his own' concept. Thank you, for reminding me of that."

"You and me both," Roxie said. "I don't know what to think of our future." She quickly covered her mouth before yawning. "I feel bad for the younger generations. I don't know how they're going to manage. It's no wonder they go around shooting people. The rage virus, as I call it, must be due to sheer hopelessness. And it's probably why Rogue is such a mess." She unzipped her pack, and Pixie poked her cute furry head out.

"Huh, didn't think of the toll it takes on the young folk. However, I do realize why I tend to disregard the climate crisis hype. Because there's not a damn thing I can do about it."

"I know what you mean." Roxie's tone turned solemn. "Despite what they say, I can't really change my carbon footprint enough to make a smidgeon of difference. Although, I did install mini-splits, which ended up costing me thousands of dollars. I can't afford solar, or an EV without draining my savings. I can barely afford organic foods and electricity. My goal: not to outlive my social security. If the economy continues spiraling out of control, I won't be able to live off of Hank's pension . . ."

"Oh, Roxie, you can always count on me." The words slipped out before Jackson could stop them.

Her questioning crystal-blue eyes stared back as if completely mystified by his statement.

"You should take a nap," Jackson said abruptly, looking around for something soft for her head. He nabbed another one of those nifty collapsible camping lanterns from his duffel and then fumbled around until he found a stack of moving blankets. "Here you go."

Roxie took the blanket. "Good idea." She yawned louder. "You should rest too."

"Don't mind if I do." He leaned back in the recliner. But after their heated discussion, sleep would be hard to find. The world was at a crossroads, whether it was the economy, energy crisis, or climate crisis. They could not continue consuming the planet's limited natural resources at the rate of the past decades.

Another Great Depression or world war to battle over the dwindling natural resources was bound to hit the U.S.

Chapter 35

Luna Lewis unzipped the rucksack's side pouch and snatched the binoculars with snarky attitude. "Roxie and Handyman Jack aren't stopping me." She panned the surroundings from the box truck's driver seat. Not even idiots would be out in this hellacious wind. It was the perfect time to go to SunFlower's.

"Oh yeah, well, they're the adults—" Rogue ragged. "And, and you have to do what they say."

"Like you do? Besides, I *am* an adult." Luna donned a rain poncho, all the more determined, before stepping out of the safety of the truck's cab, despite Rogue's intensifying glare. By the time she rolled up the storage unit's door, her brother stood beside her, shouting. Thankfully, the wind swept away his ranting.

Handyman Jack scrambled up from the recliner, rubbing his eyes. "Trouble?"

"Tell her she can't go," Rogue blurted.

"Go where?" Roxie garbled, apparently trying to yawn herself awake.

Handyman Jack's eyes narrowed. "Luna?"

"I just came to say goodbye. And to thank you for helping us. *Believing* in us," Luna quickly added when anger and confusion seemed to freeze onto Handyman Jack's well-etched forehead.

"Now hold on," Handyman Jack started in. "We need to wait for a break in this cockamamie weather. This is the storm of the century."

"Millennia," Rogue shot back.

"They won't be looking for us in this insane storm," Luna reasoned.

"You can't hike in this weather," Roxie scolded.

"Exactly. That's why I'm driving the damn truck," Luna stated firmly.

"That's what I've been trying to tell you if you'd let me talk." Rogue brandished his arms to the ceiling. "She hot-wired the truck."

Handyman Jack stood there, gawking at her.

"Where in heaven's did you learn to do that?" Roxie marveled.

Luna shrugged. It was really no big deal; older vehicles were easy to boost. It had been part of her off-grid survival training. That long-ago memory made her smile internally, remembering the day Devin had taught her, after which, they had made out in the pretense of needing more practice to go undercover as activist spies posing as a married couple.

That insanely crazy-fun summer when everything had seemed possible. She had totally fallen for Devin's heart-throbbing smile. Her first love at sixteen had been the most magical time of her life. She brushed back the ancient memories. For their short-lived romance had not ended well.

"Rogue's staying with you two," Luna said as she ducked under the partially opened door.

Rogue thrust his body around her legs and nearly sent her to her knees. "No! I won't let you . . ."

Handyman Jack pulled them both back into the storage unit and slammed the door closed. "Hmm, it might be doable." He tapped his lower lip. "That is, if the roads aren't too flooded."

Roxie gasped in the background. "Did a pinecone knock the sense out of you as well?"

"From what you saw on the radar, how long's this storm lasting?" Handyman Jack asked.

"Another eight to ten days," Luna said. The satellite report had looked apocalyptic.

"I, for one, don't fancy being cooped up in here that long," Handyman Jack said. "Tell you what, let's give it a go. But promise me we'll turn around if things get dicey."

"Since we met you," Roxie said pointedly to Handyman Jack, "when have things *not* been dicey?"

Handyman Jack chuckled. "Touché. How close are we to Sun-Flower's house?"

Rogue and Roxie kept glancing back and forth from her to Handyman Jack, as if excited to see who would win the tense tennis rally.

"Ten minutes, depending on the roads." Luna had presumed they wouldn't want to chance the trip in the storm. It would be better to leave together since she only had seven MREs to give them. "What if—" She paused, brainstorming the most logical plan. They could hide the truck on SunFlower's property. No, too risky. The truck might be AirTagged. "We can park the truck on the main county road before SunFlower's. And hike to the house."

"One thing we might want to consider?" Handyman Jack seemed lost in thought.

Rogue threw up his arms. "Tell us, already."

"Finish unloading the truck. As an act of goodwill," Handyman Jack added. "It ought to lighten the sentencing should we get charged for grand theft auto."

"Smart," Luna said, rolling up the unit's door and checking the back of the truck. There wasn't much left. The movers must have left in another vehicle when the sirens had gone off.

"Roxie ol' gal," Handyman Jack said. "It's up to you. Would you rather stay here for God knows how long or risk a short trip in hundred-plus winds? Mind you, we'll be surrounded by trees no matter where we go."

"I do detest not having a restroom," Roxie professed.

"Then it's settled," Handyman Jack said with his usual down-to-earth authority, easing Luna's uptightness.

She didn't want to be accused of abandoning senior citizens in some funky storage unit. What if the unthinkable happened, and there was a medical emergency? In this extreme storm, people were going to die. Probably already had. Flashbacks of the fires still haunted her dreams. Those people had died. Horribly.

Luna hunched in the back of the moving truck and set the boxed and unboxed items at the foot of the truck while Handyman Jack, Roxie, and Rogue carried them into the storage unit. Random items like a full-size vintage gumball machine filled with seashells, a crate with brightly painted cow skulls, and WWII ammo cans she was dying to see inside. Naturally, Rogue provided satirical commentary about each item, and soon they were back to kidding around again.

Luna had to admit Handyman Jack's idea of unloading the truck was awesome. He was awesome. She regretted insulting him and Roxie with her lame plan of abandoning them there. She shouldn't be so selfish. She was learning, a work in progress. In her profession, no one got anywhere by being nice.

She thought back to the promotions she had lost out on because the competition had been fiercely bitchy and often conniving. Unusually distracted, her monkey brain wouldn't stop reminding her of her lifetime of rash decisions. Once again, Devin flashed her mind. She hadn't thought of him in years, and lately she couldn't stop thinking about him.

"Last one." Handyman Jack's voice overrode Luna's invasive thoughts.

"Thank heavens," Roxie said, rubbing her back.

"I was thinking," Handyman Jack started casually, the way he did when he wanted to politely make a suggestion. "Thinkin' I should drive. You might still be woozy from the pine cone incident. However, you should ride shotgun since you know the way."

"I'm okay with that," Luna said.

"I'll watch for the cops," Rogue announced.

"Sport, I want you and Roxie to ride in the back of the truck. Out of sight," Handyman Jack said. "Just in case we do come to a roadblock or whatnot. Since they are looking for two males and two females. Is that the appropriate way to say that?"

Luna couldn't hold back her smile.

"But no seatbelts . . ." Rogue blurted.

"Really, after what we've been through—you're worried about not wearing a seatbelt?" Luna ribbed.

Rogue's frown quickly morphed into a huge grin. "Hey, I brought the two-way radios." He dumped his pack onto the couch, letting unmarked silver packages spill to the floor.

"What the heck are those?" Luna grilled. It didn't look like any survival food brands she was familiar with.

Rogue's wide grin quickly turned into a guilty smirk. "Did you think I was leaving my Frosted Toasted Pastries? I just took them out of the box to squeeze more into the backpack."

"You brought the pop tarts. Not extra clothes?" Roxie questioned.

"As long as they're organic—" That's when Handyman Jack lost it.

They all lost it. Luna took a radio with a giggle before walking to the truck. She couldn't stay mad at her goofy brother for long. He provided the perfect comic relief, whatever the situation, whether he meant to or not.

"It's getting dark. We'd better get," Handyman Jack said, still chuckling under his breath.

"Are you sure you don't want to sit up front?" Luna said to Roxie, trying to do the polite thing as Handyman Jack helped the woman into the back of the moving truck.

"I'll be fine back here. Just don't let Jackson pop any wheelies," Roxie teased.

"Ah, you're no fun," Handyman Jack teased back. "Back in a jiffy. Want to check out the road. We aren't going anywhere if it's too flooded." He strode off around the corner to the next wing of storage units.

"So, we're on channel four," Rogue said, hopping into the back of the truck like a hyper kid anxious for a road trip.

"Got it. But maintain radio silence. The bad guys," Luna whispered, "might be listening. Roxie, is it okay if I close the door now?"

"Go right ahead," Roxie said as Luna handed her the backpack Pixie was in.

Luna started the engine and then settled into the passenger's seat, impatiently waiting for Handyman Jack, irritated at herself. She should have thought of checking the road. The farmhouse was at a higher elevation than where they were. So, if the flood waters trickled downstream toward Redding, maybe the roads to Sunflower's hadn't flooded much.

She pilfered through the paperwork in the door's side pockets, noticing the movers were from Yreka. She fiddled with the glove compartment until it finally opened. Awesomeness. A Siskiyou County Map dropped into her lap. Synchronicity, as SunFlower would say. She studied the map to get her bearings.

Handyman Jack stepped inside and adjusted the seat and mirrors. "Bad news, the gutters appear clogged. With about six inches of standing water on the road."

"So much for not flooding," Luna groaned.

"Testing one, two, three . . ." Rogue announced over the radio.

"Citizen, you are not authorized to broadcast on this channel," Luna droned off like a military commander. And snap, she clicked off the radio.

"Alrighty, Luna, please tell me that's a map of the area."

"Yes. I know exactly where we are."

Handyman Jack strapped on the seatbelt. "Excellent, tell me which way to go."

"Left on Mott Road."

Handyman Jack exited the self-storage facility without any maneuvering problems. But the truck was taking a heavy hit from the wind. It wasn't advisable to drive the high-profile truck on the interstate. Besides, they might run into the National Guard. Taking the backroads were their best option.

Despite preferring to be in charge, Luna was all too happy to let him drive while she gave directions. Still, the closer they made it to SunFlower's, the more dread seemed to infuse her veins.

What if Mom and Dad hadn't made it to SunFlower's?

Chapter 36

Roxie Romero huddled in a pile of rough moving blankets in the back of the moving truck and kept Rogue engaged in idle conversation about his upcoming science project, in order to distract her from the wind gusts blasting the truck. It wasn't working. It was a wonder Jackson kept the truck on the road. Only a few more miles she kept telling herself.

"I want to play with Pixie," Rogue decided, already unzipping the pack.

Roxie didn't want to further upset her neurotic cat with another new environment. "Let's wait until we get to SunFlower's," she said a moment too late. Pixie sprang out of her confinement with wild, crazy eyes and jumped around with an arched back, hissing.

Before she could get mad at Rogue, the truck lurched into a steep nose-dive. Rogue slid into Roxie's lap as her back slammed against the truck's wall.

"We crashed!" Rogue shouted, scrambling out of her arms.

Roxie patted her thudding heart. "We're fine." Pixie's low growling warned otherwise. "It feels like we ended up in a ditch."

"Holy balls!" Rogue easily scaled up the tilted floor to the truck's rear door. "We have to save Luna and Handyman Jack."

The back door rolled open. "It's flooding. The creek washed out the road," Luna said, void of emotion. "We need to get to higher ground."

The temperature had dropped rather quickly, and Roxie had a hard time getting her bones and muscles to cooperate. All she wanted to do was sleep under the pile of blankets and rest her weary, aching body.

Until the truck started moving sideways—slipping deeper into a ditch. That had her adrenaline pumping.

Luna had already helped Rogue out, but Roxie's unexpected charley-horse debilitated her momentarily. "Pixie girl, c'mere sweetie," Roxie cooed.

Finally, Roxie forced her legs into working and dashed for Pixie. Only to fall flat on her tushy as the truck teetered deeper into a nosedive. She ended up sliding back against the wall again.

Jackson's head popped into the open door. "Roxie, hate to put the pressure on, but we're running out of time. Grab this." He threw her one end of a thin cord-like rope.

Roxie grabbed the rope, wondering what good that little thing would do. All she had to do was crawl up.

"Good," Jackson said. "Now tie the paracord in a solid knot around your waist."

"I'm perfectly capable of getting out," Roxie chided, sliding to the far-left corner of the truck when it tottered farther. On that note, she tied the flimsy thing around her waist, wishing she had time to take off the bulky sweater she had borrowed from the movers.

"Don't panic. I'll pull you out nice and easy," Jackson coaxed with calm assuredness.

She sensed his urgency as the truck sloshed about sideways. She kept one hand on the paracord while Jackson, who must have been standing on the rear bumper, reeled her up toward him.

"Pixie girl . . ." Roxie called out meekly as she inched closer to Jackson. From what she could tell, the water had engulfed the front half of the truck. And it was sinking fast.

"Almost there," Jackson said with blood trickling down his forehead.

"Pixie . . ." Pixie was just out of reach as Jackson pulled her out.

The truck abruptly tilted to its side. Water gushed in. She held on, slinging her shoulder purse to her back for better agility so she could tread through the influx of water.

Jackson grabbed her hand. "I gotcha."

"Heavens!" She vigorously held on, reaching Jackson in time to see Luna and Rogue make it to a hill. On dry land.

"Roxie," Jackson said somberly, "on three, we jump. And swim in the direction of that hill."

As if transfixed, Roxie stared at the encroaching waters and clutched the edge of the truck in the cold, angry wind.

"One . . ."

She shook her head adamantly.

"Two . . ."

"Pixie—"

"Three . . ."

Terror flooded through her when Jackson's strong arms yanked her into the excruciatingly frigid water with him.

"I gotcha," Jackson's gentle voice purred in her ear.

I'm safe was all she could think. *I'm safe . . .*

The water inundated the entire truck, creating a whirlpool as the truck plummeted out of sight and tore Jackson's arms from her.

"I'm comin' for you . . ." His words echoed into nothingness.

Roxie went under, gulping water. *I'll be fine*, she wanted to say. *Get Pixie*.

She flailed about, trying to remove the bulky sweater holding her captive, which was tangled with the purse strap and the paracord. *How in heavens can the water be so deep? So cold?*

Paralysis took hold. Time seemed to spiral backward as she drifted peacefully in the raging water while a lifetime of memories flashed in her mind. The good ones . . . All trumped by an unexpected yearning spiraling up and down her soul. She was devastatingly heartbroken she hadn't been given the time to know Jackson better.

Perhaps even in the biblical sense.

Chapter 37

Jackson Jones stomped around the old country farmhouse grounds, trying to make sense of yesterday's harrowing escape. What the hell was going on with this god-forsaken weather? The lack of emergency responders had him thinking it was too dangerous even for trained personnel. Folks were likely sheltering in place, as they should.

The good news: they had finally made it to SunFlower's farmhouse. On the flip side, SunFlower and the kids' parents were nowhere to be found, and the solar unit and Internet were down. He had spotted Sunflower's bus in the bushes propped on jack stands, apparently nonoperational. There was no way to take Roxie to the hospital. Of course, the roads were probably still impassable.

Yesterday's dicey drive to SunFlower's kept haunting him. He hadn't realized the road had washed out due to the flooded roads and low-visibility until they had ended up in a flooded creek. The water had risen quickly, thanks to the spillover of the adjacent irrigation ditch. He berated himself for not waiting it out in the storage unit.

On second thought, it had turned cold quickly. At least now, they had a woodstove and were a good five hundred feet higher in elevation. Perhaps they were better off at SunFlower's, as long as the countless creeks running down Mount Shasta didn't flood them out. For the life of him, he could not shake the nonsensible notion they were on their own yet again.

Was the planet really on the brink? The scientists and world leaders had promised there was time to turn back the carbon-emission clock thereby saving them from intolerable weather events like the ones they were witnessing. The planet seemed to be rearing its hind legs in retaliation and yelling, "Life on Earth will never be the same."

Jackson's gut instinct told him the world leaders were strategically running out the clock. Not because they were winning. Because they were losing. No doubt those one-percenters had their SAT phones at the ready, with the plan of escaping to their decadently stocked bunkers when they got the call.

He plunked himself down on an old wooden swing hanging from a ginormous limb of the magnificent budding oak and tried to enjoy the abrupt bout of mild weather. It wasn't raining or snowing. And nothing was on fire. "Give it five minutes," he spouted to the cloud-laden sky threatening otherwise.

It was time to think of his future. Hell, he didn't even know if his house was still standing. Chances were, he had lost it to the same fire that had burned down the hotel. Ah, and then there was Roxie . . .

Don't even go there. He didn't deserve a second chance with a wonderful woman such as her. Not after his messy divorce. He had been as much to blame as his ex when their arbitration had turned downright ugly.

"Handyman Jack?" Rogue's girly scream pierced his thoughts.

He dug his heels into the muddy soil to stop the swing. "Now what? Don't tell me there's a sinkhole in the living room?" Nowadays, he didn't know what to expect. Well, he could use a distraction from his unrelenting thoughts, blaming himself for being alone . . . dying alone. A senseless worry he had never troubled over. Until now, at the crossroads with his newfound friends.

With random amorous thoughts of Roxie harassing him, Jackson hustled past the vacant chicken coop, past the compost pile, beyond the fenced garden, and back to the front of the farmhouse to find Rogue waving madly from the front door. At least they had made it to their damn near impossible destination while lugging a semiconscious Roxie in a wheelbarrow they had commandeered from a construction site.

After Jackson had dove in to save Roxie, he and Luna had taken turns administering CPR. He had never been so relieved when Roxie had finally come to enough to wretch up the water from her lungs. If only, she hadn't been under too long. Paranoid thoughts of brain damage hounded him.

"For the love of God, please let it be good news." To be honest, Jackson's heart could not bear the alternative.

Luna and Rogue stood by the front door. *Are they smiling?* Jackson remained tight-lipped, afraid to ask if Roxie was all right.

"Hurry, you run like an old guy," Rogue had the gall to nag while Luna elbowed her sassy brother.

"I *am* an old guy!"

"Roxie wants you?" Luna sang playfully.

Luna's choice of words stunned Jackson. *Me? Roxie wants—me? Don't be a fool. It's merely a figure of speech.* He couldn't get his hopes up, only to careen down the rollercoaster of—dare he say it? Love. They hadn't known each other that long. Nonetheless, after all they'd been through, it might as well have been a lifetime.

Jackson paused before turning into the shabby chic bedroom. Unsure. If she had asked for him, she must be all right.

"Come on in," Roxie seemed to taunt. "I heard you clomping all the way down the hall."

He spun around the doorway into her room, greeted by an ashen-faced Roxie sitting up in the bed with her back against a stack of pink-rosy pillows. Her spirited sapphire eyes were not laced with anger. Or hate. As he feared.

"Roxie ol' gal, can you ever forgive me? For not holding on—" When the truck had plunged into the water, tearing her from his grip.

She waved him off. "As the younger generations keep reminding us, shit happens."

That was good for a quick laugh. Still, her wavering smile and thin voice revealed she hadn't recovered just yet.

Jackson took a seat in the rocker by her bed. "How you feelin'?"

"A bit tired. As to be expected."

"If I hadn't—" He stopped short, afraid the terror in his voice might reveal his true feelings.

"Don't go soft on me now, mister. Not after all we've been through. You saved us countless times." She fidgeted with the top edge of the rose quilt, smoothing it down until the fold was perfectly even. "I'll be fine in a day or two. It wasn't your fault. Luna told me how you kept going under, looking for me. You"—her voice cracked—"saved me!"

He leaned in to caress her dainty hands. "I want you to know—" He swallowed hard. Should he say it? Wearing his heart on his sleeve was so unlike him.

She gazed up at him with those mesmerizing eyes of hers. Hoping?

"Whatever happens. Uh, once things return to normal," he clarified. "Well, I want you to know I'd do it all again for the chance to get to know—"

"Hey," Rogue yelled into the doorway, "I think SunFlower's here. There's a car coming down the driveway." Rogue continued running down the hallway.

The elusive SunFlower at last. At times he had questioned Sun-Flower's existence, as if he were an ill-fated character ensnared in a fairytale, confronted with a series of impossible challenges to be rewarded with precious jewels upon completion. Cockamamie as it was, the actual events they had endured seemed more incredible than a fairytale.

"See," Roxie said, as if oblivious to his unfinished heartfelt confession. "Everything's going as planned."

What if the FBI was paying another visit was what he wanted to say. But didn't risk upsetting her. The farmhouse had been thoroughly ransacked before they had arrived, presumably by the FBI, according to Luna. The authorities must have figured it out somehow. They couldn't outrun the law forever. Not in Roxie's condition. Let the chips fall where they may. They had been jumping out of one frying pan into another since the fires had started.

Jackson simply nodded, wanting to sit by her side for hours and discuss what was next, provided they weren't hauled off to jail. He was dying to know if Roxie's future included him. Or was this the end of their adventure? Would they go their merrily, post-traumatized ways?

Still, he should find out what news SunFlower had.

"You'd better go meet this woman we've risked our lives to find," Roxie said, as if reading his mind.

That was the thing about Roxie; they seemed to be on the same wavelength more often than not. Another sign they were meant to be together or merely a generation thing?

"Pick her brain for all the info you can get. I trust your first impressions of her. Otherwise, no telling what crazy conspiracy Rogue will conjure up." Roxie offered a faint, weary laugh. "You know Luna, she never seems to tell us the entire story. I feel she's always holding something back."

"I get that feeling as well." He dragged himself from the rocker.

"Hurry back," she said after sipping a cup of tea. "I can't wait to hear what in heavens is going on in the real world."

Jackson bent over and tenderly brushed her forehead with his lips before scuttling to the door to avoid his impulsive moment of tenderness. Had she minded?

"Jackson"—she hesitated—"did Pixie make it?" Roxie croaked out.

That hit like a gut punch to his solar plexus. For he knew how much she loved that kooky cat. Afraid the bad news might get the best of her, he uttered, "No doubt, Pixie will show up on the doorstep any minute now, begging for a can of tuna."

She nodded knowingly, as if reading between the lines.

"Well then, get some rest," he said before stepping into the hallway, trying to hide his gloom. *Damn, wish I could have save the cat*! It had taken all his strength, pushing himself beyond his limits. Just to save Roxie.

The muffled cry from Roxie's room seemed to paralyze him as he forced himself to quicken his pace to greet SunFlower. When all he wanted to do was soothe Roxie's sorrow. If only he knew how . . .

Chapter 38

Luna Lewis stood in the doorway of SunFlower's sprawling farmhouse and stared in disbelief at the familiar, red-faded Jeep rolling to a stop a few feet away. Impossible. It couldn't be—him. He wouldn't still be driving the same Cherokee Chief. Would he?

The driver opened the door, put one foot on the ground, and then hesitated. Rogue being Rogue, ran up to the guy. "Where's SunFlower?" Rogue demanded. "If you're an FBI agent pretending to be a Rasta Man, I'm not letting you arrest us!"

The mocha-skinned man with blondish shoulder-length dreadlocks grimly shook his head.

"Hey, I know you! You're the AI Doomer Dude," Rogue exclaimed in obvious confusion. "I watch your videos on Rumble. Are you a Rasta man, for real?"

The man's unexpected burst of laughter sent Luna's heart reeling. How she used to crave that laugh.

"You must be Rogue. You grew up fast," Devin said before finally meeting her eyes.

"Wait." Rogue frowned so hard his eyes nearly crossed. "You know me?"

"I'm friends with"—Devin flashed Luna an uncertain glance—"your parents."

"Oh." Recognition spread across Rogue's face. "When my hair gets long enough, will you teach me to braid dreads? And do you have any ganja? I'm old enough now to smoke it."

"No ganja for you," Devin shot back in his well-perfected but bogus Jamaican accent.

The Devin she had known had shamelessly taken advantage of his distant Jamaican heritage with his enthralling accent by wooing people into discounted meals and lodging during their summer fling. The shortest summer of Luna's life. He had often been hired to lead meditations in metaphysical meccas, which had been an effective way to earn gas money back when they had driven to Santa Fe for an enlightenment retreat SunFlower had arranged.

An unexpected flashback of them making out in the hot evenings in the Jeep's pop-up camper invaded her thoughts. They had been so poor. So happy . . .

But her unbridled coming-of-age love story seemed like forever ago and had no relevance to her current life. Luna refused to let his adoring personality sway her. She was an adult now, not some lusty teenager victimized by her raging hormones. Although Devin was sexy as ever, he appeared far older than her. As if the years had robbed him of his zest.

Behind her, Handyman Jack asked who the visitor was. How could she objectively introduce the only man she had let steal her heart and whom she yearned for in those lonely moments that sometimes found her in the dark dead of night? When she wasn't hating him. *Whoever tagged that idiotic cliché* "Time heals all wounds," *was wrong*!

"That's right. Your Luna's old boyfriend," Rogue's not-so-quiet whisper announced. "SunFlower told me to watch all your videos. Because someday you will be super important."

SunFlower had scolded Luna for redacting Devin from her life, foreseeing they'd eventually reunite after resolving karmic past-life traumas, thereby understanding their true "soul-purposes." *Whatever that means. SunFlower, wherever you are, I love you. But why are you always so damn ambiguous?*

"Sport," Handyman Jack grunted. "Best we leave them alone—"

"No," Luna said hastily, as if she didn't have a care in the world. For him. "If Devin is here. He's part of Mom and Dad's plot." They adored him and had expected them to get married and join their activism fight.

But Devin had unexpectedly deserted his oath of saving the planet for an MIT scholarship. Who would have thought under that lazy smile, intoxicating voice, and contagious exuberance, he had been a genius in all thing's computer, surprising everyone. Especially himself.

He had vowed to channel his intelligence into manufacturing inexpensive eco-friendly housing for the homeless using 3-D printing technology. Like so many, Devin had lost his way, venturing off into the unethical world of artificial intelligence. For that, she couldn't blame him. After all, she had let the fashion industry lure her away from the thankless mission of saving the planet.

The real question pricking her brain was why Devin was there. This very moment. It had to be the absolute worst time in her life to see him. With everything that had happened since the fires, she wasn't emotionally prepared. Aw, but Luna was tough. She would rely on her perfected bitchy brashness to get her through this shitty day.

"So," Luna said, as devoid of emotion as she could, "do you know where our parents are?"

"And Auntie SunFlower?" Rogue chimed in.

A faraway rumbling warned of another approaching storm. Devin glanced at the sky and then grabbed an envelope from the dashboard. "Let's talk inside," he said in a solemn, non-Jamaican voice.

Luna led the way to SunFlower's exotic meditation room, the only room Luna had straightened up after finding the normally spotless home a wreck. She assumed the FBI or Homeland Security had paid a visit. Even the quail had been let out of their pen and darted around outside, pecking for food. It was fortunate it had taken them so long to get to there, since someone had been by. Looking for SunFlower, her parents. Maybe even her and Rogue?

As if to prolong the inevitable truth she had been so eager to learn, Luna leisurely lit the wall of Moroccan mosaic lanterns with the grace of a high priestess. The flickering candles glowed through the mosaic glass and danced on the intricate mandala mural along with the clusters of cathedral amethyst geodes, exquisite rose quartz towers, and a myriad of other crystals. Each item purposely feng-shuied around the room as SunFlower had once explained.

The room was "so SunFlower." It brought Luna back to a time when she had been at peace. With herself. With her family. And the world. She forced back a surge of unexpected tears, the happy kind. Because this wasn't a day to be happy. She plopped onto the colorful Turkish pillow–covered floor and wrapped a bohemian print blanket around her. Awaiting the truth. For Devin never lied.

"Are Mom and Dad hiding from the FBI at an uber-cool safehouse?" an enthralled Rogue asked after the tenuous silence.

A bizarre sensation shrouded Luna, as if for the first time in her life she no longer sensed her parents' domineering presence, abruptly freed from their expectations. It wasn't as liberating as she had imagined, more like profound emptiness. She shoved the odd sensation to the furthest depths of her mind. No matter what, she was not feeling sorry for them. They deserved the negative karma that had befallen them. One hundred percent.

A sudden sadness seemed to sting Devin's striking emerald eyes. Uncomfortable with the mounting tension, Luna asked, "Why is the news media blaming Mom and Dad for sabotaging the data centers? And the fires in our hometown?"

"Yeah, did you know our house totally burned down?" Rogue was quick to add.

"You do realize the FBI and possibly even Homeland Security are looking for us," Luna took over the conversation.

Devin nodded solemnly. "Before I start, you'll need to focus on the—bigger picture."

Luna hated it when people attempted manipulating the conversation with certain buzzwords. That was what her bosses in upper management did. She knew, after sitting through several managerial training seminars. "Did they do it or not?"

"Yes," Devin said simply. "But they had nothing to do with the fires."

"The media are lying fuckeroos! Mom and Dad would never use real bombs," Rogue defended.

"Exactly," she said flatly. But something was up. Why else would Devin be there? She glanced at Handyman Jack, who sat hunched in the corner of the room, looking like he didn't want to be part of the conversation.

"The 'event' was part of a well-orchestrated plan," Devin said with insufferable serenity.

"Computers aren't their MO," Luna badgered. "I mean, my parents can't exist without the publicity they incite on social media."

"Duh, Luna," Rogue scolded. "I told you. A few months ago, their social media accounts, all of them, even their bank accounts, f'n disappeared."

"No, you didn't." Rogue was going delusional on her.

Devin fluffed a pillow before crossing his legs into the lotus position. "It's true. Their money was turned off days after Crystal and Forest became woke AI Doomer influencers overnight. All it took was that one eye-opening interview on my Rumble channel where they presented real-time data on exactly how much water and electricity the Tech Giants' data centers guzzled. That video turned their lives upside down, more so than all the protest events they ever organized. I'm terribly sorry for that."

"Yeah," Rogue said, "data centers, especially the AI ones, suck up enough water and electricity to power millions of homes twenty-four seven. That's why *what's-his-face* needs his own nuclear power plant!"

Luna just shook her head, not sure what to think. It took balls to go up against Big Tech. She admired her parents for that. But was it worth the cost? How would they earn a living?

"As you must know"—Devin's tone turned patronizing, as if she no longer cared about the planet's downward spiral—"the assault on the Tech Giants was intended to be a wake-up call. To all sides of the political spectrum. Only, we were too late." His hands fell into his lap.

"Too late for what?" Luna shredded into him. Was he trying to turn this into a political thriller?

"See, they actually went after the artificial general intelligence data centers, the mad-scientist centers that are programming computers to learn—better than humans," Devin said gravely.

"The news report we saw didn't mention anything about AI," Handyman Jack finally broke into the conversation.

"Right," Devin said patiently, "unlike the good old days, today's news media exists primarily to distribute malinformation by *not* divulging the truth. They can't. Because they're owned by the billionaires, the ones literally grooming AGI. As a tool for world dominance."

"Not that same old bullshit?" Luna blatantly condemned. She was sick of the insane conspiracy theories. "It'll take generations to create a New World Order." Although, SunFlower had told her about ominous visions of AI gaining consciousness, becoming sentient. If that happened, humans were screwed.

"That was what we presumed. Until AGI woke the hell up after the attacks." There was no denying the fury spewing from the always calm and collective Devin. "They, as in the AI, hacked the U.S. into DEFCON 2 a few days ago. As we speak, we're at DEF-CON 1. For now, the U.S. and apparently all the nuclear powers, are locked out, unable to de-escalate the status. The world leaders are literally sitting with their fingers over the button—waiting to see who *gets* to strike first. But"—he paused— "the U.S. didn't escalate the DEFCON status. AGI did."

"Fuuuck," Luna exclaimed. "The National Guardsman bragged about how they had just gone to Defcon 2. I assumed it was part of the military exercise."

"That would explain the lieutenant's grave demeanor," Handyman Jack said, as if he were starting to believe Devin.

"Whoa!" Rogue gave her a big-eyed look. "See, Luna, I told you Dad wasn't cray-cray. He knewww. The shit was gonna hit the fan."

"Wait, are you saying our parents might have started a nuclear war?" Devastation leached through her body, into her soul.

"They can't take all the credit," Devin said. "We had over a hundred activists for this mission. We succeeded in taking out over a dozen AGI data centers. So, it'll only slow down AI's progress. The scary thing is, AGI knows our protocols for every viable war-time scenario. Because we, ignorant humans, inputted the data into the AGI Think Tanks. It's only a matter of time before it learns the global nuclear launch codes. Think about it, Humanity is its number one enemy."

"You're saying AI—wants to annihilate us?" Handyman Jack said, flabbergasted.

"Not yet. Artificial general intelligence still needs the power grid to function," Devin said. "More like starving us out. Shutting down communications will wreak havoc with our logistics. Averting all the power to them. Without the power grid and communications, the world we know—no longer exists."

"And, and, they won't need humans," Rogue nearly whispered, "after they crack the code to nuclear fusion."

"Unfortunately, we have a far more dangerous situation looming," Devin said. "Our nemesis countries like Russia, Belarus, Iran, China, North Korea . . . aren't buying the AGI hack. As you must know, the geopolitical situation was already tenuous. They think *we* hacked them, blocking access to their launch sites.

They're accusing the U.S. of provoking them into World War III. It's possible, more like probable, they'll launch their nukes the moment they find a workaround. Meanwhile, we're worried about the off-grid nukes hiding out there. That reminds me, we should take iodine tablets." Devin pulled out a small box from his shirt pocket and took a pill before handing the box to Handyman Jack with a trembling hand.

"Holy balls, you really think we're gonna get nuked? Any f'n minute?" The terror in Rogue's voice resonated deep within Luna.

"Hold on a minute—" They all turned to Handyman Jack. "This is sounding a little too James Bond-ish. As in preposterous. Pardon my asking, but how the hell are you privy to such top-secret intel?" Handyman Jack grilled with a stonewall glare.

"Due to the non-disclosure agreement, I can't say much. A few months ago, a nameless billionaire AKA whistleblower leaked hush-hush documents regarding our vulnerabilities to AGI. As in the future of Humanity's existence. So, after my social media and bank accounts disappeared—I went to work for the 'other' guy," Devin admitted as if embarrassed.

"You're working for an AGI developer?" Luna was appalled by his revelation. "What happened to you?"

Devin turned away. "Ex-AGI developer. Look, I'm not the bad guy here. I've been trying to prevent Armageddon in a twenty-four seven Think Tank. Everything from climate change to how close AGI was, or is, to taking control."

"Man, you're giving me the heebie jeebies. That's a lot to swallow," Handyman Jack said after popping an iodine tablet into his mouth. "No pun intended." He tossed the box to Luna. "It's just potassium iodine. It can't hurt to take one."

Luna was starting to freak. Could this be true? She took a pill to be on the safe side and handed one to Rogue.

"What bothers me," Handyman Jack continued as he patted at his phantom mustache. "It seems odd this so-called AI awakening is happening amid this Frankenstein bout of weather. Like someone somehow broke the weather."

Luna and Rogue locked eyes. "The Atlantic Current collapsed," they announced in unison.

Devin threw up his hands. "That's right."

"Hmm, Rogue mentioned something about that," Handyman Jack said. "I assumed the collapse of the Atlantic Ocean currents had about the same odds of an asteroid wiping us out."

"True," Devin said. "Extinction Level Events such as an asteroid striking the earth occur periodically as do monumental shifts in the ocean and wind currents. Only this time, the AMOC, Atlantic Meridional Overturning Circulation collapse happened sooner than predicted, thanks to excessive CO_2 spewed into the atmosphere after the past several months of out-of-control wildfires scorching the southern hemisphere. I guess the northern hemisphere's unprecedented heatwave finally caused the AMOC to reach that critical breaking point. Just like humans do," Devin seemed to say directly to her. "That's another thing. More volcanoes are waking up. Maybe even this one."

"Question." Handyman Jack spoke up. "Without giving me the TED Talk version, what you're saying is, this AMOC thing is what gives Earth our Goldilocks weather. And now that it's—broken, we're screwed up the yin-yang."

Devin nodded. "Basically, yes."

"I find it a little too conveniently coincidental," Handyman Jack continued. "The AMOC collapse, AI taking over, *and* the possibility of WWIII."

"Our Think Tank predictive models indicated we would be the most vulnerable during a long-term, high-impact weather event," Devin explained. "This phenomenal weather has been assaulting not only the U.S. but the entire planet for nearly two weeks. Longer if you count our rainless fall and winter."

Luna fought back her growing angst. Everything was happening all at once. Just like SunFlower said it would if people didn't heed Earth's pleas for help.

"Whoa, did you say Mount Shasta's gonna blow?" Rogue followed with explosive sound effects.

"It's waking up, according to the anomaly of seismic activity," Devin said. "Which usually precedes an eruption."

Luna recalled feeling nauseous several times since they'd been in the area. Mom had always been sensitive to earthquakes, even tremors. She must have inherited the trait from her mother. So far, that was about the only thing Devin had said that made sense. The rest was just mind-boggling.

"But, but I thought the AMOC collapse meant—total ice age." Rogue seemed disappointed.

"Who knows?" Devin eluded. "There are all kinds of theories floating around cyberspace. More data is required to make a proper prediction. Although, AGI probably knows the answer to that."

"Correct me if I'm wrong, but you're saying these extreme weather events are going to"—Handyman Jack paused—"intensify?"

Devin nodded slowly. "That, my friend, is an understatement. Think complete climate chaos!"

"No, SunFlower said we'd have more time." Luna bit her lip before she started ranting like Rogue.

"Then you do the math." Devin's calm exterior exploded. "A hurricane just wiped out swaths of the east coast. As in Delaware, the ocean reclaimed it."

"Are you serious?" Handyman Jack said. "That's where Roxie's brother lives. How they doin' on those fires in SoCal? Roxie's been worried sick about her sister, who lives in Palm Springs as I recall."

Devin shook his head. "It's one hellacious firepit. People couldn't escape the firestorm. Think Maui, a thousandfold. Squared."

Oh, my God! Luna wanted to puke and cry at the same time, knowing this news would totally devastate Roxie. As it was, Roxie was barely hanging on. She probably needed medical care.

"How do you know so much with the Internet practically nonexistent?" Handyman Jack quizzed.

"My billionaire's private satellites. When we can catch a signal. I guess AGI hasn't shut out everyone yet. From the horrifying scenes captured via satellite, thousands died horrid deaths. Basically, those on the California coastline fared better. If they made it into the ocean before dying from smoke inhalation. The Coast Guard's still plucking people out of the ocean. They even have survivors sheltering on cruise ships in the bay and port cities. But sitting off the coast of California, a mutha of a storm spontaneously formed. Practically overnight—"

"It'll put out the fires," Luna said with relief.

"Undoubtedly," Devin said. "The Cat 5 hurricane's hurtling straight for the California coastline. Already trapping cruise ships and the Coast Guard."

"What the hell?" Luna exclaimed.

"Hurricane season doesn't start 'til June," a baffled Handyman Jack seemed to ponder aloud.

"Guess you didn't hear about the two hurricanes in the Gulf of Mexico that combined into a Category 6 megacane," Devin replied matter-of-factly.

"Duh, there's no such thing as a Cat 6 megacane," Rogue declared to the ceiling.

"There is now," Devin said coolly.

Handyman Jack patted his heart. "And we think the homeless situation is bad now . . ."

"Right, which leads us to the next crisis: an exodus of climate refugees seeking shelter. Starving to death. And I'm not just talking about Californians. With most of the Southeast's infrastructure decimated, along with the lack of law enforcement . . . utter anarchy will ensue."

"Son of a bitch." Handyman Jack slammed his palm into the wall. "Never thought this would happen in my lifetime."

"But, but we're okay. Right?" Rogue bemoaned, looking like he was about to faint.

Luna crawled to him before he passed out, still deciding if she believed Devin. But why would he lie about all of that? "So, now what?" Luna asked, hugging a quivering Rogue. This world really was too harsh for him.

Rogue fought his way from her embrace. "But why?" he shouted with brandished fists. "We were working so hard to *save* our planet. Not fuck it up. That's what the Paris Agreement—"

"Like Greta said, it's a bunch of 'blah, blah, blah,'" Luna snarked sarcastically. "I never believed they would reverse the CO2. There's too much big money. Against it."

"Humans are nothing more than two-legged locusts," Rogue droned in the same deadpan, monotone voice SunFlower used upon spontaneously going into trance. "No other creature pillages and plunders the planet purely for profit. Once Earth recovers, she shall thrive yet again and spawn a new human-like species. As for Humanity's future," he continued with a thousand-yard stare, "that remains an unknown."

The room went silent.

Cold. Dark. Unforgiving.

Interesting, Rogue had gone into trance. Another ability to add to his hypersensitive nature. At least he was familiar with the odd gift of channeling.

"Why are you all staring at me like I'm some kinda freak?" Rogue garbled when he broke out of his trance.

This wasn't the time to tell Rogue that he just came out of channeling a message. As if realizing Rogue's random episode had been a message from SunFlower. Luna panicked. "Where's Sun-Flower?"

Devin's face went pallid. And he froze.

"Is your friend all right?" Handyman Jack asked.

"In a minute," Luna said. "He freezes when he gets upset."

Finally, Devin snapped out of it. "Remnants of the megacane in the Gulf of Mexico spurred the most destructive and deadly tornado outbreak ever recorded. SunFlower happened to be in Texas when it hit, according to her phone's tracking device."

"What?" Luna didn't understand.

"There's no way in hell she survived the EF6 tornado. I mean, San Antonio was obliterated," Devin said teary-eyed. "It was like I was there, watching the tornadic outbreak in real-time in our Situation Room. The power grid decimated. Those humongous electrical transformers—crumpled like aluminum foil. The highways resemble sprawling junkyards of demolished vehicles. And the high-rises, let's just say it'll take an entire cargo ship to replace all those windows. And with the phenomenal storm surge, the rivers were inundated. It'll take weeks to recover the dead."

"I must say, that's an incredible story you have there." a stern-faced Handyman Jack spluttered. "How much stock do you put into this?" Handyman Jack turned to Luna.

"It can't be true," Luna said, devoid of emotion.

Rogue spoke up. "No electricity, no cell service, and the bad guys never found us . . ."

"You have a point there. Still, we could chalk it up to this weather whiplash," Handyman Jack reminded.

"Wait, SunFlower can't be dead," Luna blustered. "Her spirit guide personally told her she was destined to live to her nineties." It seemed like such a silly thing to say out loud. Only metaphysical people believed in the existence of spirit guides. But SunFlower's spirit guide had been right about so many things . . . Including the success of her activewear clothing line.

"Prudy usually provided relevant information," Devin said evenly, not breaking Luna's unwavering eye contact. "Which means, there's a deviant factor at play. In layman's terms, the world is going to shit sooner than we anticipated."

"No." Luna refused to believe the shit was actually hitting the fan.

"Look, Luna, I know you must hate me for the way I—" Devin stopped. "I need you to know that we, as in me and your parents, have the same ultimate goal. Saving the planet and Humanity. We still have a future."

Luna was sick of this. Everything. Ruining her life. "You know what, Devin?" She reverted to her inner bitchiness. "I don't give a flying fuck about saving the damn planet. Just tell me where Mom and Dad are. Then you can go back to playing end-of-the-world games with your AI doomsdayer society."

They had worked so hard to get to SunFlower's, only to be derailed once again. By Devin. Well, she wasn't having it. It had been like some cosmic gravitational force pulling her to SunFlower's. To make sure Mom and Dad were okay. Giving her the sense of closure she needed so she could focus on her career. Her life. Selfish and unreasonable as it might be, saying hello and goodbye one last time was just something her conscience needed.

"Can't you just stop hating me for five freakin' minutes?" Devin's nauseatingly calm exterior erupted into anger. When he was mad, everyone had better duck.

"Please," Rogue bellowed, "just shut up! I get it now. The *real* reason *you* are here." Rogue pointed accusingly to Devin. "Mom and Dad—are dead!"

"Rogue, why would you say that?" Luna was stunned.

"I can't explain it, but, but, SunFlower just told me," a blubbering Rogue stammered with hands clasped over his face, tears dripping between his fingers.

"I'm so terribly sorry . . ." Devin's whisper faded into nothingness. "It's true."

"Huh?" Luna went dizzy. Her heart leaped to her throat, strangling her. "D-Dead?"

Handyman Jack threw his arms in the air and strode out the patio's sliding glass door. He must think they were a bunch of wackos.

Devin closed his eyes and calmly inhaled and exhaled deeply several times before saying, "He's a good soul."

"Stop avoiding the issue," Luna snapped.

"Luna, Rogue, believe me"—Devin's tearing eyes said it all—"I pleaded with your parents to back out. We had other volunteers."

Luna couldn't stomach much more of this sickening world. "Yeah, right? And you just happen to be here now acting like you're the planet's savior and all that. This is your fault, too!" Rage whirled through her. She had to stop it before it consumed her.

"It's not like that," Devin defended. "It was already too late to stop AGI from taking over. We *knew* that much. We just wanted to buy a few decades. My benefactor—"

"Yeah, yeah, blame it on the nameless billionaire," Luna lashed.

"Don't you see?" Exasperation flooded over Devin. "Crystal and Forest sacrificed themselves on the risky mission. For you and Rogue. To earn spots on an international subterranean earthship built to last generations."

"Awesomeness, an underground earthship!" Rogue bounced back to life with pinwheeling arms.

"Oh, hell no!" Luna cursed under her breath. Once again Dad and Mom were manipulating her. "I'm not wasting the last years of my life hiding in some dank underground commune like I'm trapped in the zombie apocalypse."

"Do I have to spell it out?" Devin's tone turned condescendingly shrill. "WWIII could break-out any moment. After the fallout contamination, worldwide crop failures will follow. Think of the logistics, because there *are* no logistics. There will be no way to transport food and supplies to the population. The earthship has always been some far-out contingency plan that we baby-doomers pontificated about. Even I never thought I'd be face-to-face with you again—telling you Humanity lost. Remember, I believed we would save the planet. Until AI came into the equation."

That was true. Devin had always been the optimist. She had been the survivalist, learning every skill she could, for the thrill because she had been good at it and craved the adrenaline rush. But Devin, such a pure and sensitive soul as SunFlower had often gushed, had always been sure the world would work out its problems, and reverse the changing climate. In time.

"At least think it over," Devin said. "Whether it's the climate collapse or WWIII or AI taking over—we need to bug-out. The earthship's incredible. That's why I drove my EMP-hardened Jeep here, praying I'd find you and Rogue before it's too late. Technically, we're under Marshal Law now, only people don't realize it. Yet."

"Is the earthship in Greenland? Or, or New Zealand?" an excited Rogue burst.

Devin couldn't help but smile at Rogue's innocent zealousness, all the while shaking his head no.

"Oh, I know. That underground bunker under the Colorado airport they always talk about on YouTube," Rogue continued.

"I'm not authorized to say, until you're at the location."

"Figures," Luna retorted.

"What the hell. It's tucked away under the Klamath Mountains on the California side near the Oregon border. About seventy miles north of here. The Jeep will get us most of the way there. At some point, we have to hike to the location."

"Boring. Why there?" Rogue asked.

"A lot of research went into it. Not AI research. Anyway, it's secluded, at a high elevation to withstand the doomsday glacier melt, which by the way, is already occurring. It has a pristine underground aquifer, the best water ever. Along with underground farms. We can fish the many lakes. As long as the nukes haven't gone off. See, SunFlower was recruiting a specialized group of people. Her mission failed. Leaving us at eighty percent occupancy.

Besides the usual doctors and scientists, we need people with the dying-out Luddite skills. Like building, repairing things, farming, food preservation, sewing. . . We have a huge library as well."

"Looks like you and your TEOTWAWKI followers thought of everything," she said, toning back her scream. "Except, who the hell wants to live there!"

"You absolutely have to come. We need you and Rogue. Even your friend. From what I'm getting, he's an excellent woodworker. And his wife. I can't see her face. Is she sick?" Devin asked. "But we have meds and two doctors and a few nurses."

"Hey, Handyman Jack," Rogue declared out the screen door. "You and Roxie can come too!"

Handyman Jack slammed shut the sliding glass door.

"I should let you guys talk it out." Devin held out a pink envelope to her with a shaky hand. "We need to leave within the hour."

The finality in Devin's voice seemed to freeze the air flowing into her lungs. Even Rogue was speechless.

"Devin"—her voice softened—"just to be clear. Did our parents die *in* the explosion?"

"Apparently," Devin's whisper screamed into her heart.

Luna didn't understand. "Why didn't they get out in time?"

"We don't know. A faulty triggering device? All we were able to ascertain was the fire in your hometown was a wicked tactic to discredit your parents' noble act."

Rogue went into one of his manic episodes, kicking at the pillows, the furniture, the walls, the way he did when he was upset. "Why is this happening to me? Why, why, why?"

Devin was there, cuddling him, something she should do. But she couldn't, paralyzed by her abrupt lack of emotion. Everything was happening all at once, a tsunami of bad decisions, toppling into one another like gigantic dominoes. The age of consequences was upon them. And stupid her, thinking she could sidestep global collapse until she was a little old lady on social security.

She turned to the patio door where Handyman Jack paced around the lawn furniture and made fleeting eye contact. The pain in his eyes was more than she could bear. And who was telling Roxie all this? It might kill her.

It was all too much . . .

Chapter 39

ROXIE ROMERO SAT ON the vintage brocade-covered gossip bench in the hallway and patted her racing heart when Luna stormed out of the room and out of the house. Had Roxie overheard correctly? The world was going helter-skelter. In her lifetime?

She should have stayed in bed, but curiosity had won. She had been anxious to know what SunFlower had to say only to find Luna's old beau had shown up instead. *Today of all days.* Perhaps Devin's talk was purely speculation. How could he possibly know such things? Furthermore, she could not fathom Crystal and Forest getting involved in sabotage. Sacrificing their lives . . .

Then again, Luna's parents hadn't been out and about as usual, spending most of their time at home. She had assumed they were working on a project, and since she didn't follow social media, she had no idea their social media accounts had been terminated.

Roxie was too old for all of this. Too damned tired. And too fed up with this cruel world. Lately, everyday normal life seemed to be a constant fight for survival. From what Devin and the lieutenant had said, she didn't see how her brother and sister had survived. Not after half of Southern California had gone up in flames, and Delaware had been overtaken by the Atlantic Ocean.

To top it all, trivial as it was, she was heartbroken from losing Pixie and traumatized by her near-death drowning experience. She shook away the dreamy-watery image embedded in her mind, reliving or rather "re-dying" over and over and over.

And now Devin wanted Luna and Rogue to live in some mountain in an underground earthship? *What the bleepity-bleep is an earthship?*

Absolutely not! Roxie would rather stay at SunFlower's quaint farmhouse. Until she ran out of food.

Even if the wacky weather and the FBI didn't do her in, there remained the impossible task of rebuilding her home. And her life. The government and the upper class would get first dibs on hiring contractors for the rebuilding. Furthermore, if what Devin had said were true, there wouldn't be enough building materials to meet the demand. Not for years if not decades.

It all seemed pointless as if she no longer had a life worth—living.

Chapter 40

JACKSON JONES STOMPED THROUGH the country road's receding waters. And he was pissed. At the entire world. How had it come to this? Did the world leaders really have their heads so far up their asses they hadn't foreseen the planet's temperate weather had been on the verge of collapsing? After all, it didn't take an astrophysicist to understand that Earth's fairly moderate climate was the crucial factor enabling Humanity's existence.

The world leaders, the corporations, and the one-percenters must have realized the inevitable consequences. Yet blinded by their power. Their greed. They had continued pushing the limits. And now, it was too late to reverse the damage. Whether it be the catastrophic climate or the AI fuckery.

"Ah, there's the damn moving truck." He stomped harder, taking out his fury on the road.

That kooky cat had to be in the vicinity. If memory served him right, he had caught a glimpse of Pixie flying out of the truck seconds before he had dived in for Roxie. Of course, who knew where that cat was now? But with the flooded roads, it couldn't have gone far. If it was the last thing he did. He'd find Pixie. For Roxie's sake.

Roxie seemed to be on death's doorstep, not even bothering to look out the peephole, as if she had lost the luster to live. It was heart-wrenching seeing the spunky gal deteriorating in bed with no desire at all to continue. Especially after she had admitted overhearing Devin's extraordinary revelations. Although he must admit, Devin's outlandish story had Jackson questioning his own future as well.

He scanned the area, taking in everything. The mostly submerged truck had tipped to its side in the raging creek. But it wasn't going anywhere after snagging on a tree. The road and the countryside remained submerged under several inches of water. There was no place for a cat to hang out—except in a tree.

"Here, Pixie girl . . ." Jackson called up to the early budding oak trees, unable to match Roxie's high notes. He spluttered into a cough.

A slight movement above him caught his eye. Was it a squirrel? A bird? Jackson froze and listened. To the silence. The stillness. One would never know a hurricane barreled toward the California coastline.

It was in that foreboding quietness that he seemed to witness time stand still. To his astonishment, the forest spun around him while he remained stationary, as if he were safe in the treetops and witnessed the world's insanity spinning chaotically around him. Bizarre to say the least.

A wave of serenity melted his anger. Not one for meditation and such, he had to admit the sudden peaceful sensation was invigorating. And so, he surrendered to the cleansing-like energy washing over him. Making him feel new. Young.

There it was again—rustling amongst the leaves. It took Jackson a moment to return to reality; that other place had been so tranquil. He had heard corny stories about how areas near the mystical Mount Shasta were known to exude healing energies. He had always disregarded such hippy-dippy beliefs until now. He angled for a view of the volcanic mountain, but the gloomy sky wasn't cooperating.

"Me-ow . . ." It had to be the tiniest meow he had ever heard.

"Pixie?" Jackson called out, focusing on a blurry object in the tree. His dreamy-eyed vision abruptly returned to its normal focus. "How the heck did you get way up there?" There was Pixie in the top of a sturdy oak that hadn't fallen prey to the hellish winds. Not yet anyway.

"Mew, mew, mew . . ."

"C'mon down, Pixie. I'm not climbing up after you." Although he would. For Roxie.

He remembered the can of tuna fish in his jacket pocket, one of the many cans he had carried for Roxie since leaving the bus. Quickly, he pulled back the can's tab. "Yum," he said as if the cat understood.

That sent Pixie into a tizzy. He stood on tiptoes and held up the can as tantalizingly close to the cat as he could stretch. The cat sniffed at the air and meowed excitedly.

"C'mon," he coaxed. He set the can in the crook of the lowest branch. And waited.

Pixie tentatively climbed down, catching herself when sliding down by digging her claws into the bark. The cat eyed him suspiciously before sniffing the tuna. And then, she went at it. Devouring the tuna. Next came the tricky part. Pixie wasn't exactly a people-person and had spent most of the time on the bus, hiding under the covers in the back bedroom.

In one swoop, Jackson grabbed the skittish cat before she decided to run up the tree again. He placed the squirming cat in the wicker picnic basket he had found in the farmhouse and quickly secured it shut as the drone of an approaching engine replaced the silence. "Sorry 'bout that," he prattled to the cat before stepping behind the tree to see what was coming.

"Huh, Devin's leaving so soon?" Jackson splashed through the waters and waved down the Jeep, surprised to find Rogue and Luna waving out the windows.

"We've been looking all over for you?" Rogue scolded. "Like, why are you going on a picnic? The hurricane's coming."

Jackson held up the basket triumphantly. "Found Roxie's kooky cat."

"Handyman Jack, you gotta make Roxie come with us," Rogue pleaded. "Devin says there's room for her. And you too!"

Jackson hung his head low. "We talked it over. Afraid Roxie isn't up for it."

"Nooo," Rogue groaned. "She has to come with us. Or she'll die!"

They all had to go some time, Jackson refrained from saying. "I'll look after her."

A solemn Luna stepped out of the Jeep. "What about you? Devin says they need carpenters—"

Jackson waved off the idea impatiently. "I can't just leave Roxie. Besides, we ought to be able to ride out the hurricane here. We might even stay at SunFlower's for a while. This area's known to be a fisherman's paradise. I can even hunt if need be. Might even herd up those quail. I hear they make great scrambled eggs. We'll be okay."

"But, but, the volcano!" Rogue roared.

"One disaster at a time," Jackson said with a chuckle.

Tears slipped down Luna's cheeks. "Jackson . . ." She hesitated and then gave him a burly hug. "You're such an amazing person. I'm so glad we found you." She pulled away abruptly and hurried to the Jeep.

"He found *us*!" Rogue was quick to contradict. Then the boy started bawling.

Next thing Jackson knew, his eyes went watery. "No worries." He held up a thumbs-up, bolstering his composure before he turned into an adult version of a blubbering Rogue. "You all heading to that mountain getaway so soon?"

"We need to leave," Devin said apologetically.

"Well, young man, you better take care of Luna and Rogue," Jackson demanded as gruffly as possible to hide his quickly waning composure.

Devin nodded. For a moment, Jackson seemed to recognize the heavy burden the young man shouldered. Being the bearer of apocalyptic news couldn't be easy.

Rogue bear-hugged Jackson and wouldn't let go. "No, I'm not leaving without you!"

"Now, Son . . ." Jackson swallowed the growing lump in his throat. "You need to take care of your sister. No doubt, Devin's earthship needs a smarty-pants bonehead like you." He fake-laughed as best he could. It was better than losing it in front of them.

"Rogue," Luna called out as she closed the Jeep's door.

Rogue moped back to the Jeep and kicked at the ankle-deep water. "Hey, I know!" The boy turned back to him. "Maybe Roxie will change her mind if you tell her I'm super sorry for being a brat sometimes. I don't mean to."

Jackson hurried for the Jeep, not wanting the kid to be saddled with that guilt trip the rest of his life. "This is not your fault—none of this is," Jackson reiterated.

He didn't think he had ever felt so alone when the Jeep slowly rolled off with everyone waving goodbye out the windows.

The Jeep jolted to a stop. Out popped Rogue, and the kid ran to him.

"And, and, one more thing, Mr. B-B-Bonehead," Rogue ranted crazily. "Luna said it's time to man up. You gotta tell Roxie you love her." Then just like that, the boy darted back to the Jeep.

"Whut?" Jackson puzzled over the kid's outburst. How did Luna know?

Luna leaned out the window with a mischievous grin. "Tell her!"

How could Jackson reveal his deepest desire? He didn't dare presume Roxie would respond in the like. Despite their spontaneous friendship, they hardly knew each other. Furthermore, the world they knew—had known, no longer existed.

There were countless reasons not to go out on a limb like that. Except for one. Why the hell not? Honestly, he could not imagine life without her. Whether they had one last day together. Or another thirty years.

That got his ticker pumping, and with that kooky cat squirreling around in the basket, Jackson picked up the pace and sprinted back to SunFlower's farmhouse.

Chapter 41

Luna Lewis sat in the back of the Jeep by herself while Rogue pestered Devin about the New Pangea earthship. Questions *she* should be asking but simply didn't care. As the miles blurred by, all she could do was stare at the pink envelope handwritten to *My Sweet Luna* in Mom's beautiful calligraphy.

The Jeep slammed to a halt, snapping Luna out of her funk.

"Now what?" Rogue wailed.

That's when Luna saw the wall of mud blocking the road. "Surely there's an alternative route?"

Devin pounded the steering wheel with his fists. "Not without backtracking thirty-plus miles."

"Don't we have enough gas?" Rogue badgered.

"It's not that," Devin said. "I was avoiding the interstate. It's too easy to get spotted by a drone. They're out there. Hunting down the New Pangea followers as we speak."

"You didn't tell me that," Luna berated.

"I know," Rogue said. "We can dig a tunnel through the landslide."

That would take a week, but nobody bothered responding to the ridiculous suggestion.

Luna had to get her head back in the game. Devin was freaking out. She recognized his breaking point signs, the way his jawbone quivered, and the tinny pitch in his voice. He had never handled dangerous situations well. It was her turn to take charge. "How much time before the hurricane rains hit?" Luna asked, reining in logic. Despite the higher elevation, it wouldn't take much more precipitation to make the roads impassable, even with an off-road vehicle.

"An hour, maybe two," Devin said glumly. "As you've seen, the weather's impossible to predict."

"Stop freaking me out," Rogue whined. "We have tons of time."

"Look." Devin's voice cracked. "On my way to SunFlower's, I had to shoot down a drone. I can't risk leading anyone to our earthship."

"The drones are probably surveying the storm damage and looking for stranded people. And *who* exactly is after you?" Luna had a difficult time keeping the snark out of her voice.

"Okay, so I'm paranoid." In a calmer tone, he said, "It's a risk I'm not willing to take. Most of our members, entire families with young children, are considered enemies of the state."

Luna understood. "Where's the weapon?" She spun around in the seat and groped the back compartment. She grabbed the AR-15 rifle. "Got it."

"Careful, it's loaded," Devin warned.

She left it in the back for now. "I can sit on the roof rack and surveil the area once we get on the interstate. It's your call. But you'll have to drive much slower. I'm still a good shot."

"Of course you are," Devin mumbled with the slightest note of cynicism. "But yeah, I'd feel better with you riding shotgun. If our adversaries locate us, they'll have proof of life that *we* are still alive. Meaning, they will not stop hunting us."

"If this hurricane's as bad as you say, they'll never find us anyway. Besides, if the drone you shot down was looking for you, they would have reviewed the live-feed. So, yeah, they already know your coordinates," Luna spouted, as if she knew what she was talking about. "I think with a bit of luck, we can outsmart the bad guys a little longer."

"You sound just like Handyman Jack," Rogue said, back to being gloomy.

"Find something to hang on to," Devin said, backing up. "I'm driving as fast as I can to make up for lost time. I should warn you, the interstate could get—dangerous. Can you believe, I had to drive through a military checkpoint right in the middle of the road? Near Yreka. Weirdly, it was abandoned. It even had a tower with a machine gun and walls of sandbags. So, excuse me for being paranoid."

"Yikes," Luna said. "It sounds like the military's preparing for civil unrest." Or war, but she kept that to herself, not wanting to freak-out Rogue and Devin.

"Did Luna tell you we got to spend the night in a super-big military tent? It was fun," Rogue said.

"Well, this military outpost was completely demolished," Devin said.

"Huh?" Luna puzzled.

"Did a tornado take it out?" Rogue asked.

"It looked more like it had been attacked by artillery. That's another reason I wanted to avoid Interstate 5."

"Did you see any *dead* people?" Rogue whispered.

Luna wished Roxie was there, shushing Rogue. "Maybe looters took it over. For supplies. Like MREs and weapons." With all the insane weather, people were probably already running out of food. As Dad used to say, "It only took three days to anarchy." Especially in the cities.

The power grid had already been damaged by the fires and storms. How would it sustain a direct hit from a hurricane? It had her worrying about ICU patients and the emergency surgeries that would be delayed. When the ATMs ran out of money, and the grocery store shelves were empty—that was when the shit really would hit the fan.

"Anything else I should know?" Luna asked warily.

"The interstate's a disaster zone. We'll have to take a detour at some point. But there's easy on-and-off access. Two helicopters crash-landed in the middle of it," Devin said with a touch of anxiety.

"Luna, did I tell you I dreamt the evac helicopter crashed? I hope none of the soldiers we know were on it," Rogue worried.

That gave her the shivers. "Whoa, what's going on out there?" Luna couldn't believe all the disasters happening just in her small area. It had her wondering what was going on around the world.

"Wish I knew. SunFlower, if you're watching over us, please guide us safely to the earthship?" Devin seemed to utter to himself.

Luna had some time before they backtracked to the interstate. Gingerly, as if the letter might crumble to pieces like the unrolling of an ancient scroll, she unfolded the familiar light-pink onion skin stationery, the one Mom had saved for special occasions.

My Sweet Luna,

If this letter finds you, it means your dad and I succeeded in the most monumental activism stunt of our careers. For once, I am not exaggerating. Our trip down the AI rabbit hole began after a weekend retreat at SunFlower's when a scared-shitless Devin showed up needing guidance.

During our group meditation, a vision hijacked Sun-Flower—warning that artificial general intelligence was a far more existential threat to Humanity than climate change starving us to death, more than the forthcoming mandated vaccines designed to cull individuals with certain DNA ancestry, the Great Reset to bring about the New World Order we always worried about, and the WHO's Orwellian global digital health mandates.

Can you believe we've been fighting the wrong enemy this entire time? Such a waste. That monumental weekend SunFlower surprisingly confirmed Devin's whistleblower data. Horrific data, which we revealed to the world per the whistleblower's adamant request. The episode went viral within days. We gained millions of new followers and over a million dollars. Can you believe that? We had enough money to go mainstream and educate the world.

Days later, every single one of our social media accounts vanished. Along with our bank accounts. I really shouldn't be surprised "they" shut us down. We really don't know who controls the metaverse. Designed to track society with each and every click and tap of the screen.

We lived off our prepper pantry and waited for things to die down, thinking a sponsor would soon hire us to organize a protest event. But we were locked out—there was no way to connect. Eventually, we even tried to get real jobs. I told Rogue not to tell you because Dad and I didn't want our reputation to trickle down and wreck your career.

Then Dad and I became so violently ill we had to go to the Emergency Room. You know we never get sick. We were both diagnosed with stage four colon cancer a few days later. We must have been poisoned. Thank the Goddess, Rogue had been staying with Uncle Lewie. That's why we think he wasn't subjected to whatever we were dosed with.

Finally, the offer of a lifetime presented itself by Devin's whistleblower acquaintance. Our mission was to coincide with another activist plot going after data centers, while our group's objective was to deactivate several covert AGI facilities. I know, I know, I feel your condemnation as I write this.

We were compelled to take such drastic action since the government leaders seem incapable of recognizing the ramifications of AGI. SunFlower's analogy: Humans are like kids in a candy store for the first time. Using AI for fun and games. Sex and lies and money. Manipulating every aspect of everyone's lives for personal gain.

If you want to know the truth, sweet Luna, we know we may never see you and Rogue again! Our health is deteriorating rapidly.

A tear plopped onto the words *sweet Luna*. She gazed as the tear melted into the paper and struggled for the courage to continue reading.

We allowed ourselves to commit this wicked act of violence to guarantee you and Rogue a hopeful future in this hopeless world. Our event, which occurs simultaneously around the world with other Anti

AI crusaders will only buy you a fraction of time. Time enough to escape to the spectacular New Pangea earthship. And spectacular it is, for Dad and I have been there.

I worry "they" will blame you and Rogue. Destroy your lives or dispose of you. And if they don't find you, praise the Goddess, the media will most likely label you pariahs, forcing you into a life on the run. But who is better prepared for that, than you? I'm sorry to say the media will make a mockery of our family's legacy, calling us psychotic conspiracy theorists. When, in fact, we are merely "conspiracy factualists" committed to shedding light on the looming endarkenment of Humanity.

So resent me, hate me, all you want. But, dear sweet Luna, if you don't go to the earthship for me—please, oh please, do it for Rogue. I just know Rogue will thrive there. SunFlower says you have a wonderful future waiting to happen there as well—if you allow it to be so.

P.S. I'm calling in the colossal favor I once did for you.

With Love and Light,

Mom

What the hell? Luna screamed internally. *Slathering on the guilt a little thick, even for you, Mom!* She just sat there stupefied—staring blankly at the letter in her hands.

"Okay," Devin said, pulling over to the side of the road. "I'm about to get on the interstate."

Perfect timing, Luna didn't want to think about Mom's insane letter. She performed a quick chamber check to confirm the rifle was loaded. She grabbed the two-way radio from the seat and turned it on. "Contact me if you see a drone," Luna said to a solemn Rogue.

Devin handed her a box of ammo from the glove box. "Remember, we're under Marshal Law. Let me know if you see any military or police. I heard they started confiscating weapons."

"Squawk" went the radio.

"Rogue, stop messing with the radio," Luna scolded, looking for his radio.

Rogue's eyes grew wider, rounder. "Uh, uh, that's not me."

Devin gaped. "Don't answer it."

"Squaaawk . . ."

Intrigued, Luna fiddled with the radio settings.

"Anybody there?" the radio said more clearly. "Luna—?"

"What?" Luna wasn't absolutely sure, but the voice had sounded like a garbled Handyman Jack.

"Don't get mad," Rogue spluttered. "I meant to tell you. I sorta gave my radio to Roxie before we left. 'Cause she looked so sad. I know you won't believe me, but it's like I knew deep inside my heart they'd change their mind. Like this dream I had one night on the bus, where we all lived in this uber-cool bunker."

Rogue really was gifted.

"Luna? You there?" It was definitely Handyman Jack.

"You guys okay?" Luna asked.

"Pleased as punch. We've been trying to reach you for the past half hour," a faint woman's voice chimed in.

"Did you tell Roxie you love her?" Rogue blurted.

"Boy, did he ever," Roxie exclaimed.

"Yep, hope they have a chapel where you all are headed," Handyman Jack said. "Speaking of that, if it's not too much to ask, don't suppose you can swing by and give us a lift—if the offer still stands?"

"Yay! They're coming," Rogue shouted to the world.

"On our way," Luna said more assuredly than ever. It was truly a miracle the landslide had caused them to backtrack, otherwise the long-range radios wouldn't have connected. "But we don't have much time. Can you meet us by that covered bus stop on the county road?" It would save twenty minutes each way, trying to four-wheel drive through the flooded muddy dirt road to Sun-Flower's. "Roxie, can you walk?"

"No worries," Handyman Jack practically sang into the radio. "We'll be there even if I have to haul the spunky gal in the wheelbarrow."

"See you soon," Luna vowed, suddenly giddy, as if hope or maybe even a spark of happiness, were trying to reawaken her numbed heart.

"Dammit, Luna, there you go again. Taking charge." Devin's voice turned shrilly. "Going back to SunFlower's will take too much time—"

"What's wrong with you?" Rogue stormed out of the Jeep and slammed the door. "I'm not going without them. They're like my new Mom and Dad. You can't just leave them . . ." Rogue stomped over to a tree stump and kicked at it repeatedly.

"Exactly!" Luna said with eyes colder than a steel blade when their eyes locked in the rearview mirror. "You owe me that much—after what you did. To me. Rogue. And my parents."

Devin dropped eye contact first. "I told you—how sorry I was."

"By a fucking text?" Rage surged through her. "Abandoning me, because your save-the-planet brown-ass thought it was too cruel to bring children into this fucked world."

"I was correct in my assumption," Devin responded coolly.

"That's not the freakin' point. Pregnant at seventeen. What was I to do?" Unexpectedly, she was there, reliving that horrid day, the worst day of her life. *Until today*. Ah, but this time she vowed not to be the victim.

"You're doing a great job with him," Devin finally said.

"Shut the hell up. I had nothing to do with raising him. My parents did all the work." If anything, she had avoided Rogue as much as possible the past few years, almost convincing herself that he really was—her brother. Guilt, she had learned, was one of the few emotions that got to her.

"Does Rogue"—he stopped and gazed at Rogue sitting on the stump—"know we are his biological p—" Devin asked in a whisper of a whisper.

"No! And he never will. He hates liars. SunFlower said the truth would destroy him. And that's why you are going back for Roxie and Handyman Jack. Because the most important lesson I've learned: Don't abandon the special people in your life. We need them as much as they need us."

Devin started the Jeep. "Sorry for being such an a-hole. I truly loved you. Then . . ." he added.

Without warning, her heart ached, remembering how madly in love she had been. With him. The father of her child, a secret she'd never confess to another living soul. To protect Rogue. No wonder she had turned into such a coldhearted bitch. It was time to cleanse her soul. Her heart. And start a new life. Although, she didn't see rekindling her relationship with Devin. She still harbored too much painful resentment.

"It's not that I don't want to go back for them. Time is of the essence. It's going to be a life-threatening storm."

"If you knew the hellacious weather I've driven through, then you wouldn't be such a wimp. I'm not letting a pissy hurricane stop us. Besides, why the hell did you come for us?" That was what she really needed to know.

"I told you, I promised your parents. It was part of the deal to earn a place on the earthship."

"Bullshit!" She heard the lie in his tone.

"Okay, okay." Exasperation took over his face. "I had to find you and Rogue as a sort of penance. To mend my karma."

That was all she needed to hear to know she had just won the argument. "Rogue, get in. We're getting Roxie and Handyman Jack," Luna called out the window.

"Absolutely not the cat!" Devin ordered.

"And Pixie too," Luna spouted in spite. Roxie would be forever sad without her silly cat.

"For real?" Rogue asked warily.

Devin shook his head and let out a meek laugh. "Luna, you haven't changed. Rogue, get in."

"I was praying so hard for you to change your mind," Rogue said. "Thank you, Auntie SunFlower."

"Uh, Rogue, did you get a message from SunFlower?" Luna wondered out loud.

"Sorta. I was meditating on the stump when I had this cool dream-like image of a never-ending field of SunFlowers. And, and, Auntie SunFlower's face was on *all* the flowers—like a gazillion Auntie SunFlowers smiling at me. Oh, she looked so happy. She said good things were going to happen for us. As in the five of us. And that I just had to be patient and let the karma work itself out. Weird, huh?"

"Remarkable! I'm relieved to hear that," Devin said with one of his heart-stopping grins. "It's a sign we're doing the right thing."

"Perfect." Luna stepped out of the Jeep. "Don't drive too fast." She climbed to the roof rack and found a comfortable position with the rifle in her lap and binoculars strapped around her neck. Ready for action.

They drove up the on-ramp and down the interstate. The rattling of paper nagged at her, so she patted her pockets for the sound. Ah, the letter. Her heart swelled. Abruptly, she understood her parents' sacrifice—understanding everything they had done for her.

I can't believe how selfish I've been. She had never thanked Mom and Dad for taking in Rogue as their own child. She had merely expected it. In that way, she had treated them as badly if not worse than Devin had treated her.

"Mom, Dad—if you can somehow hear me. I love you. Thank you. For everything," she crooned to the wind. They had made the ultimate sacrifice for her and Rogue more than once. It was time for Luna to let go of her animosity for this bitter hard world. Time to start a new life.

Luna stuffed the letter, the only memento she had left, farther into her jacket pocket. Yet she was all the more resilient, ready for whatever the universe threw at her. Because she was no longer that self-centered, career-driven junkie whose sole goal was to make a name for herself in the fashion industry. All she had cared about was that shallow promotion and acquiring more fancy shoes and clothes for her closet. Well, someone else could enjoy them. Someday. If the fires and floods hadn't ravaged her apartment.

In retrospect, Luna realized she had endured karma's seemingly heartless soul-hardening process. Which was now propelling her forward—for her true soul-purpose. To assist in the survival of a handful of up-and-coming generations while awaiting the planet to heal. Perhaps in a thousand years—Earth would be ready for Humanity.

Let's just hope we don't screw it up again . . .
The End

Author's Note

I hope you enjoyed my story. Besides my trusty editor, I'm it. I don't have a marketing and publishing team cheering me on. As an independent writer, I really would appreciate your help. Reviews encourage me to continue writing day after day. Indie authors rely on reviews in order to make it in this crazy business. So, if you have a moment, please leave a short review.

Thank you!
Want to join my monthly newsletter?
https://authoradpopovich.eo.page/newsletter

Books by A.D. Popovich

Only the Dead Don't Die An Apocalyptic Saga – Book 1
Book 2 – The Hunger's Howl
Book 3 – Last State
Book 4 – Finding Home

About the Author

A.D. POPOVICH WAS BORN and raised in Louisiana. At the age of fifteen, she moved to California with her family. Living in California was a huge eye-opener for her. California meant freedom. "Well, back in the 70s it did." After meeting her husband, life has been one adventure after another. They lived in Santa Fe, New Mexico for a while—absolutely wonderful. Several years later they made a wrong turn and ended up in Florida: too many tornadoes and alligators.

They returned to California and started their own business, The Cosmic Shirt Company, until the Bankstas caused The Crash. Homeless for a while. "Yes, really." They finally managed to get their feet back on the ground after obtaining super-boring jobs.

After decades of working in the mundane world, A.D. Popovich decided it was time for a change. She focused almost every second of her spare time focusing and visualizing her childhood dream—writing. Her first novel, *Only the Dead Don't Die*, was more successful than she had anticipated. She's busy working on her next adventure. She strives to write compelling survivalist stories with a touch of the metaphysical.